Praise for David L. Lindsey's *SPIRAL*

(more . . .)

Praise for David L. Lindsey's
A COLD MIND
and
HEAT FROM ANOTHER SUN

Books by David L. Lindsey

A Cold Mind
Heat from Another Sun
Spiral

Published by POCKET BOOKS

SPIRAL

DAVID L. LINDSEY

POCKET BOOKS

New York   London   Toronto   Sydney   Tokyo   Singapore

This book is a work of fiction. Names, characters, places and incidents
are either the product of the author's imagination or are used fictitiously.
Any resemblance to actual events or locales or persons, living or dead, is
entirely coincidental.

POCKET BOOKS, a division of Simon & Schuster Inc.
1230 Avenue of the Americas, New York, NY 10020

Copyright © 1986 by David L. Lindsey
Cover art copyright © 1988 Ron Barbagallo

ISBN: 0-671-73337-0

First Pocket Books printing April 1988

10 9 8 7 6 5 4

POCKET and colophon are registered trademarks of
Simon & Schuster Inc.

Printed in the U.S.A.

FOR **Joyce**
una mujer de paciencia

SPIRAL

Jerry Lowell personally didn't like the idea of dealing with Mexicans. You didn't grow up in Texas without learning a couple of things about Mexicans, and the things you learned didn't encourage you to want to do business with them. But this one had been checked out. The bankers had done their work and a $500-a-day investigator had done his work. As far as they could tell, the Mexican was fresh meat.

The fact was, Jerry was always a little antsy when he came to Houston, though he swaggered his way through it. In this goddam business you never admitted anything except that you were on a rocket and if anybody wanted to make a goddam fortune they damn well better climb on with you. But for years Houston had had this reputation of being the world's *fastest* rocket and even though it was presently sputtering, nobody expected it to fizzle out completely and some people even claimed it was going to pick up and blast right out of the universe. It still represented some of the best razzle-dazzle in the money market and you could still be surprised. The only thing was, you just never knew if you were thinking fast enough in Houston. Especially if you were from out of town, like Jerry.

Lowell mentally checked himself as he tugged at his crotch, and tried to settle his parts into the little biddy pocket of his red nylon jockey shorts. He had on his native Austinite young-buck wheeler-dealer uniform: knobby ostrich-skin cowboy boots, super-starched Levi's, super-starched tailor-made sky-blue shirt, specially made heavy-linked gold chain lying in the nest of his chest hair and peeking out of his open collar, a Bill Blass sport coat which was cut full and helped hide the fact that Jerry was getting a little thick through the middle. He shook his left wrist to make sure the Rolex Oyster Perpetual, worn loose like a bracelet so it would show from under his shirt sleeve, was indeed showing. He looked at his University of Texas Business School class ring on his right hand, big as a horse apple but a hell of a lot harder, and the specially made gold-glob ring on his other hand. He thought about his red Porsche 928S as he rubbed his cleanly shaven jaw and caught the fragrance of his own cologne. Shit, that Polo. He loved it.

He was ready for the Mexican.

Thing was, even if you made millions in Austin, you go to Houston you feel like somebody's kid brother. The city was so . . . damn big. The damn place didn't have a skyline, it had three or four of them. He stood on the forty-fifth floor of a building in one of them now. Greenway Plaza was the third-largest of what urban planners were calling Houston's "high-density urban centers," what Jerry used to call "downtown." To his left, across a seemingly solid blanket of treetops, he could see the West Loop District around Post Oak, and to his right, across more treetops, he saw the largest, original downtown. The city leaders had annexed so much land that Houston now covered nearly six hundred square miles, as much as Dallas, Denver, Atlanta, and San Francisco put together. Goddam.

But for a while Houston had been stepping back from un-bridled, aggressive land development. Dallas was easing back, too, and Austin, which for several years had been the hottest spot in the country for flipping real estate, was slowly rolling over, belly up. A few years back the big players in the country had converged on Austin like cockroaches on Karo and nobody slept in the state capital for nearly two years. Fortunes changed hands twice a day every day while good ol' boys and bankers and conglomerate reps talked deals till they were pumped up tight and red in the face, passing around parcels of land like they were coke queens at a stag party, everybody wanting to get his hands on a nice piece before she passed out. Buy in a panic, sell at a profit. Don't slow down, it can't last forever.

And it didn't. Flipping land was now just a sweet memory, like the $36 barrel of oil. Bankers were wearing slightly constipated expressions, the "thirty-day free look" was an outdated and meaningless phrase, and the city council had sucked up on development restrictions and zone changes. Times had changed.

So the Mexican was something to consider. He was already into condos and hotels on South Padre Island, he had bought some downtown property in Houston, he had hotels in New Orleans, office buildings in San Antonio, health clubs in Dallas, ski lodges in Vail, a radio station in Atlanta. He owned two homes in Houston. He had Swiss and Panamanian bank accounts. Where did he get his money? Jerry's philosophy was, who gives a shit? If it came from a clean account it was clean money as far as he was concerned. The law couldn't expect him to sniff out the origin of every dollar he turned. You couldn't put a moral meter on money.

Jerry Lowell was thinking all this over when the door behind him opened and George Crisman hurried into the conference room. Crisman was the agent. He liked to call himself a "facilitator." As a lawyer, he came across business possibilities from time to time that he knew Jerry would be interested in. He never put up any money, but if the deals went through he handled the legal work, for which he was well paid, and collected a finder's fee. When word got around Houston that Benigo Gamboa Parra was looking toward Austin, Crisman got on the telephone to Lowell, who started running his traps. Within twenty-four hours he had located some prime hill-country acreage just outside of Austin, and had strong enough verbal commitments from the principals to enable Crisman to set up the meeting. Crisman liked meetings.

"Okay, Jerry, Gamboa's on his way up. You ready?"

"Sure, sure." Lowell gestured behind him to four orange, pasteboard cylinders with metal caps. "I've got the maps, plats, aerial photographs, the works."

A woman dressed as if she had just stepped off the ramp of the new Valentino show in Paris strutted into the room followed by two men in white jackets, one carrying a silver service, the other a tray of china, silver cigarette boxes, and an arrangement of fresh flowers. It was too early in the day for liquor. The woman directed the stewards in setting the table and showed them where to put each of the four yellow legal pads, each with its accompanying fourteen-karat-gold Cross pencil laid perpendicular to it on the mahogany conference table. Crystal ashtrays by each pad, an LED calculator by each pencil. The woman left the room. Crisman checked the layout with a quick eye and followed her. Jerry glanced at the stewards, who were puttering with the details of their coffee responsibilities. Steam was beading up on the spout of the silver coffee pot when the door opened and Crisman entered again, followed by four men in suits.

"Mr. Gamboa," Crisman said, "this is Jerry Lowell."

Lowell came forward and shook hands with the first of the four men. Benigo Gamboa did not fit into Jerry Lowell's "typical Mexican" category. This guy was smooth city. Spanish, Lowell thought. No Indian blood here. Eight-hundred-dollar suits on these old boys. Jerry did not see a Rolex Oyster on Mr. Gamboa's wrist.

"It is my pleasure," Gamboa said, smiling.

He did not have a pencil-thin mustache.

"This is my associate, Mr. Sosa," Gamboa said, stepping back and gesturing an opened hand to a smaller, hawk-nosed man in a gray suit.

Jerry shook hands again. He looked at the other men, who did not come forward, and no one made any move to introduce them.

"Well, let's sit down, gentlemen," Crisman said.

Gamboa and Sosa smiled hugely and moved toward the black leather chairs on the side of the table that allowed them to face the windows and the panoramic city skyline. As they were in the process of sitting down and making room for their briefcases, one of the men who had not been introduced casually walked across the room and nonchalantly opened the first of two other doors that opened out of the conference room—an executive bath. He sauntered over to the second door, saw it was a coat closet, and strolled back to a position near the main door of the conference room. His partner was easing along the wall of windows, looking at the Summit Tower across the plaza, looking at the thin window ledge. He eventually settled near the stewards standing beside the coffee service. None of this had escaped the stewards' attention. They cut their eyes at each other and waited uneasily for instructions.

Jerry tried to ignore the background movement, walked around to the other side of the table, and sat down facing the two Mexicans.

"Everyone want coffee?" Crisman asked, sitting down.

"Yes, please," Gamboa said appreciatively.

There was small talk while they were being served, and when the stewards had done their jobs they backed away to their neutral corners and Crisman began restating the background for the meeting. As Crisman spoke, Jerry wore an earnest expression of interest in the business at hand, but noticed that the two no-names had touched the stewards' elbows, silently inviting them to leave the room. By the time they were out, Crisman was ready to get down to specifics and Jerry was beginning to recall headlines about Mexican drug kingpins and bodies found in the trunks of abandoned cars. He looked at the two no-names again. Jesus. They looked like gorilla sidemen on *Miami Vice*. Then he told himself to get real. This was typical Mexican flash. He had come to cut a land deal, and he had better get his mind on it.

"Would you like Mr. Lowell to go over the maps of the land with you?" Crisman asked.

"I do not think that will be necessary," Gamboa said, smiling. "We have done some of our own research. I think we know the attributes of the land in Austin well enough."

Crisman nodded deferentially. "Good. Then is there any information you require before we proceed?"

"I think not," Gamboa said.

Crisman nodded again. "Then do you see an offer?"

"We would be happy to offer you fifteen thousand dollars per acre," Gamboa said. "We are prepared to seal the negotiations now if you wish."

There was a pause in which Crisman played poker-face neutral, and everyone looked at Lowell. Lowell's expression took on a little bit of a frown. Just twenty-four hours before he had put down $100,000 for a free look at the

265 acres he was proposing to sell to Gamboa. He did not own the land. However, he had talked to the owners, who themselves had bought the acreage only six weeks before, and told them he was interested in working a deal with them. They told him that they were about to option the land out for $10,000 an acre, but they hadn't signed any papers. It was prime real estate, in the hills on Austin's west side, not far from the lakes and adjacent to land that was rumored to be in for heavy development by Canadian investors. Jerry thought he could smell the last real flip in central Texas.

He told the owners of the property that he thought he could get them $12,000 an acre for it if they would let him put down $200,000 for thirty days' free look. A free look simply meant that they could hold his money while he scouted around for potential backers. If he decided to buy the land the option money would go against the purchase. If he didn't buy, he could have his money back. They said they already had the solid deal for $10,000 an acre which was going to give them a $795,000 profit on a two-month investment and they didn't want to scare it off. However, it would be a week before they signed on the other option, and if Jerry would let them hold $100,000 he could have a week. Lowell never looked back.

In his eagerness to get a shot at the land, Jerry had told the owners that he thought he could put together a deal that would net them a $5,000-per-acre profit. That meant that his own profit from anything he might put together would lie in whatever money he could get over $12,000 per acre.

As the four men sat in silence, Jerry was doing his damnedest to look contemplative. If he accepted Gamboa's offer he personally would clear $795,000 only thirty-six hours after he had located the property. But he couldn't do it. Not the first damn offer, not with what he knew about the Mexican's deep pockets.

"Is that pretty much what you see as tops?" Jerry asked. He had decided to chew on the inside of his cheek and frown a little more.

"That is our offer," Gamboa said. His smile was gone, and had been replaced by a look of sincere apology.

Jerry looked at Crisman. "I'm afraid I'm going to have to

make a telephone call," he said. "You have an office I can use?"

"Sure," Crisman said. He pressed a button on a small panel near the edge of the table.

"Will you give me five minutes, Mr. Gamboa?" Jerry asked. "I'm going to have to check this out with my people in Austin."

"Of course. I understand." Gamboa smiled.

The woman who had been in earlier came to the door and took Jerry to an office down the hall. After telling him he could dial direct, she walked out of the room and closed the door behind her, leaving him alone. He stood stock still for a second, a shit-eating grin slowly covering his face. Then he slapped his left hand over his crotch, squatted, squeezed tight, and made a hook 'em horns sign with his right hand raised high in the air. He started laughing, making private wheezing sounds, as he flopped over on the leather ottoman, still gripping his crotch, raised his knobby ostrich cowboy boots, and spurred the air as if he were riding a bare-backed bull in a rodeo—which he had never, ever, even come close to doing in real life. When he had had enough of that, he got up again and tried to stop laughing. He went to a mirror and tried to compose his face, working at it, then made up his mind to go for it.

When he came back into the conference room, Gamboa and Sosa had their heads together and Crisman was just coming out of the executive bathroom. That was good. He had left them alone. Jerry went back around to his side of the desk. He wore a sober expression, as if he were going to have to deliver some bad news.

"I'm going to have to have your final offer, Mr. Gamboa," he said. "Some other players have gotten into this."

Crisman picked up his Cross pencil and screwed the lead inside. Jerry thought maybe he was going to stab it into the side of Jerry's neck if Gamboa folded.

"What will you have to have for us to get the property?" Sosa asked. Gamboa had leaned back from the table.

"I'm afraid it'll have to be seventeen thousand, Mr. Sosa. I'm sorry."

"Agreed." Sosa spoke without tension, as if he had just bought a television set.

SPIRAL

Jerry Lowell had just made $1,325,000 in less than thirty-six hours from the sale of a piece of land that he didn't even own.

Mr. Benigo Gamboa Parra had made an even better bargain. The $4,505,000 he was investing in 265 acres of prime Texas real estate was not, strictly speaking, his money.

Summer came early. By March the mild coastal winter had disappeared and spring was a disregarded season: a few pacific days in early May. In the closing days of the month temperatures had climbed to record highs and the usual spring rains, seemingly confused by the brevity of the season, were few and slight. The heavy gray pillows of Gulf clouds that could pile up unexpectedly and darken the day with torrents of warm rain never paused, but drifted quickly on the southerly breezes passing over the city in bright white spumes that gave way to clear skies by midmorning. June ushered in two straight weeks of thermometer readings over a hundred, and by July Houston was locked into one of the hottest and driest summers of the city's history. It was the time of the long days, and at night, of Sirius, the dog star.

The old Belgrano home was on the southeastern edge of the city. When the mansion had been built more than a hundred years before, it had been part of a large estate that lay deep in the isolated coastal lowlands, almost in the floodplains of the bayous that wriggled their way toward the back bays of the Gulf twenty miles to the east. Built in the nineteenth-century southern tradition, it had been constructed of brick and limestone with wide wooden verandas on both floors that were meant to take advantage of the meager and torpid Gulf air that made its way across the surrounding miles of scrub-brush flats and into the east Texas woods of cypress and loblolly pine. The house was situated in the center of a cypress grove encircled by a high wall, its pediment crowned with sharp wrought-iron fleurs-de-lis.

Now all that was left of the estate lay within those same dun-colored, crumbling walls. The big cypresses and oaks remained, casting a perpetual twilight of shadow over grounds which had been unattended for so long no one remembered them otherwise. The old house itself was hidden, obscured by the wild undergrowth of dead weeds and grasses, lost within the matted tangles of coral and butterfly vines. The once wooded countryside had been scored and cross-hatched by the shaggy streets of one of the city's Latin barrios that had crowded and bullied itself right up to the pitted estate walls. The Houston Ship Channel was less than a mile away, and in the near distance toward the bays the barrios died away where miles of oil refineries, stark and sprawling, attached themselves to the channel like noisome tumors.

The entrance to the Belgrano estate faced Chicon Street in the core of the barrio, its graffiti-smeared walls abutting the sidewalk, its badly rusted gates sagging over a strip of bald caliche that went from the street to about three feet inside the gates, the span of an arm's reach through the wrought-iron bars where the smooth paving stones had been plundered over the years. The body lay in this patch of chalky dust.

It was approaching nine-thirty in the morning and the dry heat had already stirred the insects in the parched undergrowth on the other side of the high wall. The edge of the dead man's right shoulder and the tip of his splayed-out right shoe were just now being touched by the thin light of the morning sun; the rest of him was in the blue shade, suspended on the white bed of caliche dust in his own silence and in the rasping drone of the insects.

He lay on his back, his legs straight out and parallel to each other and to the gate, his left shoulder up under the bars themselves as if he had been trying to crawl under. He was dressed in a charcoal-gray suit with stripes of a lighter gray, the coat neatly closed with a single button above his waist. A soiled white shirt, open at the collar and without a tie, showed above the V of his coat lapels. His hands were placed properly inside the coat pockets, the thumbs outside as if he were posing for a quaint old-fashioned photograph. He wore a pair of scruffy black lace-up shoes, but the laces were missing, the empty eyelets giving the impression of dispossession. He appeared to be a Mexican in his early thirties, chunky, not tall.

In the very center of the man's lead-colored forehead, just above his eyebrows, a single carpenter's nail protruded from his skull. There was no mess; it was very neatly done. One end of a tiny black string was tied to the nail, and to the other end of the string was tied a large red ant. The ant was trying to walk away from the string, and in doing so was clambering back and forth in a shallow arc across the dreaming gaze of the man's opened eyes.

Chapter 2

Scenes of homicide, Haydon thought as he stood over the reposing body, were contradictory affairs. The minimal constants, by definition, never varied: a criminal death; a Cain, an Abel. The variables were infinite: time and space and circumstance. It was not when or where or why men murdered that made homicide investigations a tedious business. It was the surety of it, the inevitability that during every single day that dawned man could be depended upon to prove again that even after thousands of years of progressing civilization, he was utterly incapable of controlling his earliest criminal impulse. In this one thing man was frighteningly consistent, and incorrigible.

The sun was steadily rising overhead, pushing the shadows farther back into the gloomy drive. The cheap suit was dusty. Whoever had put him here had wrestled him around in the caliche until they had maneuvered him into the position they wanted. Though they hadn't bothered about the ashy blotches on the dark material, they had taken the pains to straighten his coattails so that they were not tucked up under the dead man's back. Haydon noticed too the socks. See-through gray nylon with dark vertical stripes. Tropical.

It wasn't an ugly scene, but it was definitely disconcerting, because of the peculiar lead pallor of the bloodless olive flesh, and, of course, the nail and the tethered ant.

"You ever see anything like this before?" Mooney asked. He was holding between two fat fingers the last bite of a fried pie he had bought from a vending machine as they left the station.

Haydon shook his head as his dark brown eyes studied the corpse with a singularity of concentration that precluded any further response. He stood with his arms crossed, his straight lean frame seemingly at odds with the inherent disorder of a homicide scene. His thick sable hair was neatly barbered, the temples beginning to have enough gray in them now so that it was one of the first things you noticed about him. He was conscious of the broad band of sun falling across the shoulders of his suit, penetrating like a heat lamp, drawing the perspiration from the pores beneath the high collar of his shirt. Ever correct, his silk tie tightly knotted, his shoes polished, he stood over the shabbily dressed corpse and tried to place the dead man's odd mien within the framework of something sensible.

Behind him, outside the area of the crime scene roped off with Day-Glo yellow plastic tape, he could hear the four uniformed officers talking to the crowd of fifteen or twenty people that had gathered on the sidewalk and street blocked off by the patrol cars. Haydon did not like to be overheard at a crime scene. Every patrolman who knew anything about working homicides knew that.

In fact, Haydon's reputation for adhering to a personal, and sometimes eccentric, code of conduct was notorious, and reached far beyond the police department. Foremost was his obstinacy in demanding absolute privacy for his investigations, as well as for himself. He sustained a relationship of constant tension with the news media, and detested having either his cases or his name mentioned in any context. He considered having his picture reproduced the ultimate desecration. This obsession had been strained to the breaking point in the past by the fact that he had been the principal investigator in a number of sensational cases.

In addition, Haydon's personal life was guaranteed to attract media attention at the slightest opportunity. He was the only son of a respected and prosperous international lawyer whose death had left Haydon with a considerable inheritance. Aside from his work, he lived a very private life with his wife, Nina, an architect, in the family's old and spacious residence in a fashionable part of the city near Rice University. It was the natural inclination of those who did not know him well to wonder why he worked at all, much less as a homicide detective. But at age forty, and after thirteen years in homicide, Haydon had long ago dispelled those questions among his colleagues. In the police department his reputation was quite different, though perhaps no less enigmatic.

"You figure it's some kind of gang deal?" Mooney reached into his pocket and took out the waxed-paper package the pie had come in. He wrapped the piece of pie in the paper, dropped it into his pocket, and sucked the sweet off his fingers.

Haydon shrugged. "If it is, they're being uncharacteristically creative."

By now there were a few flies coming around, even though there was nothing to attract them. There was no blood. If the death had been the result of the nail, the mess it would have caused had been left somewhere else, and the man's face meticulously cleaned.

The crime-lab technicians and medical examiner's investigator arrived at the same time, and the uniformed officers moved the crowd back even farther as the vans rolled up. The police photographer was the first to step over the tape and approach Haydon.

He glanced at the body, turned to Haydon to say something as he reached into his camera case, and then jerked his head around to the body again.

"God Almighty," he said. "What is *this?*"

"There's an ant tied to the string," Haydon said. He didn't know this photographer. "You'll see it when you get closer. It's up near his hairline. I want sharp close-ups."

Mooney sauntered over to speak to the coroner's investigator, an older man and a former homicide detective himself. Together they started measuring the scene as Mooney sketched the layout on the back of an envelope he had gotten off the dashboard of the car.

Haydon moved over nearer the high wall and looked at the caliche, the gates, and the driveway. The paving stones where the driveway began again inside the wall were buckled and tufts of dead grass the color of dried corn husks grew through the cracks. The drive made an immediate turn to the left about fifty feet beyond the gates, and disappeared around a corner of scorched brush and weeds. Haydon stepped to the gates, picked up a small caliche clod, and threw it into the weeds. He could hear the grasshoppers popping against the parched undergrowth. The keening insects drowned out the sounds of the city.

Backing against the wall in the narrow border of what was left of the morning shadow, Haydon faced the sunlight as he took a pair of tortoiseshell sunglasses out of his jacket pocket and put them on. While the photographer and then the coroner's investigator did their work, he looked across at the crowd.

There were three or four high school kids in the tribal dress of their particular barrio. One, a girl with a single yellow dangling earring, kept her hand over her mouth and her head turned half away from the ugly scene as though she could not bear to watch it, though her eyes never left the body as Finn did what he had to do to take the corpse's temperature. A few middle-aged women hugged themselves and talked quietly in a little wad off to one side. A redheaded delivery man whose uniform name patch said "Red" and whose bread van was parked down the block in front of Montoya's grocery popped his gum and alternated his attention between the dead Mexican and the perky nipples under the thin tank top of the girl with the yellow earring. There were a couple of older men who appeared to be regulars from La Perla bar across the street, and a barber wearing a white short-sleeved nylon smock and a cigarette tucked behind his ear.

There were four or five others, but none of them caught Haydon's attention as individuals. They were merely "crowd," the back of a head, a blank face, a quarter profile.

When they were through, Mooney and the coroner's investigator started toward Haydon. Finn, whom everyone but Haydon called Jimbo, was probably fifteen years older than Mooney, and was his physical opposite. Tall and thin, he seemed prematurely bent with age. His octagonal rimless glasses had sunk deep into the sides of his nose, and he always had one or two white patches on his face where he had had skin cancers burned off.

"You got a nice one here, Stuart," Finn said.

"It looks like it," Haydon said. He guessed from the fidgety way Finn was pulling back his lips and repeatedly clenching his even white teeth that he was breaking in a new set of dentures. "Are you through with him?" he asked.

"All I'm gonna do."

"Then let's take a look."

The three men stepped over to the body and squatted down. Haydon leaned over and sniffed at the dead man's mouth, then turned his attention to the feet. The guy hadn't been particular about how he treated his patent-leather shoes. They were scuffed and scratched, the heels worn considerably on the outsides, and the toes turned up slightly, indicating the shoes were too large for his feet. Haydon shoved a yellow pencil into the instep of one shoe and pushed it off the foot. He turned it over in the dust with the pencil and read the brand name on the inside. They could make out only one word in the sweat-stained leather: Canada.

"Canada!" Mooney snorted. "A Mex'can from goddam Canada. Beautiful."

Ed Mooney had none of Haydon's reserve. He was overweight, and gaining. He was Irish, impatient, garrulous, prejudiced, and profane. They had been partners for four years, ever since Haydon had stuck his neck out to get Mooney transferred from vice to homicide. It was a move Mooney had coveted for years, but was always denied because his own irascible personality had created bad blood for him in the upper echelons of the department, where such decisions were made. The two men had been friends since the academy, and their opposite personalities, instead of clashing, meshed like cogged wheels.

They looked at the hole in the big toe of the thin sock through which a dirty, horny toenail protruded, and another hole, larger, worn at the heel. Haydon wondered about the missing shoelaces.

Carefully, he probed the suit pockets. Nothing in the inside coat or lapel pockets, nothing in the trousers pockets. Leaning against the gate, Mooney and Finn gripped the body by the right shoulder and lifted it while Haydon quickly checked the hip pockets. Nothing.

Haydon felt the stickiness under the cuffs of his shirt, the briny sweat soaking into the lizard band of his wristwatch. Feeling his own clothes becoming a blotter for perspiration, his attention was drawn to the damp spots on the dead man's coat pockets which concealed his hands. He reached down and pulled at the right coat sleeve, pinching the cloth just below the elbow. There was some resistance, from the beginnings of rigor mortis, Haydon thought, and he held the coattail with his other hand as he jerked firmly at the sleeve. When the hand finally came out, it pulled the lining with it.

"She-it," Mooney said.

The hand lay palm up in the dust, and in the stiffening cramp of death the fingers had contracted into a claw with five bloody stubs where the fingernails had been. Three of the fingers had been wrenched into impossible angles, one bent completely back over itself. The pocket lining was crusty with the coagulating blood serum that had seeped from the wounds.

"He pissed off *some*body." Finn turned his head and spat in the dust.

Haydon rose to a crouch and pulled on the dead man's arm until he had dragged his left shoulder out from under the gate. He straddled the body and, stooping, pulled the other arm from the other pocket. Again the pocket lining came out with the hand. Again the disfigured stubs.

Squatting down again, Haydon examined the fingers. At first he thought the fingernails were missing, then he realized they simply had been mashed beyond recognition. The ends of the fingers had been flattened by something, and then they had swollen, making it difficult to tell exactly what had been done to them.

"Goddam. Somebody really did a job on this tamale," Mooney said.

Haydon glanced at his partner. Ed Mooney didn't enjoy these as he used to. His face was flushed, and it wasn't completely attributable to the heat and his increasing obesity.

Turning his attention once again to the dead man's face, Haydon saw that his features were predominantly Indian. It was impossible to determine if he was Mexican, Salvadoran, Colombian, Cuban, Guatemalan, or what. Houston was a refuge for people from all over Latin America. A refuge, and sometimes a staging ground. The corpse had started a mustache, which had only a few days' growth, and there was a relatively recent scar about half an inch long in the shape of a shallow crescent at the lower corner of his right eye.

"Gases building up in there," Finn said, pointing at the pink emerging between the corpse's slightly parted lips. "It's pushing his tongue out. We'd better get him into the cooler."

Haydon didn't say anything. He was looking at the nail in the forehead. It was a large galvanized finishing nail and extruded at a slight angle about an inch out of the pewter-colored skin. Though the wound at the nail's entrance was clean and bloodless, it seemed to Haydon a particularly sinister form of mutilation, more chilling even than the condition of the tortured hands.

The ant was still alive, but motionless except for a single wavering antenna at the edge of the man's oily hairline. Haydon took the pencil and prodded it. The ant moved about an inch before it stopped again, its head down next to the ridge of thick hair. The string was tied just in front of the insect's bulbous abdomen.

Haydon put the pencil in his pocket, and the three men stood.

"Nail didn't kill him," Finn said flatly.

"I don't think so either." Haydon was looking at the ant. "I guess you can take him," he said. "If Vanstraten's there would you tell him we're coming over, and ask him if he would wait around for this one?"

"Sure thing," Finn said, and he motioned for his assistants to bring the gurney.

Haydon and Mooney moved away as the coroner's assistants collapsed the aluminum gurney, wrestled the corpse onto the sheets, covered it, raised the gurney, and wheeled it to the back doors of the van.

"You want to give this to the Chicano squad?" Mooney asked. "This guy definitely ain't Irish."

Haydon shook his head slightly and looked away. He looked down the street, squinting into the morning sunlight. He wondered how many homicides he had investigated in morning sunlight. He would like to know. In fact, he wondered how many kinds of morning sunlight he had stood in and looked at dead people. A few came readily to mind. The deep gold light in which the old man had lain. His name was Petersen, and he had replaced every window in his odd little house with amber glass. He had been dead three days when they got there, and his cat was sitting on his chest, having eaten one side of the old man's fat lower lip. Mr. Petersen and his cat, levitating in the thick gold light. There was the cool blue light of a January dawn in which he had viewed the body of one Jamie Frank Carlisle, whose assailant had shot him point-blank in the navel, and had left him sitting in the backseat of his car with his bare feet in a Styrofoam ice chest full of cold water. He remembered the eerie apple-green light on the teenaged girl he had seen only minutes after a spring hailstorm. She lay nude and face down in a vacant lot, raped and strangled, white hailstones in her black hair, and a solitary one, tinted aqua by the light, melting in the small depression above her hips. The pearl light on the waterlogged breasts of the prostitute Sally Steen, who surfaced in the steamy water of Buffalo Bayou, like the Lady in the Lake. He remembered . . .

"You'd think it'd rain," Mooney said.

It took Haydon a moment to come back. "It will," he said.

"Yeah," Mooney snorted. "And then everything along that goddam Braeswood will flood again. I'll tell ya, the city oughta issue scuba gear over there. Hell, I wouldn't care if it didn't rain for a year. A little drought would do that damn swamp some good."

"Let's keep it," Haydon said, referring to the case. He had taken a handkerchief out of his pocket and was wiping his forehead, lifting his sunglasses and going over the straight bridge of his nose.

"Hell, I don't care. I'll bet it's gonna be a queer mess. They're vindictive little shits. They'd do something like this."

"Maybe so," Haydon said, but he didn't believe it. The contrivance of the nail and the ant was not an act of spite or venomous retaliation for spurned or unfaithful love. It was a calculated performance, too specific to have been done in a moment of hot, unreasoning passion. And the tortured fingers. There had been method in their mutilation; it was not a random viciousness. This would be worth investigating. He would like to meet the man who had tied the string.

"I got the name of the old *mamacita* who stumbled onto the guy. You didn't want to talk to her, did ya?"

"We can interview her later if we need to," Haydon said,

neatly refolding the handkerchief and putting it back in his pocket.

Mooney looked at the wall and the gate as if registering their existence for the first time. "This place deserted, or what?"

"It looks deserted, doesn't it?" Haydon said, not answering the question. He moved to the gates and looked through the wrought-iron grillwork again. "No one saw anything, I suppose," he said, turning around and facing the street.

"Nothin'. First two officers on the scene talked to the people who came up. Nobody knew *nada* about *nada*. The barber—there was a barber here—was the one who found them. He came along across the street to open his shop and saw her over here layin' right beside this dead guy. He didn't know what the hell. Thought there was some kind of slaughter, bodies everywhere. He's the one put in the call. Then he comes over here, sees Mama squirming, figures out that she'd just fainted, and helps her up."

Haydon thought a minute. He looked both ways along the sidewalk, and then out to the dusty street. Traffic was occasional, but picking up. The morning light was already turning harsh.

Chapter 3

Blas Medrano Banda rolled over on his side and looked out the open window at the late-morning sunlight. It was impossible to relax; the bed was really little more than a cot. The best thing he could do was to shift positions regularly on the limp sheets and let the blue plastic blades of the fan that sat in an empty chair push hot damp air over his body. Despite the drought, the humidity remained high, especially here near the bayou. Sticky was as close to dry as anyone ever could hope to be in this city.

He had learned long ago that patience was the great art in these affairs. How many hours had he spent letting his mind range along the continuum that was his memory, a boundless entertainment that could evoke an equally boundless spectrum of emotion? Now, it was patience that was required. To achieve true patience you had to play games with time, to select a discrete point in Plato's moving image of eternity and hold it in your mind, even against its will. Boyhood. Father Donato. And the subject of patience. The priest stood in front of the classroom of boys, at his wit's end. *Quo usque, Catilina, abutere patientia nostra?* "How long, Catiline, will you abuse our patience?" Cicero always had served Father Donato well, even in his frustrations. And in that school in Guadalajara there had been many frustrations.

A tug horn bellowed in the late-morning heat. It sounded foreign to him. From an oak tree beyond the dry weeds, the deep fluting of a mourning dove drifted through the window, sad and comforting, as if calling him home. He imagined that it had flown all the way from Jalisco, over the hundreds of miles of desert and brown mountains, just to sit nearby and call to him, beguiling his memory.

Why else had the priest come to mind just now? That had been so long ago, before Blas had lost his faith, not in God—he never thought of God anymore—but in men. What is it when an exile begins to think of home again? Not a real exile, but a man like himself, a kind of disobedient Jonah in search of Tarshish. Or, more accurately, hiding from God. Hiding from God. That was an oxymoronic proposition, Father Donato had said. And later, when Blas had turned his back on the hopes the priest had held for him, and embraced instead a politic and philosophy so radically different, the old man had something very much the same to say. But by that time he was approaching the end of a long and cruel illness. He was frail and dying, everything made him cry. It didn't matter.

Even the drought in this city was a source of nostalgia. They had been here four days, and every night he went outside to walk in the grounds, thinking and smoking cigarettes. When he moved against the weeds, the thistle pods clacked their shriveled seeds like the gourd rattles the Huicholes filled with cockleburs, locked in the purgatory of dry weather. At times he could smell the dust too, hanging in the night air like a moistureless fog churned up by the cars that passed on the poorly paved street beyond the wall. In all his years of traveling, he had come to realize that dust smelled the same the world over. And yet, always, in every place, it reminded him of home.

At this moment, though, he looked out the window to the white light of a clear day. He wore only a pair of khaki pants, which he had rolled almost to his knees. The old house had thick walls and deep window ledges, and on this one sat a jug of water, from which he occasionally wet his hands, and ran his fingers through his black hair until it was damp and pressed back from his forehead. He lay on his side and waited.

Ireno was overdue. He registered that fact. He would like to be able to say he wasn't worried about it. If he were Indian, like Ireno and Rubio, he would have the proper psychology for this, the blank-faced patience for which they were famous, and which the *mestizos* and *criollos* attributed to simple-minded passivity. But Blas knew different now. He had worked with Ireno long enough to know the almost Zenlike patience for what it was. Ireno could watch the lanky body of Death walking toward him across a mile of flat, shadeless desert and wait for Him with a serene and steady pulse. It was in the mind, or rather, far back in the place where the mind is not mind, but soul.

Blas listened. Old houses creaked in the hot weather. Only a few minutes earlier Rubio had passed his doorway and told him something was going on outside. He thought of the two of them, Rubio and Teodoro, peering from the edges of the shades, straining to see, but not be seen. He could feel the intensity of their combined anxieties, like a tangible energy in the silence. Like the heat in the house. He lay on his side and waited, his back to the empty room, to the door that led to the rest of the empty house, to the incident on the street. It was a test he gave himself, to see if he could remain detached. He wondered if someone would come into the room and shoot him in the back of the head.

He heard the boards creaking under the footsteps in the corridor, and someone stopped in the doorway behind him.

"Blas!" Rubio's voice was a harsh whisper. *"Es la policía.* They are doing something at the gates."

There was a flutter in his chest, and then his heart caught its stride just as he turned over and sat on the edge of the cot.

"What do you mean, 'doing something'?" The old floor was rough under his bare feet.

"Something. I don't know."

Rubio's speech was marked by an occasional muted whistle from a notch in his lower lip where two white teeth—an incisor and a canine—were permanently exposed in the groove of dark flesh. An old knife wound from his youth, his first taste of violence, Blas thought. A bitter pun, for Rubio had indeed consumed more than his share of it since then.

"There are people. Police cars." Rubio was not easily alarmed. He had had far more experience than any of them. He was good on the streets, knew his way around in the barrios of San Antonio as well as Houston. Blas looked into his Indian eyes, and saw the coyote.

"Are they coming in?" He stood and reached back for the Heckler pistol that had been on the window ledge beside the water jug.

He followed Rubio down the hallway and into another room, bare except for its two cots and two chairs draped with wadded clothes. There were a few wooden packing cases on top of which automatic weapons lay in various stages of disassembly. There were two windows on the street side of the room, and as Blas moved toward one of them a young man stood back to give him his place.

It was Teodoro Anica's first trip, and he was eager to do well. He never relaxed. Despite the heat, he never undressed to his underclothes like the others; he was not going to be caught off guard. As Blas squatted down to the windowsill and carefully lifted the shade, he could feel Teodoro watching him. He knew the young man was trying to read something in his face. The adoration angered him. He had no patience with Anica's zealous eagerness to do the job.

The Indians kept their thoughts to themselves. God knew why they were doing it. They were outcasts as far as the Brigade was concerned, but the Brigade used them because they were the best at what they did. Prejudice had its practical limits. Blas himself tried not to think about it at all. It had to be done and he was doing it, so to hell with it. Teodoro, however, wore his Brigade pride on his forehead. Blas and Teodoro shared a cultural history: a *criollo* heritage, family wealth, staunch conservatism, fierce Catholicism, the Byzantine experience of the Autonomous University of Guadalajara, the fervent secrecy and brotherhood of the Brigade. But he felt no kinship. The boy's enthusiasm was repugnant to him.

"Binoculars!" Blas whispered, and reached back an open hand as he kept his eyes locked to the slit held open with the thumb of his other hand.

Teodoro grabbed the Zeiss glasses from a small bag by his cot and handed them to him.

"Hold the shade," Blas said. Teodoro crouched beside him and held the slit at precisely the same lever. Blas put the

Heckler automatic between his knees on the floor and adjusted the binoculars. *"Poquito más."*

Teodoro raised the shade slightly, and Blas rested the front of the lenses on the paint-chipped sill. The weeds and matted vines were so thick he could see only glimpses of the street through the loops of brown vegetation. He saw the police cars and made out the crowd along the sidewalk. They were looking at something, and the way they were gathered it appeared that the gates were indeed the center of everyone's attention. Suddenly a man stood from behind a blur of weeds, and continued looking down at his feet, his big stomach forcing apart the loose sides of his sport coat as he wiped at the sweat on his face. Then a second man stood. He was taller, trim, well dressed. He wore a tie, a light summer suit; he stood straight and his hair was neatly combed.

Two other vehicles arrived, both vans, and Blas recognized the morgue wagon. The sweat under his arms turned cold.

"Damn!" He jerked away from the window. "Stay here. I've got to get a better look."

He didn't want to think. He concentrated on what his legs and feet were doing, down the stairs, turning, down again and into the entrance hall. At the bottom he doubled back, and burst out the door at the rear of the house that opened onto the long porch. Crouching, he followed the porch to the end of the house, paused, then stepped silently off and scrambled to the thickest undergrowth in the direction of the front gates. The cypress trees cut out the sunlight as he inched along on the spongy mat of desiccated leaves and twigs.

The scratchy transmissions of the police radios were audible now, but he still couldn't see anything. He crawled a few yards on his stomach and elbows until he came in line with the drive that led from the gates. The granular debris of dead cypress leaves stuck to his sweaty forearms and stomach and bit into his elbows as he raised the binoculars. He was fifty or sixty yards from the gates. At this distance the binoculars brought everything right up to his nose.

He twisted the focus adjustment, overcompensated, twisted it back, ignoring everything but the area at the bottom of the gates. The body came into focus, lying in the caliche. He recognized the suit first, and then Ireno's profile. Goddam,

SPIRAL

goddam. He stared hard, his eyes trying to crawl right through the lenses as he touched the eyepiece for even sharper magnification. Holding his breath, he saw the nail. He knew what was tied to it. *El hijo de la chingada!* Lucas Negrete had left a message, and in doing so had brought the police right to the gates. It was an arrogant maneuver. And clever. The game had begun in earnest.

Haydon and Mooney turned off of Old Spanish
Trail Road, a wide commercial thoroughfare that stretched
from South Main across to Interstate 45 and resembled anything but a trail, and drove along the median-divided drive.
The new building was situated at the edge of dozens of acres
of asphalt which served as additional parking for the Medical
Center's South Extension. Signs at both ends of the lot, one
at Bareswood and one in the grassy median at Old Spanish
Trail, told you where you were. There were gates and chain-
link fences surrounding the lots. The medical examiner's office sat just outside the gates.

The lobby of the new office smelled of fresh masonry and
caulking and paint. Haydon wondered how long those odors
of optimism and new beginning would last. He and Mooney
showed their identification to the receptionist and walked
through to one of the four autopsy rooms.

Dr. Harl Vanstraten was standing to one side of the room
slipping into his surgical gown. Even from across the room
his tall, thick-chested frame seemed in clearer focus than everything else. His thinning hair was cleanly parted, his face
could not have had a closer shave, and his sharp Nordic features caused one not to be surprised by the Germanic inflections in his speech.

"A real whodunit, huh, Stuart?" Vanstraten was smiling
as Haydon entered, his baritone echoing slightly in the starkly
furnished room.

He turned aside to a glass cabinet and removed a new pair

of surgical gloves from an open box. Adding talcum to the insides, he shook them gently before inserting each massive hand, beginning with the right.

"I went with Renata last night to see a play at the Alley Theater," he said, working with the gloves. "First time in weeks."

Haydon looked at his friend's broad back. "Did you enjoy it?"

Vanstraten laughed and turned around. "I don't know. There was a minute, near the end of the first act, when it didn't hold my attention, and my mind wandered to something here—a woman who died for *no* apparent reason during a rape—and except between acts when I somehow managed to talk about the play with Renata, I don't remember a thing. Excuse me. I've got to change the tapes."

Haydon watched him round the corner to his office, and tried to imagine his predicament. Vanstraten was an unrepentant daydreamer, which infuriated his wife because he also liked to work the social circuits, where he was a popular figure. He loved being around people, but often he didn't pay any attention to them. If he saw or heard something that triggered a change of direction in his thoughts, he was gone. Sometimes he recovered in time to save himself, and sometimes he didn't. It was an embarrassment for Renata, but rarely was anyone ever offended by this eccentricity. Vanstraten's mind traveled in oblique channels, and to destinations most people never knew existed.

Two aluminum autopsy tables stood side by side in the center of the almost phosphorescent light of the room. Over each table a chrome microphone hung from the ceiling alongside a single silver-bowl surgical lamp. Above that, frosted skylights let in the clean, bright daylight. The Mexican was the only cadaver in the room. Jimbo Finn stood beside him, awkwardly stooped as if he had a catch in his back. The Mexican's head was wrapped in a plastic bag which was taped around his neck. Finn wasn't going to let the ant get away from him.

When Vanstraten came back he was kneading his surgical gloves, tightening the membranous latex around the fingers. He got straight to business.

"You have pictures, Jimbo?"

Finn nodded. "Sure do."

"Well, Richard, shall we proceed?"

Richard Hull had been at the morgue nearly ten years, and was the only diener of the several employed there whom Vanstraten would allow to assist him. He was an easygoing black man, almost as big as the medical examiner himself, who handled the cadavers in a deferential manner, as if they were still in possession of their emotions of fear and embarrassment at their situation.

As Haydon, Mooney, and Finn watched, Vanstraten and Hull began removing the dead man's clothes, carefully undressing him as if they were his valets. The process was awkward, for the rigor mortis had become even more severe than it had been when they had gone through the pockets an hour or so earlier. Vanstraten went over each piece of clothing with meticulous attention, noting especially the stains in the suit pockets. As he finished with each article of clothing, he gave it to Hull, who put it in a plastic bag, sealed it, labeled it, and set it aside.

With the removal of the last sock, the Mexican lay naked on the grates in the aluminum table that kept him above the circulating water that would carry away the blood. It was at this point that Haydon first noticed the odor of disinfectant and heard the gurgling of the lavage troughs.

Vanstraten took a pair of scissors, cut the masking tape around the man's neck, and removed the plastic bag. The ant tied to the nail looked even queerer now than it had when the man had lain on the dirty sidewalk. The ant had sought refuge from the air conditioning in the corner of one eye, where it had curled up in a ball the size of a small pea.

Vanstraten hissed through his teeth. "Very good. I've never seen this before. Not a nail with an ant tied to it. No, never." He shook his head and pulled the ant up, dangling it on the string. "A big ant," he said, stooping down and looking at it eye to eye. "Tied with thread. Black polyester thread." A huge man concentrating his inquisitive energy on the riddle of a small red dot. He shook his head again, snipped the string, and let the ant drop into a clear plastic vial that Hull was holding, and quickly capped. The plastic vial was labeled and put on the top shelf of an aluminum cart Hull had rolled over near the table. It was the first specimen of many that would crowd the cart in various bottles, jars, pans, and jugs before Vanstraten finished.

Without being asked, Finn stepped forward with his camera and began photographing again. When he finished, Hull and Vanstraten turned the man over and Finn took more photographs. Then Hull and Finn lifted the grated tray holding the body and transferred it to a nearby gurney, which Hull rolled down the hall to radiology.

While they were waiting, Vanstraten said, "And when did you find this fellow, Stuart?" They moved to one side of the room near a desk, and Vanstraten lighted a Dunhill cigarette from a red box that lay on the desk. He offered one to Haydon, who shook his head. "Sorry. I forgot. You're sticking with it, huh?"

Haydon nodded. "I still smoke cigars, but only a few a day."

Vanstraten regarded him with a slight smile. "Very good, Stuart." He held up his cigarette and looked at it. "So, when did you find him?"

"We got there about nine-twenty, nine-thirty. I understand he was found shortly after nine o'clock."

"And this ant business. What about that?"

"I don't have any idea."

Vanstraten snorted, wrinkling his forehead. "Can you imagine? This is truly innovative. What do you suppose? A warning? A signature?"

Haydon shook his head. "Simple human cruelty," he said.

"I think this will be a very strange one," Vanstraten mused, not disappointed at the prospect.

"They're all strange," Haydon said. "They're all routine and they're all strange."

"A little philosophy," Vanstraten said, grinning.

"Yes, exactly." Haydon looked at the pathologist.

Vanstraten laughed, and the doors to the X-ray room swung open as Hull and the radiologist wheeled the body back in place under the bright lights. Mooney and Finn came over from where they had been talking about Houston's high percentage of available office space, and the autopsy began.

Pressing the floor switch to the microphone, Vanstraten began a monotonous statistical recitation: date, autopsy number, John Doe number, and persons present at the autopsy.

The data of his external examination: height, weight, skin condition, body development, fat distribution, color of eyes, hair, condition of ears, mouth, neck, genitalia, damage to the hands, discolored areas around the lower abdomen, below the left nipple, below either kidney, and on the genitalia.

With his scalpel, Vanstraten quickly made a large incision down the man's chest in the shape of a Y, the upper branches of which started at the front of each shoulder, crossed below the nipples, joined at the bottom of the sternum, and continued down the middle of the abdomen, and around the navel to the pubis.

Assisted by the docile Hull, Vanstraten cut the skin away from the ribs so that it could be folded back on either side, exposing not only the ribs themselves, but the abdominal cavity as well. With long-handled shears that looked like snub-nosed branch trimmers, Vanstraten began cutting the ribs, starting at the bottom and working upward in an outward curve to the clavicle. When this had been done on each side, he lifted out the entire section, including the breastbone, and set it aside, revealing the contents of the chest cavity. At this point the entire inner workings of the dead man, from throat to pubis, were ready for Vanstraten to examine.

"Now is the time to be philosophical, Stuart," Vanstraten said, smiling at Haydon. He gestured at the cadaver. "This is what we are. Rich and poor alike, we each possess this marvelously complex system that makes even the most sophisticated computer, with all its dazzling microchip capabilities, look like a child's toy. The human intellect is not capable of constructing so delicate a system . . . not in a million years."

It was true, Haydon thought, not in a million years. And yet, what man could not achieve by force of intellect, he could cause by simple brute passion. Any pair of grunting fools could play God. He looked steadily at the cadaver, hoping he could manage somehow to see it differently. But in the end, he thought, they *are* only playing. They have no idea . . . no idea at all, what they really have done in those brief, greedy moments. It seemed quite absurd.

He watched as Vanstraten began what would become an exhaustive investigation. It occurred to him that in one sense, they would learn more about this man in the next hour than the man had ever known about himself. Like an ancient seer, Vanstraten would search the coils of the body as if he were reading the entrails of a sacrificial lamb, as if each organ had a voice, and each voice a tale, and the sum of their tales a confession. And yet, in another sense, they would remain forever ignorant. Of this man's true essence they would learn nothing, nor could they ever hope to. They would never see in his face the animating spirit, never hear the sound of his voice or his laughter, never sense in him the subtle changes of embarrassment or grief. That unscientific thing that is life had already escaped them.

The autopsy was a long one. Vanstraten knew that when Haydon requested his personal attention to a particular cadaver it was only because Haydon himself found it to be one of more than routine interest, and desired more than a routine explanation during the process. Therefore, the pathologist's narration was deliberate and detailed, with numerous parenthetical elaborations that would not appear in the formal report.

When the time came for Vanstraten to dissect the cranium and remove the brain, Haydon turned away and walked out of the room and into the hall. It was long and white and empty. The years of having to watch autopsies had disciplined him. He was seldom disturbed by them, only with children and some women. But during the past five or six months something had begun to happen during the cranials. He first noticed it as a vague uneasiness that he thought was a temporary quirky reaction to a routine he had gotten used to many years before. But it didn't go away. Instead he became increasingly agitated by this process to the point that he would perspire and his heart rate would skyrocket. Once he thought he was going to faint. Now he simply refused to watch them; they had become unbearable. It was not nausea that affected him, but something more. It was, he thought, something like fear, though he knew that made no sense. Still, it was something like that.

He could hear Vanstraten's narration through the door. When the pathologist began his instructions to the secretary who would be typing the report, Haydon knew he was through. He took a deep breath and went back into the room.

"That's it," Vanstraten said, looking at Haydon, who did

not approach the autopsy table again but lingered near the door. "Let me wash up and I'll give you an overview. Come."

Haydon nodded, and followed Vanstraten toward his office. Behind them Hull had sealed the plastic bag of organs and placed them into the now empty body cavity. He began folding the body skin back over it in preparation for the final suturing, which he had already begun.

When Vanstraten returned to his office from an adjoining scrub room he was already lighting a Dunhill. He was meticulously dressed in one of his famous three-piece suits with their hint of an older European cut. French cuffs in place, with cobalt porcelain links. Vanstraten had dressed in exactly this manner and style since Haydon had first met him, never succumbing to the trendy whims of popular designers. He didn't own a blow dryer and his hair had never touched the top of his ears. Sometimes Haydon thought he looked as if he had stepped out of a time warp, the close-clipped and stiff-shirted days of prewar Germany. His hair was freshly combed.

"You'll have the typed report in a day or so," Vanstraten said, sitting down in his chair behind his desk. "He was beaten to smithereens, Stuart. It's that simple. He died instantly from the trauma to the heart. But he suffered a lot before that came along. Almost all of the other damage was antemortem. The heel to the sternum was the *coup de grace*. The nail was hammered in a good while after he had died, most likely."

"How long had he been dead?"

"Guessing, I'd say he died four or five hours before he was found. The rectal temperature at the scene was normal, and was just a few tenths off that when we began autopsy. Under normal conditions a person who dies will retain normal body temperature for the first four or five hours after death. Then it will begin to fall off at a fairly predictable rate. Under *normal* conditions."

Haydon looked out the window of Vanstraten's office. Mooney and Finn were nowhere around. Hull had finished the suturing, and was now sponging off the body.

"I think . . . it seems to me that he was beaten by very experienced people, Stuart," Vanstraten added, putting out his cigarette. "In a street fight, a brawl, the head receives a huge amount of punishment. People like to kick their adversaries in the head, pound it on the pavement, against a wall. But aside from the nail, this man's head didn't have a mark on it. Also the marks on the epidermis were few, considering the kinds of injuries he received internally. Someone knew his business very well.''

''And the hands?''

''Deliberate torture. I saw the X-rays while I was back there.'' Vanstraten held up his hands for illustration. ''The first one or two digits on several fingers of each hand have been smashed to the texture of coffee grounds. His wrists are dislocated and deeply cut by ligatures. I would guess he was hanged by his wrists and beaten for part of his ordeal.''

Haydon didn't say anything.

Outside, the autopsy room was empty except for the naked dead man on the shiny aluminum table.

Both Haydon and Vanstraten had chosen professions that turned upon riddles. They knew that method and detail and persistence were the instruments of their craft, but that often intuition was the key to discovery. Vanstraten had just employed the first three. Haydon eventually would come to rely upon the fourth.

ooooooooooooooooooooooooooooooo **Chapter 5**

When Haydon came out of Vanstraten's office, Mooney and Finn were waiting by the reception desk talking about the best place to get barbecue.

"Jimbo's going over to Lockwood's for lunch," Mooney said, hitching up his pants. "Wanna grab a bite with him?" It was pretty clear Mooney had already answered that question for himself.

Haydon looked at his watch. "I'd like to go back to Chicon and talk to that barber first," Haydon said. The truth was, it would have been impossible for him to have swallowed anything at this point. To that extent, his loss of detachment was debilitating. "I can stop by there and pick you up on my way back."

Mooney glanced at Haydon out of the corner of his eye. "Naw, I'll go over there with you. We'll eat later."

"Hell, look, you guys," Finn said, clinching his new teeth with a death's-head grimace. "Let's just meet over there when you're through. We'll have a late lunch. I ain't starvin'. What time? An hour?"

Mooney looked at Haydon.

"That's good, Finn," Haydon said. He didn't care. "We'll see you at one o'clock."

Haydon drove as they pulled onto Old Spanish Trail and headed east in a sunlight so bright it made your eyes water. Mooney began taking off his suit coat, groaning, getting caught in his own sleeves, getting frustrated, jerking his arm out, and piling the wadded coat wrong side out on the seat beside him. Then he started fiddling with the air-conditioner levers, shoving them on high, jacking around with the vents on his side of the dash until they were all focused on his pink face, which always looked overheated.

"I shoulda been a Mountie," he said, slapping down his sun visor. "Work in cold country, ride a lazy horse, wear a red jacket to match my face. Sam Browne belt." He snorted. " 'Member that Mountie came down here, testified on that Cammarata business? All those wiretap tapes. Slick." A chuckle. "Thought our bail system was shit paper. Couldn't figure it. Let 'em all get away, he said. Arrest 'em, and let 'em go, he said. What's that? Said no wonder we got all this scum on the streets. Actually got hot about it." Mooney touched a vent to fine-tune it. "A damn good point."

Haydon didn't say anything, and they rode in silence for a while, passing MacGregor Park, crossing Brays Bayou, under the Gulf Freeway overpass. Haydon could tell Mooney wanted to say something, and finally he did.

"That autopsy get to you today?" He didn't look at Haydon, but fine-tuned another vent as if the question were of secondary interest, incidental. "I noticed you ducked out."

"I've seen enough autopsies," Haydon said. It seemed noncommittal enough.

"I don't like it when they do the heads, either," Mooney said. This time he adjusted the sun visor.

Haydon was surprised. Mooney had noticed. He wondered how many cranials he had walked out on before Mooney first spotted what he was doing. Not many, he guessed; Mooney had been watching him for a good while.

"This been bothering you awhile, huh?"

Haydon didn't want to go any farther with it. "Not really," he lied.

Even with Nina, Haydon wasn't the kind of man who allowed himself to be examined at close range. Mooney knew this, of course, and Haydon knew he knew it. That's why he was interested in Mooney's fumbling approach. Had his own behavior been so uncustomary that Mooney would go against the grain of things to draw him out?

"You see something enough, something outta the ordinary like that, it gets to you," Mooney said. "No matter who you are. Seems like people go through phases, or something."

Mooney thought a minute. "We've known each other, what, twenty years, now?"

Fifteen, Haydon thought. Mooney always exaggerated. Nothing had ever been good enough for him just the way it was.

"But I bet I never told you about Patty Sherrill."

"I don't think so," Haydon said. He was now going to hear about Patty Sherrill.

"Used to be a matron in vice. Retired now. Worked there forever. We used to go out for a drink once in a while after the shift. She was ten, twelve years older than me. Had lots of stories." An attribute worthy of great esteem in Mooney's books. He slipped his feet out of his shoes. "Jesus, that feels good. Patty had the dubious pleasure of frisking the gals we brought in. She told me one time she must've frisked two thousand of them over the years. Not a pleasant job, considering the kind who come in there. You know, you just do it, ignoring the damn thing. Just do it, and get it over with.

"Well, one long summer it just happened that all these gals were handling tons of drugs. Naturally, it was necessary for Patty to go over these baby dolls to see what they'd stuffed in their gashes. Seems that was a favorite place. She frisked so many that she began to have this funny feeling about it. She sort of got the heebie-jeebies when she had to do it. Couldn't really figure out what was happening to her, like she was going to freak out every time. She couldn't close her mind to it anymore. Started doing just the opposite, paying attention to these things, close attention, like she was *studying* them. Shape, size, texture. She got gynecological about it.

"Then one week she had this dream."

Mooney looked out the window. "Goddam, look at that." He pointed down the street at several men pushing a car along the shoulder to a gasoline station a block away. "Mexicans." He shook his head. "Stuart, you been driving around this city, what, all your life. How many times you see Mexicans pushing some ol' junker to a gas station? You can't count 'em. I don't know. I mean, if they've got the money to put gas in it when it runs out, why the shit don't they just put gas in it *before* it runs out? These guys probably passed that station fifteen minutes ago. I don't know. Like to push cars, only thing I can figure. It's a cultural ritual."

As they drove by, Mooney got close to the window so they could see him, and shook his head at them in an elaborate display of disgust. One of the men threw his head back and cursed him, then shot him the finger. Mooney laughed, satisfied, and sat back.

"Patty had this dream," he said, picking up the thread of his story. "A twat nightmare. She had it every night for a week. Same dream. She chased twats. That's what was strange about it. Seems like they should have been chasing her, but they didn't, was the other way around. All colors of hair on these things, all kinds. She told me about 'em, had a whole detailed catalogue of different types. Hell, she'd been scrutinizing the things all summer. They had these little legs, a whole flock of them running from her, jigging jerky fast, like in the old silent films, their hair streaming in the breeze, and every so often one would turn around, still running, and snap at her. Some of them were snapping without even turning around. Said she could hear this clatter of snapping. She said in her dream she wore a surgical glove on her head like a shower cap, all the fingers sticking up and waggling like a rooster's comb. She was terrified one of those twats was going to turn around and go for her, but they never did, and she kept chasing 'em. Seven nights straight."

Mooney shook his head, "Mondo bizarro. Then one night she didn't have the dream, and she never had it again. That was it. Never did feel funny about the job anymore. Just put the whole thing out of her mind. Cured. I asked her, Patty, what the hell you chasing 'em for? She said she didn't know, but she thought maybe it was something Freudian. After that she went on frisking twats for another six years until she retired."

Over the years, Haydon had heard hundreds of Mooney's baroque tales, but never this one. Everything reminded Mooney of a story. But Haydon couldn't ignore the fact that it seemed to be didactic, a modern morality tale for Haydon, who in Mooney's psychoanalytic assessment, it seemed, suffered from the same type of job-related disorder as Patty the Matron. The healing moral seemed to be that if Haydon just hung in there, nature would run its course, and he would eventually be "cured." People went through phases, or something.

Mooney remained curiously quiet after this offering, but the story gave Haydon something to think about until they reached Chicon.

The sun was a few degrees off the meridian and the asphalt of the street was getting soft as Haydon parked the tan department car next to the curb and turned off the motor. He and Mooney immediately rolled down their windows.

You had to understand Chicon to appreciate it. It ran through the center of one of the barrios near the shipping channel, and like most of the city, it had an abundance of trees, which gave it the quiet attractiveness associated with shady places everywhere. And there were times, if you were not too much of a realist, when it was even beautiful: when it rained and the fog rolled in from the coast and you saw the street through a gauze that obscured the details, and at night when the darkness rounded off the rough edges, and the streetlights made magic of common things, and glittery signs in beer-joint windows lied.

But in midday Chicon was more rough edges than anything else. It had two lanes with room for cars to parallel-park along the crumbling curbs. The asphalt was crazed and the dotted yellow line that marked the center of the street had almost paled to invisibility. Both sides of the street were lined with chunky telephone poles from which draped a ropy confusion of heavy black cables that were strung back and forth across the street as if every other one were an afterthought. The signs on Chicon were consumer-targeted: *"Salem que frescura!"* *"Qué pareja,* Canadian Club!"

Across the street to his left was the graffiti-covered wall that protected like a shell the dead kernel of the old house. A grocery stood on the corner in the next block, and beyond that a store with a sign above its door that said *"Ropas Usada."* Beside that was Tres Marias lounge. The two blocks in front of him contained a small drycleaning shop, a shoe shop, Los Cuates lounge, an auto-parts store, a bakery, La Perla lounge, and the barbershop.

The lounges, more accurately cantinas, were the unrepressible bane of the neighborhoods. There were as many as three to the block in this barrio around Chicon, and they were consistently the sites of many of the city's homicides. They were usually small, dank little places, often a converted house that sold only beer and wine. A large number of their customers were young undocumented workers from Mexico and El Salvador who had already fulfilled their number-one dream in the land of opportunity: to own a gun. It was a necessary thing, to defend their machismo and to protect the money they had earned to send home—but were afraid to deposit in banks—until they could get to the Western Union office on Friday night. In the glare of the noon heat these lounges seemed deserted, but Haydon knew that if he paused in their opened doorways and looked into their damp shadows he would see the lonely daytimers sitting in kitchenette chairs at wooden tables, sweating like their brown bottles that left dark rings on the wood.

Haydon wiped his forehead with his handkerchief. The temperature inside the car had swelled rapidly in the few minutes without the air conditioner.

Mooney looked through the windshield at the picture window of the barbershop and saw the barber cutting hair and glancing out at him.

"That guy looks like a barber, all right, but he's not our barber," he said.

"Let's see what he says."

As Haydon walked around the front of the car to the sidewalk, he heard a parrot squawking from one of the shady backyards a few houses away. From Mexico. There was a burgeoning and lucrative black market in parrots, but hundreds of them died every year from heatstroke and suffocation as Mexican *fayuqueros* stuffed them into a variety of cruel hiding places in every kind of vehicle crossing the border. The huge colorful birds that had lifespans equal to that of a man were always in great demand in the drab streets of the barrios.

The barber shop was in a small frame building with asbestos siding. The front door was approached from the sidewalk by ascending three cement steps, but to get to the steps you had to slide around a telephone pole that was inexplicably installed in the center of the sidewalk and aligned with the center of the steps. Herrera had coopted the pole, in defiance perhaps, and painted it barber-pole red, white, and blue up to a height level with the roofline of his shop. It was the most obvious sign on the street. Sparrows had nearly covered the transformer at the top of the pole with their frumpish nests, and their chalky droppings whitened the sidewalk in a two-foot diameter around the pole.

The barber nodded at them as they came into the shop and sat down in the chrome armchairs covered in pea-green vinyl that were lined up against the wall opposite the two barber chairs. Haydon picked up a copy of *Impacto*. The cover of the magazine was dominated by a Mexican vocalist smiling brilliantly and singing into a chrome microphone. He wore a shiny, lead-blue suit and was standing against a flamingo-pink background. Mooney looked through a scrungy copy of *People*. The barbershop smelled of sweet tonics and scented powders.

The barber put the finishing touches on the middle-aged man in the chair and whirled him around to check out the new job in the long mirror behind the chair. The man looked at himself out of the corners of his eyes as he twisted his head, then nodded and said, *"Bien."* The barber stripped the apron from around the man's neck and dusted inside his collar with a little round brush into which he had shaken scented powder. The man got up from the chair, paid, and went out the door, using the candy-striped telephone pole to steady himself as he descended the steps.

Haydon put down the magazine and stood, as the barber looked at him and shook out the striped apron, popping it twice.

"We were looking for Ernesto Herrera," Haydon said, reaching in his pocket and presenting his shield.

"You talkin' about my brawther, Ernesto," the barber said. "I'm Ricardo." He smiled and flashed a single gold incisor. His long upper lip was adorned with a thin mustache that rose in two upright lines at the center.

"Your brother's not here?" Haydon asked.

"Naw, he's gone home for lawnch. He won't be back here till two." His face sobered quickly. "Hey, that was bad business over there, huh? Ernesto, he tol' me." He paused. "Man, I seen ever'thing aroun' here, you know. Shootings

. . . cuttings . . . beatings . . . but this one, it's the first *nailing!*''

He could hardly keep his face straight until he got it out, a kind of staccato throat laugh followed by, ''Shit!'' Haydon guessed he had pulled that on every customer he had wrapped his apron around that morning.

Behind him, Haydon heard Mooney say sarcastically, ''Oh, that's a pisser.''

''When do you close?'' Haydon asked.

''Close? Six. Nine on Thursdays, but this ain't Thursday.''

''I can find your brother here until six?''

''Oh, sure, sure. You can catch him later. Ernesto will be happy to talk to you about it.''

''I hope he's got a better feel for comedy than his 'brawther,' '' Mooney said, standing, and preceding Haydon out the door.

Another customer was coming in as they were going out. ''Hey, Javier,'' Herrera said brightly, *''Qué dice?''* The striped apron popped twice.

They stood on the edge of the sidewalk and looked across to the gates. There was nothing along the wall to indicate what had happened there earlier that morning. They crossed the street and approached the iron gates. Haydon looked through at the dead undergrowth that surrounded the house.

''Lock's on the inside,'' Mooney said. He reached in and lifted it, looked at its bottom, and dropped it quickly, shaking his hand. ''Shit!'' He licked his burned fingers. ''Brass facing's scratched around the keyhole.'' His suit sleeve was smeared with rust from the old bars. He didn't notice.

He stepped over to the gate hinges next to the wall and examined them. ''Rust's been worn smooth in the joints of these pillar brackets. Not regular use, maybe, but recent.''

''Can't really see anything in there,'' Haydon said, and they turned and walked back across the dusty street to the car.

Haydon started the motor, and Mooney turned the air conditioner on high, and they waited a moment for the compressor to begin producing tempered air before they rolled up the windows.

They followed the wall of the estate to the end of the block and turned left. Equidistant from both corners of the back wall there was a tall wrought-iron gate with perpendicular bars. Haydon stopped the car and got out, leaving Mooney in the idling car as he crossed the street. Here the hinges were definitely worn and the padlock was well oiled. Haydon looked down at the dusty ground just inside the gate, where a solid stand of brittle bamboo sprang out of the powdery earth. Above him, rangy cypresses and oaks hung their heavy branches over the top of the wall. There was little else to see.

He went back to the car, and they continued slowly around the block, straining to get glimpses of the house before turning toward Harrisburg on Chicon.

∞ **Chapter 6**

Haydon took a rain check. He just wasn't in the mood for barbecue or conversation, so he dropped Mooney off at Lockwood's, where Finn said he would gladly bring Mooney by the station when they were through.

Retracing their earlier route down Old Spanish Trail, Haydon turned north on Fannin, passing along the western edge of the Medical Center. There was construction at the entrance of one of the hospital's parking garages, and a policeman was stepping out in the street to stop traffic and let cars out of the garage. To his left Haydon caught glimpses of the cool green acreage of Rice University. At the Outer Belt Drive he entered the sprawling grounds of Hermann Park, its irrigated green spaces as refreshing as rain in the harsh glare of summer sunlight.

He worked his way into the left lane just before reaching the Reflecting Pool, where he turned left on Sunset Boulevard. Within a few minutes he was pulling through the pillared gates at the house and making the shallow turn on the brick drive to the porte cochere, where he parked the light tan department car in the shade.

As he opened the front door the coolness of the old house greeted him like a calming spirit. When his father had built the house of limestone quarried from the central Texas hills in 1943, he had said the heavy finished stones would insulate them from the sweltering tropical summers; like a cave, it would hold a natural coolness. He hadn't been far wrong, though he might have underestimated the severity of Houston summers. Still, the old house did not require much air conditioning, mostly to remove the humidity, and its marble and granite floors were always pleasantly cool. In a real sense it was a refuge, from heat and turmoil. There were days when Haydon didn't want to leave it at all.

Haydon took off his Beretta, laid it on the hall table next to the library door, and walked through the dining room to the kitchen. Nina had her back to him, making sandwiches on the butcher block in the middle of the large square room.

"I hope it's someone I know," she said, without turning around.

Haydon stopped and looked at her. Her cinnamon hair was up in its familiar chignon, a wisp or two coming loose at her neck above the collar of her fawn silk blouse. The blouse was tucked into a white linen skirt that reached just to her ankles, revealing a glimpse of her white stockings in low-heeled shoes that matched the blouse. He always liked her in summer colors, which contrasted well with her dusky skin.

She whirled around.

"It'd better be you," she said, breaking into a smile when she saw him. Then she turned back to the sandwiches.

"Make you nervous?" he asked, putting his arms around her waist and hugging her.

"You don't make me nervous," she said.

"But you didn't know it was me."

"You always do that," she said, putting a piece of smoked ham in her mouth. "You want Poupon on this?"

"You should've put on an apron," he answered, taking one out of a drawer. "Yes, and just plain cheddar. None of the smoked."

"I like the smoked stuff." She ducked her head as he looped the top of the apron over it and tied it behind her waist.

Haydon stepped over to the refrigerator and got out a jar of olives and a cucumber. With a paring knife he sliced the cucumber into thin strips and put several on each of the two plates that Nina had laid out.

"Are you going to work at home this afternoon or at the studio?" he asked, dishing up olives for each of them.

"At the studio," Nina said. She put romaine lettuce on each sandwich, and then slices of tomato. "It's just too much trouble," she said, cutting the sandwiches. "I'm past the sketching stages on these. I'll need the parallel bar, all that."

"Which plans are these?" Haydon was opening a bottle of white burgundy.

"The courtyards for Loeffler and Mancini."

"Have I seen those?" He poured some for each of them in bistro glasses.

"Yes, you've seen them." Nina picked up her plate and a glass, paused and kissed him, and went into the sunroom overlooking the terrace. Haydon followed her, put his things on the glass table beside hers, and looked out the windows to the lawn and the small lime grove.

"I haven't been down to the greenhouse in three days," he said. "I need to check the humidity system. Pablo said it was all right last night."

"If he said it was all right, why do you have to check it?"

He ate a cucumber strip and continued to look outside. "I didn't check on Cinco before I left this morning, either." Haydon missed seeing the old collie lying in the shade on the terrace.

"Sit down, Stuart," Nina said. "Eat."

They ate silently for a few minutes, and then Nina said, "What did Dr. Boren say about Cinco last night?"

"He's just getting too old. The summers are too hard on him."

"Is he in any pain?"

"Boren doesn't think so. Just worn out. Said it wouldn't hurt him to sleep so much. Said he might as well."

Haydon sipped his wine.

"So. How was your morning?" Nina changed the subject. It hadn't been a good time to ask about Cinco.

"Spent most of it watching an autopsy."

"Great."

"Well, this turned out to be an interesting one."

"Great."

Haydon grinned. "You asked."

Nina smiled back. "You would think I'd learn." She chewed an olive and raised her glass. "Here's to you, handsome."

"You want to change the subject?"

"Please."

"Where's Gabriela?"

"You don't listen," Nina said, shaking her head and taking another bite of her sandwich.

Haydon looked at her. "Well?"

"Ramona Salazar took her out to do some last-minute shopping."

"That's right," Haydon said. "I forgot. Has she gotten her passport renewed?"

"I did."

"Has she gotten her flight ticket yet? I heard some of the flights were being canceled because of the trouble down there."

"I did."

Gabriela Sauceda had begun working for Haydon's parents when she was a young girl and they were living in Mexico City. She had moved to Houston with them a year before Stuart was born, and Haydon had never known the home without her. When his parents died, he and Nina had moved into the family home. There was never any question that Gabriela, who had never married, would stay on. Haydon's father, Webster, had been a beneficent patron from the beginning, helping her gain her American citizenship and seeing to it that she had substantial financial security beyond her position with them. Every summer she was given a month off to visit her family in Mexico City, and over the years the Haydons' lives had become intertwined with the Saucedas as Webster, and then Stuart himself, had helped a string of Gabriela's nieces and nephews come to the States to attend a variety of universities.

Gabriela saved little of her salary for herself. Year after year, monthly checks went back to her family, of which Gabriela was the oldest of five daughters. As her sisters married and had young families, it was Gabriela's money that enabled them to keep her parents out of poverty. When they died, Gabriela continued sending money, though the assistance was not great when divided among the four sisters. She took an active interest in the welfare of her eight nieces and nephews. There were only eight, because Gabriela had been a quiet but emphatic influence in educating her sisters. She had impressed upon them the belief that it was far better to use birth control and pray for divine indulgence than it was to fill their houses with children and pray for food. Her sisters were remarkably responsive to Gabriela's guidance in all matters, and Tia Gabriela had become a familial saint in Mexico, revered and adored. Her annual trips home were occasions for great rejoicing within her extended family.

Nina and Haydon both thought about her as they looked out to the sunlit terrace. Then Nina said, "I finally said something to her about Ramona."

"Oh?" Haydon turned to her. "And?"

"She was a little stiff about it at first, as we expected. It was when we were making the casserole last night. I said that since I was getting busier at the studio I was having less time to help her. I tried to make it sound as if it would be a convenience to *me* if we got someone to help her. Of course, she said she didn't need any help, and that she never expected me to help her. I said I knew that, but we both enjoyed it. Only now it was getting hectic for me and we ought to go ahead and get someone to take my place. Anyway, we went around like that a minute and then I brought up Ramona's name as soon as I could because I know how much Gabriela likes her."

Nina sipped the burgundy.

"She said, well, maybe a few days a week. I said it was entirely up to her. Anyway, we worked it out. Ramona is going to start working with her a little at a time. I suspect she'll be on full-time in a couple of weeks."

"You've already spoken to Ramona?"

Nina nodded. "She's perfectly willing to follow Gabriela's lead. I told her that was just part of the job. She knows Gabriela well enough to know that it isn't going to be easy for her to admit she's getting too old to look after everything properly. Ramona's a sweet girl. And she owes a lot to Gabriela, too. Gabriela's treated her like a daughter."

"When I left this morning I heard her in the kitchen singing 'La milagrito en la maizal.' She can't be too upset."

Nina smiled. "She'll love it."

They finished eating, and while Nina was putting things away in the kitchen Haydon decided to check on Cinco and the greenhouse. He stepped into the brilliant sun on the terrace and walked to the steps. Pablo had turned on the sprinkler system to the left of the terrace, and a fine mist was drifting across toward the lime trees, carrying the rich fragrance of damp plants into the hot air. Two bluejays and a scattering of grackles were walking around on the grass enjoying the mist, and a mockingbird had taken up his post in a flamboyana, soaking wet and going through every note in his repertoire as if there were no tomorrow.

Haydon went through the lime grove toward the greenhouse. He checked the bird feeders hanging in the ebony trees outside, and then went in. He looked at the meters on the wall inside the door. The temperature was all right, the humidity was perfect. While he was standing there the fans in the ceiling kicked on and stirred a gummy breeze through the upper reaches of the frosted-glass roof. Everything was fine. He quickly walked along the slate paths through a miniature landscape of rising and falling terrain and limestone "cliffs," trees rising toward the highest part of the ceiling. Everywhere there were bromeliads, hanging from the trees, lodged in the crevices of the tons of rocks amid vines and ferns, along the spongy "jungle" floor. The exotic colors ran from brilliant to drab, and Haydon enjoyed every one of them.

After a moment, he turned and walked back down the path and out the door. He followed a brick walk along a border of cherry laurels to the white bathhouse, and rounded the corner to an open-air shower protected by latticework. Cinco lay on the cool bricks; a ceiling fan mounted on the shadow box overhead stirred a sluggish breeze. Again Haydon noticed the fragrance of the wet plants across the lawn.

He squatted down and started scratching Cinco behind a mottled old ear that failed to perk up as it used to. The collie opened an eye, and when he saw Haydon his tail stirred on the bricks.

"How you doing, old friend," Haydon said. He sat down and continued to scratch behind Cinco's ear. He looked at the collie's brindled muzzle, which was getting so gray it was losing its golden color. Cinco gave a jerky sigh and began a prolonged deep moan of gratification at the attention. His eyebrow perked as Haydon talked to him, but his eye slowly closed. Haydon rubbed the thin coat that used to be thin only in the summer when Cinco shed profusely to accommodate climbing temperatures. Now it was thin the year round.

Haydon looked through the latticework to the sprinklers

across the lawn. He wondered if Cinco smelled the wet plants, if he enjoyed it as much as Haydon. He wondered if he was cool, or burning up. That was the worst thing about not being able to talk to him. Haydon didn't really *know* how he was doing. He could tell himself that Cinco didn't seem to be miserable, Boren had said he wasn't suffering, but then how did Boren really know? Time had taken on another meaning for the old dog, or maybe another value. Haydon could not feel that it was all the same to him now. If he didn't see the end of it just ahead, at least he must perceive that it was different. What occupied an old dog's mind in the long days of his end? Did he remember; did he find pleasure in it; did he have regrets? Did time play tricks with his memory, or did he finally understand the truth of it?

vvvvvvvvvvvvvvvvvvvvvvvvvvvvvvv **Chapter 7**

The black stretch limousine with smoked windows pulled out of Charlie T's parking lot in Greenway Plaza, turned west on Richmond, and headed directly into the full glare of the midafternoon sun. It was followed by a midnight-blue Mercedes. Both cars moved easily with the flow of traffic headed toward Loop 610. In the Mercedes, two men in business suits somberly watched the traffic from behind dark glasses, frowning into the sharp, colorless light. They had eaten well during a long lunch at a table a few feet away from the man they had been hired to protect, the man who had been conducting business with three other men over *côte de veau*. The late heavy meal, the heat, and the monotony of the traffic congestion all combined to make them feel sluggish.

As they passed Weslayan and crossed over the railroad tracks, the two cars pulled out of the left lane in preparation for turning right on Post Oak Road as soon as they emerged from under the expressway overpass just ahead. Approaching the traffic light at the access road, the limousine driver noticed a frustrated motorcyclist in the left lane trying to get his attention. The cyclist's face was hidden behind a mirrored visor, but he managed to signal to the driver that he wanted permission to cut in front of him before the light turned so he could cross over to the access road. He had waited too late to change lanes. The chauffeur shrugged and motioned for him to go ahead.

The cyclist waved his appreciation and eased the motor-cycle in front of the limousine. When he got squarely in front of it, his motor stalled, and he began working frantically with the fuel line against his left leg, glancing anxiously at the traffic light. The chauffeur cursed and raced his engine. Two cars behind the limousine, a second cyclist, also wearing a mirrored visor and straddling a powerful racing bike, shot out of Guiton Street and roared toward the intersection on the gravel shoulder at the edge of the pavement.

The traffic light flashed to green. At that instant, the cyclist in front of the stretch limousine suddenly started his bike and in one smooth movement turned it perpendicular to the traffic as he jerked a machine pistol from his windbreaker and pointed it at the windshield. Simultaneously, the second cyclist slid to a stop beside the two guards in the Mercedes, who were just now realizing something was happening. Before they could react, he fired two brief bursts from his own machine pistol, blowing out the Mercedes's windows and splattering the two guards all over the inside of their car. The Mercedes lunged forward, bashing into the rear of the limousine as the first cyclist opened up on its windshield. In the convulsion of sudden death, the chauffeur jammed the accelerator to the floor, and the sleek sedan smashed into the surprised gunman, who continued firing as his cycle was plowed under the front end of the heavy car. In a shower of sparks, gunman, cycle, and limousine ground along the pavement, through the intersection, and crashed into the sloping cement embankment of the overpass. With its engine whining at full tilt, the stranded limousine's rear wheels spun out a thick cloud of black rubber smoke as it shimmied against the embankment where it had pinned the mutilated gunman.

The second cyclist roared up beside the crazily jumping limousine and, with cool professional efficiency, raked its darkened windows with short bursts from his machine pistol, blowing glass into the air and across the intersection. When the magazine was empty, he calmly replaced it and pulled closer to the front of the limousine. He seemed to hesitate, but only for a moment, before he fired several bursts into the half-concealed body of the other cyclist. The rest of the clip he emptied into the gutted windows of the passenger compartment.

He paused to reload one last magazine, unhurried, prolonging the mad scene as if he controlled the flow of time and had no cause for fear. Then, swiftly, he cradled the gun across his lap, jammed his bike in gear, and with the engine revving wildly, swiveled through the scattered cars of the stunned motorists in the intersection. Crouching low over his handlebars, he careened into a left turn and disappeared onto the up ramp of the expressway.

Chapter 8

It was a few minutes after two o'clock when Haydon pulled into the parking garage at the department headquarters on Risener Street, only an hour before the end of his shift. The police department had recently completed a renovation program that for three years had kept the building in a state of perpetual disruption with an architectural autopsy not unlike the one Haydon had watched earlier that morning. The building's viscera of electrical wiring, air-conditioning ducting, and plumbing that had draped from the ceilings, cluttered the hallways, and turned the offices into obstacle courses had now been shoved back into the ceilings and walls and sutured with new plaster, paint, vinyl wall covering, and spongy acoustical tile.

But the greatest change at headquarters had been in security. The administration had implemented a strict new security system that was long overdue. There was now a twenty-four-hour lobby check of all visitors. Security officers were stationed at the elevators and in the hallways, and anyone not in uniform had to wear an identification badge at all times. Access to some restricted areas required special electronically sensitive identification cards which made it possible for security officers to monitor traffic in the building.

The homicide division was definitely a brighter place to work now, and less cluttered. The clunky metal desks that had been there since the 1950s were gone. The small offices that surrounded the squad room and used to hold four desks with just enough leg room to squeeze in sideways now held four or five carrels with open space in the center of the room. Each carrel faced the wall and had its own desktop, shelf, light, CRT, and telephone. It was easier to stake out your own territory and protect it, if you were inclined to do that sort of thing. But there were still no windows.

"So this gal drove a sandwich wagon out around East Gulf Bank Road where those office parks are, those little miniwarehouses and shit. You ever look inside one of those sandwich wagons?"

Mooney paused to take a swig from the mouth of the halfpint carton of milk. He was trying to save his ulcers from the barbecue and hot sauce, onions and beer.

"They're not your luxury-mobiles. And in this one, Lolly's old man had let the air conditioner go out, so she drove around in that little van sweatin' like a Baytown whore."

There were four men in the office, Martinez and Clavo from the Chicano squad, Weaver from robbery down the hall, and the old veteran Dick Small—a name that had not been easy to live with—who had already heard the story three or four times, but liked it so much he listened every time Mooney told it. Haydon had memorized it too, but it sounded as if Mooney had been polishing it.

"Lolly, she always wore these jeans that looked like they were a threat to her circulatory system. Tight as a Jew banker." Mooney sat his milk carton on the edge of his cubicle desk. Keeping his face straight, he said, "And she always wore a white T-shirt. Nothin' underneath." He looked at everybody in the room, then cupped both pudgy hands just above his Buddha stomach, and began a slow grin. "Now, Lolly was blessed with a coupla jugs that had a life all their *own*. I mean, these puppies wagged their tails, and sat *up*. Nipples the size of Susan B. Anthony silver dollars. When she walked up to you and stopped, it took those babies a full minute to settle down, and I guarantee you, you couldn't look at anything else for the next sixty seconds."

Haydon nodded to the room in general, took off his Beretta, and put it in his carrel drawer. He got his blue coffee mug from the back of his desk, and while Mooney continued he walked outside to the coffee machine. He saw Dystal through the glass window in the lieutenant's office. He was talking to one of his detectives sitting across the desk from him, and he was saying something he wanted the detective to take to heart. Dystal's massive shoulders were hunched around his neck as he leaned on his log-sized forearms and slowly moved a thick index finger laterally back and forth, his eyes locked onto the detective as he made his point.

Taking his time with his coffee, Haydon stirred it more than he needed to, hoping Mooney would make it short. Then he decided he didn't want to wait. He walked around the perimeter of the squad room until he found an empty office and went in.

The first call was to the Harris County clerk's office. It didn't take long. The second one was long distance, to the office of the Texas secretary of state. He took a lot of notes, and asked for clarifications of spellings.

Just as he put down the telephone after the second call, a burst of laughter came from the corner office across the squad room. Mooney's punch line. He waited a minute longer until everyone had drifted out of the office before he walked back.

Mooney was stuffing his milk carton down into a trash can already overflowing with old computer printouts. His face was still flushed from laughing. He always laughed at his own jokes, no matter how many times he told them.

"You missed some good barbecue, Stuart. Shoulda gone with us."

"Next time," Haydon said, sitting down at his carrel. "I just called the county clerk's office. That old house over there is owned by a business. The Teco Corporation."

"Whatever that is," Mooney said, uninterested.

"Then I called the secretary of state's office and got the names and addresses of the officers of the corporation. They're all Mexican nationals."

Mooney looked up. "No shit?"

"The registering agent has a Mexican name, too. His office is over on the Southwest Freeway. We'd better go talk to him tomorrow."

Mooney bobbed his head up and down, holding his wrist up to Haydon as he tapped his watch face. "The operative word there is *mañana*. I was kinda hoping to sneak out of here a little early today. What do you say, Stuart? It's already two-forty."

Haydon looked at his coffee. He didn't know why in the hell he had poured it. As both men stood, getting their guns out of the carrel drawers, they became aware of a commotion out in the squad room and heard Dystal's booming voice. Haydon looked out just in time to hear Dystal call his name. He stepped to the door and saw other detectives coming out of their offices into the squad room, looking toward Dystal.

"Everybody listen up," Dystal was bellowing. He had walked out toward the middle of the room. "We just got a call on a shooting out at Richmond and the Loop. Coupla boys on motorsickles pulled up to a limo and opened up on it with automatic weapons. Shot up a Mercedes behind the limo, too. Four or five men down, includin' one of the sickle boys. Lapierre and Nunn are first out, but they're gonna need a lot of help on this one."

He called out the names of five teams of detectives who were nearing the end of their shifts. He wanted them to stay and work through.

Haydon turned around to his desk and called Nina.

Chapter 9

It couldn't have happened at a worse time for traffic. It was approaching four o'clock and the afternoon sun was burning in at an angle just above the overpass and the traffic overhead was at a standstill. The motorists who happened to be stalled above the intersection had ringside seats to a first-class slaughter. The traffic on Richmond was being diverted north and south at Weslayan, causing forty-five-minute delays on its feeders to the Southwest Freeway as well as those at Westheimer and San Felipe. The inbound traffic on the west side of the Loop at the Richmond intersection was easily diverted onto the access roads, thereby creating a relatively isolated crime scene below the overpass where the limousine and Mercedes had finally come to rest.

Haydon had to put gas in the car at the motor pool, and there were two blue-and-white units ahead of them. By the time they got to the intersection, the crime-scene ribbons were already in place, including a ten-foot-wide aisle of ribbons stretching along the north side of Richmond to the Guiton intersection. All the bodies were still in place. The crime-lab and morgue vans were standing with opened doors, and several teams of detectives were peering inside the two cars and talking to motorists who had been at the intersection when the shooting occurred.

Haydon parked about fifty yards from the intersection, and he and Mooney got out and started across to the wrecked cars. Bob Dystal spotted them and came to meet them, his bearish frame leaning slightly forward as his size-twelve boots pounded the hot asphalt. He was cutting a wedge of Tinsley's chewing tobacco with his pocket knife, which he then folded closed with one thick hand as he placed the tobacco in his mouth. He squinted in the sunlight despite the drugstore sunglasses.

"Hell of a thing," Dystal said as they approached, turning and walking with them. "Looks like some kinda 'sassination." He quickly recapped what they believed had occurred, based on the stories of the motorists who had witnessed the shooting. They stopped at the Mercedes.

" 'Cordin' to his driver's license, guy behind the wheel here is . . ." Dystal flipped through a creased and sweat-stained pocket notebook. "Raul Saenz Sales. Guy on the other side is . . . Vicente Gonzales Gonzales."

They looked through the shattered windows at the two men, who sat in their seats as if dozing, Saenz leaning his head against the splintered remains of his window, Gonzales with his head thrown back against the headrest, his mouth open as if snoring. There were holes in their faces and upper torsos, but the entry wounds were not that unpleasant. However, both men were plastered to their car seats by massive amounts of blood that had been blown out their backs and splattered across the backseat and windows.

They walked over to the limousine. All six doors of the car were open. Some of the detectives backed away to give them room.

"First guy here in the backseat is Jerry C. Lowell from Austin," Dystal said, referring to the notebook. "Guy over there is Ramón Sosa Real, Mexican driver's license, Mexico City address, and that fella there is George L. Crisman, here in Houston. Chauffeur is Esteban G. Moreno, Houston. There was lease papers for this thing in the glove box in Sosa's name."

The limousine reeked of feces and blood. The men would not be identifiable without first being scrubbed at the morgue.

"What did they use?" Haydon asked.

"Aw, shit," Dystal growled angrily, spitting a squirt of amber juice. "There was forty-five casings all the hell over the place."

"Mac-10s."

"I 'magine. People said they saw the boys shooting, saw

'em changing clips in the 'pistols,' but they didn't hear nothing. So I guess they had silencers too. Real slick.''

"You said one of the motorcyclists was killed?"

"Yeah. Come on around here."

They followed Dystal's beefy shoulders around to the front of the limousine. The car had climbed up on the slope of the embankment, curling the motorcycle up under its front wheels as it went. A man's bare thigh, split lengthways to the bone, which showed white through red flesh, stuck out from under the rear wheel of the motorcycle. His head, with the bullet-shattered helmet still firmly buckled, was lying under the cycle's engine. One of the header pipes coming off the engine had ripped loose and smashed through the mirrored visor, wedging itself into the space where his face should have been. Haydon could smell the burned flesh. The rest of the man was ground up under the motorcycle, out of sight. Bright green radiator coolant and blood ran down together and formed a marbled puddle under the glistening black panel of the limousine's front door.

"I doubt if the boy'll have an ID," Dystal said. "I can't tell if his motorsickle's got a license plate."

"Was there return fire?" Haydon asked, suddenly noticing the bullet holes in the cyclist's helmet.

Dystal shook his head slowly, looking at the mess at the front of the limousine. "One little detail there. Witnesses say that when this one got plowed under here, the second shooter rode up after blowing away those two boys in the Mercedes, and finished him off." He turned his dark lenses to Haydon. "How ya like that?"

Another detective walked up and started asking the lieutenant about the procedures for removing the bodies. Dystal turned, talking to him, and walked away.

Mooney stepped to the rear of the limousine and surveyed the layout of the intersection.

"They picked a good spot, Stuart. Regular stop-and-go traffic flow gave them time to get in place around the targets. No place for the limo, or the Mercedes, to evade in the bumper-to-bumper traffic once the shooting started. Easy access to the expressway, and the cycles could hump right on past the stalled cars by squeezing between the lanes. A police car couldn't have pursued them even if it'd been sitting right here at the time it happened.''

Haydon nodded. "Doesn't look like an amateur hit, does it?''

The falling afternoon sun was not yet low enough to take on color, and its fierce white light reflected like scattering sparks off the chrome of the parked and moving cars. Pale splashes of red and blue from the police units skittered up and down the shallow angles of the cement embankments and overpass girders. The car radios echoed to one another through the underpass and mixed with the loose rumble of traffic.

The medical examiner's investigators were going over the bodies systematically, beginning with the two men in the Mercedes. They were followed by the police photographer, and then the crime-lab technicians.

Peter Lapierre stood in the middle of the intersection with a clipboard and pencil giving instructions to several patrolmen with measuring tapes. He made meticulous notes as they called out distances and dimensions, length of skid marks, sizes of scratches, and angles. No one surpassed Lapierre in analyzing a crime scene, and each team of assisting detectives already would have been assigned a specific aspect of the scene on which to make a report. Lapierre and Nunn would cover it all, and coordinate the investigation.

Haydon and Mooney followed the aisle of ribbons that stretched along the edge of Richmond to Guiton. Nunn was there with a couple of patrolmen, walking along with their heads down looking into the grass that grew along the shoulder of Guiton. Farther down, a patrolman and a woman from the crime lab were squatting and looking at something on the ground.

Nunn looked up as they approached.

"A mess, huh?" he said, squinting into the sun.

"Sure is," Mooney said. "Find anything?"

Robert Nunn was a good partner for the punctilious Lapierre. He was a slightly built man in his early thirties with a blond, neatly trimmed mustache and lanky hair. He was a dedicated detective who unfailingly took advantage of opportunities to attend special law enforcement seminars and courses. His only interests were his work, his wife, and twin daughters, whom he worshiped.

"Nothing," Nunn said, taking off his jacket and slinging it over his shoulder. There was a dark patch of perspiration between his shoulder blades. "The shooter who got away came out of this street. It seemed to me he was probably parked along here somewhere waiting for the limo to come by. If he waited very long I thought he might have smoked a cigarette or something. Chewed some gum, ate some peanuts, drank a Coke." He laughed and shook his head. "Left me a note, maybe."

"No tracks from the cycle?" Haydon asked.

Nunn ran his fingers through a hank of hair that was falling over his forehead and pushed it back.

"Well, we think we've got something," he said, turning toward the woman and patrolman fifty yards away. "They're trying to get a moulage."

Mooney continued talking to Nunn as Haydon walked along the shoulder to the woman in a white lab coat. She was on her knees now, mixing a latex base with a catalyst, stirring quickly, testing the consistency.

"The dust is awfully fine, but the spray fixative ought to help a little," she said to the patrolman, who was on his knees too, holding two pieces of cardboard on either side of the faint track in the sand. She was young and had her sandy hair pulled back in a ponytail. "If you mix this stuff too thick, it'll break down the original when you pour it in. If you get it too thin, it's not going to want to set."

They didn't pay any attention to Haydon as he stood behind the woman and looked over her bent back. The track was small. The shoulder along the street was mostly coarse gravel, with very little sand where a tire could make an impression. He was surprised they had found even this much.

Carefully, the woman poured the latex mixture, now the consistency of thick milk, into the indentations of the original print in the sand. Designed to be quick-drying, the pinkish liquid was set in just a few moments. When she peeled it up, the moulage was far more effective than Haydon was expecting. The herringbone pattern of the tread was clear and unmistakable.

"It's sharp," she said, pleased. "Maybe it was a new tire."

Haydon turned and walked away. The lab technician and the patrolman had been so intent on what they were doing that neither of them had given any indication they knew he had been there.

"What kind of a motorcycle was it?" Haydon asked, walking up to Nunn again.

The detective grinned. "I was just telling Mooney that that depends on who you talk to. Only three people out of all that traffic around here noticed. Two guys said it was a Kawasaki, third guy said there was no doubt about it, it was a Suzuki." Nunn looked down into the grass again. "It was probably a Harley."

"Anyone know if the shooters were Anglos or Latins?"

Nunn shook his head. "They were wearing visored helmets with mirror finishes. I guess they might be able to tell about the one over there, although it looks to me like his face is a total loss."

"Thanks, Robert," Haydon said. "We'll see you later."

Nunn nodded, and kept his eyes down to the side of the road.

As they approached the Mercedes, Dystal was going through the rest of the papers in the wallets of the two Mercedes passengers.

"These boys work for a security firm here in Houston," Dystal said, holding up plastic ID cards. "Personal Security."

"They should've seen one more film strip," Mooney said dryly. "Another half hour of training."

The men in the Mercedes were the first to be moved from the scene and put into the morgue vans. Then the police wrecker came in and towed the Mercedes away. Another morgue van backed up to the limousine. It was then that Haydon noticed the four television cameras being pointed down at them from the overpass above, and two reporters recording "on the scene" coverage as the bodies were dragged out of the open doors of the limousine and wrestled onto aluminum gurneys. It wasn't Haydon's case, so he kept his mouth shut and backed out of sight under the overpass.

When the last of the four men had been loaded and the van pulled away from the scene, a second wrecker backed in and started hooking onto the rear bumper of the limousine. The detectives gradually left what they were doing and gathered around the crushed cycle with their backs to the sun. Now they would see if anything could be learned from what was left of the dead assassin. As the wrecker driver put his truck in gear and eased away from cement embankment, the twisted metal in the limousine began to groan and pop. With a shrill grating sound the car slid down the incline, and the motorcycle came with it, embedded in the grille and the front of the motor. The helmeted rider came with the motorcycle, his torso clinging to the cycle. His legs dangled free, almost severed. There would be no face for identification.

No one said anything as the attendants from the third morgue van began pulling the rider off the distorted motorcycle. He came away in three parts, which they laid in approximate order on a collapsed gurney. There was a windbreaker mixed in with some of him, and Dystal had the attendants lay it aside so he could go through its zippered pockets. They were empty. The blue jeans pockets were empty. The jogging shoes were like a billion other pairs. With the last part of him the machine pistol fell out on the pavement, bent double with two fingers pinched in its creases. The morgue attendants covered the reassembled cyclist with a sheet and loaded the gurney into the van.

The wrecker drivers pried as much of the motorcycle off the limousine as they could to prevent loose parts from falling in the street as they towed it in. When the wrecker finally pulled away, the last morgue van followed it past the bright markers of the red tape and into the traffic.

The detectives stood in a loose group next to the cement pillars in the middle of the overpass and compared notes, listened to the general summaries of the information that each of them had gotten in the last hour and a half. Pigeons roosting on the trusses overhead burbled in the high shadows. The sun was still a couple of hours above the horizon, and the heat under the overpass was dry and harsh.

When they had gone over most of the known facts, there was a brief silence before Dystal said, "Okay, Pete, have you got everything covered?"

Lapierre referred to his notes. "Marshall and Coates will take the two men in the Mercedes. Singleton and Watts will take the Austin man, Lowell, and Crisman. Haydon and

Mooney will get Sosa, the chauffeur, and the leasing company. Nunn and I will follow up on the prints, the DEA, and ballistics. I need to get together with you to work out the rest of it.''

"So far so good," Dystal said. "Anybody want to put in their two bits before we get outta here?''

No one said anything. They knew what was next.

"Okay," Dystal said with a massive sigh. "We got to get some positive IDs, and notify families. Could take all night, so let's get going. Everybody check in tomorrow morning, sleep or no sleep. I want to stick with this thing till we have something *meaty.*''

chapter 10

The office of Executive Limousines was on West-heimer, not far from Chimney Rock Road and the Galleria. Haydon parked in the empty parking area in front of the white one-story building and walked up to the front door as Mooney went around back to the service area. The sign on the door said they were open from nine o'clock until six. It was five forty-five, but the door was locked. Haydon walked along a covered walkway beside a flowerbed of tattered zinnias to the side of the building and followed Mooney around to the back.

Two black men were washing a limousine in one of the stalls, and Mooney was talking to them.

"They're closed," Haydon said, walking up to them.

One of the men wearing rubber boots and a rubber apron looked at his watch.

"They not 'sposed to close till six."

"That's what the sign says, too," Haydon responded. "But the door's locked."

The two men exchanged glances over the top of the limousine, and then the one closest to Mooney looked toward the rear of the building and pointed his chin at a Lincoln sitting near the back door.

"Thas the boss's ca' right theah. You jus' bang ona back doah. He ain't gone."

"What's his name?" Mooney asked.

The man bent down and dipped his washing mitt into a bucket of foamy soap. "Val-ver-de. Jimmy Val-ver-de. *Mista*

Val-ver-de.'' He grinned at his partner over the top of the limousine again and went back to smearing the car with giant sweeps of sudsy water.

Mooney said to the man, "How many of these damn things you wash in one day?"

"Too many," the man said, "fuh what I gets paid."

"Damn right, Pooch," his buddy agreed.

"What's the matter? Valverde a cheap-ass?" Mooney asked. He was warming up. By the time he got through with them, he would have learned more than they had ever dreamed they would tell a white man, especially a cop.

Haydon turned and walked to the back of the building. The rear door was flanked by a row of fat junipers planted in both directions to the edge of the building. He knocked on the door. No response. He knocked again, harder, and called Valverde's name.

Someone called back, but Haydon couldn't understand the words. He waited, and suddenly the door was jerked open.

"Yeah? Yeah?" A man in his late thirties was looking around at him from behind the door, which he did not open all the way. He was irritated, and wasn't trying to hide it. "We're closed," he said.

"Mr. Valverde?"

"Yeah. Right." He looked Haydon over. "Who are you?"

Haydon held up his shield. "Detective Haydon, with the Houston Police. I need to talk to you a few minutes."

Valverde looked at his face now, instead of his clothes. "What's the matter?"

"I've got some information for you. May I come in?"

"Information? What information?"

Haydon nodded, but didn't say anything more.

"Okay. Hold on." Valverde closed the door, opened it immediately. "Gimme five seconds," he said, and closed it again.

Haydon patiently returned his wallet to his pocket. He looked around at Mooney, who had pulled off his coat and tossed it over his shoulder as he chatted with the two car washers. They had stopped what they were doing and were leaning on the limousine grinning and listening to Mooney.

"What's the matter?"

Haydon turned to see Valverde standing with the door wide

open. His attitude was still challenging, but there was an underlying note of concern that he was trying hard not to give in to.

"Mr. Valverde, one of your limousines has been involved in a collision. I need to ask you a few questions."

"A wreck?" Valverde grimaced. "Where? A bad one?"

"May I come in?"

"Yeah, okay. Come on. My office."

Valverde turned and motioned for Haydon to follow him. They walked a few yards down a short dark hallway with imitation woodgrain paneling. The shag carpet smelled musty. Looking at Valverde's back, Haydon noticed that one of the hip pockets in his trousers was turned inside out and caught under his belt, causing his pants to pucker at the waist. It looked as if he had put them on in a hurry.

They turned into an office on the left. A desk and credenza of dark wood faced outward from a corner. There was a portable television on a wire stand with a VCR hookup, a collection of cheap-brand liquor on a cart with wheels, and a sofa with nappy brown fabric. Haydon would have bet that everything had been purchased in one load from an office-furniture outlet, at reduced prices. There were photographs on the walls of the Houston skyline at night.

There was also a brunette, a decade younger than Valverde. Haydon's impression was that she didn't quite fit into the setting. She seemed a little rich for Valverde's blood. Her cool pink silk dress clearly had cost more than Valverde's desk, which she was pretending to tidy up.

"We can finish this later, Celia," Valverde said with a cocky tone of double entendre as he walked around behind the desk where she was killing time.

"I'll finish posting the receipts, then," she said, having to squeeze past him. Valverde didn't give her much room.

As she walked by Haydon, she cut her eyes up at him and said, "Excuse me," her smile hidden from Valverde by the angle of her head. Haydon watched her walk out the door. She had nice legs, and they were bare.

Haydon looked at Valverde, who stood behind his desk with a cocky grin. Valverde knew the girl had class, and he was proud that Haydon had seen it. With typical hustler reasoning, he thought that having a girl like that around boosted his own rating on the sophistication scale. It never occurred to him that he only suffered by the comparison. As Haydon watched Valverde light a cigarette with the macho flourish of the postcoital smoker, he wondered why the girl was slumming with such a creep.

Haydon pulled the carbon copy of the leasing paper found in the glove box of the limousine from his pocket and handed it to Valverde.

"A couple of hours ago this limousine was ambushed by two gunmen on motorcycles. Your driver, Esteban Moreno, and the man who signed these papers, Ramón Sosa Real, were two of the four killed."

Valverde looked as if Haydon had slapped him across the face. "God bless!" He sat down hard in his chair. He looked at the leasing papers. "Goddam! What the hell *ambushed!* What's this *ambushed?* What happened?"

Haydon briefly told him what had taken place. Valverde looked at him without blinking, incredulous. He put out the cigarette he had just lighted.

"We need to find out if Sosa has an address here in Houston," Haydon said. "We have only his Mexican driver's license with an address in Mexico City. I'm assuming you have more complete information than what is on that leasing agreement."

Valverde stared at Haydon, and slowly started shaking his head. "Son of a bitch," he said vaguely. "It was an *Ogara* Caddie, for Christ's sake! Damn thing cost fifty-five thou! Goddam!"

"Your car is at the police station downtown. You can make arrangements to pick it up after our crime-lab people are through with it."

"I not believin' this," Valverde whispered. "Incredible."

Haydon glanced at the flashing blue digital numbers on the VCR. The tape that had been playing was on hold. A rental box lay on the top of the machine. The film was *Swedish Holiday.* Triple X.

"Mr. Valverde, do you have more information about Mr. Sosa?"

Valverde looked at Haydon, his mind finally coming around to the question. "Uh, yeah, but listen." He swallowed hard, put his hand to his bottom lip, and massaged it between his thumb and forefinger as he thought. "The thing is, I deal with a lot of very wealthy people here. They're . . . discreet. I tell them this information's confidential." He looked up at Haydon with an expression that pled sympathy for his position.

"I really need to move quickly on this," Haydon said, stepping over to the end of the sofa. He leaned over and pulled at something sticking out from under one of the cushions. The panty hose that stretched out slowly between Haydon's fingers and the sofa were sheer, pale pink with a tiny rosebud pattern. Without saying anything he held them up, folded them carefully, and laid them in one of the letter trays on Valverde's desk.

Valverde looked at him, pursed his lips contemplatively, and nodded. He got up, walked over to a filing cabinet, and pulled a manila folder from the files. He flopped it down on his desk and sat down again.

"Look," he said. "Really, this guy is, was, one of my best all-time customers. I mean, it'd be nothing for other people like him just to go to some other service if they don't like the publicity I'm getting here. Know what I mean? They don't need me. I need them."

"It'll be all right," Haydon said.

Valverde rolled his eyes in resignation and handed Haydon the leasing application.

Haydon looked at it. "This was filled out in 1983."

"Right. He's been using me since then. My best customer."

"Is this address still good?"

"Yeah, I guess so. The drivers go there."

"Is this his address?"

"That's what it says."

"This is a little vague. Under 'occupation' it says 'Executive.' "

Valverde shrugged. "I don't hassle them about details. This city's full of executives. That's why I call this place Executive Limousines. I cater to the upper-echelon types."

"How often do you lease to Sosa?"

"He's had that one four months straight. Pays a month at a time."

"And before that?"

"Month here, three months there. A regular thing."

"How regular?"

"Two, three times a year."

"Does he request a special driver?"

"He likes Moreno. Been using him a couple of years."

"Why?"

"He's trained. Security. Couple of my drivers have evasive-action training. You know, reverse outs, handbrake turns, J turns, spotting tails, cloak-and-dagger all the way. That's a big thing now. Everybody's afraid of being popped off. Terrorism. I sent a couple of the guys to this three-day course. If some of my clients feel more comfortable having a driver with that kind of expertise, then they can have him. I charge about twenty percent more for their services."

"Are they pretty good at evasive action with a stretch limousine in heavy traffic?" Haydon asked.

"Hey, look," Valverde said defensively. "I send them to the damn school. They're certified."

That was it, Haydon thought, that was Valverde's mission in life, what he dedicated himself to perfecting: getting ahead while covering his ass, all in one fluid motion.

"If Sosa was concerned about security, why wasn't he using an armored limousine?" Haydon asked. "Did he ever request one?"

"I don't have any," Valverde said. "I used to. I had one. But it's just too big an investment. Besides, if somebody really wants their man that armor shit isn't going to stop them. The KD-2, that Teflon-coated stuff, cuts it like butter."

Haydon kept his eyes on Valverde. "You know a lot about KD-2, Mr. Valverde?"

"Look, I read that shit in the magazines," Valverde explained, defensive again. "People in the business, security people, talk about it all the time. I told you, it's a big thing now."

Haydon switched subjects. "What bank does Mr. Sosa write his checks on?"

Valverde looked at Haydon. The man was transparent, Haydon thought. You could see his mind working all over his face. This clearly was a question with different implications.

"I don't remember," he said.

"Then check in your files there," Haydon said.

"I don't keep those kinds of records," Valverde said. "Nobody does."

"Does Sosa sign the checks, or is someone authorized to do it for him?"

Valverde thought about that.

"Maybe your secretary remembers," Haydon suggested.

"Sosa signs them, I think. Yeah, Sosa."

"Has he always paid by check?"

"Right."

"For three years?"

"Right."

"He's your best customer, always pays by check, and you can't remember the name of his bank?"

"Right."

Haydon looked at Valverde in silence. He found the man depressing. Like his furniture, he was several notches down from where he pretended to be. You could buy his respect at outlet prices. You could get him at lower-than-ever reduced rates. The only problem was that when you had bought him, and got him out in the light where you could get a good look at what you had, there would be the sudden sinking feeling that you still had paid more than he was worth.

"Mr. Valverde, this is a homicide investigation," Haydon said. "You can be prosecuted for concealing information, or providing false testimony."

Valverde continued to stare at Haydon. Then, with resignation, his head sagged between his shoulders.

"He's always paid me in cash," he said glumly. "The guy always carried big bucks. These people, they live in a different kind of world from you and me. Okay? He wants to pay me in cash, what am I gonna do? Say, 'Gee, thanks, but I'd rather have a check.' I'm not going to offend the guy. That kind of money, it was nothing to him. Pocket change. Literally. You don't want to get picky with people like that. Shit."

Haydon listened.

"Look. These wealthy Mexican types, they're a class act. He doesn't flash the stuff. Very discreet. Just a clean, white envelope. Thank you very much. *I'm* not going to offend the guy."

"You didn't suspect anything?"

"What! What?" Valverde suddenly became animated,

leaning forward over the opened manila folder, his eyes widened, his shoulders bunched up around his neck as he spread his hands palms up on the desk. "Suspect! What am I supposed to suspect? When the hell did cash get to be a dirty word? My old man used to be proud he didn't have no debts. Paid for everything in cash or he didn't get it. I got to 'suspect' cash now? *Cash,* for Christ's sake!''

Valverde was laying it on too thick. Haydon had had enough of his dramatics. "I'll need Esteban Moreno's address," he said. "Does he have a family?"

Valverde fell back in his chair again. His face was drawn. This was the part he had dreaded.

"A mother, a brother, and a sister," he said flatly.

"They've got to be notified. Someone has to identify the body."

"Oh, shit. This is terrible."

"Give me the address," Haydon said.

There was a long silence.

"Look, the guy worked for me for two and a half years," Valverde said with resignation. "I'll do it. I'll tell them."

"Do you know the family?"

Valverde closed his eyes and nodded. When he opened them again, he looked at Haydon and tilted his head toward the front office.

"That's his little sister was in here. Celia Moreno."

Haydon took Mooney back to the police station, where he would start the paperwork on their part of the investigation and type up a report on the Belgrano killing, which would have to be put on the back burner for a while. Before he left the station, Haydon called Nina at her studio and told her he was going to be working late, maybe all night. She said the courtyards were coming slowly anyway, and since he wasn't going to be home she would send out for a sandwich and work late too. She promised him she would be home by midnight.

Sosa's home was, of course, in River Oaks. Haydon was not surprised. Sosa's Mexico City address had been in Lomas Altas, one of the most prestigious and fashionable sections in the western part of the city. Former Mexican president José López Portillo's flamboyant sister had built an extravagant mansion there with questionable funds during her brother's administration. Sosa kept high-ranking company.

There were no walls or gates protecting the Italianate residence on Inverness, but tall hedges screened the entrance itself from the quiet avenue in front. In the falling dusk, Haydon did not at first see the guards who stood beside their cars at the driveway entrance. As he turned off the street and eased between the hedge that loomed above the car, two men in business suits stepped out of the blue evening and into the beams of his headlights. They made no effort to hide their automatic weapons.

Lowering the window, Haydon held up his shield at the

74

same moment a sharp beam from a powerful flashlight played into his eyes. It stayed there. His temper flared, but he held his tongue and fought the urge to slap down the flashlight as he put the shield in front of his eyes. He could see nothing behind the glare, but he could hear the second man talking to someone over a hand-held radio.

There was a scratchy response, and the man with the flashlight said, "You may continue, señor." He pointed the beam along the paved drive as a gesture of escort. "Please accept our apologies for the inconvenience."

Haydon was surprised they hadn't asked whom he had come to see, which was just as well, because he didn't know if Sosa was married, had a family, or lived alone.

He put the car in gear and drove toward the long, softly lighted loggia that stretched across the front of the house. A man hurried down the steps to wait for him, and was there to open the car door by the time he turned off the motor.

"Please," the man said as Haydon got out of the car. He gave a nodding salute, and indicated that he should be followed. Haydon had the odd impression he was expected, that he was the only one who didn't know what was about to happen next. Their footsteps made rasping sounds on the footlighted stones as they quickly ascended. At both ends of the loggia men with automatic weapons leaned on the shadow side of the columns, and yet another stood at the door itself. Haydon knew there would be no legal impropriety in this ostentatious show of weaponry, but it rankled him nonetheless. He resented the state-of-siege mentality that seemed more appropriate in the Middle East, or in Latin America itself. He was irritated, too, because it reminded him that this was just a more overt representation of an attitude that was increasing among many wealthy United States citizens as well. Especially in Texas, where the right to bear arms was sacrosanct. For the most part, that right had been judiciously and cautiously exercised in the past, but this seemed no longer to be the case. There was a cowboy on every street now. The state bristled with arms.

As the heavy wooden front door swung open, Haydon was greeted by a thin young man with tortoiseshell glasses. He wore a suit and a heavily starched Oxford-cloth white shirt with a buttondown collar.

"Please come in, Detective Haydon," he said, stepping back for Haydon to enter a vestibule dominated by a curving double stairway of dove-gray marble that reached to a balcony on the second floor. A heavy chandelier hung from the high ceiling, adding brilliance to the polished marble. "My name is Efren Gamboa. My father is waiting to talk to you in the library."

Gamboa? Haydon didn't say anything. Apparently he didn't need to. Everything seemed to be going according to schedule. Someone else's schedule.

The two men walked across a floor inlaid with a black marble labyrinth pattern that encompassed the entire entryway to a pair of carved wooden doors. The young man opened the doors, and they entered a spacious and richly decorated room. Haydon quickly saw that it was a library in name only, furnished with the kinds of volumes that are the stock items of interior decorators whose clients want the appearance of erudition. Huge tomes of matching leather bindings with gold imprinting lined the mahogany shelves. There were rows and rows of matching sets of dark leather volumes accented with others in red and green morocco, and the butter-colored spines of parchment bindings. Massive folio volumes lay on their sides in the lower shelves. A heavy library table dominated the near side of the room. It was decorated with a giant antique globe on a brass stand, and excellent pieces of pre-Columbian statuary under individual Plexiglas canopies. No room here for spreading out one of the volumes from the shelves and perusing its expensive pages.

The young man led Haydon past the table to a sitting area with an oval arrangement of creamy Roche-Bobois leather armchairs around a large oriental carpet as precise and detailed as any Haydon had ever seen. It was Chinese, with gul motifs in cream and rose.

A man in his early sixties stood from one of the plush chairs and gravely waited for the young man to bring Haydon to him. As they approached, the older man stepped forward and extended his hand.

"Please let me introduce myself, Mr. Haydon. I am Benigo Gamboa Parra. Mr. Sosa worked for me."

Haydon shook Gamboa's hand.

"You were expecting me?" Haydon asked.

"Not you specifically, but the police."

"How did you learn of his death?"

"Mr. Haydon," Gamboa said, his expression one of sadness and world-weariness, "I am preoccupied with security. That kind of tragedy does not occur to someone in my employ without my immediate knowledge."

"But how did you learn of it?" Haydon persisted. His tone was polite, but emphatic.

"Of course." Gamboa understood, and nodded in deference to Haydon's position. "I was in another limousine at the time. We had radio contact. We heard the firing and my driver brought me back here at once. My security personnel have a police scanner. They followed the developments." He looked at his son, who excused himself and left the room. "Please, sit down, Mr. Haydon."

Gamboa himself sat down, and unbuttoned his suit coat so that the garment would hang more comfortably. It was tailored of silk the color of ashes, and complemented his wavy gray hair. He wore glasses, slightly tinted.

"I know you have questions. I will do everything I can to assist you."

"I'm sure you have no idea what provoked this attack," Haydon said curtly, keeping a tight rein on his temper.

The tension in the flat tone of his voice was not lost on Gamboa. He looked at Haydon for a moment as if he were giving him time to relax. The Mexican's eyes were alert, though the flesh around them was sagging from age. There was a sense of melancholy in them that suggested his life had not been without other tragedies.

"I have a million ideas, Mr. Haydon. I do not live with this absurd security without reasons." Gamboa touched his glasses and smiled tiredly. "For many years I have been active in Mexican politics," he said simply. He seemed to find that explanation enough.

"You are still active?"

Gamboa shook his head. "I retired after my service in the José López Portillo administration. The stresses are as real for the mañana Mexican public servant as for your own distinguished government officials. When President Portillo left office it was a good time for me to leave as well. A good time to retire. I have devoted a large portion of my life to my country. It was a duty. It was right that I should do it. But a man does not live forever. I have a family to consider. True, as you have seen, my children are mostly grown, but in Mexico we stay a family longer than is your custom here. I am not too old to enjoy my children, or to help them with their careers.''

"You have other children?''

"Two sons, two daughters. Efren is my second son. He has been in law school at Harvard. The alma mater of our President de la Madrid. A good selection for a young man.''

"What is your relationship with Sosa?''

"Ramón has been my close friend and associate for many years. Before I entered political life, I was a businessman who had been blessed with some success. Since I could not continue my commercial pursuits while I was in politics, I retained Mr. Sosa as my representative. Something like your blind trust here in the United States. He looked after my interests, while I tried to attend to the interests of Mexico.''

"Do you have any idea why he was assassinated?''

Gamboa shook his head again, slowly closing and then opening his eyes.

"No. They were not after poor Ramón. They thought *I* was in the limousine.''

Haydon studied him. "You seem sure of that.''

"As I said, there is a purpose for the security.''

"You believe your life is in danger from opposing political factions in Mexico?'' Haydon was still missing the point here. Gamboa was using his charming paternalism to sidestep the obvious intent of Haydon's questions.

"Mr. Haydon, Mexico is full of fanatics. It is our shame and our pride. After all, one could call the fathers of our revolution fanatics. Yours too. But all Mexicans are fervent people, not just the 'movers and shakers' as you call them here. Perhaps there are some fanatics who disagreed with my politics. No man can expect to be loved by everyone. Certainly not a man in government. If he were, he would not be doing his job. It is not realistic.

"In Mexico there are those who feel that a man has committed a crime simply by virtue of his wealth. There is much to be hopeful about in my country, but there is no denying that many people are still uneducated. Ignorance among our poor is a plague for all of us, because the disappointments they face in life causes them to grasp at weak reeds for hope. They are taught by some to hate those who have more than they. They are told that their poverty is a direct result of our wealth. Their bitterness is corrosive and unavoidable, and their exploitation by leftists is understandable.''

Gamboa sighed and looked around the room.

"Mexico has its problems, Mr. Haydon. They may appear primitive to you. You may wonder why we cannot pull ourselves together for progress. Why we cannot educate our people, why there is the terrible gap between the rich and the poor, why we cannot be more economically productive, more honest. More like you North Americans.'' His eyes settled on Haydon. "Well, for all our faults we are not deceiving ourselves. We may have to look over our shoulders while we step into the twenty-first century, but we will be there along with everyone else. And another generation will have engaged the complexities that challenge us. There will be more answers. There will be more hope.''

An expression of resignation slowly replaced the light that had momentarily illuminated the dignified Gamboa's eyes.

"In the meantime we must face the realities of the situation,'' he said. "To answer your question: I do not know who would want to assassinate me, Mr. Haydon. I only know that I must never let down my guard. I can never have enough eyes to watch. I can never have enough ears to listen.''

Haydon sat silently, breathing the rich aroma of the leather upon which they sat, and looked at Benigo Gamboa. He wondered at the complex truth behind what he had been saying. He did not believe that the old man had only these vague notions of who the assailants might have been. While it might be true he had many nameless enemies, Haydon was sure that *these* enemies were known to him.

"Mr. Gamboa, did you know any of the other men killed in the attack?''

"Yes.'' Gamboa nodded heavily. "Yes. There were two security men in a Mercedes. I did not know them personally. They were hired from a local agency. There was the chauffeur of the limousine. He has driven for us for several years. Again I did not know him personally. Sosa made all those kinds of arrangements. And then there were Mr. Crisman and Mr.

Lowell. This morning Mr. Sosa and I met with these two men to discuss the possibility of my buying some property in Austin from Mr. Lowell.''

''He was a realtor there?''

''A land developer, yes.''

''Crisman was also a developer?''

''No. He is an attorney here in Houston. We were meeting in his office in the Coastal Tower building in Greenway Plaza. He had been the contact between myself and Mr. Lowell. We came to a verbal agreement this morning and I asked the two men to lunch. We dined together at Charlie T's. A long lunch, because we talked at greater length about the land. We had more drinks after lunch, and then we left. Ramón and Mr. Crisman were going to take Mr. Lowell to his hotel—''

''Where was he staying?''

''The Westin Galleria. And then Ramón was to take Mr. Crisman back to his office.''

''Why didn't you go with them?''

''I frequently leave in a separate vehicle from the one in which I arrive at a restaurant or business meeting. It is something my chief of security arranges.''

''Were you expecting this attempt?''

''No more so than at any other time, as I have said.''

''Why did the security men follow the limousine instead of following the vehicle in which you were riding when you left the restaurant?''

''I don't know the particulars. All of the logistics are handled by my security chief, Lucas Negrete. You may talk to him about it.''

Security chief. Gamboa still used the language of a government official. But somehow Haydon thought that was less a habit from a past vocation than it was the confident vocabulary of a man who simply viewed himself as being as important as any dignitary regardless of whether or not he was attached to a political authority.

''Has Mr. Negrete been with you long?''

''Four years, almost five.''

''What members of your family are living with you in Houston now?''

''Only the son you met. My wife and daughters are in and out from Mexico.''

"And your oldest son?"

"He has his own business in Monterrey, and his own family. He comes occasionally."

Haydon thought a moment. "Mr. Gamboa, can you think of anything, any information, that might help us in this investigation? Are there any specific political groups, leftist groups, opposing factions, dissidents with known or suspected contacts in Houston, that might be even remotely involved in this?"

Gamboa shook his head slowly, even as Haydon was speaking. "No one," he said with a wan, apologetic smile. "In fact, I do my best not to think about that sort of thing at all. There is no profit in that kind of worrying. I let others do that for me."

Haydon nodded, then stood.

"You'll make arrangements to notify Mr. Sosa's family?"

"Of course. I will personally send someone to his wife. My people will make all of the other arrangements regarding the body."

"Thank you," Haydon said. He was irritated with himself. He had the uncomfortable feeling that he had allowed himself to be manipulated in this interview, an interview *he* had conducted. "I'm sure I'll be talking with you again."

"Certainly." Gamboa stood also, and walked with Haydon to the library doors.

As they stepped out into the entrance hall, Efren Gamboa turned from the front windows, where he had been standing with his arms folded staring out to the soft light of the loggia. His face bore a seriousness uncharacteristic in a young man his age. He also seemed unaccustomed to the blunt bulge of the weapon beneath his suit coat.

Chapter 12

They sat inside under a dim ceiling light as insects circled above them in a slow flittering dance, the only moving things in the room. A large square floor fan was wedged into one of the windows. It was turned on high, creating a breeze that dissipated to a slothful stirring of the old home's musty odors by the time it reached them across the spacious room. They could have gone outside on the long upstairs gallery, but instinctively they sought cover. Outside, a guard kept watch from among the relic weeds and the cypresses.

Blas Medrano had stopped lighting the cigarettes off one another and was now smoking them meditatively rather than emotionally. A weathered wooden table sat in front of him, covered with brown, grease-stained butcher's paper from which they had eaten the tamales and tacos bought at a neighborhood café. There was a bottle of wine, nearly empty, and three glasses.

Blas stared at Professor Daniel Ferretis's *guayabera*. It was made of polished cotton with fancy needlework on the front panels. There were also two perfectly round spots of orange grease on the front. He wondered if the professor knew. Rubio was smoking too, his cigarette resting neatly in the notch of his lower lip, as he absently pecked the wooden table with a key. Blas could not tell if there was a rhythm to the pecking, or if it was simply an idle noise to accompany the drone of the fan.

Ferretis suppressed a belch and poured a bit more wine into his little glass. His hair was receding—he could not have been past his late forties—and he had a decided paunch. He was soft-looking, a result of his occupation in front of a classroom and behind a desk. His features were small, and he set them off with a pair of Cazel eyeglasses, the heavily square, reddish-brown kind that were popular in Europe. He was clean-shaven, and high on each cheek a blotch of pink glowed as if he had just been slapped, a natural flush that grew even brighter when he was hot.

"So you think Ireno told Negrete's men *everything?*" Ferretis asked, irritated.

"Everything he could think of," Blas said. "And probably some lies, anything, everything. Negrete's techniques are not primitive, and after a while his victims will say anything, hoping he will stop. Then Negrete is faced with having to separate the truths from the lies."

"Then why did you go ahead with the ambush?"

"Precisely because I knew Negrete wouldn't be able to make that critical separation. Not really knowing if it was going to happen or not, he went ahead and let Gamboa out on the streets, but took the half-measure precaution of switching him to another car at the restaurant. He got lucky."

"But he knows about this place."

"He does now, but when he dumped Ireno's body out front he wasn't sure. He couldn't risk getting in trouble with the local police by raiding us, so he dumped the body and settled back to see what would happen."

Ferretis downed his wine and said, "So I'm at risk."

"Of course, and the others. Anyone, anything Ireno knew about."

"Son of a bitch," Ferretis snapped. He thought a moment, then said, "I'll tell them in Guadalajara about Teodoro. Or do you want to do it?"

Blas shook his head. "You do it."

"I'll tell them he died firing from his motorcycle, like a true soldier. I'll tell them you, personally, were with him. His father will be proud," Ferretis said.

"Yes, you tell them that, Professor. It was such a wonderful thing Teodoro did from his little Kawasaki."

Ferretis looked across the table. The tone of sarcasm in Medrano's voice was unmistakable. He had never met Medrano before, but his reputation among the *tecos* was remarkable. That was why he was here. In the matrix of that murky shadow world in which he moved and lived, he was renowned, but Ferretis hadn't expected to find a man so at odds with his profession. Especially this profession.

Blas felt the professor's eyes on him, but he didn't care.

"Do you remember the prayer of the Teco Brigade, professor?" It was a rhetorical question; he didn't wait for an answer. "I remember every word of it, though I memorized it a long time ago. There is a phrase: '. . . sprinkle my blood jubilantly over the countryside of my homeland so that those who come after me will return to that place and say: He died for God, and for Mexico.' My God, that's wonderful stuff," he said caustically. "Don't you agree, professor? Teodoro Anica: Martyr of the Select Guard." He fixed his eyes on Ferretis, and the tone of his voice became almost casual. "It means nothing, you understand. Perhaps even less than nothing."

Ferretis returned the gaze. What was this? This son of Apolinar Medrano Mallen, this legendary *teco de choque,* seemed to be walking very near the edge.

"Do you want me to ask them to send someone else to take his place?" Ferretis asked, ignoring what Blas had just said.

Blas shook his head again. "It won't be necessary." He cut his eyes at Rubio, who wasn't looking at anyone, keeping his own counsel. Wise coyote. It was the way to survival. Then Blas looked at the professor, who was now pouring himself another glass of wine. He drank some of it. He had a lot to think about. Months of planning were in the balance, and the professor was feeling the tension of the scales.

The grinding whine of an industrial crane loading merchant vessels in the ship channel rode the heavy air through the windows with the moist, muddy smell of the bayou. As the crane moaned to a muffled stop, the odd ululation of an owl moved through the cypresses. Blas was almost embarrassed by the melodrama of the irony. A moment from an unsubtle film. How could real life be like this? If the other two men had noticed, he did not know it, for he avoided their eyes.

Perhaps the professor did not notice. He was an economist,

a political historian. Subliminal life was not his concern. His concern was with the life he could touch and effect, preserving democratic systems of government, stopping the creeping cancer of communism that gnawed in the bowels of Latin America and threatened the heart of the United States. He was concerned with Jews and Jesuits and counterrevolution. And secrecy.

If Rubio heard the owl, he did not acknowledge its irony, either. But then he would not have recognized it as such. It might have been a symbol to him, a totem, a sign that spoke to the darker currents that streamed with the Indian blood in his veins. He would have heard it as the coyote hears it, as the voice of a hunter who sees and thrives in the absence of light, who covers his actions with night.

When the owl called a second time, Ferretis set his glass on the table.

"This time, Blas, there can be no mistake," he said. "No one expected it to be easy. Negrete is formidable. But we can risk only one other attempt. The shooting was a spectacular event by U.S. standards. They're not used to that kind of thing here."

"They'll think it was drug-related," Blas said. "And so will everyone who watched the evening news, or will read tomorrow's newspapers."

"You're probably right," Ferretis said. "But it won't take the police long to sort that out. If you miss him this time, and it makes the papers like this shooting, they're going to track it down. Negrete will lead them to you. He can do that without risking any adverse publicity for Gamboa. He's good enough to do it."

"He's already done that," Blas said.

Ferretis looked at Blas. "How are you going to do it?"

Blas disdained the question. The professor's desire for the details, for the vicarious pleasures of battle, was repellant to him. Like an armchair general, he liked to talk war, to imagine the smell of cordite, to imagine the rush of adrenaline, to imagine the acts of heroism, to imagine the encomiums of victory. The rearguard were despicable to Blas, not because they conducted war without risk, but because they had not the power of mind to imagine the truth: the smell of vomit and blood, the rush of panic and horror, the acts of cowardice, the despair of defeat. There were too many professors, too many generals. And far, far too many Teodoro Anicas eager to be blown to hell for high-sounding words and pompous ideals.

"It will be quick," Blas said. "And soon." He was fully aware, however, that the professor was only doing his job. Guadalajara was monitoring the squad's pulse. They did it everywhere. They called it "networking," but Blas often thought of it as a web. Every time he moved, the strands quivered and a message was telegraphed to Mexico. It was only tolerable because he knew the professor also had his burden of spies. *Las orejas,* the ears, were everywhere. It was the nature of the Brigade to be suspicious, to stay informed.

On the other hand, it was his nature to survive too, and he knew that the only true secret was that which existed solely within one's mind. If it took any other form it was endangered, and risked betrayal.

Ferretis started to say something else, but Blas cut him off. "Let's look in the cases," he said.

He motioned to Rubio, who had been sitting quietly, wedging his key into a crack in the old table. As he had listened, he had worked it in deeper and deeper. Now he jerked it out and reached down for the first of two five-inch Samsonite briefcases sitting on the floor beside them. Blas cleared away the greasy paper and Rubio set the briefcase in the middle of the table. The professor produced a key of his own, unlocked the latches, and snapped them open. As Rubio unloaded the money, Blas began counting it. They were all $20 bills. They were secured in $1,000 straps, fifty bills in each strap. When he finished counting them, there were 250 straps on the table. A total of $250,000.

They returned the money to the briefcase, and Blas put it back on the floor as Rubio hoisted the second briefcase to the table. They followed the same process, counting and repacking another $250,000 in $20 bills.

"They each weigh a little over twenty-five pounds," Ferretis said, pouring another glass of wine. "I weighed them on my bathroom scales after I had to haul them across campus."

Blas didn't say anything. He wondered why the professor

wanted to weigh them, since their weight had no bearing on the transfer. Did he have that much curiosity for the trivial?

"This will petrify them." Ferretis's eyes had found the middle distance of deep thought. "They'll all be wondering how far down the pecking order this justice is going to penetrate."

"When will they announce the reason for the assassination?" Blas asked. He was lighting another cigarette. His throat was raw and he could no longer enjoy the taste of them.

"As soon as it happens."

"It's going to cost us," Blas said. "Already we've lost Ireno and Teodoro. As soon as they make the announcement, the other targets are going to put on heavy security. As touchy as this one is, the losses in the other teams are going to be worse."

"They knew that," Ferretis said testily. He peered at Blas through his heavy frames. "Look at the squad members we've lost all over Central America, in San Salvador, Tegucigalpa, Guatemala City, all over Mexico. It's a war. You expect it. But it's got to be done, especially now with the Nicaraguans wearing East German socks, and licking Karl Marx postage stamps. A weak government is an invitation to defeat. There is no national security with a weak government. Gamboa and the others like him were incautious, and grasping. Their greedy self-interest has jeopardized Mexican economic stability. In their own way they've paved the road for communism. We'll make examples of them. Before de la Madrid's term expires. We have an eye on him too, and his ministers. From now on they'll all have to answer to us, and to justice."

Blas looked at the professor, whose cheeks were glowing after his pompous little outburst. Blas could dredge up no sympathy for the professor's dogmas. He felt no real passion for Benigo Gamboa, or for López Portillo, or any of them. The old man had done nothing the men who wanted him dead hadn't done. His crime was not that he had sinned, but that he had sinned so egregiously. It was not that he had stolen, but that he had marauded; not that he had seduced, but that he had raped; not that he had killed, but that he had decimated. Though Blas understood the distinctions, recognized the disparity in degree, he simply wasn't offended by it. Rather, he saw offense in the justice as well as in the crimes.

But it didn't matter. Years ago he had chosen his course, and though he no longer believed in it, it was too late to change. Too late now to protest in fastidious indignation.

But the professor's excitement was understandable, for he was riding a wave of enthusiasm. He had sat on the council that had conceived this stratagem, and had been influential in drawing up the list. Though he was a Chicano and not a Mexican national, he was much admired by the radical right in Mexico, and had lent his political expertise to their causes. He fervently believed in the domino theory, and felt that the extreme situation in Nicaragua called for extreme situations farther up the line. Although he wrote papers expanding on these views and published them in academic and private-foundation journals all over the world, he was cautious never to attract personal media attention. He had no desire to be seen or to become a public figure. In his mind the real shapers of history were the unseen ideologists, the men who moved in the strong, unobservable undercurrents of political thought, influencing the course of nations from their small, overcrowded offices, whence they were summoned in secret by the media-vain politicians for consultation and advice.

In the politics of Latin America, the professor could see a more immediate result of this kind of influence than was possible in the United States, where the process was more sclerotic. And in Mexico in particular, he could sense changes in the wind. A skillful hand could make history there by defending democracy and freedom in a clear-cut way. It was certain that Marxism was a living, breathing threat in the Americas. It had to be stopped, then driven out. Extraordinary means were justified.

"Do what you have to do," he said suddenly. "There's more money if you need it. The importance of this is incalculable."

"I don't need any more money," Blas said.

The professor was sweating profusely now. He took off his glasses and wiped the brow of his nose with the tail of his *guayabera*.

"I won't be back unless you send for me," he said, returning the boxy frames to his small nose. His magnified eyes looked across the table.

"Fine." Blas nodded. "We're leaving tonight. When it happens, you'll know it."

"Good, but you've got to leave a message at the dead drop—the new one we've agreed on—when you leave for Mexico. I've got to know that."

Blas tipped his head.

"And check the drop twice a day so I can get word to you in an emergency. Otherwise we won't use the drop at all."

They stood.

"Buena fortuna," Professor Ferretis said. Rubio led him out of the dingy room, down the stairs, and out onto the porch, where he was escorted through the tangles of the unkempt grounds to the tall gate that opened to the street at the back of the estate.

Blas walked out onto the upstairs veranda and looked toward the sparkling monuments in the city to the west. He smelled the dust from Chicon that hung in the barrio air, and thought again of home. There was very little he could do about the way he felt.

Haydon left Gamboa's and drove to Shepherd, changed his mind about going back to the police station, and turned south. He thought about Gamboa, the siege atmosphere around his place, and the fact that he really hadn't learned much from the old man. It had been a long day, and, as with all new cases, the files on this one consisted mostly of questions and they didn't even have nearly enough of those. But something bothered him. At the back of his mind he had already stored some information that could be helpful, but it was buried beneath the quick-paced events of the last five or six hours. He let his mind roam, hoping that eventually it would close in on something.

While he was waiting at a traffic light he remembered that Nina wasn't home. He looked around to see where he was, and remembered a little steak house not far from the Southwest Freeway. He started looking for it, spotted it, and cut across traffic into the parking lot. The place was gloomy in the black-and-red tradition of tavern design, but he had eaten there before and the steaks were good. He chose a corner table and ordered a thick filet, medium well with baked potato. He passed up the salad bar, and sat at the table, staring at the tablecloth.

Starting at the beginning of the day, he reviewed the events methodically, running the film a second time, trying to see the little things he'd missed before. By the time the waitress brought his food, a moth had gotten under the copper sheathing of the miniature English inn lamp sitting in the center of

the table and had begun to incinerate. Haydon blew out the candle, which made his corner even gloomier, but he didn't mind. He could tell the difference between the baked potato and the steak and he could see the cup of coffee.

He ate without enthusiasm, his thoughts returning once again to the day's events as he chewed the steak and gazed at the tablecloth, which had a ragged thread in the weave of its herringbone pattern. Suddenly he stopped chewing. He remembered what had been buried at the back of his mind, or he thought he remembered. He reached out and touched the ragged thread, and stared at the herringbone pattern. He would have to check it out. Definitely, he would have to check it out.

He got up from his chair and went out to the pay phone in the lobby to call Mooney.

"Steak, shit!" Mooney said. "You know what I'm eating? A submarine sandwich stuffed with mayonnaise and shredded lettuce. Watts went out and got them for us. His idea of a great meal. I don't even believe I'm eatin' this for dinner, for Christ's sake."

"I'll bring you the bacon they wrap around the filet," Haydon said. "I've got some interesting information about Gamboa. Anything there?"

"Naw," Mooney sounded bored. "Everything's outgoing right now."

"Will you be at a stopping place in about forty-five minutes?"

"I'm always at a stopping place."

"I've got an idea I think we ought to check out."

"I'm ready. Maybe we could drop by a quickie seafood place."

Haydon hurriedly finished the filet. It would sit like a stone in his stomach, and if by some odd chance he actually got home by twelve as he had agreed with Nina, he would not be able to sleep for hours. The waitress had disappeared, so Haydon decided to forgo the second cup of coffee. He quickly sipped the last of the original cup, put two dollars on the table—a generous tip, considering—and walked to the register near the front door. The waitress was there, talking with the young man behind the register, who had showy white teeth and heavy black eyebrows that had grown together.

"Oh, God, I'm sorry," she said when she saw Haydon, and began fishing in her apron pockets for the check.

"It's all right," he said. "I should have told you I was in a hurry."

She quickly calculated the total with her ballpoint pen, and took the time to turn the ticket over and write: "Have a nice day! Candi," in a rounded script that went all the way across the back.

Outside, Haydon unlocked the car and ran the air conditioner a minute before he pulled onto Kirby. He drove to Shepherd, where he jogged over to Memorial Drive and followed it all the way to the police station.

The homicide division looked as if it were working two full shifts at the same time. Haydon and Mooney were back on the street in fifteen minutes. By the time they got to the edge of Chinatown on Preston, they saw a ghostly jet of vapor pouring out of the air-conditioner vents. There was now no cool air, only a kind of heatless exhalation. It was leaking Freon.

"Well I'll be goddamned," Mooney said, his voice rising. "This is the shits." He angrily slapped off the air conditioner and rolled down his window, as Haydon did the same. Mooney took off his tie, which hadn't been tightened around his neck since five minutes after he had gotten to the office early that morning, and stared through the streaked windshield, sulking. No steak, and now no air conditioning.

"You know," he said, after stewing a few minutes, "there are few enough goddam amenities on this chicken-shit job without having the air conditioner crap out. I mean, an *air* conditioner. In this goddam sump of a city it's an absolute necessity! Like public utilities, for Christ's sake." He reached down between his legs and pushed the seat lever. His side of the seat slammed back as far as it would go. "And I'm surprised they don't have us running around in some kind of little Chink-shit cars, too," he said, apropos of nothing. *"That's* when I'd tell 'em to kiss my ass, and take early retirement."

Haydon had been hearing a lot about early retirement from Mooney lately. Quite a few of the detectives were discouraged by the new, stringent policies imposed on the department, and Mooney was no exception. Haydon agreed with their reasons for discontent and was a little embarrassed that the new austerity measures obviously posed no hardships for him.

But aside from that, Haydon had been concerned for a good while that Mooney didn't seem particularly happy. In a fast-paced city that placed a premium on youth and health-spa physiques, a paunchy, red-nosed cop pushing forty-five was not exactly in the mainstream of the A crowd. Mooney was facing the lonely middle age of a lifelong bachelor, and his social life was quickly losing altitude. He was watching a lot of television at night, alone.

"See if there's a flashlight in here anywhere," Haydon said. Mooney reached under his seat and felt around. He turned with a groan and looked in the backseat.

"There's a little one back here," he said. "I doubt if it's got batteries. If it does, the bulb'll be broken."

They followed Harrisburg into the East End, past a monstrous coffee packaging and distribution plant that produced odors that always reminded Haydon of the smoldering fires of a jungle village in the Yucatan, past Eastwood Park, a used-furniture store darkened and ripe for burglary, a meat-processing plant, the railroad tracks, a thrift store, a dance hall called Latin World with palm trees along its sidewalk and a painting on its wall of a pair of dancers in thirties-style tuxedo and slinky dress leaning into a sweeping tango.

Turning into the darker streets, they entered Chicon two blocks from the Belgrano estate. The neighborhood cantinas offered them bouncing Mexican music with wheezy accordion rhythms and the simple chords of amateur guitarists. They crept past Los Cuates and La Perla, seeing the men and women lounging in the night shadows outside, cigarettes glowing in parked cars. The sweet smoke of marijuana drifted to them from the hot, murky evening like the heavy perfume of a sad and indifferent woman.

Haydon continued past the cantinas and stopped across the street from the empty barber shop of Ernesto Herrera. From where they were sitting they could see a faint glow of amber light in the second floor of the old house.

"Somebody's there," Haydon said, his voice low.

"You don't want to go up and knock on any doors, do you?" Mooney asked.

Haydon smiled. "No. There's a gate at the back, like a door in the wall. I want to double-check it. That's all." He turned, stretched over the back of the seat, and grabbed the flashlight. He held it under the dash and flipped it on. A yellow beam lit Mooney's shoes in the floor of the car.

"Well, whattaya know," Mooney said sourly. "Not exactly high-performance, though."

"It's good enough," Haydon said. "This will take only a minute."

He put the car in gear and eased away from the curb, around the corner and down the street on the east side of the house. The top of the high wall was darkened with cloudy branches of trees growing on the other side. Haydon went to the end of the block and crossed the intersection into the next block. He cut the lights and parked in front of a little shotgun house with its windows thrown open. There were no lights on inside, but they heard a radio.

"Okay," Haydon said. "Let's walk back and cross the street to the rear wall. The gate's right in the middle. All I want to do is check the ground just inside."

They locked the car and took the hand radio with them, the volume turned down. Haydon carried the flashlight and Mooney followed with the radio. They rounded the corner on the opposite side of the street, staying in the shadows of the banana trees growing next to the fences inside the yards. When they were opposite the gate they paused, then crossed.

The streetlight that should have been at the corner of the block was out, so they were in a prolonged half-light when they stepped up on the sidewalk next to the wall. Mooney turned his attention to the street as Haydon cupped his hands over the lens of the battered flashlight and guided a dull beam along the edge of the wrought-iron gate. When he found the latch where the lock was supposed to be, he was surprised.

He straightened up and put his mouth close to Mooney's ear. "It's not locked," he said. "I'm going to ease it open."

Mooney turned to the gate and put his hands on the hinges to help deaden the squeak they anticipated. Haydon inched it open. It squeaked sharply once, and Haydon crouched to the ground, directing the flashlight beam on the few feet of open ground between the gate and the dense stand of bamboo. He saw the powdery dust he had remembered, and then he saw the other thing, the narrow herringbone pattern of tread marks, clear and precise in the fine dust. Instinctively, he followed them with the beam to the bamboo. The rear end of a motorcycle glimmered through the stalks.

Haydon heard a dog on another street, a high-pitched quivering wail that dropped to a deep chesty baying a split second before the point-blank barrage of automatic-weapon fire opened over his head with an explosion like the end of the world. Though he could not possibly have seen it, he was aware of Mooney being blown off his feet, being hurled out the gate with an awesome grunting bawl that had no comparison in Haydon's experience. Unreasonably he screamed too, heard his own voice syncopated between the spitting solar brilliance of each rapid explosion. He came up with the Beretta in both hands to meet the stunning muzzle fire with his own deafening blasts into the bamboo.

Then silence.

For an instant the hush was disorienting. His body was as rigid as bone, his arms holding the Beretta straight out in front of him.

Suddenly every dog in the barrio raised an incredible yowling. Haydon staggered from his crouch, caught himself with his left hand, his ears ringing, the Beretta still pointing at the stand of bamboo. He was trembling, crabbing backward to the gate, suddenly realizing he might have emptied the fifteen-round clip, wondering if he could fire again if he had to. He stumbled backward over Mooney, the dogs filling his head and scrambling his thoughts, remembered, felt the numb coolness of shock coming as he lunged out of the line of sight of the opened gate, remembered again, jumped back into the open, and began dragging Mooney sideways to the protection of the wall. He knew Mooney was dead. He felt dead, and in Haydon's mind the black spillage that was still spreading incredibly quickly over the pale sidewalk and in which Mooney seemed to float so lightly under the dim, distant source of illumination proved he was dead.

The straining whine of a car engine on the other side of

the block. Louder as it approached the front of the old mansion, shouting coming from beyond the wall, yelling, only a few voices, the deep-toned jangling of iron gates, and the car screaming away into the city night.

He sat on the gritty sidewalk, leaning against the Belgrano wall with Mooney's head in his lap. He was thinking about Mooney's ulcers when he remembered the radio, and saw it winking at him from the gutter.

~~~~~~~~~~~~~~~~~~~~~~~~~~~~~~~~~~~~~ **Chapter 14**

He listened to the dispatcher call for the nearest units—officer down, which would bring everyone on the East Side—and then she asked if he was all right. He said he was. Homicide picked it up and Dystal was on, his west Texas drawl tightened by what he had heard. Dystal asked if it was bad, and Haydon said Mooney was dead. Dystal asked if he was all right, and he said he was. They were on the way, the lieutenant said, and kept talking, and Haydon knew why and didn't care and turned off the radio.

The empty sidewalk stretched on either side of them like a luminous chalky border against the wall. No one was coming out of the houses, which was good, because he didn't want them to, and after a minute there were fewer and fewer dogs barking until the last one stopped. He watched the black pool spread to the edge of the curb, where two or three rivulets broke loose and went over the side. He knew there would be a lot of it, so it didn't bother him. He wanted a cigarette. Dystal would have one when he got there, or maybe one of the patrolmen who would be there first. His clothes were plastered to him with sweat, enough of it to soak through his suit, enough to make his face slick, to form a drop on the end of his nose and make the corners of his mouth taste salty.

In his mind he stood back and looked at himself. It was an unreasonable thing for him to keep Mooney's head propped up with his thigh, but it didn't seem right that he should let it on the sidewalk. Not now, while there were just the two of them and they still shared whatever it was that tied them together. After the others arrived the situation would become official and it wouldn't matter anymore and he could put Mooney's head on the sidewalk. When the others entered into it—he almost thought "intruded"—the strange intimacy of a closely exchanged death would vanish. Mooney's departure would become a "case."

Mooney's head was surprisingly heavy. Haydon looked at the enormous swell of Mooney's stomach and remembered the corpse that had lain next to this same wall, but on the other side of the block. That was only this morning. He remembered the shoes without laces, and he looked at Mooney's shoes to check. He looked at Mooney's hands. And, realizing now that he had been avoiding it, he looked at Mooney's face. Even though he was only a foot or so away, he could not see his features distinctly. He could not get a clear picture of what Death looked like, having come to make its roost in Mooney's body.

He looked up and let his eyes settle on a nothing part of the night. He thought that it was a good thing he didn't have cigarettes with him because if he had he would have smoked one and it might have seemed a callous gesture to the first officers to arrive—him sitting there with Mooney's head in his lap, smoking a cigarette. Mooney wouldn't have given a damn, but it wouldn't have looked right all the same.

He was not, initially, aware of the sirens, rather it was as if he thought of them first, and then heard them. They were distant, frail and distant.

Mooney had been still for so long Haydon half expected him to heave a big, fat man's sigh as he often did on stakeouts when he had to sit cramped up in a car for long periods of time. But there would be no such sigh from him now, because Mooney wasn't there. Mooney was lost. Roosting Death had performed its magic, and shunted him into oblivion, to a place that even Death forgot. That was part of the magic, the heart of its hopelessness. He remembered the words of Catullus, "Lost is the lost, thou knowest it, and the past is past." Haydon saw the infinite black vacuum of never again.

He simply waited, cradling what Death had done on a hot night, dreading the approaching end of their tranquillity.

chapter 15

The streets on all four sides of the block occupied by the Belgrano estate were closed off by police cars, and teams of officers were going door to door to each of the houses that faced the mansion walls. Fractured beams of flashlights crisscrossed in the darkness through the brushy undergrowth of the grounds, and every window in the old house was lighted, its bare rooms exposed to the surrounding night.

Dystal had been in the fifth car to arrive at the scene, though he was the first man from homicide. Before the others arrived, he took Haydon aside and listened to his story. He was easygoing, but not lax in wanting details. Haydon was aware that Dystal was watching him closely. He had expected it. Haydon had not acted responsibly in deliberately cutting off the radio, leaving Dystal to wonder what was happening, and with no idea of what he would find when he got there. He had every reason to expect the worst.

After Dystal had made Haydon go through it a second time, and then began backtracking with questions, Haydon realized there was more at play than the lieutenant's need to know. Haydon had to have his facts straight. He would have to repeat his story to each of the three teams that investigated officer shootings: the department's shooting team, the representative from the internal affairs division, and the Harris County district attorney's investigators. Dystal was testing him, coaching him. He wanted to know for himself if Haydon would be able to handle it, and he wanted to help him do it if he could.

It was the beginning of a long night. The parts were played by the same actors who always played them, but the cast had been expanded with additional characters. Besides Dystal, there were several teams of detectives, as there had been that afternoon, and the shooting team investigators. There were two other homicide lieutenants, the captain, and one of the assistant chiefs. The afternoon's terrorist-style assassination had already put the upper echelons of the department on alert. When they arrived at the scene at the Belgrano estate and learned that Haydon and Mooney had been investigating Haydon's suspicion of the presence of a motorcycle at the scene of another Latin killing earlier that morning, their worst fears broke into the open.

Standing in the street, thirty yards away from the empty white outline of Mooney's body on the stained sidewalk, Haydon did his best to review the events of that morning to the small crowd of detectives circled around him. There was as yet no written report about the morning's incident, since it had quickly taken second place to the investigation of the assassination that had occurred a few hours later. Nor had he yet had the time to write up the results of his interviews with Valverde and Gamboa. A great deal of the information he had gathered during the day and relayed back to Mooney still had not been recorded, since Mooney had been busy initiating his own inquiries up until the time he had accompanied Haydon to the Belgrano address. It was obvious that before either investigation could progress much farther, Haydon would have to sit down and produce a detailed report.

After he had recapped the new developments and answered a few questions, there was little left to say. The administrators gradually moved aside to discuss cosmetics, their immediate concern being the news cameras and reporters held at bay behind the barriers across the street. The officers huddled together to compare notes, to work out the strategies they would have to answer for the next day. Haydon and Dystal were alone again.

"Have another one of these things 'fore we go in there," Dystal said, tilting his head toward the house and shaking out a cigarette.

They leaned against the fender of Dystal's car and smoked, and as Haydon raised the cigarette to his lips a spasm of ungovernable twitching seized his upper arm. He almost lost the cigarette, then dropped his hand to his side, hoping that Dystal hadn't noticed.

"I don't guess you gotta go through with this part of it," Dystal said.

Haydon knew that as they had stood in the street talking with the officers and other detectives, Dystal had caught him glancing toward the flashlight beams raking the bamboo.

"I ought to," Haydon answered. It seemed he should have said more, but he didn't.

Dystal nodded, and let it go. "Pete'll be out here in a second. He's about got 'em all squared away in there." He pulled on his cigarette. "Ol' Pete," he said.

Haydon could smell the hot oil from the engine of the car they were leaning against, and he listened to the periodic popping and cracking of the metal in the hood and firewalls as the engine cooled. He heard someone cough and spit on the other side of the wall, and the faint conversational voices of men in the dark.

Suddenly these minutiae were essential to him. As long as he could make sense of them, as long as they fit together in the increasingly unreal fabric of the night, he would be able to maintain his emotional equilibrium. He strained to pull in even more sensations: the subtle colors still discernible in the night; the soft chinking of a nervous hand worrying pocket change coming from the group of administrators plotting strategy off to one side; the distinctive cadence of a woman's voice coming from the news vans behind the barricades.

Lapierre appeared in the opened gate of the wall and motioned to them. Together Haydon and Dystal stood up from the car and tossed their cigarettes aside. They approached the sidewalk and stood on either side of the bloody sheet that someone had thrown over the place where Mooney had lain.

"Okay," Lapierre said, in an oddly preparatory tone. "The shooter is seven feet from where you were standing, Stuart." He shined the bright beam of his flashlight into the dense bamboo directly in front of them and illuminated a ragged path torn through the stalks. "That was your line of fire," he said. "First him, then you, from a slightly different angle."

They stood there, looking at the narrow path of shredded

poles at shoulder height. Closer, the bamboo was torn lower and climbed on a rising trajectory where Haydon had fired from a crouching position.

"I guess he didn't see," Haydon said. It wasn't clear what he meant.

"We've cut a path around here," Lapierre said.

They followed him through a narrow opening the investigators had cut to the body. It did not go in a direct line, but approached the site in detour to avoid contaminating the evidence of the pattern of fire. The bamboo was so dense they didn't see the flashlight of the waiting patrolman until they were several steps away. He stood to one side of the body, which was draped with a sheet. Though Haydon had been sweating profusely all evening, he had forgotten about it until Lapierre bent down to uncover the body. Then he was conscious of it again, seeping from every pore, a maddening, strangling dampness.

The shooter lay on his side in a small opening hacked out of the impenetrable bamboo, his legs scissored as if he were running. His blood was splashed like black sludge across the rigid stalks that had been at his back. Haydon's stomach clenched, his hearing filled with the constricted surging of his own blood driven through his arteries. His eyes focused on the entry wounds. They were not clean. The slugs, having been deflected from a true course by the bamboo, had wobbled and tumbled into their mark. Two slugs had hit his face: one took his left eye into his head, the other blew out his right cheek. A neck wound. One, he thought, in his chest.

Haydon stared until he heard Dystal say, "Ever seen him?"

Haydon nodded. "It's Jimmy Valverde . . . the limousine service."

"Goddam." Dystal almost jumped. He spoke to Lapierre. "Better get somebody over there, seal the place off." Then to Haydon, "You sure?"

"It's Valverde," Haydon said, staring at the man who had liked to take cash, and had played with the body of Celia Moreno.

The thin, unsteady beams of the flashlights made the sprawl of the dead man quaver before Haydon's eyes, and when they played across the rails of bamboo, the bamboo jittered like the jerky images in a shadow play. Haydon felt as if he were

Geco-BAT 9mm parabellum cartridges, a plastic soft-drink case filled with empty Dos Equis beer bottles, yellowing copies of several Spanish-language newspapers published in Houston. A copy of *Penthouse* lay on the windowsill that faced the street.

"Not much here," one of the detectives said. "Just this stuff." He handed Lapierre a Guadalajara newspaper—"Published last week," he said—and a small paperback book. The paperback was a copy from one of dozens of serial novellas published in Mexico each week, popular soap operas printed in sepia ink in a comic-book format and relating tales of passion, betrayal, romance, and tragedy.

"And these," the detective said, looking at Lapierre as he handed him three of four copies of a cheaply printed magazine called *Replica*. These, too, were printed on comic-book paper, their covers variously decorated with lurid illustrations of what the headlines said were threats to democracy: leering bespectacled Jews casting glances over their shoulders hunched in cabalistic conspiracy; effeminate homosexuals in mincing postures corrupting children with offerings of candy and pornography; a political cartoon caricature of a giant-sized guerrilla in camouflage clothing with long hair and a hammer and sickle on his beret swallowing one by one the countries of Central America as he reached a grasping claw toward Mexico; a conspiratorial black-robed Jesuit whose fanged teeth echoed the traitorous symbols of the sons of the church in the murals of Siqueiros.

"Let me see," Haydon said. Lapierre gave a copy to Haydon and Dystal, and the three of them looked through the magazines.

"What the hell is this?" Dystal said.

Haydon fought to stay on his feet. With deep breaths, he sucked in the stale air of the old house, the dead, dusty air of the barrio.

chapter 16

La Colombre d'Or was an anomaly in a city of contemporary glass hotels eager to attract large numbers of guests to their atriums, escalators, coffee shops, and theme restaurants. With only five suites, it was probably the smallest luxury hotel in the world. It occupied an old mansion on Montrose Boulevard that once had been the twenty-one-room residence of Walter J. Fondren, one of the founders of Exxon Oil. As a hotel, it was operated in the manner of an elegant and refined auberge intended to make its guests feel as though they were visiting in the home of a warm and wealthy friend. Each of the five suites was furnished in different antique period pieces and original artwork, and was daily supplied with fresh flowers, fruit, a box of chocolates, French toiletries, mineral water, and a complimentary decanter of brandy. A staff member was assigned to each suite, twenty-four hours a day, and the guests were indulged with quiet discretion. Each suite had a private telephone line. There was no switchboard.

He arrived a little after ten in the evening without reservations, hoping he would be lucky. He was. While he registered, the concierge arranged for his three oxblood leather suitcases to be taken to the only remaining available rooms. He then selected his dinner from the evening's menu and asked that it be served in the dining room of his suite. Across the small lobby, diners visited quietly in the softly lighted dining room that presented its large windows to Montrose. The glittering pillars of downtown rose beyond the dark trees of the old neighborhood that was Houston's equivalent to Paris's bohemian Left Bank.

Glancing first into the small bar and then into the library that served as a sitting room, he turned and walked up the dark walnut stairway to his rooms on the second floor.

The valet had left all three bags sitting at the foot of his bed, as he had requested. The drapes had been pulled back from the windows that looked toward downtown and only two lamps had been left on. The suite was large and comfortable, and smelled vaguely of furniture oils and the French Provençal dinners that were being served downstairs. He stepped over to a small pedestal table and poured two fingers of brandy into a glass. He tasted it, felt it heat his throat all the way to his stomach. The aftertaste was excellent, but he was starving. It would go to his head. He took another sip, and looked around the room, walked into the sitting area, then into the dining room, and back into the bedroom, feeling the slight movement of the wooden floors, hearing their subdued groan beneath the Persian carpets.

He stood in the middle of the room, holding the brandy and thinking. The knock on the door startled him. It was too soon for dinner. But it *was* dinner, and he watched the valet and maid move the flowers from the center of the table and set the china and silverware in place, and then the serving dishes with the *carré d'agneau*. Watching them, he was shocked at how long he must have stood there, so unaware of time, so comfortable in limbo. They finished and stepped back, waiting. He thanked them and asked them not to stay.

He sat alone at the head of the table and ate in the dim light, which he preferred. The lamb was better than he had expected—in fact, it was superb—and he made a deliberate effort to eat slowly, to savor the sautéed vegetables and the mint jelly. He had chosen a heavy Guatemalan coffee from the list, and asked that they serve it strong. It had been perfectly brewed.

Turning to his right, he glanced out the windows, saw lights of every kind beyond the panes, and staring back at him through the glinting sparks a pair of eyes with a freakish hollowness that stopped his breath. It was not the strangeness that startled him; it was the recognition. How had he come so far, gone so far? He was beyond himself, beyond the man he once thought he saw and understood through the lens of his youth. The man of these eyes was somewhere else. This man who held the piece of skewered lamb on the end of a silver fork, this man whose face he examined in the reflection, whose cheekbones . . . whose cheekbones . . .

Once Father Donato had struck him. Donato had heard every kind of provocation from the young men he taught. All of them understood things they believed no one had ever understood before, certain they saw more clearly than the plodding priests who taught them. They offered heretical theories, they flirted with damnation, and yet Donato maintained his emotional equilibrium through it all. He did not denigrate their expositions, but sought always to guide their curiosity, to use the momentum of their own interrogations to lead them to more refined truths. Only on one occasion did Blas ever see him loose control. Just once, and Blas was all the more shocked because he had not known he was approaching perilous ground.

It was after he had entered the Autonomous University and had long given up his early thoughts of entering the Jesuit order. Donato had forgiven him that, too, and though he said he had seen it coming, the disappointment was something he could not so easily hide. Blas had known for a long time that he had become more than just another student to the priest. He was a son. This they both understood.

Inevitably his involvement in the university's politics became more important to him than everything else. He was a *teco*, the unblinking eye of justice, condemner of corruption, exposer of fraud, one of the select guardians of democracy. Enlightened by the conservative political philosophies predominant at the university, he became an ardent proponent of a new kind of revolution in which Jeffersonian ideals played a greater part than did the grand-sounding concepts that had risen out of the Revolution of 1910, and which were dragged out of the mothballs by Mexican politicians whenever there was an election and then promptly returned to the mothballs the day after they were sworn into office. Between elections, they ruled by corruption and deceit.

He was in his fourth year at the university, and was trying to explain to Father Donato the importance of the *teco* philosophy. The priest, whose wavy black hair had grayed dramatically in the past year, listened to him with steady, dark eyes. There had been no amusement there, no pleasure in the young man's excitement at discovering a new truth, no enthusiasm for the grand convictions of this new philosophy. When Blas finally paused in his audacious dialectic of the pious right, Father Donato's hand came from nowhere and struck him across his jaw. Blas distinctly remembered the force of it, and the single motion of his own reflexive action as he came to his feet swinging a doubled fist he somehow stopped inches away from the priest's unflinching glare.

"You-do-not-create-by-destruction," Donato hissed. "Not with people." The tears in the Jesuit's eyes were instant, coming as if to spite the fire that was also there. "Did I teach you *nothing*? Blas! Did I delude us both?"

Blas had stormed out of the room without saying a word, but the remembrance of Donato's eyes followed him. Those eyes, set deep in the hollow wells of his skull, reflected the same anguish as the eyes he now saw staring back at him from the night beyond the glass.

He turned away from the windows and laid down his fork. He looked at the few pieces of lamb on his plate. Had that highly charged conversation been one of politics or theology? Both disciplines had to be lived as they were learned or they did not possess the value of conviction, and were meaningless. Father Donato had seen an abyss between them, yet Blas had not been aware of having crossed one. The distance separating them had been spanned unnoticed, and the priest's blow had spun him around and revealed it. Father Donato could not have been more surprised than Blas himself. His had been a radical departure, but somehow he had failed to recognize it until his confrontation with the priest.

After that, Blas had spoken with his rejected mentor only one other time. It was two years later, and Blas had already begun the career that would eventually suck from him everything the priest had given. But he had heard the priest was quite ill, and in an awkward effort to rekindle a lost friendship, he went to visit. It was an unsatisfactory reunion. After a few false starts at conversation, Blas related a recent dream in an effort to amuse the older man. It had been a strange dream, a kind of fable of confusion, of loss, and of being lost. The frail priest began to cry. Perplexed and embarrassed, Blas turned around and walked out. They had not even really talked. Six weeks later, he heard that Father Carlos Donato had been found dead in his rooms.

Lord God of the Armies, General in Chief of the Brigade, let me be first in holy combat, do not refuse me the vanguard. Give courage to my burning heart that I might obey without question.

Lord God of the Armies, give me the satisfaction to see the victory, but if it is too much to ask, let me die for you, so that my soul can enjoy you for century after century. Sprinkle my blood jubilantly over the countryside of my homeland so that those who come after me will return to that place and say: He died for God and for Mexico.

Lord God of the Armies . . .

Perhaps Father Donato had indeed seen the future. Perhaps he had seen in Blas's dream the foretelling of his ultimate defeat in a realm of struggle far more tragic than his misguided politics. Blas would never complete the puzzle of God because he had lost the key piece, somewhere within himself. He had lost the understanding mind, the gift of discernment. To him the moral landscape had become a vast and empty plain with no distinguishing landmarks to guide him. Good and evil had disappeared.

Blas put his napkin on the table and stood. He looked at the dinner that no longer appealed to him, and turned and walked into the bedroom. Grabbing the first suitcase, he threw it on the bed and turned the combination to the first three digits of the Belgrano address. He snapped open the latches and took out plastic-wrapped packages of new underclothing, new socks, new shirts, new neckties, two boxes of new Ferragamo shoes, a new shaving kit. From the other side of the suitcase, he unpacked two new Ermenegildo Zegna suits, two pairs of dress pants, and a new sport coat. He had bought them at three separate stores within a two-hour period, the suits first so that they could be altered while he finished shopping. He had paid lavishly to have the alterations done immediately. They bowed and scraped, and did it. Money, he had long known, was the blood of the true aristocracy.

When he had put everything away, he sat the empty suitcase beside the armoire and hoisted the second one onto the bed. He dialed the first three digits of his father's telephone

number, and the latch snapped. Carefully, he laid open the
two sides of the suitcase. He folded back the flap covering
one side and removed a canvas airline satchel, a piece of
plywood eighteen inches square, a small handsaw, a packet
of screwdrivers with red plastic handles, a shrink-wrapped
toggle switch, and several packets of wood screws of various
sizes. Everything still had the hardware store's price tag.

From the other side of the suitcase he removed a plastic
sack that had been stapled closed. "Post Oak Hobby Shop"
was printed in yellow on the side of the sack. He ripped it
open and took out a green-striped box with a red triangle
above the words "Futaba: the Number One Choice for Remote Control Models." Tearing off the end of the box, he
slipped out a Styrofoam molded carton containing a two-
channel radio transmitter, two servos, a receiver, and a power
pack. It was a nice set. Gringos made everything so easy.
You just walked into a store and bought it. Incredible.

The first problem was sawing the board to fit into the airline bag without anyone hearing it. He turned on the stereo
near the bed and selected a channel playing jazz. A saxo-
phone was conveniently raking the scales. He placed the board
between two chairs with a newspaper underneath to catch the
sawdust, approximated the dimensions, and started sawing.
It was slow because he had to pause when the music softened,
but the new saw was sharp and it went quickly. He put the
board on the bed and arranged the receiver, one servo, and
one power pack near one side. Using the long screws from
the hardware store, he made everything stationary and
stretched the flexible antenna the full length of the board for
maximum reception potential. Next he took the switch and
placed it beside the servo and fastened it to the board with
shorter screws. With the switch off, he connected one end of
a small push rod to the toggle with copper wire, and then
wired the other end of the push rod to one of the little holes
on the servo disk. He made sure the wire was taut when the
switch was in the off position, and then he connected the
servo to the power pack and the receiver. One more item;
he wired a small light bulb to the two lead wires coming off
the toggle switch. It was ready.

He lifted the board off the bed and turned out the lights.
Feeling his way, he walked across the suite and sat the board

at one end of the dining table. He went back to the bed, checked the batteries in the transmitter, and telescoped the antenna. He flipped on the switch. There were two channels on the transmitter, and he had made sure to wire the servo controlled by the control stick on the right. The dim light on the power indicator dial was glowing ready. He tilted the control stick to the left, being careful to notice how much play it had before it activated the servo across the room. There was very little. The servo exerted pull on the push rod immediately. He pushed the stick all the way and the light bulb flashed on. He tilted the stick to the right and the light went off. To the left on, to the right off.

He tried it several times. On. Off. On. Off. On. Sitting in the dark, he stared across the suite to the light. He concentrated on the center of it until his eyes created the illusion that he was looking at it through a long dark tunnel. It grew, slowly at first, then with increasing speed like a rolling, expanding ball of fire until it encompassed his entire vision in exploding brilliance.

Off.

Chapter 17

When Haydon drove through the gates and saw the lights on downstairs, he knew that Nina had already heard. It was Dystal. He would have called her. He parked the Vanden Plas and had started up the steps to the front door when it opened and Nina stood in the entry with the soft golden light behind her. She had already dressed for bed, her hair down, her gown hiding her feet. Her face was almost obscured in blue shadow, but he recognized in the attitude of her body the mosaic of her emotions. In that instant, everything she meant to him was summed up in the recognition of that complexity. There were no words in language that would have enabled him to articulate what he instinctively understood about her at that moment in the doorway.

She put her arms around him as he stepped inside, and they held each other, the dim light from the lamps in the entrance hall keeping back the night that approached, but could not enter, the opened door.

"I'm so sorry," she said after a minute, her voice smoothed by the meaning of her words.

"Bob called you?" he asked.

He felt her nod.

He pulled away, but kept his left arm around her, away from the blood-soaked right pants leg.

"Let's go upstairs," he said. "I want to clean up, and then we'll talk."

They went up the stairs together, and he was aware of the extraordinary satisfaction he got from feeling her body under his arm, moving in step with him, alive and reassuring as if her very presence was the signal to him that it was over.

As he entered the bathroom and turned on the light, the first thing he did was to look at himself in the mirror. He was surprised. At first he thought he looked as if nothing had happened. He wondered if he was supposed to *see* that he had stood next to a friend who had been killed. What was that supposed to look like? But there was no difference.

Yet, as he continued to look at himself, he saw that there were differences. The distinctions appeared gradually, like the details of a photograph in a tray of developing solution.

First, there was the blood. Speckles of it the size of pinheads on the left shoulder of the suit. He couldn't imagine how they got there. It didn't seem possible, remembering what had happened. But there they were, and there was a rusty smear of it on the right side of his chin. Then with revulsion he remembered holding Nina. Had she touched it? But her head was on his left side, the left side of his chin had touched her hair. The left side? His eyes returned to the speckles. He didn't even know whose blood it was.

Swearing, he wrenched off the coat and threw it on the floor. He turned on the shower, wanting to hear something besides his own breathing.

Again he turned his attention to the mirror, searching for some visible evidence of what he had been through. He looked at the feathering of gray mixed in the sable hair at his temples, the first hints of wrinkles at the corners of his eyes. They were not new. Keeping his eyes on his eyes, he removed his shirt and threw it behind him. He looked at his chest, his shoulders, his neck. He was in good shape. He put his hands on the vanity and leaned closer. It was there, something was different, but he couldn't see it. In two weeks, a month, he would see it. An additional line by the eyes, half a dozen more gray hairs. He couldn't see them now, but they were predetermined. He wondered where, precisely, they would be.

He straightened up, took the Beretta from the small of his back, and laid it inside one of the towel cabinets. Turning from the mirror, he stooped and took off his shoes, and then his socks and pants. He threw everything in the corner on top of the suit coat.

He stood under the freshet of cold water as if it were the oxygen that kept him alive. He concentrated on the way it felt, the manipulations of the individual jets from the shower head. He heard the bathroom door, and opened his eyes. Through the blur of water he saw Nina come in and begin picking up his clothes. Impulsively he started to stop her, then didn't. He simply stood there and watched her remove his wallet and shield from his coat. He had forgotten about them. She went through his other pockets and laid the coat aside, then picked up his pants. She removed his comb and handkerchief from the right hip pocket, some change from the front pockets. Suddenly she jerked them away from her, held them out. He watched her stare dumbly at the blood on his pants leg. She hadn't seen it downstairs. Oddly, he felt ashamed that she should find it, as if she had caught him in an infidelity, or a secret baseness.

It was an absurd reaction. He closed his eyes and stretched out his hands to lean against the cool marble wall.

Nina had gone downstairs and made them both large and strong gin limes, which she brought up to the bedroom. Haydon turned the lights off, and they sat together on the small sofa under the slow sweep of the ceiling fan and looked toward the night through the tall bedroom windows. After a few minutes of silence, he started talking, and told her everything that had happened that day, from the first victim until the last. Twice he had to stop when he was telling her about Mooney, emotion strangling him until he couldn't breathe, couldn't go on. She leaned her head against him in the dark, and he waited until she stopped crying.

He was himself surprised at how strange a day it had been, including his telling of it. Never before had he been this free with the details of his work. He had narrated the day's events with an even, thorough completeness, and though he spared her the brutal specifics and an examination of his own emotions, he had shared more of it with her than he had expected to. He simply began talking, knowing she would want to hear and knowing, perhaps subconsciously, that for the first time he wanted her to hear it.

When he finished they sat quietly, and Haydon could feel Nina's relief. It was the sort of thing he should have done on many occasions in the past. He didn't know why he hadn't, but was glad that this time he had.

He held the tall cold glass to the side of his neck. He could feel his carotid throbbing against it.

After a moment she said, "What about his family, Stuart?"

He had already thought about that, on the sidewalk.

"None in Houston. I think there's a sister in Atlanta, a brother in, I believe, Arlington, Virginia. Captain Mercer will have that responsibility."

"Are they married?"

"I've heard him talk about his sister's children. His brother . . . it seems to me he isn't married either."

"That would be unusual, wouldn't it? Two bachelor brothers. Never married."

Haydon nodded. It seemed that for the most part everyone was accepted as being more or less average, until he was dead. Then people began to look at him more closely than they ever had before, and discovered that he was unusual. The truth was that everyone was unusual beneath the surface, but few people ever took the time to look there. It was a human failing to accept people as they presented themselves. Yet, to do otherwise was emotionally expensive and, some would argue, injudicious. Yes, Ed Mooney was an unusual man, more so now than this morning, and he would become even more so tomorrow when the media began their background interviews and the newspapers printed profiles of the friendly homicide detective everyone liked. An especially tragic loss.

"What happens next?" Nina asked.

"Tomorrow I go in and work on the report. I'll have to do that before anything else. A lot of people have to have copies of the details." He sipped the gin. "I'll have to talk to the various men investigating the shooting."

"They'll put you at a desk?"

"For a while. They almost have to, until I've talked to the investigating teams at least."

"Then what?"

"Then it's up to Bob, Captain Mercer, and maybe the departmental psychologist as to when I can go back to my regular schedule."

"Is that the way it's always handled?"

"Yes." He knew what she was thinking. "The psychologist is routine in officer-related shootings. And especially in something like this . . . with Mooney."

"When you go back, will it be on the same case?"

"I hope so."

"You want to continue with it?"

"Of course."

"How do you feel about the investigation itself?" Nina asked. "What do you think is happening?"

Haydon drank the last of the tall glass. His low tolerance for alcohol and Nina's strong mixture were working compatibly to sedate him. He was glad for a reason to give way to dissociation, glad for an excuse not to care so intensely.

"I don't know," he said. "But it's going to be complicated, and everyone realizes that now. I suspect it'll be a long, involved investigation, and what we can dig up during the next few days will be critical. A bad time to be deskbound."

"But can't you still work on it? Isn't there always a lot of paperwork? You don't have to be on the street to contribute to this."

"No," he said. "I don't have to be."

His eyes had adjusted to the darkness by now, and Haydon could see the shapes of the furniture in the dark. He could see the black slate mantel clock sitting on a bookshelf across from them, and could hear it ticking. The clock was old and not expensive, German works and French case. He had another old one in the library; both he kept because of the measured catching of their escapements. The sound of time circumscribed, and quantified.

He lay awake only briefly with Nina in the crook of his arm before he slept. But it was a fool's sleep, throughout the night. Twice he found himself completely awake, sitting up in bed sweating, his heart crazily out of rhythm with his breathing. Nina was sitting beside him. She didn't speak. She didn't have to. After the second time, he got up and went into the bathroom and drank some water. He washed his face and looked at himself in the mirror. When he came back to

bed he slept, but only fitfully, running in the murky border-
lands of dream and hallucination. Again and again he suddenly was staggered by the deafening, blinding bursts of
point-blank gunfire coming from the paling of black bamboo;
over and over he was jolted by the awful grunting bawl of
Mooney's dying astonishment.

Chapter 18

Haydon sat on a wooden bench inside the open-air shower of the bathhouse and looked at the splinters of early-morning light breaking through the lime trees. He wore only his pajama pants and sandals. A cup of coffee sat on the bench beside him as he leaned over and fed a piece of breakfast ham to Cinco, who was lying on the bricks in front of him with his front paws crossed, chewing patiently. After the collie swallowed each piece, he looked at Haydon with his old watery eyes to see if there was more. When Haydon showed him the next piece, Cinco flopped his tail twice on the bricks and Haydon handed it over. The routine was unvarying until the ham was gone.

As Cinco sighed and slowly reclined on the bricks, Haydon sat back against the bathhouse wall and sipped the last of his coffee. The stone was cool on his naked shoulders. These few minutes in the new morning air with the birds gabbling and bickering at the feeders in the trees in front of the greenhouse were far more calming than the night had been. Knowing that Haydon needed to get downtown early, Nina had gotten up before him and had breakfast ready by the time he came down. They had eaten together in the sunroom, and then Haydon had come down to check on Cinco. The morning had restored sanity. Nina, and the morning.

She knew he had to go in to the office, yet she begged him to stay home, said no one could possibly expect him to be there. And in most circumstances, she would have been right. But Mooney's death had not been an isolated incident. Some-

119

how it had played an integral part in the scheme of a larger investigation. No one but Haydon could provide the information the department needed. Only he and Mooney had talked to certain people, gathered certain information. Only he had made certain correlations. There was no way he could change that, no way he could shut his eyes to the responsibility.

He was on his way downtown before the worst of the traffic hit the streets. He wasn't looking forward to going back into the squad room, facing the awkward, even painful way in which the other detectives would want to tell him that they were sorry, that they understood how he felt, but wouldn't be able to because in the end men didn't know how to comfort men. He had seen it before, how they subdued their own emotions in deference to the survivor, to his struggle to comprehend why Death had brushed past him, and laid its hand on the next man instead.

If Haydon could have his way, he wouldn't speak to anyone for a month. He would retreat behind stone walls, withdraw behind silence. But he could not have his way in this, and rather than seeing no one, he would see everyone.

When he walked into the homicide division, it was six-thirty, half an hour before the day shift began. The place was relatively quiet. He walked straight to his office without looking left or right and flipped on the computer terminal. He avoided looking at Mooney's carrel as he removed his coat and hung it behind the door. Out of habit he started to go out and get a cup of coffee, but he checked the impulse and sat down at the screen.

He had been typing only ten or fifteen minutes when he heard Dystal say, "You get any sleep last night, Stu?"

Haydon swiveled his chair around to face the bulky lieutenant, who was leaning against the doorframe holding a steaming mug of coffee.

"It was all right," Haydon said. "How about you?"

"Got home late, got up early." He was freshly shaved and smelled of Mennen's aftershave. Sometime within the last couple of days he had gotten a new haircut. He looked squeaky-clean, the tips of his brown boots shiny from beneath the bottom of his brown suit pants. But his fresh appearance disguised the effects of a night that probably had yielded only a couple of hours' sleep. Haydon knew without asking that before going home last night, Dystal had made a grim trip to the morgue.

"I'm gonna set a meeting for the whole bunch of us at eight," Dystal said. "We got a lot of catching up to do. Since you're not going to have a complete report till later on, I'd appreciate it if you'd just get up and tell your story." Dystal sipped at the coffee tentatively, looking at Haydon for a reaction. "A to Z. Everybody's gonna want to know, and everybody needs to know. We got nearly thirty-five detectives on this shift who'll be locked into this thing till something breaks. This way you get it over with in one dose and all the guys'll get the facts they need. You do that?"

"Okay," Haydon said. Dystal was right. "Have you got a cigarette?"

Dystal pulled the white pack of generics out of his shirt pocket and shook one up for Haydon. He lit it with his chunky Zippo, which still snapped smartly when Dystal closed it despite being so old there were only traces of the nickel plating still left on the case. The bulldozer insignia welded to one side was nearly smooth from years of rubbing against pocket change. The cigarette was terrible, as Haydon knew it would be, but he inhaled deeply anyway.

"Thanks for calling Nina last night," he said.

"I didn't think she needed to be surprised by that," Dystal said. "It's tough."

What he really meant was, he'd wanted her to be prepared for whatever state of mind Haydon might be in when he got home.

Lapierre and Nunn came in together and said good morning. Since Lapierre had been put in charge of coordinating the two investigations, Dystal told him what he thought he wanted to do about having Haydon speak to the other detectives.

"That's good," Lapierre said, looking at Haydon with his calm, smoky eyes. "We need to put everything in perspective as soon as possible. Robert and I are working on a list of players, and their relationships. Stuart, if you'll look over the list in a minute we can have it duplicated in time to hand out at the meeting. Can you think of anything else we could give them?"

Haydon shook his head. "I'll try to have the report before I leave today." He heard the division room filling with the day-shift detectives. By now everyone had heard about Mooney, from other detectives or on the news, and the usual noise that took over in the mornings was decidedly subdued.

"Okay," Dystal said, straightening up. "I'm gonna get busy. I'll make the announcement over the intercom in a few minutes. See you in a little bit."

When he turned away, he pulled the office door halfway closed behind him.

Without saying anything else, Lapierre and Nunn turned to their work as Haydon swiveled around and faced the computer terminal. For the next forty-five minutes he didn't stop working on the report except to go over the list that Lapierre had mentioned.

At eight o'clock, everyone filed into the meeting room. All the desk chairs were full, and a few stood or squatted on the floor against the walls. Dystal said some words about how the investigation would be conducted, and then turned it over to Haydon, who began relating the essentials of his and Mooney's activities from the previous morning until last night. He tried to anticipate questions by relating the sequence of events in considerable detail, as if he were reciting the report he would later type. The detectives listened quietly, and Haydon knew that each of them was following his story point by point, looking for the fatal mistakes that could have prevented Mooney's death. If he had been in their place he would have been doing the same thing, not as an indictment, but as a kind of self-test. If it had been them and their partners instead of Haydon and Mooney, would it have ended the same way? If chance was the only guilty party, which of them would have been talking this morning and which would have been in the morgue?

When Haydon was through, Dystal asked if there were questions, and when there were none Haydon sat down. Lapierre got up and started handing out copies of the list.

"The first thing I ought to tell you," Lapierre said, "is that we didn't get a hit on *any* of these names from the computers in our narcotics division, or from the DEA's computers. Well, that's not quite right. The chauffeur of the limousine had a couple of marijuana busts, but that's it. Some of us were betting on leads in that area, but we're not going to get them. That covers the DEA files in Mexico too. They just don't have any records of those names. Something may come up later, under aliases maybe, but as of now, nothing.

"However, the cache of literature we found last night in the house at the Belgrano address seems to be pointing us in another direction. The next thing we need to do is to get with the FBI records, and conduct a thorough search on radical right-wing political groups to determine if there are any connections here. The neofascist type of propaganda is familiar to us by now, but the difference in this instance is that it was all printed in Spanish, the target of the assassination is a Mexican national, and it's possible the shooters are also."

Haydon sat through the next hour only half listening to Lapierre's measured and methodical briefing followed by assignments to the various teams of detectives. Although he was himself presenting a controlled, even detached, appearance, he resented the cultural practice that called upon them to react to Mooney's death with a businesslike demeanor. He was as guilty as the next man regarding this, and he knew that Mooney would have done the same. Death was a complicated event for the survivors. If there was a proper way to deal with it, he did not know it. Even in the most sophisticated societies, perhaps more so in sophisticated societies, death remained the single most confusing event in the human experience. The one true disappearing act for which there could never be an explanation, or any real understanding.

He had finished the report, been debriefed by the DA's investigators, by the detectives from internal affairs, and by the shooting-team investigators. Now he had gone across the squad room and was looking through the glass wall into Bob Dystal's office. Dystal was trying to get off the telephone, and motioned for Haydon to come in.

"All righty," Dystal was saying. "You bet. Uh-huh. You bet. Appreciate it. Talk to you later." He hung up the telephone and leaned back in his swivel chair in a kind of controlled stretch that made the chair creak and pop as if it were about to explode. "Sit down, Stu," he said, and he rubbed his face with his thick, chunky hands.

Haydon came in, closed the door behind him, and took the

chair in front of Dystal's desk. He was tired, too. The day had been interminable.

"You've talked to the DA's people, and the others?"

Dystal nodded. "I don't think there's goin' to be any problems."

"How long?"

"A few days, I guess."

"At a desk?"

"Yeah." Dystal looked at Haydon. "They're a little squeamish, Stu. All the shooting that's been going on. They don't want to give the media anything to rake them over the coals about. Being real cautious on this."

Haydon sat there a moment. Dystal pulled out a drawer and propped a boot on it. He picked up a rubber band, looped his big thumbs inside, and started strumming it with his ring fingers.

"What's on your mind?" he asked slowly.

"I'm going to make a request for a brief leave of absence."

Dystal studied him from under his eyebrows, fiddling with the rubber band. "Leave of absence," he said.

"That's not out of line under the circumstances."

"No," Dystal said, shaking his head a little. "I don't think anybody'd see it as being outta line." He shot the rubber band into the metal trash can with a hollow thunk. "Except maybe me."

Haydon waited.

"Somehow I can't see you wanting to take a breather just now," Dystal said. "How come I don't think you're just going to sit this thing out?"

"I just need to be away from it a few days," Haydon said.

"You mean you just don't need to be tied to a desk a few days," Dystal countered. "A kinda crucial time for this investigation."

Haydon didn't say anything. He was giving Dystal his chance to play it by the rules, take the request at face value.

The big lieutenant's face seemed suddenly heavy, and weary. The pressure and the lack of sleep caught up with him in a physical change that took place as Haydon watched. Dystal brought his booted foot down off the desk drawer, and he turned in his chair to face Haydon.

"Listen to me, Stu." He stopped, his eyes sagging. "You

gonna make me do this? Have I gotta tell you what you're doing? You're gonna be stepping all over us, or we're gonna be stepping all over you. The first time one of the guys comes across your tracks he's *got* to report it. We're gonna have to haul you in. I mean, I can't even think about this it's so stupid.''

"I need a few days' leave of absence," Haydon repeated, as if Dystal had never said anything. "I feel emotionally and physically exhausted," he said, using the rote phrasing he had heard in the department's bureaucratic handling of such cases. "It would do me good. I could get something from Fry to corroborate that. They're going to want me to talk to him anyway.''

Dystal grabbed a piece of paper that had been lying on his desk and wadded it up, staring at it, thinking. He wadded it thoroughly, tightly, into a small compact ball, pressed it and molded it with his blunt fingers in the palm of his hand until the muscles in his massive forearms rippled and bulged. His jaw muscles worked just as hard. Then he stopped, opened his hand, and let the marble-sized pellet roll onto the desk, where it came to rest against the clear Lucite ashtray in the shape of Texas with the rattlesnake rattles embedded in the bottom.

He looked up.

"I'll do the paperwork for it before I leave tonight." He started to say something else, but stopped. Then he said, "I'm gonna trust you to let me know something when I need to know it.''

"If I hear anything," Haydon said.

Chapter 19

Haydon walked directly out of Dystal's office and through the squad room to the third-floor corridor. He didn't look left or right, didn't speak to anyone, didn't give anyone a chance to speak to him. He took the stairs instead of the elevator, the gritty sound of his quick-paced footsteps amplified in the emptiness of the stairwell. Staring straight ahead, he strode out the rear door of the department headquarters and into the flat heat of afternoon, hurrying across the asphalt of the motor pool service yard and into the parking garage. The elevator door didn't open fast enough, didn't close fast enough. The ride was agonizingly slow. He didn't wait for the air conditioner to cool down before he wheeled the Vanden Plas into the down ramp of the garage, his tires screeching in the tight turns.

Not until he was out of the garage, and headed downtown on Washington, did he feel any sense of relief from the tightening in his chest. If he hadn't been through this before, he would have thought he was having a heart attack. But he knew himself, to that extent at least, though it had taken him years to recognize the signs for what they really were.

He had felt the first twinges of claustrophobia while sitting at the computer terminal finishing the report. It had been difficult to concentrate on the details, and several times he had found himself simply staring at the screen, unaware of what he had written. Before he had finished, he knew he would not be able to continue within the framework that the department inevitably would impose on him. By the time he walked into Dystal's office the decision was behind him. As far as he was concerned, he was out of it. It had taken a tremendous amount of self-control to get through the conversation. He wanted out from under the restrictions of the department. If Dystal hadn't gone along with him, he would have resigned. It was suddenly that important to him. Within half an hour's time, it had become an absolute necessity.

Even in the four-o'clock migration that had already begun to curdle downtown traffic, he was less than five minutes away from the RepublicBank Center, which was only six blocks away across Buffalo Bayou, and the Gulf Freeway. He pulled into the garage entrance, took his ticket from the buzzing dispenser, and started looking for a parking place.

Again the sound of his own footsteps followed him across the granite paving of the northern arcade of the main floor. From a pay telephone he called Frank Siddons's law firm on the forty-eighth floor and asked for Mitchell Garner's office.

Garner was a young man in a hot field. He specialized in international law, and together with another attorney represented all the firm's clients involved in Mexican litigation. Haydon's father, whose own legal practice involved a great deal of Mexican law, had been responsible for convincing Frank Siddons nearly eight years earlier that he should acquire some Mexican specialists for his own firm. The first man Siddons hired, Edward Rhodes, had been an authority on Mexican business law, and then in 1980 Garner had been hired away from a political position with the State Department because of his expertise in Mexican politics and criminal law. After Haydon's father died, both Rhodes and Garner had helped Haydon with the legal complications of his father's considerable Mexican involvements, as well as handling the periodic paperwork involving Gabriela's nieces and nephews.

When Garner came on the telephone, he immediately expressed his sympathy.

"I was eating breakfast and flipped on the television," he said. "Usually I don't do that, but I'd just told Janice . . ." He paused awkwardly, as if embarrassed. "How are you holding up, Stuart?" he asked.

"I'm all right," Haydon said. "But I need to talk to you."

"Of course, sure. Come on up."

"I'd rather not. I don't feel like seeing Frank right now, or anyone else, really. Could you come down?"

"Sure. Where are you?"

"I'm on the ground floor now, but why don't you meet me on the bridge at the third level?"

"You want to go somewhere we can sit down?"

"No. The bridge would be best."

"I'll be right there."

Garner appeared at Haydon's side without speaking. He was breathing noticeably, his chunky frame beginning to take its toll even in the short brisk walk along the corporate corridors. His blond, prematurely thinning hair was cut short, still reminiscent of the conservative influences of Washington. He wore only white or pale blue shirts with button-down collars and striped ties. In the last year or so he had ventured into braces for his trousers. They looked good on him, suiting his style and manner.

"I'm sorry to get you down here like this," Haydon said, turning to Garner. "I appreciate your taking the time."

"No trouble." Garner tried to hide a hard swallow.

Haydon saw the curiosity in Garner's eyes.

"I'll get right to the point," Haydon said, glancing again out over the space. "The address on Chicon where Ed was killed last night was the site of a killing that Ed and I had caught early yesterday morning. A man was found lying on the sidewalk outside the gates of this large old house that appeared to be unoccupied. After we made that scene, I ran by the county clerk's office to find out who had been paying the taxes on the place. It turned out that for the last four years they were paid by a corporation. The Teco Corporation."

Haydon thought Garner's eyes narrowed slightly at this, but he didn't stop.

"Last night, when we got inside the house, we found some interesting literature in one of the bedrooms. It looked like radical right-wing material, even fascist. Anti-Jewish, anti-homosexual, anticommunist. Pretty strong propaganda. In Spanish. The stuff was printed in Guadalajara, Jalisco. I got in touch with the secretary of state's office in Austin, and found out that the corporation was registered four years ago. All the officers are Mexican citizens. A couple live in Guadalajara, a couple in Colima, several in Mexico City." He took a piece of paper out of his pocket and handed it to Garner. "The registering agent is a Mexican-American here in Houston: Enrique Cordero Rulfo."

Garner looked at the list of officers. His face was set, and Haydon had the impression the names weren't of as much interest to him as something he had already heard.

After reading each name, Garner shook his head and looked at Haydon. "I've never heard of the Teco Corporation," he said, "but I think I know what it is." He looked at the piece of paper, not seeing it, but thinking. He folded it, unfolded it, ran his fingers along the crease. Watching him, Haydon realized he had never before noticed that his friend's nails were manicured.

Garner seemed unsure how to begin. He turned square to the railing and stared straight across through the massive windows that reached up from the floor, looking out onto Louisiana Street.

"That attack on the limousine is tied to this, too, isn't it?" he said.

"It's almost certain."

"The news said they got a Mexican named Sosa, Sosa Real."

"That's right. You know him?"

"I think I might."

Haydon wondered how many Sosa Reals Garner "might" know. He decided not to say anything about Gamboa.

"I don't know, Stuart. I'll just tell you what comes immediately to mind. Okay?" He frowned thoughtfully. "The states of Guadalajara and Colima are centers for some of the most right-wing political thinking in all of Mexico. In Guadalajara, much of this attitude grows out of the Autonomous University, which was founded by conservative, wealthy Catholics decades ago. The university system there is dedicated to inculcating its students with right-wing philosophy. Nothing wrong with that, naturally. The National University in Mexico City more than balances it out by leaning all the way in the other direction. However, in reality, the university in Guadalajara is much more than an educational system with a conservative philosophy. It's been charged that it receives funds from the U.S. Agency for International Development and the CIA, and has been a haven, a sort of safe house, for many of Anastasio Somoza's infamous *guardia*. It is also the seedbed, the center, of a secret order, called *los tecos*."

"I don't know the word," Haydon said.

"It's an abbreviation of *tecolote*. Owl."

Garner leaned his forearms on the wrought-iron rail, frowning, considering how to continue. He raised one hand and massaged the tips of his fingers across his forehead, where a glaze of perspiration had begun to glisten. He looked at his fingers with a slight frown and rubbed his hands together.

"Very little can be substantiated about this organization. The *tecos*, I mean. It's an obsessively secret movement. However, it is clearly a neofascist order, and rabidly anticommunist. Anti-Jewish. Fanatically Catholic . . . the *tecos* are not tolerant of liberal or mainstream Catholicism. They are extreme in the extreme. For instance, when Pope John Paul II visited Mexico in 1983, their propaganda publications depicted him as a homosexual drug addict, and the Antichrist. These people are crazy. What makes them serious, Stuart, is their backing, and the people involved in their various levels and factions. The *tecos* are supported by a certain element of wealthy conservative Mexican politicians and businessmen. They have a close relationship with the administration of the Interamerican Development Bank, people in power in strongarm Latin American countries, connections with the Fascists International. They are militant."

Garner shifted his weight to his other foot, and unfolded the list of names of the Teco Corporation officers.

"The *tecos* used to be the Latin American affiliate of General John Singlaub's World Anti-Communist League. A few years ago it became evident that they were too extreme even for the league. They were eventually expelled. They've been named by a defected deathsquad member in Honduras as having a significant hand in the deathsquad activities there, as well as in other Central American countries."

"What do you mean, none of this can be 'substantiated'?" Haydon asked. "You don't sound like you're giving me speculation here."

"It's the same problem you'd have in acquiring court-admissible evidence against them," Garner said, shaking his head. "You know they're guilty as hell, but you can't put your hands on facts that will hold up. No one has ever produced unimpeachable evidence that the *tecos* are involved in violence in Mexico, or anywhere else in Latin America. Also, as a *New York Times* reporter told me, 'The way you get substantiation on the *tecos* is the same way you get dead.' There aren't a lot of people who want to ask probing questions about these people in Mexico.''

"And how does all this relate to Sosa?"

Garner looked at Haydon. "You know it's not Sosa, don't you?"

Haydon looked over the railing into the immense heart of the building.

"Gamboa's name wasn't in the news," Garner said. "But it's him, isn't it? He's the target."

"Yeah, it's Gamboa."

"Okay, then. Your field of suspects numbers in the tens of millions. Right now Benigo Gamboa is one of half a dozen men who have earned the wholehearted contempt of practically the entire Mexican population."

"As a part of the last administration, López Portillo's?"

"He was minister of public works."

"You think the *tecos* are trying to kill Gamboa?"

"Knowing their politics, knowing his crimes, I'd look into it very seriously."

"But that kind of pillaging of the public coffers by a departing administration is a longtime Mexican tradition," Haydon said. "The presidents and their cabinets have always left office with stolen fortunes. It's been the biggest unofficially acknowledged scandal in the western hemisphere."

"It's the same old song," Garner admitted, "But 'the people' are wanting to rewrite the last verse. You been keeping up with things down there?"

"Not closely."

"With López Portillo, Mexico's institutionalized corruption got out of control. You know how much those guys got away with?"

Haydon shook his head. "Millions, I imagine."

"Well, it really got zany with Luis Echeverría Alvarez, who was president from 1970 to 1976. It's estimated that Echeverría—personally—got away with between three hundred million and one billion . . . American.''

Haydon looked at Garner skeptically.

"These figures are CIA-substantiated," Garner said soberly. "Then comes José López Portillo, 1976 to 1982, Echeverría's *tapado,* chosen successor. He takes—personally—between one billion and three billion."

"Rumored?"

Garner shook his head. "There's confirmation."

"CIA again."

"They know a lot," Garner said. "Uh, sometimes the information comes around in odd ways, but the bottom line is, you can believe it."

"And Gamboa was part of that."

"He was one of the worst, one of the grandest *sacadolares*—dollar looters—of them all. From 1979 to 1982 he and guys like him, big businessmen and top-level bureaucrats, took from between fifteen and twenty-five billion dollars out of the country."

"In anticipation of the peso devaluation."

"Right. By the time that happened in the closing months of López Portillo's administration, along with the nationalization of the banks, these people were home free. Fortunes—I mean *fortunes*—were already in banks outside the country. Secure. Then prices skyrocketed. Price of oil on the world market plummeted. Mexico became the world's second-greatest debtor nation. Now old Juan Doe can't even buy flour for his kids' tortillas, but these boys have mansions all over the world."

Haydon didn't say anything. In their silence he could hear floating up through the three stories of the arcade the muffled hum of the crowds pouring from the elevators into the cavernous lobby below, hundreds upon hundreds ferried down from the stone towers of the building. So far removed, Haydon thought. He felt utterly alone. The day before yesterday at this time Mooney had been following his daily routine, settling down in front of his television with a bottle of beer to watch the evening news. Yesterday at this time, he had been back at the office plowing through the paperwork of an investigation in which he was soon to make a heavy investment.

"Benigo Gamboa Parra got out of the country with nearly one and a half billion," Garner continued, almost pensively. "Homes in Los Angeles, Miami, here, Gstaad, London. He's into real estate. A son in law school at Harvard. A son in the importing business in Monterrey. He's got a couple of daughters and a wife who compete for the world's best-dressed list.''

Garner turned so he could look over the rail with Haydon, shoulder to shoulder. ''While he was in office, he was the center of several controversial financial scandals, which isn't an easy thing to accomplish in a society that accepts corruption the way they do.''

''What kind of scandal?''

''Probably the biggest one involved something that's just recently surfaced in the news again. As ministry of public works, his office was responsible for awarding building contracts. A large number of the downtown buildings in Mexico City were built by the government. Naturally Gamboa gave the contracts to the construction firms that agreed to cough up the largest kickbacks. In order to be able to afford his financial demands, the contractors had to save money on their expenses, which meant they took shortcuts with their construction methods and materials. They undercut the building standards, put less rebar in the concrete, used less cement in the concrete, used shallow excavations for foundations, cut corners in every conceivable way . . . then paid off the building inspectors.''

Garner shrugged and shook his head. ''Then in the earthquake government buildings collapsed like sand castles, which is about what they were. Of course, Gamboa was long gone by then.''

He looked at Haydon. ''He's a bastard, Stuart. With government officials and business leaders like him—and Mexico has more than its fair share of them—it's a wonder the country is solvent at all. The guys have devastated their own people for personal gain. It's incredible.'' He paused. ''The truth is, Stuart, if someone kills him, the world will be a better place without him.''

''You said the *tecos* were backed by wealthy Mexican businessmen and politicians,'' Haydon said. ''Doesn't that exactly define Gamboa? How did he come to be at odds with his own people?''

''They're not his kind of people,'' Garner said, shaking his head again. ''I know, it would seem like they've got the same interests, but they don't. Gamboa's theory of acquiring personal wealth was to milk the public, steal from them with both hands with total disregard for the long-term effects on them. If the economy collapses, to hell with it. He'd catch a plane out of there and live somewhere more pleasant. He was perfectly willing to sack the Mexican economy to enrich himself. He and Portillo. To them it was an expendable resource.

"The thinking behind the *teco*-associated businessmen is quite a bit different. Sure, they're definitely out to make their fortunes at other people's expense, but they're looking at the long term. They're strongly nationalistic; they don't want to destroy Mexico. They may keep a stranglehold on it, controlling various industries, businesses, and political parties with Mafia-style corruption, but they don't squeeze the system to death. They give it enough air to keep it breathing, to keep it alive. They'd even like to see the country flourish, as long as they can stay behind the scenes and pull all the strings. They know what will happen if they kill the source of the golden eggs. Gamboa's crime was that he didn't give a shit about the goose."

Haydon stared down into the cavern, thinking. After a minute he said, "You ever heard of Lucas Negrete?"

"Jesus. Now there's a bad man," Garner said. "Does he figure into this, too?"

"Somehow," Haydon said.

"Damn, Stuart, what the hell's going on here?" Garner's forearms were on the railing again, and his fingers were turning the square of paper, tracing the edges, turning, tracing the edges.

"The position of chief of police of the federal district of Mexico City was a plum under López Portillo," he said. "It was a license to outright banditry. He gave it to his friend Arturo Durazo Moreno, who, at the time, was actually wanted in the United States for drug trafficking. As warlord of the federal district, Durazo became fabulously wealthy, scooping up the graft that came to the top like cream.

"He was as ruthless as he was greedy. He formed his own personal brigade of secret police, called the Jaguars. Negrete was its head. They were legalized terrorists, protected by the Mexican government. Negrete is famous for organizing an incident later known as the Tula River Massacre. As Durazo's number-one lieutenant, Negrete was responsible for collecting tribute from the Colombian drug cartels who used Mexico City as a stopover before final shipment north. At one point, a group of these Colombians tried to cut Durazo out. I guess they got a little cocky. Negrete arranged a meeting just outside the city on the Tula River one night to discuss this. The Jaguars killed eighty-seven Colombians. That kind of crap. Story after story. You wouldn't believe it.''

Haydon said, ''According to Gamboa, Negrete is his 'security adviser.' ''

Garner whistled softly. ''You've got something serious here, Stuart. This is for the FBI.''

''They're already on it.''

''But the HPD is continuing to pursue it?''

''That's right.''

Garner shook his head and took his pen out of his pocket again. He wrote a name and an address on the square of paper and handed it to Haydon.

''I've done some work related to the *tecos* for this woman,'' Garner said. ''I'll have to call her first, see if it's all right for you to talk to her. The woman's been through a lot. I would understand if she refused.''

Haydon took the paper and nodded. ''I'm grateful,'' he said. ''But do me a favor, Mitchell. Tell her . . . my situation. Tell her it's important to me.''

ぶぶぶぶぶぶぶぶぶぶぶぶぶぶぶぶぶぶぶぶぶぶぶ **Chapter 20**

They drove the rental car east on Navigation, while behind them the glittering spectacle of the city came alive against the peachy afterglow of sunset. In front of them the streets of the East End were gloomy and sullen. After Wayside they got their first glimpse of a lighted derrick, and then down the fall of a side street the splayed fingers of dock cranes at the Turning Basin. Then at Seventy-seventh, Navigation made a forty-five-degree sheer to the right and swung around parallel to the ship channel. Suddenly the freighters loomed off to their left across the Booth Rail Yard, leviathans berthed in rank and sluggish waters, groaning in their slips, stained with seepage, draped with lights against the night. In the lambent glow of millions of small globes, the web-world of the wharves lay in a netherscape of cranes and derricks, masts and cables, warehouses, silos, elevators, tugs, and barges. They passed Canal Street on their right, and then Navigation rose, climbing above it all, spanning Brays Bayou, which wandered back into the city. In the near distance the long, graceful, and incandescent arc of the Sherman Bridge crossed the ship channel just below Brady Island.

On the other side of Brays Bayou, they turned off Navigation onto Cypress and crossed a small low-railed bridge to Brady Island and a sprawling well-lighted parking lot. The lot was only a third full. It was still too early for most of the diners who came to the two upscale restaurants that sat next to each other on the channel side of the island, their dining rooms looking up the channel toward the Turning Basin. They drove to the left toward Shanghai Red's, a restaurant with a movie-set atmosphere, an imitation of somebody's idea of the rusty tin warehouses in that infamous Chinese port. Passing slowly by the front, they looked down the rows of cars and continued past Brady's Landing, the larger, more exclusive establishment.

At the end of the parking lot, there was a chain-link fence separating it from a collection of warehouses with low-pitched roofs. They drove to the end of the paved lot and rounded the fence to a strip of asphalt drive, and then around a screen of dead sunflowers to a caliche lot. There were no port authority warehouses on the island, but across the narrow channel where the freighters lined the wharves they could see the long numbered sheds of the official Port of Houston. On the other side of the warehouses, near the northern foot of Sherman Bridge, a cluster of streetlights indicated the gates of the main entrance to the port. To their left the warehouses were continuous into the basin and back out to the island on the near side of the channel.

Blas parked at the edge of the caliche, facing three freighters sitting prow to bow at warehouses 27, 28, and 29 across the cut of water. Bumper-high weeds in front of the car marked the island's northern bank, a five-foot drop to the channel. He cut the lights and the motor.

"Let's get out so we can hear," he said. He reached up and flipped off the switch on the interior ceiling light, and they opened the doors in darkness.

Sounds were distant and muffled, a chugging gasoline motor across the water, a humming electric motor on the lighted deck of one of the ships, the voice of a man unseen on the deck of another, the heavy clanging chunk of a water-lock door slamming shut.

"Shit," Rubio said.

"What's the matter?"

"This is no good. I don't like it." When he was tense, the hissing from the notch in his lip was more pronounced.

"Why?"

"I don't like the water, doing business around the water."

"It's all right," Blas said. What *he* didn't like was Rubio's sudden wariness. It didn't give him anything to lean on. If

Rubio was nervous, Blas was doubly so. He relied heavily on the Indian's instincts.

"Uhmmm." Rubio's tone was skeptical.

Blas took a deep breath, the stench of creosote and bad mud.

They watched the docks, and were looking in the wrong direction when an inboard launch emerged from under Sherman Bridge, its powerful engines grumbling in the heavy water as it steered into the center of the channel. When it was a hundred yards away it turned slightly toward them, approaching at a shallow angle, throttling back its engines until they finally stopped as the launch drifted in to the overhanging weeds in front of them. Then silence.

It was too dark at the margin of weeds and water for Blas to see what was happening. He could see the far side of the launch sitting quietly, bobbing in the ripples of its own wake. He saw no movement on board.

Rubio moved the safety on his Mac-10 and concentrated hard on the weeds above the launch. They heard footsteps on the fiberglass hull, and then someone jumped. They could hear one man breaking dry weeds as he climbed the bank.

"Fuckin' weeds," the man said, his head breaking the plane of tangled undergrowth, and then the whole man stepped out onto the caliche. He was wearing a port authority uniform and a gimme cap with an NRA patch. "Hey, boys," he grunted in a low voice, looking at them. He was stocky, his stomach straining the buttons of the uniform, and his sleeves were rolled up tight over lumpy muscles. "Ya'll sure you're in the right place? I was expectin' a particular friend. You boys sure ain't him."

"We are with the Teco Corporation," Blas said, using the prearranged wording. "Ireno López spoke for us."

The man looked at them a moment, sizing them up. Then said, "Oh. Well, I guess you know what you're doin'."

Blas relaxed a little, but not too much. He was afraid if the man didn't do everything in exactly the right, magical way prefigured in Rubio's psyche, the Indian would blow him back into the launch.

"Just the two of you?" the man asked.

"Yes."

"Good," he said. "I'm Tucky Waite." He extended his

hand and shook with Blas, and then with Rubio, who almost
didn't go along with it. "You boys got names? I like to know
names."

"My name is Blas, this is Rubio." Goddam Texans, he
thought. How he hated their familiarity. It was as if it never
entered their heads that someone might not like them. Blas
caught the smell, the salty stink of beer and old sweat.

"I'm by myself in that boat there," Waite volunteered,
hitching up his pants. "Took me a second to get it tied up,
too." He grinned at them. He was in his late thirties. When
he reached up to tilt back the bill of his cap and scratch a
sweat-plastered hairline, Blas saw the black image of a tattoo
on his thick forearm. "Nobody follered you on the island far
as we could tell," he said. "Everythang seem okay to you?"

Blas nodded. As a matter of fact, it did, but who was
"we"?

"Okay. Lissen, back there at Shanghai Red's there's a
black-'n'-silver '85 Chevy pickup truck in the parkin' lot.
You go back in there and foller that boy out. We gonna have
to get to a little better place to do our rat killin'." He looked
at Rubio's Mac-10. "Nice little guns." He sucked at a tooth
thoughtfully. "But you ain't gonna need it, I don't thank. Tell
you the truth, those thangs make me kinda nervous." He
gave Rubio a slow grin, and winked. He threw a look at Blas
as he turned and started back into the weeds. "Just foller the
truck. I'll meetcha there."

"How far is it?" Blas asked.

"Not far," Waite said from the darkness. They heard him
crashing through the weeds, and then the hollow thunk as he
hit the fiberglass hull of the launch.

When they got back to the parking lot, the pickup was
already pulling out of one of the aisles. It was jacked up on
mud wheels, and a whip antenna mounted on the side of the
bed behind the driver was bent over and snapped into a catch
beside the rain gutter. Two chrome fog lights were mounted
on top of the cab.

Blas stayed a short distance behind the truck, leaving
enough space to avoid being pinned in if someone cut them
off from behind. The cross streets and trees grew sparse, then
disappeared altogether and gave way to flat, grassy stretches
littered with occasional abandoned sheds and shacks, and

pieces of rusting machinery. They crossed two rail spurs and moved into the tinted glow of a chemical plant and oil company terminal whose tower lights reflected off the clouds of their own effluent.

The long ascent of the Sherman Bridge on Loop 610 rose in front of them, and they passed under it, coming once again into streets and trees and houses, a shabby district of shotgun shacks, a few bars and cafés and vacant lots surrounded by a shallow loop of the ship channel, wharves, a rail terminal, and Sims Bayou.

An arm came out of the driver's window of the pickup and indicated a left turn. Blas followed, but dropped farther back.

"Why didn't he use his blinker?" Rubio asked warily.

Blas shook his head. He was wondering too. He had carefully watched the side streets, waiting for the tail that never appeared.

Again the arm came out of the pickup window, this time a right turn. They were entering the wharves now, rows of sheds, and alleyways and beyond that the mammoth cylindrical profiles of oil storage tanks. They passed the warehouses and slowed to an idling crawl as they came into a long corridor of tanks. In the crossaisles Blas could see an occasional small pier on the channel, less than a hundred yards away.

When the pickup turned into one of the aisles, Blas and Rubio lowered their windows. The car filled with the sour air from the petrochemical plants and refineries farther down the channel toward Pasadena. They stopped at the last storage tank on the aisle. In front of them a small road, white with crushed shell, ran along the edge of the channel where a short wooden pier jutted into the water. At the end of the pier Blas saw a tin shed, and the rear of the launch peeping out of the shed.

The pickup door opened and a gangly young man stepped down out of the cab and looked back at them. He also wore the ubiquitous gimme cap, and a dark T-shirt tucked into jeans which were themselves tucked into high-topped cowboy boots. His jeans were cinched to his thin hips by a western belt that sported a buckle half as big as a hubcap. As he looked at them, he reached into his hip pocket, took out a round tin of Skol, and put a pinch into his bottom lip. Then he started toward them.

Blas opened the door and got out before the young man reached the front of the car.

"Ya'll ready?" the kid asked.

"Yes."

"Okay. Tucky's down there in that shed. He's got what you're lookin' for."

"Is he alone?"

The kid nodded. "Your man goin' with us?" He looked at Rubio in the car.

"No." Blas motioned for Rubio to get out and said, "I think the two of you need to stay here. I'll go alone."

"That's not how Tucky said we was gonna do it," the kid said solemnly. His bottom lip was stretched tight, holding in the Skol.

"I can't leave the car alone," Blas explained.

The kid looked at him with an uncertain frown, and gave a flashing glance at the rental car. The jaundiced reflected light that filled the sky rippled across his face as the clouds from the chemical plant drifted like a foul fog above them. "I see what you mean," he said.

Blas was sure he didn't, but it was a good sign that he wasn't going to make it a point of protest. Then in the sky-glow Blas saw the wire, and the plug in the kid's ear. He was sure, too, that he was hiding a transmitter as well. These people were careful.

Rubio leaned against the fender of the car and laid the Mac-10 across the hood. The kid looked at it, looked at Rubio, then at Blas.

"When you get out there on the pier, stick to the right side," he said. "They's some shaky boards about halfway to the shed." He looked Blas over. "You ain't takin' a Mac," he said. It wasn't a question.

Blas didn't respond, knowing the kid had said it for the benefit of Waite on the receiving end of his wire. He looked at Rubio and then started toward the crushed-shell road. As he crossed, he looked both ways. To his left, the city; to his right, a weedy stretch of flat bayou bottom, and a little farther down scattered freight cars on the edge of a rail terminal.

He had no doubt there were others out there, not just the redneck and the skinny youth. He kept to the right as instructed, and approached the dark opening of the shed. As he got closer he made out the green glow of a kerosene lantern shimmering off the water onto the shed ceiling. He paused ten feet from the opening.

"Come on in," he heard Waite say. "It's all right."

There were moments in every operation when you openly subjected yourself to blind risk. There was no other way to do it, if it was going to be done. You put your trust in something senseless, and you had no right to expect what you hoped you would get. These were the moments he used to live for, but now he only feared them. His mouth filled with the dreaded and familiar taste of iodine as the image of Teodoro, firing and falling under the roaring limousine, played across the green haze that filled the doorway.

As he stepped inside, he saw the stocky hulk of Waite sitting on the prow of the launch, one foot on the pier. He quickly surveyed the layout of the shed. There wasn't much, only the pier and the launch. Unless someone was hiding in there, they were alone. The only sounds were the soft lapping of water against the fiberglass hull and the hissing of the lantern which hung by a wire from one of the rafters.

"This is the sticky part." Waite grinned.

"I need to see what you've got, first," Blas said. He saw the wire coming out of Waite's shirt pocket and snaking up to his ear.

" 'At's what I mean." Waite laughed. "I wanta see what *you* got."

Blas began unbuttoning his shirt and pulled it open to reveal the money belt.

"Well, I'll be goddamned," Waite said, genuinely surprised. "Just like that." He stood and stepped over to one of the stubby pilings. Grabbing a cotton cord, he hoisted up a crab basket and plopped it up on the pier. He squatted down over the basket and took out a brick-shaped package wrapped in black polyethylene. From a scabbard on his belt he took a single-blade K-Bar knife and flipped it open. With a delicate flick of the blade, he made a clean three-inch hole in the plastic. He stood and stepped back, grinning at Blas.

Blas knelt and pinched off a pea-sized piece of the gray putty-textured block. He tasted it, then took a small vial from his pocket and dabbed some of its contents on the sample.

"There's thirteen point seven five pounds in that cake,"

Waite said. "There's three more cakes in the water here. Fifty-five point one one five pounds. Twenty-five kilos of RDX, on the nose."

Blas stood, took off the money belt, and handed it to Waite. "You count," he said.

While Waite emptied the money onto the prow of the launch, Blas hauled up the other three cakes and tested them, laying them in a row on the boards of the pier. When he was satisfied he rewrapped them and started buttoning his shirt, tucking it into his pants.

Waite finished, and swung around on the launch.

"I'm satisfied," he said. "How about you?"

"Not quite. The primer."

Waite looked slyly at Blas and produced his slow grin. "That's right," he said. "That was in the deal." Taking the money with him, he crawled into the back of the launch and rummaged in a wooden crate until he came up with a coffee can with a plastic lid. "Catch," he said, and tossed it to Blas.

"PETN," Waite said. "The best."

Blas checked the contents of the can and nodded. They were good products, fresh and stable. Sometimes the fabled "arms merchants" of the underworld could come up with some garage-sale-quality material.

"I brought somethin' for us to haul your shit in, too," Waite grunted, picking up a small blue ice chest. He jumped onto the pier with it and took out a sack of crushed ice and a six-pack of beer. He put the four cakes of RDX in the bottom of the chest and covered them with the ice, then took the cans of beer out of the cardboard container and put them on top. "You better carry the detonators," he said. "Wait a second." He took one of the beers off the ice and popped the tab. "You want one?"

Blas shook his head. Jesus Christ.

Each of them took one end of the ice chest, and they started out of the shed. They walked the length of the pier, taking it slow around the loose boards in the center, and then crossed the road to the pickup.

"*Bueno*," Blas said to Rubio as they approached the car.

Rubio backed around the car, opened the trunk, and held the lid while Blas and Waite set the ice chest inside. After he slammed the lid, the three of them walked around to the front of the car.

"Well, it was sure good doin' business with you boys," Waite said, summing up the deal as he sipped the beer, one hand resting casually in his uniform pocket. He acted as if they had just come in from running their trotlines together. "Now I'm goin' to tell my folks to let you out. We had us a little backup," he explained almost apologetically, nodding at the tops of two of the storage tanks that flanked the road. "Cissy, Ruby," he said, speaking into his shirt pocket. "Ya'll let 'em out. We got ourselves a deal down here." Then to Blas, grinning, "Those gals got infrared scopes. Couldn't do shit without the little ladies." A loud suck at the beer. "Can ya'll find your way back?"

Blas nodded. "We'll be all right." If this man was for real, they had made a discovery. He and Rubio turned and got into the car.

"Good enough," Waite said, congenially stepping to the car window and leaning on the door in a neighborly fashion. "Ya'll tell your people if they ever need anythang else, look us up. We're purty good folks to do business with."

Blas started the car and put it in gear as Waite stepped back to let him pull away.

"Ya'll have a bang-up time." Waite grinned and saluted them with his beer can.

Rubio didn't put the Mac-10 on safety until they had once again passed under the Sherman Bridge and turned onto Broadway.

They sat for a moment in the bruised lavender light that preceded dusk, in that hour of day during Houston summers when it seemed as if time had ceased, and night would be held forever in abeyance.

"You want to talk about the *tecos*." She spoke with the unflinching directness of one who had decided not to be intimidated by misfortune.

"That's right," he said.

"He told you how I know them?" she asked, referring to Garner.

"Only that there had been a personal tragedy."

" 'A personal tragedy.' " She repeated the phrase as if it were a reference to someone else. "How much do you know about them?"

She listened quietly as he told her. She didn't look at him as he talked, but stared straight ahead almost as if she were trying to ignore him, or what he was saying.

When he finished she said, "I saw the news last night and tonight, about the attack on the limousine. This is what you are investigating?"

"Yes."

Laying her head against the white boards that formed the high back of the old chair, she gazed out to the darkening courtyard. She seemed to be trying to calm the noticeable rise and fall of her breasts, a sign of emotion she apparently could not control as easily as the placid expression on her face.

Using the thumb and middle finger of her right hand like a comb, she ran her hand from her brow to the back of her head, clearing the wandering strands away from her dark eyes. She said something to herself in Spanish, and then, "What do you want from me?"

"Anything you can tell me about the *tecos*."

"They are madness," she said. "Madness. That is what you should know first of all. They are blind in one side of their brain, and in the other side they have a fire. God's favorite sons, defenders of all that is right and holy." She looked at Haydon. "Do you know . . . God could save His world immeasurable agony if He would allow all His favorite sons to be stillborn. Then the rest of us, the less loved, would not have to cry so much for mercy in this life, as well as in the next.

"Mr. Garner told me the policeman who was killed last night was your good friend. I am sorry for you. It is the only reason I agreed to talk to you. I don't know your heart, Mr. Haydon, but I hope you are a man capable of hating. If you had not had . . . 'a personal tragedy,' I would not have seen you. I do not want to be around dispassion. If you hate, even in a small way, I want to help you. Perhaps you will learn to have a great hate, as I have."

She turned away, swallowed, and ran her tongue lightly over her lips as she stared at her lap. Then she looked up again, in control, and said, "If you think you are dealing with the *tecos*, then you will be dealing with a particular element of the *tecos*. *Los tecos de choque*, the shock troops, the truly secret part of the Brigade.

"The owl was chosen as a symbol of the Anticommunist Brigade of the Autonomous University of Guadalajara because this bird's eyes are always open, vigilant. The 'anticommunist bastion in Mexico,' they call themselves. Their detractors interpret that symbol quite differently. They say it was chosen because they do their filthy work under cover of darkness."

She shrugged, and shook her head wearily. "The simple fact is, they are the death squads. Who do they kill? Communists. How do they know when someone is a communist? After all, the Communist Party is legal in Mexico, just as it is here. Do they kill those communists in the Communist Party? No. The *tecos* make their own list. And since the *tecos* are an extreme-right-wing entity . . ." She left the sentence hanging.

"Can you tell me anything about their method of operation?" he asked.

"The attack on the limousine was typical," she said. "Mexicans, all Latin American killers, have always favored the gun. The terrorists in the Middle East have been using bombs for over a decade, but the Latin Americans? No, for them it is still the guns. And they like the motorcycle. Aside from its obvious advantages of mobility, it suits the image of machismo. Cowboys. The bombs are too . . . impersonal.

Latins like to be personally involved with the people they kill. It's more visceral. *Mano a mano!*

"But that could be changing," she added. "In March two Chilean government security men were killed by a bomb in a hotel room in Concepción. They were lured to it by an illegal radio broadcast. In June a car bomb exploded outside the presidential palace in Lima. It was attributed to the Shining Path group of leftists. I think there will be more and more of this kind of thing, the bomb."

"Do you have any names?"

"I have rumors of names. In Mexico there are mutual support groups, parents and family of the *desaparecidos.*" She looked over at him. "Do you know that word? In translation it has a hauntingly passive sense to it: 'the disappeared.' One suddenly becomes nonexistent. Lost."

She paused, as if contemplating the meaning again for herself, as if she were counting a rosary with a single bead.

"We meet regularly and compare notes," she continued. "To coordinate ways of protesting to the government, initiating efforts to find our missing. It is a frustrating task. Mostly fruitless. However, over a period of time we have compiled considerable information. Some of it is from eyewitness accounts. Some of it is circumstantial, placing persons at certain places when certain things occurred. Some of it is speculation. Most of it would not hold up in a court of law, perhaps. But we are parents and husbands and wives, not federal prosecutors, and we do what we can do. It is not a sin that one's efforts amount to so little; the sin is to do nothing."

"Do you have access to this information?" Haydon asked.

She nodded. "The reason I am in Houston is to try to organize support for our work on this side of the border. There are families here who could help us. There are legal pressures that can be brought to bear in some cases. People need to know."

"What can you give me?"

She was quiet, looking past the salmon cinder blocks that had faded even more, everything going pastel, colors washing away in the thin, warm summer light.

Without speaking, she rose from the deep seat of the old wooden chair. As quietly as she had come onto the porch, she disappeared through the screen door into the darkness of the house. Haydon waited, and after a few moments heard the sharp click of a lamp switch. Through the gauzy screen of the open window next to his chair, he saw a doorway beyond the front room, a sallow light falling across the back of an open door like an old painting yellowing with aging lacquer. He saw her bending shadow against the paneled door. The light went out. He imagined her bare feet beneath the hem of her long dress as she moved through the darkened room.

Another lamp came on, this time in the living room. Haydon looked through the window again and saw her sitting in an old armchair in a cone of dull light, a thick expanding folder in her lap. She was going through it, flipping through papers, pulling a scrap out, looking at it, putting it back, going through others. Finally she paused, holding what appeared to be an envelope. She was holding it lengthwise, reading something from it, as if a note had been jotted there. Reaching down to a low table by the chair, she picked up a pencil and wrote something on another piece of paper she had also gotten from the table, then continued looking through the file.

Haydon waited.

After a while the light clicked out in the living room and she emerged once again from behind the screen door. She walked over to Haydon and handed him a piece of paper, though it was too dark for him to read it. She did not sit down again, but stepped to the edge of the porch and picked one of the flowers from a begonia, toying with it as she looked out to the dying light in the courtyard. Crickets filled the quiet, throbbing in their familiar, alien language. Her simple dress and long, unstyled hair transformed her into the *indio* woman she might have been. In the graceful pitch of her hip, darkly outlined against the deepening evening, Haydon saw a woman of the Grijalva.

After a moment she said, "Only occasionally do we come across any connection to the States. Usually it has to do with someone who has fled from the *teco* fear in Mexico, and come up here to live with relatives or friends. Even though they cross as illegals, we help them when we can. We don't think of international relations, or of immigration quotas, or of going through the process of requesting political asylum. As you know, that doesn't seem to be working for the Latin Americans right now anyway.''

She was referring to a painful truth. A person was far more likely to be granted political asylum if he was coming from Poland or Iran than if he was coming from Guatemala. A refugee had to be fleeing from the ''right'' evil government.

''However, this man—this Rubio Arizpe—whose name I have written on that piece of paper has on two occasions pursued his victims into Texas. He killed one in San Antonio, one here in Houston.''

''You're sure about this?''

''The same way I'm sure about the rest of the information. *We* are sure. I couldn't prove it in court.''

''Have you checked with the police?''

''Both killings are unsolved. A friend, a lawyer, in San Antonio checked with the homicide division there to see if they could trace this name. They checked their computer, the National Criminal List or something . . .''

''The National Crime Information Center.''

''Yes, that. But there was no mention of this man.''

''Did they check their local intelligence files?''

''Yes. Nothing.''

''How about here?''

''Yes. Mr. Garner did that for us here. Nothing.''

''What do you know about this man?''

''Only that he is from Guadalajara, and has been identified several times by the families of *desaparecidos.*''

''Do you have a photograph of him?''

''No.''

''Why do you think he was the one who pursued these people to Texas?''

''Probably because he has spent a lot of time here, and knows his way around.''

''But he's a Mexican national?''

''As far as we know.''

''Have you checked to see if he has family here?''

''Yes. There are only eight Arizpe surnames in the telephone book, but none of them admit to knowing him.''

''The same in San Antonio?''

She nodded.

"If you don't have a photograph of him, how are these people able to identify him?"

"As I told you, we compare notes. This man was recognized by someone in Guadalajara who knew his brother, and had seen them together. So we knew his name. From there it was always easy to know when he participated in something—that is, if there were witnesses. They always described him as the man with *un iabio muesca,* a notched lip. His lower lip, near the center. A cut, I think, not a natural deformity. A double misfortune for him, because he is always recognized."

"Is there anything else about him that is distinguishing?"

"He is an Indian. He is not very tall, and quite dark. That's all I've ever heard about him. Except for the things that only wives and daughters and mothers care about."

"What's that?"

"That he is cruel."

Haydon looked at her. In the dying light he could see the muscles in her throat. They were taut, strained, and he guessed that this woman had not known a peaceful night for a very long time.

"Thank you," he said. He was quiet a moment and then asked, "How long have you been doing this?"

"Three years." She hesitated, looking at the small flower in her fingers. "My 'personal tragedy,' Mr. Haydon, is that I have lost a son and a husband to the *tecos.* I have lived in that shadow for six years. I know what I am talking about."

Haydon heard the word again. Lost. It had never struck him so peculiarly as last night on the gritty sidewalk of the Belgrano, and here, now. Morally or spiritually without hope. Lost. Wasted, as of time or opportunity. Lost. As of defeat. Lost. If a thing is gone, but can be found, it is misplaced. But if a thing is gone, and cannot be found, it is . . . lost. As of Mooney. As of husbands and sons. "Lost is the lost, thou knowest it, and the past is past." The mystery of never again.

In the deep violet light that suffused the porch, Haydon still could distinguish the flowers of the bromeliads, and the lighter blooms of the begonias. He still could distinguish the passive Mayan profiles of the clay urns, and the sorrow that had no end in the eyes of Renata Islas.

Chapter 22

In half an hour he was slowing the Vanden Plas a block from Gamboa's, passing a parked car he recognized as surveillance. He pulled up to the drive, his shield already out, holding it up to his lowered window as he turned in, and was immediately stopped before his rear wheels were even off the street. There were the same figures in front of his headlights, the same glimpse of automatic weapons intentionally displayed, the forms of other men moving, turning, and looking toward him from the darkness outside the beam of his lights. The flashlight again, playing across his face; again he held his anger.

"Will you use only your parking lights, please?"

Haydon cut his beams.

The man at the window peered at Haydon's shield. He was a different man from the night before, slightly paunchy, with tight skin, a heavy mustache.

"Can we help you, señor?" He lowered the flashlight beam.

"I would like to talk to Mr. Negrete. Mr. Gamboa said he would be happy to help me."

"Is he expecting you?"

"No."

The man stood up out of the glow of Haydon's dash lights and spoke to someone on the other side of the car. Haydon watched the man's neck work inside his tight collar, his head lost in the dark. There was a good deal of back-and-forth conversation, and Haydon wondered if there had been any

kind of instructions from the police about him. The car idled.
Several men in conversation now. A radio transmission. Finally the man's face came down into the glow of the dash
lights again, framed in the window.

"Señor Negrete asks if ten o'clock tomorrow would be a
good time for you to meet him."

"No."

The man frowned, and bent closer as if he hadn't heard
Haydon correctly. "Pardon, señor?"

"I said no. Tomorrow is not a good time. Right now is a
good time. This is not a social call. It's official police business."

The man stared at Haydon a moment, and then his head
went back up into the dark again. A shout across the lawn,
the crackle of the radio again, another shout coming back.
The man's face in the window again.

"If you will follow this man," he said, and directed the
strong beam of his flashlight to a figure in front of Haydon's
car.

Haydon idled the Vanden Plas along the drive, its amber
parking lights glowing on his escort's back. This time, however, they went a short distance past the lighted steps of the
loggia across the front of the home, to a narrow drive that
opened up through a wall of shrubbery. The escort turned
and stopped, motioned for Haydon to cut his motor and parking lights. He came around to the door and opened it.

Haydon got out of the car and the escort was already at his
side, closing the door behind him. Without either of them
speaking, they started down the drive through an arbor of
trees, the escort carrying his machine pistol casually at his
side, a small buckle on its strap clinking rhythmically. It was
the only sound other than their footsteps on the pavement as
they walked toward the pale, sea-green glow of landscaping
lights at the end of the drive. They emerged into an open area
with a lighted pool, the water as motionless as a sheet of
aqua-tinted glass. Sidewalks meandered through lush foliage
flanked by tiny lights which indicated their course long after
the walks themselves had disappeared into the dark.

They proceeded between the near end of the pool and a
tiered terrace at the back of the house, turning and following
the pool edge toward a bathhouse at the far end. Two or three

additional guards lounged in cabana chairs in the bathhouse, smoking as they watched them approach, their swarthy faces reflecting the aqua light from the pool.

Haydon's escort spoke to them in Spanish, and they responded tiredly. The boredom of encamped soldiers. Just as Haydon thought they were going to enter the bathhouse, they turned right into the dark along one of the lighted walkways, continuing through stands of banana plants and hibiscus. There were fireflies out in the darkness, flickering, as if some of the tiny sidewalk lights had detached themselves and floated free.

They came to a dimly lighted bungalow with a stone patio in front covered with a palm-frond roof. The escort spoke to two guards in bamboo chairs, and without pausing opened the front door, stepping back to let Haydon precede him.

The bungalow was rustic only on the outside. Inside there were the familiar television monitors and panels of electrical paraphernalia for the surveillance equipment that guarded the houses and grounds of many of Houston's wealthy. There were telephones, spare sets of portable radios lying on top of a filing cabinet. A pot of coffee, looking strong and not fresh, sat on a hotplate near the door. Two machine pistols and a suit coat hung on a nearby wall rack. The room was almost cold with air conditioning, and was full of shadows. The only light came from a couple of low-wattage desk lamps, and the ashy luminescence of the television monitors. It stank of stale cigarette smoke—strong tobacco, long-dead butts, smoke on top of rancid smoke.

The escort closed the door, and Haydon found himself alone with a thin man in his late forties who stood behind a desk in a tie and white shirt, looking at Haydon from slightly swollen, red eyes that seemed unusually large for his head. His face was long and narrow, with an equally narrow nose that was prominently beaked. His upper lip was small, slightly pinched toward the center, and in the low, unnatural light, he appeared considerably darker than most Mexicans, though he did not have Indian features. He wore his straight hair well oiled, cleanly parted. A large handgun was clipped in a shoulder holster under his left arm, and he was smoking a cigarette from which he puffed twice before he spoke.

"I am Lucas Negrete. How can I be of help to you?" He

extended his hand to Haydon, but the sobriety of his expression did not mesh well with his words or actions. His handshake was firm, and he gripped Haydon's hand a moment longer than seemed necessary, looking intently at Haydon as he did so.

"I need to clarify a few things regarding your position in our investigation," Haydon said, pulling his hand away. The strength of Negrete's clasp stayed with him.

Negrete looked at him without expression. "Are you confused about something I said earlier?"

"I don't know," Haydon said. "I haven't read the report."

Negrete's face remained passive. "I do not understand."

"The detectives who spoke with you today are conducting the formal investigation of this shooting," Haydon explained. "But the 'incident' has various levels of complication. So there are various levels of the investigation."

This indirectness was not going to be lost on Negrete. Mexicans had invented the fine art of dissimulation, as Negrete's boss had ably demonstrated the previous evening. For them, it was the natural way to deflect confrontation, or to gloss unpleasant hard facts, or simply to lie. Directness implied commitment. One had to be flexible in life; circumlocutions left the options open. Haydon expected that this cultural familiarity with indirection would work in his favor. Negrete was not likely to question Haydon's unorthodox procedures. That was something else with which he felt sure Negrete would be familiar.

Negrete nodded, slightly closing his eyes, and took a last drag on his cigarette before he extinguished it, with precise attention, in a glass ashtray already filled with butts.

"Please sit down, Mr. Haydon," Negrete said, offering a chair opposite the desk from his own. He sat down also, and leaned his forearms on his desk. His slight frame gave the impression of taut sinew, lean muscle.

"When I spoke with Mr. Gamboa last night," Haydon began, "he indicated to me that he had no idea who might want to kill him. He told me a little about his work in politics, mentioned that all politicians found themselves with enemies, and could only guess that, perhaps, the threat came from someone harboring a political grudge. Is that your assessment also?"

"That is certainly a possibility," Negrete said. "Of course. But, really, it is not so much my business to know the ideologies of someone who might want to harm Mr. Gamboa. That would be impossible in any event. I am his security officer only. It is the duty of my men and myself to protect his life, and that is our sole concern."

Negrete had picked up a hand-held radio when he sat down, and while he answered Haydon he slowly pushed the end of its extended antenna with the palm of an open hand until it had completely disappeared into its case.

"You have no suspicions? You don't have any idea who might have launched this attack?"

"I wish I could help you," Negrete said. He laid down the radio and reached for the pack of cigarettes on his desk. He offered one to Haydon, who refused, took one out for himself, and ran his fingers along its sides, smoothing the paper, watching his fingers smooth the paper.

"*Los tecos de choque,*" Haydon said, watching Negrete's face, "seem to be implicated here."

"Really?" Negrete was not surprised, and did not act surprised as he lighted his cigarette. After he spoke the single word, he left his mouth slightly open, allowing the inhaled smoke to leak out of his lips and nostrils like one of those cast-iron skull ashtrays Haydon had seen in the house of a murdered biker.

"You had no suspicion of that?"

"None, señor."

"You know who they are?"

"I have heard of them."

"What have you heard?"

"Only gossip and rumors."

"About what?"

"I have only heard the name," Negrete said, dismissing the subject with a wave of his hand. "I do not even remember the circumstances, the reasons." He paused. "Maybe, I think, they are some kind of communist terrorists."

This last remark was almost an afterthought of insolence, but it told Haydon that Negrete knew, and it gave him his first glimpse at the way the man's mind worked.

"Do you know if the *tecos* have ever operated in the United States?"

"How would I know something like that?"

The lamps on the desk were at an unfortunate height for Negrete, throwing uncomplimentary shadows on the peculiar proportions of his features. As he drew on his cigarette, his long cheeks sucked in, emphasizing his protruding cheekbones. The mannerism, together with the irregular configuration of shadows, created the effect of rapacity.

"Have you ever heard of Rubio Arizpe?"

"No, señor." The answer was too facile, the tone too flat.

Haydon decided to try a different tack. "How many men do you have working with you? Here in Houston?"

"Six."

"I'll need their names, their addresses, and their visas. If you can't give them to me now, then I'll have someone pick them up in the morning."

Negrete showed neither false nonchalance nor bravado. His face didn't change at all.

"Why would you need these names, Mr. Haydon? Are some of my men suspect?"

Haydon looked at Negrete. He wanted to get beyond the studied facade. "I can appreciate the pressures of your responsibility. It's not an easy task . . . trying to protect a man like Mr. Gamboa. Perhaps it's not even possible. But my concern is that you keep that responsibility in perspective." He paused for emphasis, then spoke with deliberation. "This is not López Portillo's Mexico. Arturo Durazo does not control Houston. Buffalo Bayou is not the Tula River."

This time Negrete's mask of weariness and mercenary control failed him. His eyes glistened, and the hard gristle of a jaw muscle rippled quickly across his coarse complexion, then relaxed. Haydon actually felt a change, a quickening energy between them. It was a surprising sensation, unlike the simple anger which Haydon had anticipated.

But in a few fleeting seconds Negrete had composed himself, and spoke in the same tone he had so far maintained.

"I am afraid you may have come upon some misleading information, Mr. Haydon. I think, perhaps, you should reconsider your sources."

"My sources are good."

Negrete tilted his head in acquiescence. "I don't know what you may have heard, señor, but I can assure you my only concern here is protecting the life of Mr. Gamboa. I have no desire to make myself unwelcome." He looked at the cigarette in his fingers, studying the rising smoke. Watching him, Haydon was startled to see something new. Negrete's eyes, which Haydon had noticed only for their swollen redness when he first came in, were actually the only features on his strange face that possessed an evenness of symmetry. They were, in fact, handsome, or, rather, beautiful, the clichéd almond eyes of beautiful women.

As Haydon stared at this phenomenon, Negrete suddenly looked up from the burning cigarette and met his stare. There was a moment when they simply looked at each other, and then Negrete said, "However, I hope you yourself realize that Mr. Gamboa is not without influence in the United States, as well as in Mexico."

Haydon did not respond immediately. He looked at Negrete steadily, unhurried, letting silence emphasize in advance what he was about to say.

"In this case, Mr. Negrete, I can promise you that will not make the slightest difference. In fact, it's totally irrelevant. I'm here to tell you, you're going to be watched. Your record in Mexico is documented. If I decide your presence here is 'inconsistent with the public welfare,' I'll pull your file. I'll have you deported within twenty-four hours."

Negrete stood abruptly, his long face sunken as he held his hand to his mouth, and sucked on the cigarette. When he took it away he asked, "Do you have any further questions?" Smoke seeped around his lips, obscuring them. His beautiful eyes seemed to swim in oil.

Haydon felt a hot flare in the pit of his stomach. He was suddenly infuriated, not at Negrete's imperious gesture of dismissal, not at his cat-and-mouse evasiveness, nor his insolence. Haydon was enraged by the Mexican's impatience, as if Haydon's investigation did not warrant his full attention, or his genuine respect, as if the killings of the previous twenty-four hours could be disregarded with a haughty gesture of brusk intolerance.

He stood slowly, thinking as he rose that he did not know what he was going to do or say when he finally was standing, his own eyes locked on the lovely shape of Negrete's, the beauty of which seemed a sick thing in such a man. When he was at his full height he stretched out his arm until he brought a pointing finger to within an inch of the bridge of Negrete's nose.

"My partner was killed by these people." He spoke in a carefully measured cadence, but his voice was tight, his throat was dry, seared by anger. "You have an involvement with them . . . which means you have an involvement with the killings . . . which means you have an involvement with me. I own a piece of you, Mr. Negrete, and when the time comes I'm going to come and get it."

He kept his finger in front of Negrete's nose as the Mexican's soft eyes stared past it to meet Haydon's glare. The longer they stood there the angrier Haydon got, but Negrete didn't speak. They were stone men, the only movement around them being the smoke from Negrete's cigarette, which rose in a thin wavering current between them.

Suddenly Haydon turned and stalked out of the bungalow, the smoke trailing behind him into the torpid night. The escort who had brought him stood up from where he had been squatting, talking to another guard. He saw something was wrong at once, glanced back at the door of the bungalow, then hurried to catch up with Haydon, who did not wait but strode ahead alone between the borders of pinlights and banana trees. He hurried past the cabana and the pool again, the terrace tinted green from the landscaping lights high in the trees, through the dark tunnel of shrubbery to the front drive.

The escort ran ahead and opened the door of the Vanden Plas. Haydon started the engine and flipped on the headlights. He was out of the drive before Gamboa's men had a chance to play their parts.

As he drove away he took several deep breaths and tried to calm himself. Jesus Christ, what did he think he was doing? His first impulse was to castigate himself: it had been a stupid stunt; he hadn't been rational. He knew better. Then in a fleeting moment he saw that none of the old arguments seemed valid. What had he done, after all? He'd lost his temper. Mooney had been *killed,* for God's sake, and he was berating himself for losing his temper. Which extremity of his reality would be the first to fracture? Which end would snap, dropping him into the endless fall?

He was still a block from the entrance to his drive when he saw the cars parked along the curb on either side of the gates. There were three of them, and his headlights caught the large, bright call letters of their stations on the sides. They recognized the Vanden Plas, and he saw the doors fling open as cameramen and reporters piled out into the street. He pushed the remote control for the gates, and without slowing any more than necessary to make the turn, swung in between the opening wrought-iron grilles, scattering the newsmen, who shouted questions at him through the closed windows and lighted the car in the bright flare of their strobes. The gates closed behind him without his having to hear a single question. He had resolutely kept his eyes in the path of the headlights, not wanting to see their faces, the ghoulish black holes of their gaping mouths.

The front of the house and the porte cochere were far enough from the gates to make the cameras useless, and by the time Haydon got out of the car, he heard them starting their cars in the street. They knew that had been their only shot. There was no use in hanging around.

The house was dark except for the light in the porte cochere and in the entry hall. He let himself in and turned off the outside light as he locked in the security system for the night. It felt good to be home. As he walked across the entryway, he looked up along the curving stairs for the lamplight in the hall outside their bedroom door. There was none.

Nina was either not in bed yet or had uncharacteristically left it off. Gabriela was long since asleep in her wing of the house.

He noticed there was no mail on the small Italian table in the hall as he walked past it, and then he saw the pale change of color on the marble floor, the timid light of a single lamp. She must have heard him, for as he walked into the room her eyes were already focused on the doorway.

She smiled slightly and raised her face to him as he came across the room and bent down to kiss her. She sat in one of the leather wing chairs, her feet pulled up under her and a copy of Marguerite Duras's *The Lover* in her lap.

"I'm sorry there was no way to warn you about them," she said.

"Have they been out there long?"

"All night."

"You should have gone to bed," he said, stepping over to his desk and turning on the lamps with green glass shades.

"I assumed there would be a lot to do," she said. "But I wasn't expecting you to be this late."

Haydon pulled off his jacket, hung it on the back of his desk chair, and loosened his tie as he walked over and sat in one of the other chairs near her.

"I'm sorry," he said. "I should have called."

"You want something to drink?"

He shook his head and leaned back and looked at her, crossing one long leg over the other. Even before he said anything, he saw that subtle transformation in her face. Every time he saw this, he couldn't decide what had happened. Not a single muscle flinched, nothing moved, but something communicated the essence of what she was thinking.

"There have been some changes," he said, feeling the concern in her eyes which did not leave him as she slowly closed her book.

He told her everything, starting at the beginning as he had the night before, but this time he structured the framework of the investigation for her. He gave her background about the major characters, went into detail—as he had not the previous night—about the killings, told her what he knew about the *tecos*, and about Renata Islas. He spoke unhurriedly, taking time for elaboration, clarification, background. The more he talked, the more he found to tell, confiding hunches and suspicions, wondering at possibilities, his mind ranging through the obscurities of every fact he knew, every osmotic exchange between himself and what he had seen and heard and felt during the last forty-eight hours. He even told her of the thoughts and emotions that had led to his decision to pursue the investigation independently only hours before.

When he finished, he was staring at the spines of the books across from him. He couldn't think of anything else to say. Not about the case.

Nina didn't speak immediately. She studied him quietly, and then laid her book on the lamp table beside her chair.

"You have no doubts about this?" she asked.

He looked at her. "You know I do."

"But you're going to do it anyway."

"Yes," he said. "I have to."

"You have to?"

He realized immediately how inane that must have sounded. It told her nothing at all about what he was really feeling.

Almost apologetically he said, "He was standing right behind me, Nina, holding his hand over the gate hinges so they wouldn't squeak. He was hungry, for Christ's sake. . . . We . . ." Haydon fought to control his voice. "Within all reason, logically, it should have been me. I was in *front* of him. He may have been shooting at me . . . Valverde. I know he saw me, decided to fire. . . . I bent down, but it seemed like I'd been down, I don't know, ten, fifteen seconds. It couldn't have been the timing."

Haydon stopped, waited a moment. His heart was hammering, and he tried to take a deep breath without letting Nina see it, an absurd deception. Why was he doing that?

"Even while my ears were still ringing from the gunfire I knew I'd fired, but I didn't remember actually doing it—I was staring right into the darkness and thinking: God—I'm alive! I'm alive! A flood of thoughts, emotions, very clear, very distinct, but disordered. Incredible . . . Unabashed relief, euphoria, at being alive. I don't remember fear so much as horror. Then immediately guilt, enormous guilt. As if *I* had been responsible for whatever the hell had just happened. For Mooney dying. Him! Yes, Christ, not me. Him!" Haydon clamped his hands into fists. "As if his death instantly became my talisman. *Surely* it couldn't happen to both of us.'' He paused. ''Then, the bald, undeniable truth of it hit me: it meant nothing, the euphoria, the guilt, the sorcery. None of it meant anything at all. It just as easily could have been me. There was no reason why he was dead—already I knew he was dead—and I was alive. I mean, it was . . . pure . . . random chance.''

Haydon was sitting forward in the chair, his forearms resting on his knees as he looked at the long fingers of his hands, palms down, spread open in front of him. He looked at the plain gold wedding band on his left hand. Thirteen years. On his right, the gold signet ring he had purchased during a trip to Italy, alone, when he was eighteen. Its face was still unengraved, blank, a youthful concession to magical thinking that he never had brought himself to resolve. Twenty-two years. He felt Nina's eyes on him, and knowing that he was going to be talking at cross-purposes, he continued anyway.

''I read an article,'' he said. ''It must have been a year ago, or more, about a group of physicists studying the mechanics of turbulence and disorder. Chaos.'' Still looking at his hands, he moved his right one as if placing something on a surface. ''If you put a cigarette in an ashtray in a closed room, the smoke will rise in a straight unwavering column. Up to a point. Who knows what point, but suddenly the column of smoke will break up into swirls and eddies, for no 'reason' at all. No principle of physics explains this phenomenon. It simply happens. It's the same with storm clouds, turbulent winds impossible to predict, incapable of being understood.''

The long face of Lucas Negrete, his solemn, almond eyes studying the smoke from his own cigarette, sprang into Haydon's mind. He was startled, momentarily caught off balance. Then he pushed the image aside and talked past it.

''These physicists,'' he said, ''have a theory that chaos is not totally random, that it, too, operates within a system of laws, though they are as yet unrecognized, undefined. For instance, they can't tell you *why* the smooth column of smoke suddenly begins boiling and churning and falling apart, but they *can* tell you that it won't suddenly shoot out in a straight line to the side and travel horizontally. It will never do that. The reason it won't is that it is constrained, limited, by a certain physical law, a constraining element. They call that element the 'strange attractor,' and it represents the boundary of the randomness of chaos.''

He looked at her, but she said nothing. He didn't really expect her to. He took his opened hands and rubbed them over his face. When he continued, he spoke as much to himself as to her, as if he were audibly thinking through the problem.

''Reason has such an enormous density for us,'' he said, ''that we can't imagine living without the unfaltering pull of its gravity. Traditionally, disorder has been the outer limit— where chaos begins, reason stops. In a very real sense these men are trying to exorcise the idea of the irrational. It's a way of conquering the fear that accompanies the inexplicable.'' He hesitated. ''I'm not sure I believe there's an answer to every question, a 'reason' at the core of every act, or thought. But I can understand why they want to believe there is. You've got to seek the answers, or you find yourself at the mercy of the questions.''

Nina stared at him. He saw her nostrils working, a potent signal that she was having difficulty controlling her temper.

''I don't understand that,'' she said.

''I just want to get to the bottom of it.''

''Don't tell me you really think the odds are in your favor.''

''No. But then, this isn't something where the odds enter into the decision.''

''Not for you maybe.''

The reprimand stung. He knew she was right, and he knew that wouldn't be the end of it.

''You know how I feel about your work,'' she said. ''I'd like to see you get out of it, but not like this. Not discharged at the end of this investigation because you were a rogue cop.''

''It's not going to come to that,'' he said. ''I've lived too many years with that incident in the cemetery to repeat it.''

''Have you, Stuart?'' Nina shot back. ''Did it really change you that much? Do you really think you can let the system handle the justice—this time?''

Haydon felt the full force of her words. Nina had never been one to dance around the hard questions, but neither was she given to vindictiveness. She had been hurt, and she was hurting in return. It wasn't typical of her, and he hated to see it. He saw how much pain he had caused her and it shamed him; and, paradoxically, it showed him how much she wanted to protect him.

"I'm not going to do something like that again," he said. "I'm not even sure I *could* do it again. You know me better than that."

Nina kept her eyes on him.

"Look," Haydon said. "I've worked within the system long enough to know you don't get a free hand in these things. There are bureaucratic procedures. They're necessary to prevent abuses, but they're not expedient. Sometimes they encumber an investigation. I just don't want to play the games this time. I've told Dystal I'll keep in touch. And I will."

"You'll be running greater risks," Nina said. "You won't have backups, you won't have support systems. No one will know where you are."

"I've thought of that," Haydon said. He looked at her.

"And what do you think about it?"

"I'm going to have to ask you to help me. I'll let you know where I'm going, what I'm doing. If anything goes wrong you can get in touch with Dystal."

Nina stared at him.

"I don't believe you," she said. But she did believe him.

Then neither of them spoke. They simply looked at one another, Nina trying to see something that wasn't there, Haydon unrepentant, having no reason to do otherwise.

Then Nina turned away, looking across the room toward the refectory table. He wished he knew what was going through her mind, exactly what she was thinking. Her eyes moved back to him, and then she stood and wiped a strand of hair at her temple and crossed her arms. She walked across the room, around the end of the refectory table, and to the French doors that looked out onto the terrace. She peered out the glass, her back to him. Her gown of pearl silk fit close above her hips, then fell like a thin sheet of water past her thighs. Turning, she came back around, slowly passing a decanter of brandy on a table, reaching out a bare arm to touch its crystal top in a gesture of nervous preoccupation. Then she stopped squarely in front of him, challengingly.

"I don't know what you think you're going to do," she said angrily. "I don't see how any of this is going to make any difference. It's bigger than you think. The politics of Mexico, you know what that's like . . . you don't . . . It's insane to believe you could do anything, alone." She searched for the right words, frustrated. "If it's . . . for God's sake, you killed the man who shot Ed. What do you *want?*"

Her voice cracked a little. They both heard it, and he saw her face tighten, angry at herself for letting it happen. She jerked around with her back to him and walked to the fireplace, wiped at another strand of hair, rubbed a bare arm, and came back toward him. He knew what she was feeling, that he had stepped out of character, had made the extra effort to bare his feelings to her about his work, something he had attempted rarely and had never done satisfactorily in all the years of their marriage, and she had come back at him with a total lack of understanding of what he had been trying to say. But she was wrong. She hadn't let him down, not now, not ever, not in any way at any time.

Still facing him, she started to say something else, but changed her mind. For a moment she stood like a wax figure, her features empty of expression. Then her eyes softened, and he saw her shoulders slowly relax. She stepped toward him, lifting her arms to him, the lamplight behind her penetrating the silk as if it were spun of something finer, rarer than fabric. He saw the swell of the sides of her breasts, the exact lines of the space between her slightly parted thighs.

"If ever I come to the point that I think I understand you," she said, taking his face in her hands, "it will be the end of us. I don't believe I could bear it."

He put his arms around her hips and held her, his head cradled against the flat of her stomach as he inhaled her special fragrance, felt the slow movement of her breathing, the shape and texture of her body.

 "**W**hat did he have to say?" Benigo Gamboa sat behind a baroque seventeenth-century French desk with gilded sphinxes facing outward from its corners. The two men were in a small private office off the formal library, and Gamboa was dressed for bed in white shadow-striped silk pajamas and a burgundy silk robe that sagged on the left side from the weight of a family crest braided of heavy gold thread. Muted light, falling from a fixture recessed in the ceiling above him, illuminated only the desk and the front half of his body in the otherwise dark room. His wavy gray hair was immaculately groomed, as always, but was in stark contrast to his weary expression and the unattractive bruises his tinted glasses cast around his sagging eyes. The ornate desk was clean. There was not a single piece of paper on it, not even a letter opener, or a small decorative tray, or pen set. It had been a long time since Benigo Gamboa had needed such utilitarian items to conduct his business. Now he worked only with his voice. His words and his wealth were sufficient.

 "To tell you the truth, I think he was fishing for something," Negrete said. He sat in an armchair in the twilight margin of the darkness, his cigarette burning bright as he sucked on it, then fading as he blew the smoke into the circle of jaundiced light where Gamboa glowered back at him.

 "Fishing?"

 "And warning."

 "I don't need any fucking riddles," Gamboa said.

 "He told me that this was not Portillo's Mexico. That Durazo did not control Houston." Negrete chose not to mention Haydon's reference to the Tula River.

"Son of a bitch." Gamboa snorted. "What the hell does he think he is doing?" He fell silent, brooding.

From the darkness a whorl of smoke wandered into the light. Negrete said, "He knows something about the *tecos.*"

Gamboa, who had slumped in his chair as he thought, now lifted his head and fixed his glare on the faint form of Negrete.

"He said the *tecos de choque* were implicated in the assassination attempt," Negrete said.

"He *said* that?"

Negrete nodded in the darkness. It was doubtful that Gamboa could see him. "He asked me if I had ever heard of Rubio Arizpe."

The old man showed no emotion, but Negrete knew that for Gamboa, hearing Arizpe's name was like getting bad news from his doctor. Suddenly, life no longer could be taken for granted.

"This Haydon, he knows something," Negrete said. "He was warning me off. He was very pissed about his friend who was killed."

Gamboa stared grimly across the desk. Negrete thought he looked drawn. Old and drawn. This *teco* business was scaring the hell out of him. As it should. Fanatics had to be feared like devils and madmen. The normal addictions of other men didn't have any hold on them; they couldn't be bribed with pesos, or pussy, or power; they couldn't be bought. Beyond a certain point, they didn't even think like other men. You couldn't reason with a fanatic. For his part, Negrete too was nervous. Protecting Gamboa in Mexico, where everybody ignored the rules equally, and most of the police and *federales* understood the practicality of the *mordida,* and let you handle such business in your own way—that was one thing. But trying to keep the old man alive on this side of the border, where you had to keep glancing over your shoulder for the police as well as for the *tecos,* that was something else.

"Arizpe." Gamboa said the name softly, almost as if he had been pronouncing the name of his beloved mistress. He studied the darkness in front of his desk, staring like a sullen old dog.

Negrete could not determine if his boss actually was looking at him or simply looking in the direction of his voice. Gamboa was asking the questions. It seemed an odd reversal of setting: the spotlight on the inquisitor, while the questioned sat in the protection of the darkness.

"That little pussy-lipped *chingón*," Gamboa said, with no particular enthusiasm. "Those fucking maniacs have sent their best boys, anyway, huh?" He found a grim pride in the fact that he had warranted the very best, even in assassins. "He said nothing about Medrano?"

"No."

"How did he get Arizpe's name without Medrano's?" A faint smile of amusement. "That's funny, huh? He doesn't know too much, this smart cop. You don't have to worry about him."

Negrete bridled inwardly. Good. Very good, Señor Gamboa. He wouldn't have to worry about this detective, just as he wouldn't have to worry about the limousine routes. Gamboa had been impatient with Negrete's elaborate precautions, but Negrete had insisted. It was only a gut feeling that had made him switch Gamboa to another car when they left Charlie T's. The old man hadn't wanted to, had gotten huffy in the parking lot when Negrete decided on the last-minute switch, had almost refused to do it. Then the *tecos* blew the limousine to hell. Gamboa had never said anything about it. He just threw a tantrum about losing Sosa, that was all. No "Thank you, Lucas, for saving my life once again." Nothing. So now, Negrete didn't have to worry about this detective. Thank you, Benigo, for this very good advice. In these matters, Gamboa had made only one good decision: to hire Lucas Negrete.

"Those shit *tapatios*." Gamboa's mind had shifted to the enemy. "Their dog-shit pride. Their fucking honor. They don't know the meaning of the word 'pragmatism.'" He turned his head aside in disgust. "Fucking romantics." His shoulders were hunched as he placed his forearms on the shiny burled surface of the desk and with the thumbnail of one hand absently traced the swirls of wood grain, pressing occasionally, making shallow crescent dents in the finish. Then he looked again to Negrete's darkness.

"So what are you doing?"

"We're still trying to find—"

Gamboa's hand shot up. "No names," he snapped.

"The guy with the explosives, the name we got out of Ireno. The boys found his house and they're watching it, but he's not coming around. Not yet."

Gamboa looked at the top of the desk and slowly swept an open hand back and forth across its smooth, burnished surface as if relishing the feel of its glossy finish. Negrete watched him. This was the side of Gamboa that only Negrete saw, the side Gamboa hid from the rest of the world, from his family, his associates. It was the side of him closest to his soul, the true Benigo, the side Jesus Christ would lay bare on the Judgment Day before Satan sucked him down to hell. At least that's what those owly Catholics believed. The *tecos* believed in justice. Negrete saw it differently. He saw Benigo living a very nice and comfortable life and it didn't make a shit what happened to him after he died. The truth was, being a badass had been a wonderful thing for Gamboa. It had gotten him everything he ever wanted, and for the past five years Negrete had clung to him like a pilot fish. When the good things came to Benigo, they came to Lucas too. Being this man's security guard was a hell of a lot better than being a Jaguar for Durazo. This work was more respectable, not so dirty, not so dangerous. At least it hadn't been until the *tecos* came into it. Now it was as dangerous as anything he had done for Durazo in Mexico City. The *tecos* were threatening not only Gamboa, but a very comfortable living that Negrete didn't want to see come to an end.

Therefore he could not have agreed more with what Benigo Gamboa said next.

The old man abruptly stopped his hand in midsweep and pressed the open palm on the glossy surface of the desk. When he lifted it, there was, for a moment, a moist spectral print of his splayed fingers which gradually evaporated in the dry, climate-controlled atmosphere of the room.

"I don't give a fuck how you do it, Lucas," Gamboa said, looking up and into the darkness between him and Negrete. "I don't care if you have to pull their nuts out through their nostrils, but I do not want these *tecos* to make another run at me. Let them know how it is." He paused. "Every time you get your hands on somebody connected to them, kill him.

Con venganza. I want to eat this owl bite by bite," he said, crimping the fingers on one hand and snapping it closed, opening it slowly and snapping it closed again, as he spoke. "And I want him to watch me taking every mouthful. I want him to know what it feels like to be eaten alive, watching my mouth closing on him, from his asshole all the way up to his fucking head."

He was not aware of having actually awakened, for the night had afforded very little sleep. Rather, he simply opened his eyes and looked up at the morning light burning on the sienna wood of the bed posters, felt the eddying breeze of the ceiling fan, and was thankful the dreaming was over. In the wakeful moments of life, at least, he was allowed a sense of transition from one experience to another. The night world had been unmerciful, hurtling him from one perception to another in a never ceasing, never slowing succession of phantasms. As he lay there, his single overriding emotion was that of relief at seeing the morning sun.

Nina was not in bed. His watch said eight-forty. He threw off the sheet and went into the bathroom to wash his face and brush his teeth. Coming out, he grabbed his light cotton robe off the foot of the bed and started down the stairs. He smelled breakfast before he was halfway down, and he hurried through the dining room to the kitchen, where he found Gabriela squeezing oranges.

''*Buenos días,*'' she said, wiping her hands on a towel and reaching for the coffeepot. ''Coffee?'' She looked at him and frowned appraisingly as she poured the dark Colombian brew into his cup. ''You don' look like you slept too good,'' she said.

''I didn't.'' He pulled the cup and saucer toward him across the massive butcher block they used as a work table in the middle of the kitchen. ''Where's Nina?''

''On the terrace. You ready to eat? We got *migas.*''

"Has Nina eaten?" He poured cream into his coffee, stirring until it was the right color.

Gabriela shook her head. "Jus' coffee, tha's all. She wass gonna wait for you. You ready?"

"Sure," Haydon said. "How about you?"

"I've already eaten, twise," Gabriela said, grinning. "I'm no lazybones."

Haydon took his cup through the sunroom and out onto the terrace, where Nina was sitting in the webby shade of a flamboyana. The two morning newspapers were sitting on the table, but Nina was again reading her book, her bare feet propped in another chair, a cup of coffee sitting on the wrought-iron table beside her.

"How long have you been up?" he asked, standing near the doorway, taking his first sip of Gabriela's coffee.

She looked at him and smiled. "Good morning." She lifted her wrist and looked at her watch. "Since six-thirty. I woke up, and couldn't go back to sleep. How do you feel? You did a lot of twitching and tossing last night."

He went over to her and sat down in another chair at the round table. Nina never looked bad in the morning; sleep refreshed her as it was supposed to, even when she got only a little of it. That was one of the first really personal things he had ever noticed about her.

"How about you?" he asked, not answering her.

She smiled. "I've had better nights."

The newspapers were face up, and he could see the headlines about the shooting at Richmond and the West Loop, and Mooney's death. The stories took front-page space for the second day. There was also an item about a tropical storm that had grown to hurricane status entering the Gulf of Mexico, early for the hurricane season.

He reached for the *Chronicle* and pulled it over in front of him. Police spokesmen were saying that it hadn't been established that the deaths were related, but the waffling was obvious. Reporters were not going so far as to draw their own conclusions, but in light of the little information coming from the police department, they stated facts that allowed readers to make their own judgments: Detectives Ed Mooney and partner Stuart Haydon had investigated a death Tuesday morning at the same Chicon address where Detective Mooney was killed Tuesday night. Both detectives were among the investigators at the scene of the ''terrorist-style'' assassination on Tuesday afternoon. Motorcycles were used in the assassination, and a motorcycle and ''motorcycle workshop'' were found at the Chicon address where detective Mooney had been killed Tuesday night. One reporter had speculated that the Mexican, Sosa Real, had been the intended target of the assassinaton, rather than the two Americans in the car with him.

There was a boxed article farther back in the first section, accompanying the continuation of the lead story from page one, which explored the potential of ''Latin terrorism'' spreading to the United States, specifically Texas. Several experts and authorities were interviewed who said that indeed what had happened on the West Loop had been a ''classic'' terrorist-type assassination. They speculated about the reasons for it—increased drug trafficking from Latin America, increased political and economic tensions in Central America and neighboring Mexico, increased activity of illegal aliens in all Texas cities—and said they feared this would not be the end of it.

A second sidebar article said gunshops in the city had done a booming business on Wednesday.

Benigo Gamboa Parra's name was never mentioned.

Haydon shoved the paper away and reached for the *Post* just as Gabriela brought their breakfast on a tray and set it on the table. Haydon poured fresh coffee for each of them and returned to the articles in the *Post*. He ate indifferently, paying more attention to the newspaper. Though there were more photographs in the *Post*, the information was essentially the same. After he read the last article, he leaned back, the cool wrought iron pressing into his bare back.

''Did you read these?'' he asked.

Nina nodded, wiping her mouth on a napkin. ''Not much there, is there?''

He shook his head. ''I imagine Captain Mercer's being pretty tight-lipped, but I suspect the truth is there's really not much to be tight-lipped about.''

''What are they going to do?''

Haydon stuffed one hand in his robe pocket and set his cup in the saucer. ''They're going to hope for the lifesaver: an anonymous tip. I imagine everyone's working his snitches, the Alcohol, Tobacco, and Firearms agents are running their traps, the FBI's counterterrorist teams are doing the same. Probably the DEA in Guadalajara is trying to help. And Interpol.''

''Who's going to be coordinating all this?''

''I guess Pete has drawn that impossible task.''

''Impossible?''

''With this many agencies involved, 'cooperation' is wishful thinking,'' Haydon said. ''It's sensational investigations like this one that can make or break a career, and agencies are an extension of their administrators' egos. The FBI ought to have a head start. They've got a special division for this sort of thing, but I doubt they're going to want to share a heck of a lot of information. Everyone else will resent that, and will have a tendency to do likewise.'' He sipped his coffee. ''You won't read about it in the newspapers, but agents are going to be tripping all over each other. Whoever has the best informant network is going to win this one.''

''What about what Renata Islas told you?''

''I imagine the DEA in Guadalajara has people who can provide information on the *tecos.*''

''I mean about this man with the scarred lip.'' As always, Nina was going straight to the central issue, central for Haydon, that is.

''She said there was no police record of him,'' he answered evasively.

''That's my point. Aren't you going to pass that on to them?''

''Yes.''

Three bluejays came out of nowhere, falling and screeching out of the bright morning light and into the flamboyana. They fought shamelessly, like an ill-mannered family taking their squabbles into public with no sense of disgrace, thrashing about in the branches, shaking loose a scarlet shower of broken flowers, and then they were gone.

''When?''

''As soon as I check it out,'' he said.

''How are you going to do that?'' Nina was being unusually curious. He liked that, but what he didn't like was the irrepressible twinge of caution he felt about answering her. It was peculiar, having the gut reaction of wariness—the sixth sense he depended upon to keep him alive—to a question from Nina. There was no reason for him to feel that way except for the fact that she was showing the kind of interest in the case that, if exhibited by anyone else, would have put him on Haydon's checklist. He didn't like it. He didn't like the way it made him feel. It was a sensibility that belonged "out there," not at home.

"I don't believe these people could operate in Houston as they've been doing without some kind of backup system here to support them," he said. He tilted one of the newspapers and shook off the ruby debris of flowers. "They've got to have some kind of collaboration. Someone up here has to deal with someone down there. I think that the someone here is the lawyer who was the Teco Corporation's registering agent, Enrique Cordero Rulfo."

Nina picked a fragment of a leaf, a fragile piece of filigree, out of her coffee cup. "Don't you imagine he's already been questioned?"

"I should think so, but the only connections to him they know about are the obvious ones, the ones in the newspapers. He's going to be ready with responses to questions about those."

"So you're going to ask him about Arizpe?"

Haydon nodded. "I'll need to talk to him anyway. He's really the only lead I've got."

"Because he deals directly with the *tecos* in Mexico."

"Well, that's a good working assumption. But there could have been an intermediary. Cordero might not have dealt with them at all. And even if he did have direct contact, we can't assume he knew anything about the death squad here. They might have kept him in the dark about that. Sometimes it's a lot cleaner for them that way, in the event a lawyer's legal services are ever needed for criminal defense."

Nina closed her book and laid it aside.

"So what do you think?" she asked.

Haydon drank the last of his coffee. "I think it looks bad," he said. "I think Gamboa's going to be assassinated no matter what any of us do."

Nina's eyes flared in surprise, and then she frowned. "Why are you so pessimistic?"

He shook his head and was aware of a trace, a slight mist, of perspiration on his upper lip.

"Because we're dealing with the wrong side of the coin," he said. "The FBI's got informants in all sorts of foreign dissident groups operating in the states, but Mexicans are not seen as that kind of a threat. Mexico is a staging ground, yes. A number of radical groups work from there. It's a kind of out-of-bounds territory. The FBI has thwarted numerous terrorist missions which were being planned in Mexico but were to have been executed in the States." He stared at a tiny yellow stamen he was rolling between his fingers. "But the Mexicans *themselves* have never been seen as the source of political terrorism. Up to now their political dissidents have been regarded as a relatively benign sector. Activists in name only. That is, if you're talking about the left wing. But this business is coming from the political right, 'our' people down there. We're simply not going to be ready for it."

Haydon stood and gathered what was left of the *migas,* got a fresh cup of coffee, and walked down to the bathhouse. Cinco had been dozing, but either heard or smelled Haydon before he rounded the corner of latticework to the open-air shower. He was struggling to a sitting position, his ragged old tail making a flopping effort at a wag. Haydon sat down on the bricks beside him and scratched his ears, holding the bowl of *migas* on the bricks so it wouldn't scoot away while Cinco ate. Gabriela had as much affection for the old collie as did Haydon, and every meal she prepared now was prepared for four.

Haydon watched Cinco eat. He thought of the numbers of hours they had spent like this, sitting together in summer shade or winter sunshine, each following his own thoughts, and neither having the remotest idea what preoccupied the mind of the other. They had nothing in common but the unexplained pleasure of the other's company.

When the old collie finished, he glanced at Haydon from under his hoary eyebrows, then sat blinking lazily a few minutes. After a while he lay down again and closed his eyes. Slowly he moved a front paw on the bricks until he touched Haydon's leg. He pressed against it in a feeble stretch, and left it there with a sigh. His breathing became rhythmic and content. Haydon didn't have the heart to move for a long time, and finally, when he did, Cinco was asleep.

Haydon's main concern was that he *not* get to Enrique Cordero Rulfo before the other detectives. The last thing he wanted was for them to run across his trail the first morning after he had taken a leave of absence. He didn't have to worry. Dystal had come out of the chute running. The first thing Cordero said was, ''What's the deal here? I just went through this with HPD detectives not two hours ago.''

''I'm sorry,'' Haydon said, putting his shield back into his pocket. ''But the administration decided to handle the incidents as separate but parallel investigations. There's no proof they are related, so they're taking this approach initially, hoping the double-teaming will give us a break.''

Cordero looked at Haydon from his high-back chair behind his desk and nodded skeptically. The office was a little warm, despite the fact the red miniblinds were screwed down tight to block out the glare that came off the traffic whining past on the Southwest Freeway outside the window. Cordero's office was in a business park complex, and was flanked by a computer software company on one side and a beauty supply company on the other.

''God.'' Cordero rolled his eyes impatiently. ''I don't know what I could tell you I didn't tell them.''

''May I sit down?'' Haydon asked.

''Yeah, go ahead,'' Cordero said with resignation. He jammed the plastic top on a Bic pen and tossed it onto the desk with a pile of papers.

''Maybe I won't ask the same questions,'' Haydon said.

Cordero tilted his head to one side and smirked. He was in his mid-thirties, a little on the chunky side, with a clean haircut and a fat neck that ran over the collar of his white shirt. His eyes were slightly bulbous and his mouth was cherubic, as if someone had squeezed his cheeks together and told him to say "chubby bunny." His olive complexion had an underlying tone of copper.

Haydon tried to put himself in Cordero's position. According to the Teco Corporation charter, Cordero had been the registering agent four years ago, which must have put him in his middle to late twenties. The corporation was formed by wealthy and formidable businessmen. They could have asked any of the city's larger firms to represent them. Instead, they got this young man whose "firm" must have been in a far less substantial position then than it was now, and it certainly wasn't impressive now. Haydon was willing to wager that he was a relative of someone on the board. A nephew. Not, perhaps, a brilliant nephew, but one who had graduated from one of the lesser law schools on either side of the border, and could be depended upon to fill out forms correctly, to file the annual franchise tax report correctly—which was probably a negligible effort, since the corporation didn't actually function as a business—and to conduct essential errand-boy business on this side of the border.

Haydon reflected on all this as he looked at Cordero's chubby-bunny smirk. He decided he would not begin with a question, but with a sobering bit of advice that would go a long way in cutting through the bullshit Cordero was obviously ready to dish out.

"One of your clients is going to require a change in legal counsel," Haydon said. "He's up to his neck in the kind of trouble that's way out of your league, Mr. Cordero." He paused. "You tell Rubio Arizpe he's going to need a new lawyer."

Cordero looked as if a glass of ice water had just been dumped on his crotch and he was trying, unsuccessfully, to ignore it. Using his elbows on the armrests, he scooted up in his black vinyl junior executive chair and raised one leg a little as if he wanted to break wind. He didn't respond, perhaps couldn't.

Haydon arched his eyebrows expectantly, but Cordero

didn't say a word. He only twisted his blocky head on his spongy neck. The smirk had been jolted into an expression of apprehensive discomfort. Cordero's swagger had been pitifully superficial. There could be no doubt about his reaction to Arizpe's name.

Haydon promised himself he would try only one more risky shot. He knew Lapierre's tactic would be orderly and correct, concerned as much with protecting the integrity of the evidence against inadmissibility in court as with obtaining the evidence in the first place. There would be no "fruit of the poisonous tree" doctrine applied to evidence in Lapierre's cases, especially this one. The disadvantage to that approach in this instance was that it was slow. Haydon had no doubt that Lapierre's men would return within hours with a search warrant to go through Cordero's files, that Cordero hadn't been told this, and that before this morning's visit he hadn't anticipated it. Haydon also had no doubt that Cordero was alerted to the possibility now, and that between now and the time the detectives returned, Cordero would purge his office of most, if not all, potentially incriminating or informative documents.

"You understand what's coming down, don't you, Mr. Cordero?"

"What do you mean?"

"You've seen the news, you've been through the interviews?"

Cordero nodded, trying to seem smug, but not really being successful, because it was all over his face that he didn't see where Haydon was taking this.

It was a legitimate concern, because until this moment Haydon himself didn't know what he was going to do. Suddenly it was apparent to him that talking to Cordero was not what he wanted, because Cordero was not going to tell Haydon what he needed to know. Cordero might be a little thick intellectually, but he definitely wasn't suicidal. And besides, there was no assurance he even knew what Haydon needed to know. What Haydon wanted was what Cordero *had*.

"I'm going to be honest with you, Mr. Cordero," Haydon said, standing and leaning on Cordero's desk. "If I were you I'd be nervous. You're fronting for an organization that has killed seven people in the last forty-eight hours. One of them a policeman. The FBI is going to be all over you. We're going to be all over you, and—if it hasn't occurred to you before, now's the time to give it some thought—you are our only contact with the *tecos*. You're in a tight spot and we're going to bring to bear every conceivable pressure to make it tighter.''

Cordero shook his head abruptly, and his ample cheeks waggled. ''Somebody's messed up,'' he said. ''I do work for the Teco Corporation, sure. You know that, sure. But this man . . . I don't know this man, this Rubio . . . Arizpe. Somebody's messed up about that.''

''No one's messed up, Mr. Cordero.''

''*Some*body's messed up.''

''No,'' Haydon said.

''Sure as hell did.'' Cordero's voice was a little stronger as he tried to rally his position. He pushed himself up with his elbows again.

Haydon pulled out one of his cards and wrote something on the back.

''If you ever want to talk, off the record, here's my home telephone number. You could ease things on yourself considerably.'' He put the card on the edge of Cordero's desk. ''I wouldn't wait too long,'' he added.

He turned and walked out of Cordero's office, closing the door behind him. The front office was so small he had to turn immediately to see the nameplate on Cordero's secretary's desk. Linda Solis was as plump as Cordero, and had the highest-riding breasts Haydon had ever seen. They formed a tight cleft in the sharp V neck of her red dress, swelling proudly toward her little oval chin. He smiled, thanked her, and went out into a hallway.

He walked quickly toward the next corridor, looking for a telephone. When he found it, he dialed home, then grabbed the telephone book that was hanging from a wire cable. He found what he wanted, talked to Nina a few minutes, and hung up. Not knowing how long he would have to wait, or where Cordero's car was parked, he returned to the main hallway and stood against the wall near the back door so he could see Cordero's office.

He had to wait longer than he expected—nine minutes—before Cordero came churning out into the hall and exited through the front door. Haydon followed, and got to the glass door just in time to see Cordero ripping out of the parking lot in a new Oldsmobile, headed for the upramp to the expressway. He waited five minutes before he walked back into Cordero's office. It had been almost twenty minutes since he left.

"Hello," he said to the secretary. "Back again. I got a call that Mr. Cordero wanted to see me."

The secretary's eyes widened, and she tilted her head with its stiff bonnet of black hair. "Really?" She thought about it. "Well, I don't know. He just left," she said, her voice emphasizing the last word. Her expression made it clear the situation was unfathomable. Haydon guessed that Cordero didn't let Ms. Solis in on many of his business secrets.

"When will he be back?"

"He didn't say." She softly drummed the red humps of two false fingernails against the bottom of her chin as she looked at him.

"Maybe I'd better wait a few minutes, in case there's been some mistake."

"Well, that will be fine." She smiled. "I can't imagine."

"May I borrow your telephone?" Haydon asked.

"Oh, sure." She smiled and touched it, moving it an eighth of an inch toward him. She remained in her seat as Haydon stood over her and dialed. While he was waiting for it to ring, she cut her eyes up and caught him looking at her décolletage. She smiled and decorously placed the plump, tapered fingers of one hand over her bosom, but removed them a second later to shuffle some papers around on her desk.

Speaking into the telephone, Haydon asked if there were any calls, said yes to a question, and then hung up. He thanked Ms. Solis, who sweetly said he was very welcome. He sat down in one of two chairs to wait and picked up an old copy of *Private Pilot* magazine. He thumbed through it, and then looked at the mailing label. It appeared that chubby bunny had a personal interest in flying. Ms. Solis received a call, and Haydon cut his eyes up from the magazine and watched her. She giggled at something, said she surely would tell Mr. Cordero, said goodbye very sweetly, and smiled to herself as she jotted down a message. Haydon returned to the magazine. Ms. Solis typed eight or ten characters on her red

IBM Selectric and then stopped to get something out of her purse under the desk.

She was digging in her red handbag when the telephone rang again. Haydon watched her, holding the magazine. She listened, her face changing to an expression of sobriety, then disbelief.

"No . . . no, I'm not married. A sister, yes. Yes, it's Juanita, no . . . Juan-it-a. Are you sure? Are you *sure!* When was this? . . . But she don't even drive! Yes. Oh, my God!" She did the Father, Son, and Holy Spirit over her straining cleavage. "Seventeen-seventeen Cord. No, no . . . C-o-r-d. Yes! Oh, my God!" She did the Father, Son, and Holy Spirit with her humpy red fingernails. "I'll be right there. Tell her I'm coming, tell her I'm coming." She began to cry. Huge, generous tears sprang from her eyes as if from suddenly squeezed fruit. Mascara streaked her cheeks. "Yes! Yes, right now. Goodbye . . . bye!" She slammed down the telephone.

"Is there a problem?" Haydon asked.

Linda Solis frantically crammed everything back into her purse. Not looking at Haydon, she said, "That son of a bitch Roland has got my sister in a car wreck. I *know* it's that guy. Juanita don't even *drive.*" A sob broke loose, and she grabbed a tissue from a flowery box beside her IBM Selectric. "I gotta go to Ben Taub. You tell Mr. Cordero where I am. I gotta go right *now!*"

She hopped up from her chair, came around her desk, and headed for the door, digging in her handbag for her car keys. She stopped halfway out the door and gesticulated with a jangling wad of keys that would have made a janitor envious.

"Lissen," she lectured. "If you have to leave, you flip this latch when you go out. Don't forget it. My God, I'll get fired." She wheeled around with a loud snuffle and pumped down the hallway toward the foyer door.

Haydon waited until she was outside before he walked to the door and flipped the latch. He stepped over to the copying machine and turned it on, then went into Cordero's office. There were three filing cabinets. The drawers were marked alphabetically.

~~~~~~~~~~~~~~~~~~~~~~~~~~~~~~~~~ **Chapter 27**

Enrique Cordero followed the flow of traffic west on the Southwest Freeway, under the Almeda interchange, and off on the Elgin exit. When Cordero was nervous he chewed his fingernails like a dog gnawing a bone, and right now he was driving with his left hand and had his right elbow up in the air as he tried to get at an available piece of cuticle on the outside of his ring finger. He worked at it persistently, but his mind was far away as he turned into the streets near the University of Houston campus.

He was surprised to see Ferretis standing under a tree at a collection of newspaper cages across the street from the little café where they were to meet. Cordero was sure Ferretis recognized his car, yet he didn't budge from his place on the sidewalk as Cordero pulled into the parking lot and drove to the back of the restaurant. He walked around front and saw that Ferretis was still there, concentrating on his newspaper. It was almost noon, and the kids from the university soon would be heading for the dozens of eating places around the campus for lunch. Cordero went inside to get a booth. Ferretis wouldn't talk to him unless they had one of those high-backed booths. Ferretis was picky.

He chose the last booth near the front, which meant there would be someone only on one side of them. He slid into the booth and noticed that from where he sat he could see Ferretis through the front window. He was acting strange. Cordero ordered a Mexican Corona, and told the waitress he was waiting for someone. He gnawed on a fingernail and watched

Ferretis, who bought two more newspapers, perusing their major sections leisurely before he finally looked around, tucked them under his arm, and stepped off the curb to cross the street.

When Professor Daniel Ferretis came inside behind a couple of girls who had made an indecorous rush for the door to get in front of him, it took a minute for his eyes to adjust to the tavernlike dimness of the little café. Finally he saw Cordero in the booth, staring at him. It had taken Ferretis six months just to train the stupid shit not to wave at him like an idiot. It had taken him a year to train him how to arrange a meeting by telephone without giving away what he was doing. Cordero had been the thorn in his flesh. The café's worn-out air conditioner was turned on high, and a greasy-smelling breeze was shoving its way among the tables and booths.

Ferretis walked over to Cordero and sat down in the booth, tossing the newspapers into the seat next to him.

"What were you doing out there?" Cordero asked.

"You have shit for brains," Ferretis said. He put his forearms on the Formica table in front of him. "Were you followed?"

Cordero looked at him quizzically. "No."

" 'No.' " Ferretis shook his head, mocking Cordero's dull-wittedness, and a lock of his longish straight black hair which always seemed in need of washing fell over his eyes. He pushed it angrily out of his way and glared at Cordero through his heavy Cazal eyeglasses. "This is the first you've thought about it, isn't it?" Ferretis said. "Well, *I* thought of it. I was trying to find out if you'd led a parade down here."

The waitress came, and they ordered mechanically, without looking at the menu.

Cordero ignored the rhetorical question. "The police have been to see me," he said. He tucked his elbow into his belly and went at the cuticle on the ring finger from another angle.

Ferretis looked at him. "Cordero, was that a *surprise?* The police?"

"No, of course not. But they came twice."

"What do you mean?" Ferretis took off his Cazals and polished his thick lenses with the tail of his *guayabera.*

"Two detectives came about nine-thirty. Asked me everything you said they'd ask."

"And you told them everything they wanted to know," Ferretis said sarcastically.

"No! I was cool. They didn't press me. I said I'd never met anyone with the Teco Corporation. It was just another piece of business. I'd accepted the client by mail. A routine corporation thing. I took care of their annual tax business for them, my secretary paid the monthly bills on the Belgrano place. I never even went over there. All the stuff we talked about. It was smooth."

"Smooth. I'll bet." Ferretis was irritated because one of the air-conditioning vents in the ceiling was adjusted so that it blew directly on him. He was sweaty from standing outside for so long, and he could feel the breeze blowing through the thin, damp shirt. It felt good right now, but in three minutes he would be chilled.

Enrique Cordero's cheeks bulged like a trumpet player's as he took a huge mouthful of Corona and held it a moment before swallowing. "Honest, Daniel," he said. "No problem. But the second detective was strange. He came a couple of hours later. Said he was part of a parallel investigation. He told me to tell Rubio Arizpe to get a good lawyer, one better than me—"

"What!" Ferretis lurched forward on his elbows. "What did you say?"

"I said, he told me to tell—"

"No, goddammit! What did you *tell* him?"

"Nothing."

"Nothing?"

"Yeah. I didn't say anything."

"Goddam!" Ferretis said in a hoarse stage whisper. "What did you do? Give him one of your boiled-egg stares?"

"What'd you want me to say?"

"You're missing the point, Enrique. You're missing the point! What happened, for God's sake?"

"He said I was in a tight spot, being the only contact with the *tecos,* and they were going to squeeze me—the police and the F.B.I."

"And . . ."

"And I said I'd never heard of this guy Arizpe."

"And . . ."

"And he gave me his card in case I wanted to talk to him off the record."

Ferretis leaned back. "Jesus." In a perfect world people wouldn't have to do business with other people's relatives. "Let me have the tape."

Cordero reached into his suit pocket and pulled out a small cassette, which he placed on the table. Ferretis popped the tape into a player he had brought with him and inserted an earphone. He rewound the tape, which Cordero hadn't thought to do, and listened to the interviews. This was a precaution he had decided to take as soon as he learned the Belgrano safe house was likely to be exposed. Since Cordero was the only one connected to it, he was in the most vulnerable position, the one most likely to be questioned. There was no way he could rely on this dim-witted nephew to tell him exactly what he had told the police. This way, at least, Ferretis would get the story straight. He could hear for himself how badly Cordero had screwed up.

The tape lasted about forty minutes, and he listened to it as he ate his chicken-fried steak, mashed potatoes, and black-eyed peas, which he washed down with several glasses of instant iced tea. He ate with his right hand while he used the middle finger of his other hand to block out the increasingly noisy café sounds. He completely ignored Cordero while he ate, and listened to the tape. Dessert was included with the price of the rubbery steak; a square of dry white cake with a yellow sugar icing which Ferretis dispatched in three bites. He finished eating before the tape was through, and sat picking his front teeth with the corner of the bill the waitress had left when she made her last pass to fill his iced-tea glass. He looked at an obscene limerick penciled on the Formica next to the chrome napkin dispenser.

Finally he jerked the earphone out of his ear by its wire and flicked the rewind button on the player.

"You have Haydon's card?" he asked.

"Yeah, right here." Cordero had to go into three pockets before he retrieved it.

Ferretis took the card and looked at it, turned it over, and looked at the telephone number Haydon had written on the back. He put the card in his pocket and glared at Cordero, who was working on his second Corona and had now made his ring finger as raw and red as the end of a wiener.

"I'm not sure I buy this parallel-investigation thing," Ferretis said. "That doesn't sound right, for some reason." He was going to ask Cordero what he thought, but dismissed the idea as he looked at the round-eyed nephew sitting across from him intent upon becoming the first man Ferretis had ever known actually to devour a piece of his own anatomy.

"Enrique," Ferretis said. "Listen to me. I want you to go back and get everything out of your files that relates to the *tecos*. I want those corporation papers to be the only evidence the police can get their hands on. You have any names anywhere in there, you get them out. Then I want you to go back to Mexico—"

"But the police said—"

"Goddammit, it doesn't matter what they said. You leave. Don't fly. Don't cross at a border station. Go to our condos in Brownsville, and let Hernán take you around to Matamoros by boat. *Comprende?*" Ferretis leaned forward, and spoke deliberately and with emphasis. "Enrique. Go straight from here to the office. Do it in a hurry. Put gas in your car, and drive straight through to Brownsville. Don't go back to your place. *Comprende?*"

Cordero nodded. He looked scared. He was such a rabbit. This stupid nephew could bring the whole thing down. Still, Ferretis himself could not risk going back to clean out the files. Better Cordero than he, and if Cordero could get out of the country, they would have some breathing room. He hadn't expected to have to do this so quickly. He knew he couldn't depend on Cordero, but he would never know what madness had possessed the otherwise reliable Valverde to fire on the detectives at the Belgrano. It was *that* killing that would bring down on them the full force of the law in the form of a massive investigation. The killing of Detective Ed Mooney had been that unpredictable and unforeseen variable that is the ever present hidden threat of every clandestine operation. No matter how precise the plan, no matter how practiced its execution, you are, at best, playing long odds against an unknown factor.

"You'd better get going," Ferretis said. "When you're finished at the office, and are on your way out of town, stop at a pay phone and call me.''

Cordero nodded again.

"Any questions?"

Cordero shook his head, swallowing.

"Okay, get going."

Ferretis sat at the booth and ate the ice out of his empty tea glass. He took the business card on which Haydon had written his telephone number out of his pocket and stared at it once more. How in God's name had this man gotten hold of Rubio's name? Rubio had no personal U.S. connections. It was Ferretis's understanding that Arizpe had made runs into Texas before, but it was strictly business. He was a loner, had left no trails. The people in Guadalajara even said they had gone so far as to check the National Crime Information Center files—no trace of Arizpe or Medrano. How the hell did this cop know?

Yes, he remembered the name. This man was the dead detective's partner, and it *was* odd that he should have called on Cordero separately from the other detectives. Odd enough that Ferretis believed it was significant, and significant enough that he believed it to be threatening. On the other hand, everything unexpected was going to look threatening now. He couldn't afford to let himself do what Valverde had done. The operation would not survive two such blunders. He, at least, had to be analytical, and be ready to react rationally to the unexpected.

It had been a little over thirty-six hours since he had talked with Blas. He didn't have any idea how the shooting at the safe house would affect the plans Blas had set forward, whatever they were, but Blas had said "soon." Would it be sooner now, or later? The killing of the policeman had stirred up a hornets' nest, which couldn't make it any easier for him. But Blas had been through this sort of thing before.

The question was, just how important was it that this detective knew of Arizpe's existence, and possible involvement? Was it a critical enough factor that Ferretis should use the dead drop to warn Blas and Rubio? Ferretis tried to sort out the implications of having learned this. In the first place, why would a detective conducting an investigation of this kind tip his hand like that? Why would he "warn" a prime suspect?

Only one reason came immediately to mind, and the more Ferretis thought about it the more it made sense: Haydon didn't know anything about Rubio Arizpe. He was kicking the bushes, trying to flush out game. He was hoping to panic someone. It was the gesture of a man who didn't have anything to lose by doing it, because he didn't have anything to risk. Ferretis would take his chances. He wouldn't use the dead drop. Yet.

In the meantime, he had to keep the situation from unraveling at the edges. He had just spoken with the main loose thread. Cordero was the immediate worry. If he hadn't called back within the next two or three hours, he would have to be found. Cordero could not be permitted to talk at any great length with the police, even though he knew practically nothing about the assassination.

The second problem was that the *tecos* had not consulted with the Mexico City station on this because it involved hits in the United States, and moreover one of the targets was one of their own men. However, Gamboa had caused them problems, a lot of problems, and they might not be all that disturbed if something happened to him. But the *tecos* did not want to run the risk of being waved off, so there had been a high-level gathering and the decision was made to go ahead without consultation. Now he was sure they were on to them, but he had received no frantic "meet" signals, which he had been anticipating since the shooting at Belgrano. This seemed ominous to him, though he had no intentions of answering such a signal should it come before either Gamboa was dead or the attempt was called off.

The third problem was Celia Moreno. He had expected to hear from her, too, by now.

All things considered, the *tecos* were running a dicey operation.

Haydon didn't really know what he had found in Cordero's files. He had copied an address book he came across in a bottom drawer of Cordero's credenza, which he hoped would contain names not found in the more obvious Rolodex on Linda Solis's desk. The files themselves, the drawers and drawers of Pendaflex folders, were too voluminous. He looked for the names he already knew but, not surprisingly, did not find them. Nothing else seemed of any value until he came across the metal file box of bank statements. These turned out to be confirmation that aside from the fact the *tecos* had owned the Belgrano place for four years, they had been operating in Houston for a good while prior to the shootings of the last few days. *Tecos* activities were not confined to Mexico.

From the bank statements it appeared that Cordero was acting as the bursar for the organization in Houston. There were statements for checking accounts on three separate banks. It seemed that Cordero and his secretary drew their salary checks from one of these accounts, which was in the name of Cordero's firm, Enrique Cordero Rulfo, Attorney. The second account was in the name of the Teco Corporation. Taxes, utilities, and maintenance on the Belgrano property came from this account. Deposits were always in cash. A third account, again in the name of the Teco Corporation, received regular monthly cash deposits in the same amount and had regular monthly cash withdrawals in the same amount, so that the account maintained no fewer than $2,000 at any time. The regularity of the amounts of deposit and withdrawal were obviously intentional, and there were probably two reasons. First, the *tecos* did not want to attract the attention of bank examiners, who, since the scandals about money laundering, were attentive to large, erratic cash flows. Second, it appeared that Cordero was expending funds for a specific purpose, not randomly as needed, but always in the same amount, to one or more persons or organizations.

For whatever reasons, Cordero was definitely a conduit for finances. Haydon suspected that much of that money was funneled to Executive Limousines, or to Valverde personally. There was nothing he could do about the files there, since Dystal had secured them the night of the shooting. But he could try the next best thing. He only hoped that Celia Moreno would talk to him, and that once again he would be second in line, not first.

She lived in a condominium on Woodway not far from the West Loop. It was in the heart of high-dollar life, about $60,000 per annum above what she should be able to afford being the secretary to Jimmy Valverde. Her roommate answered the door wearing a pair of loose-fitting shorts that looked like a tailor had spent two hours on them and a shorty top that stopped an inch below her breasts. Her streaked blond hair was held out of her eyes with a white sweatband, and pink leather weights were strapped to her wrists and ankles. Giorgio perfume floated out to him on a stream of cool air and the throbbing beat of exercise music.

Celia, it seemed, had gone to her brother's funeral at ten o'clock that morning, and was over at her mother's house with the family. Haydon asked if she knew the address. Raising her arms, the roommate stretched to the beat of the music behind her and exposed the soft curve of the bottoms of her breasts. Sure, she said, did he want to come in while she got it? Haydon said he would wait where he was. She grinned at him, stretched higher, and told him the address. As he walked down the tiers of steps banked with wisteria and Algerian ivy, he wondered how close the relationship was between Celia Moreno and her roommate.

The Moreno family lived north of downtown in the Latin neighborhoods around Quitman and North Main. Haydon found the street, but didn't have to hunt for the address. The cars of family and friends were parked under the trees on either side of the quiet residential street, and when Haydon got out of the Jaguar he could hear the crowd of people talking in the backyard of the pale blue house on the corner. He could smell the pecan trees in the midday heat.

As he walked along the pavement he passed half a dozen little kids, still in their funeral dress clothes, playing tag between the bumpers of the cars. He spoke to them in Spanish, but they simply stared at him as he went by. He heard one little girl ask another in English what the man had said.

Haydon stepped between the cars and entered the side yard. He walked by a stand of plastic sunflower windmills sticking out of the grass, their yellow petals motionless in the mottled shade. The low chain-link fence that enclosed the backyard was hidden under a solid bank of honeysuckle. The gate was already open, and Haydon entered the placid confusion of a large family gathering. Tables covered with cloths surrounded the outer edges of the yard, laden with dishes of homemade food which the women had sensibly organized by meats, casseroles, vegetables, salads, breads, desserts, and an assortment of drinks. A washtub of beer sat on the ground at the end of the last table.

They were already eating, a few people milling around the tables getting seconds. Several women stood behind the tables fanning flies off the dishes, while others occasionally came in and out through the screen door at the back of the house with additional dishes or fresh batches of iced tea or red punch. People were sitting on anything they could find. Most of the men were making do by squatting, or getting comfortable on the grass with the children.

Two young Chicanos spotted Haydon immediately and rose from the grass and came toward him with their paper plates in their hands and scowls on their faces.

They spoke to him in Spanish, and then immediately in English.

"You lookin' for somebody?" the larger one said, cocking his head back. He had a healthy girth, and it looked like one more slice of barbecue would split his britches.

"I'm looking for Celia," Haydon said.

"Which one?"

"Esteban's sister." This had an unpleasant effect on the

two *vatos*, who acted as if Haydon had made a questionable comment about Celia's virginity.

"You a fren' or what?"

"We've met, but I don't think she would remember my name."

"What *iss* you name?"

"Stuart Haydon."

"We got a family thing here," the other one said. He looked as if he limited his suit wearing to weddings and funerals. The dress pants he had on now were too large, with the crotch halfway to his knees.

"Maybe you better come back some other time, huh?" The chunky inquisitor shifted his weight.

"I really need to see her now," Haydon said. "If you would just tell her—"

"Hey," the big man said forcefully. "I said later."

This was loud, and the conversation at their end of the yard came to a halt as everyone looked around to size up the situation. Haydon didn't see a single pair of eyes that weren't glaring at him.

Just then the screen door opened and Celia came out helping an old woman negotiate the porch steps. Haydon assumed it was her mother. As soon as they got down the steps, Celia looked up to continue across the yard and noticed the quiet. She followed the eyes of the crowd to the yard gate and saw Haydon looking back at her. She stared at him for a lot longer than he would have liked before she gave her mother to another woman who had come up beside them. The inquisitors had been watching her since the door opened, and when she flicked her head they turned and walked away from Haydon without saying a word.

As she approached him, Haydon was surprised to see her smile. She laced her arm through his and turned him with an adroit maneuver as together they walked out the backyard gate to the side yard between the cars and the wall of honeysuckle. She didn't say anything until they came to the large trunk of a pecan tree near the cars, then she let go of his arm abruptly and squared around to face him.

"How did you know I hadn't told them I was a detective?" he asked.

"I relied on it," she said coldly. "This is a hell of a time to try to talk to me."

"I'm sorry," he said. "But I felt it couldn't wait." She was smaller than he remembered, but no less pretty. The black linen looked even better on her than the pink silk. The pale gray pearls were perfect.

"Why weren't you with the detectives who came by this morning? That's what I expected."

Haydon was relieved. "It just didn't work out that way," he said. "I'm sorry about your brother."

She looked at him as if she couldn't believe he had had the bad manners to say it. "Jesus!" She shook her head, looked toward the backyard, and then back at him. "What the hell do you want?"

He was surprised to see tears in her eyes, and decided on the spot that he wouldn't try to finesse her. He didn't have the time or the patience right now, and besides, she was too savvy for it.

"First," he said, "let's agree that we'll play straight with each other from the start, and get it over with. Okay?"

She looked at him, waiting. Haydon would have to take his chances.

"I'm going to assume you told them you didn't know what they were talking about when they asked you about the *tecos*." He paused, looking at her, trying to see something. "I'm also going to assume you are far more intelligent than you were pretending to be the other afternoon in Valverde's office, and that you will recognize an opportunity when you see it."

Her expression didn't change.

"I'm willing to stick my neck out," Haydon said. "But I want you to know ahead of time that if you take advantage of this, I will be in a position to respond and will not hesitate to do so. All I want is honest answers, and in exchange I'll agree to help you in any way I can, if you want it."

She still wasn't saying anything, but the stubborn stance was gone, and she was listening. He could see she was trying to think ahead.

"You've seen the papers about Valverde?" he asked.

"Yes, I saw it." Her expression softened a little, but there was more on her mind than compassion, or even grief, for that matter.

"I'm on temporary suspension. It's almost mandatory in an officer-involved shooting," he said, bending the truth. "But I'm continuing the investigation independently." He let her sort out the implications in that. "There are three reasons I think you should tell me what you know," he continued. "One, because I'm going to find out later anyway. Two, because helping me now will buy you leverage later, when you're going to need it. Three, because I believe you did not know your brother was going to be killed along with the rest of them and you are now beginning to have second thoughts about your involvement."

"You're a confident prick, aren't you?" she said.

"I told you I didn't want to waste a lot of time, and I've got a long way to go. Those are my hunches. You tell me where I'm wrong."

"One question. If you're on 'temporary suspension' working 'independently' on this thing, explain to me why your word will be good back in the real world. If you're not legitimate, neither are your promises."

"I didn't say I wasn't legitimate," Haydon answered. "I've been given off-the-record liberties. You can't expect me to explain the details."

"Why not? That's what you want from me, isn't it?"

"You're failing to recognize a small distinction between us. I wasn't involved in an assassination. I'm not going to need any help trying to avoid spending the rest of my life in a federal prison because I've been involved in a political assassination."

She looked at him without expression, and then a slow, cynical smile changed her face.

"Christ, if you only knew," she said. She gave a humorless little laugh and looked away.

Haydon studied her as she started fighting back tears again. He tried to remember the face of the girl who had brazenly smiled at him behind the back of her lecherous boss as she walked out of the room leaving behind her pink panty hose. She had known quite well her tryst with Valverde was apparent to him, but she had shown absolutely no embarrassment. Either she had been truly unaffected by being caught, or she had covered admirably, playing the part to the hilt. In either case she was going to be interesting to deal with.

Haydon glanced toward the gate and saw the two *vatos* sipping beer and looking at them. She saw them too, and turned back to him.

"You'd better go," she said, wiping the corners of her eyes. "Come on. I'll walk you to your car."

As he turned, she played the part again, putting her left arm casually around his back at his waist. He felt her hand pause a fraction of a second on the Beretta in the small of his back, and they both stiffened. In an instant Haydon's mind flashed back to the two *vatos,* and just as quickly her hand was off the gun, but stayed on his back as they approached the Vanden Plas.

He unlocked the car and opened the door, letting out the pent-up hot air as he reached into his pocket and took out another card. Using Celia as a blind from her two cousins, he wrote his telephone number on the back of the card and handed it to her.

"This is my home number," he said. "If you want to talk."

She slipped the card between the buttons in the linen dress. She didn't say anything.

Haydon looked at her. "I'm not going to be sitting still," he said. "The offer's not open-ended."

Celia Moreno said nothing, but backed away from the car. Haydon got inside and slammed the door. He started the motor and pulled away from the rows of cars. He didn't look back at her in the rearview mirror, and wondered later if she had stood in the street watching him leave, or if she had immediately turned and walked back to the mourning family behind the honeysuckle fence.

Driving home, Haydon thought about the John Doe and the tethered ant. The investigation had gone so far so quickly that he was no longer important. And it was not likely that he would become important again. When it was all over he probably would be buried as John Doe and the enigma of the ant would be buried with him. Haydon wondered what would have happened if another team of detectives had caught the case. What if he and Mooney had not been first out? He would never have seen the motorcycle tracks in the dust, would never have forgotten them and then remembered them, would never have gone back with Mooney to double-check, would never have had to sit on the dark sidewalk with Mooney's head in his lap, watching the black rivulet of Mooney going over the curb and into the dusty gutter. Jesus Christ. It was such an incredible thing that it kept forcing its way back into his thoughts. The finality of it; Mooney's complete and irrevocable absence.

He drove through the gates onto the brick drive, and into a spray of water that covered the windshield, melting the world beyond the glass. He turned on the wipers and let them pump a couple of times as he drove out of the reach of the sprinklers and pulled up to the front of the house. As he got out of the car he looked back at the curve of the drive and saw steam rising from the dampened bricks. The sprinklers on either side of the gates had obscured the wrought-iron grilles in a heavy mist that billowed and fell in the still heat.

Haydon consciously relaxed as he walked through the entrance hall and into the library. He tossed the copies he had gotten from Cordero's office onto the refectory table and took off his coat. Through the French doors he caught sight of Pablo down on the bright emerald swatch of lawn, crossing toward the lime trees with a pair of clippers.

At that moment Nina stepped out of a thin slice of shade on the west side of the terrace and into the sunlight. She was holding a garden hose, watering the terra-cotta urns of bougainvilleas that lined the limestone balustrade. She wore a shirtwaist dress of white summer linen and was barefoot. As she moved from one urn to the other, she ran the water on the slate floor to cool it off, then stepped into the dark puddle, wriggling her toes and frowning in the unrefracted light as she put the hose into the urn and watched the water bubble in the soil around the bougainvillea. She was intent, and Haydon knew what she was thinking about. Nina did not have a wandering mind. When she watered the bougainvilleas, she thought about watering the bougainvilleas.

He moved around his desk to the French doors, stood there a moment watching her, then tapped on one of the small panes. She turned at her waist, the hose still in the neck of an urn, and shaded her eyes with her free hand. She saw him, smiled, and indicated she had two more urns.

He nodded and waved, and she turned back to the flowers as he continued watching her, the white dress, the sunlight, the remembered smile. He didn't want to take his eyes off her, and thought how remarkably she contrasted with the depressing events that had preoccupied him during the last two days. She represented all that was positive in life, unencumbered by the solemnity of death, free of fear and the dread of fear. She was his counterpoise, sustainer of his often dubious equilibrium. They had been so long together that he had come to accept her presence and the rhythm of their life together almost as he accepted the rhythm of his own breathing. Almost. Looking at her, he thought what a rare thing she was, and he hoped he would never be guilty of taking her for granted. He turned away from the windows.

Sitting down at the refectory table, he picked up the stack of pages copied from Cordero's address book. Some pages had only one entry, and a few of the others were blank. The entries were as varied as anyone's address book, though there were a lot of entries with Mexican addresses and telephone numbers. Haydon flipped through the pages one at a time, reading all the names, putting check marks by those that he wanted to come back to, sometimes for no specific reason.

On the bottom of the last page, and written at an angle across the lines of the address book, were four rows of a series of letters. Two of the series were darker than the other two, indicating that perhaps they had been erased and written over, the pencil markings showing darker on the abraded surface.

Codes, in Haydon's experience, were usually simple from the perspective of the designer, though he knew this was not so in those instances where cryptography was an integral part of the profession, as in the military or in intelligence work. But in the cases he came across, where an ordinary citizen was simply trying to make an unobvious record for future reference, and did not want the record to be immediately understood by a casual observer, the codes were not complex. And in many cases, they were based on some system involving the twenty-six letters of the alphabet, and/or the numerals 0 through 9.

Haydon began by making a few assumptions: that Cordero had written the four lines; that the four lines were a list; and that the list was composed of names, or telephone numbers, or a combination of both. If the letters represented telephone numbers, and there were only four, it said something about Cordero that he simply didn't memorize them and avoid this kind of evidence.

Taking a legal pad off his desk, Haydon began jotting notes about the combination of letters in front of him.

If each letter represented a single-digit number, only the second and fourth series had the proper amount of numerals—ten—to represent an area code and telephone number. The first and the third series had eleven.

All the letters in each of the four series were from the first ten letters in the alphabet, except for the initial letters in the first, third, and fourth series, which were V, W, and L respectively.

Where doubled letters occurred, they were vowels, except in the second series, where the initial letter F was doubled.

When coded to the alphabet so that A represented 1, B represented 2, and so on, none of the combinations of numbers that resulted were legitimate area codes or prefixes in the Houston area. If the coding was reversed so that A represented 26, B represented 25, and so on, the results were equally unsuccessful.

He was studying the list, searching for patterns and dissimilarities, when he heard the terrace door to the hallway open and close. Turning in his chair, he waited for Nina to come around the corner.

"Any luck?" she asked, appearing in the doorway with the backs of her wrists resting on her hips. Her hair was a little wild, wiry with humidity, and trying to break out of the clasp at the back of her neck. The heat on the terrace had enriched her complexion, brought a brighter color to her cheeks. She blew at the hair curling around her forehead and wiped at it with the back of her hand. "Let me rinse my hands," she said. "And we'll talk." Then she was gone from the doorway.

When she returned, she brought a tall glass of iced water with mint leaves crushed in the ice.

"You want some of this?" she asked, pausing at the door.

"No, thanks," Haydon said.

She came in and sat down, and put the glass on a cork coaster she had brought with her.

He showed her the copies of the bank statements he had copied in Cordero's office, along with the pages from the address book. Then he explained what he was trying to do with the series of letters.

Nina shook her head, looking at the pile of papers, and his legal pad covered with his trial-and-error efforts to unscramble the code.

"I don't know how you manage to straighten out evidence like this," she said. "None of it seems to go together."

"Sometimes you don't straighten it out," he said, loosening his tie. "And about half the time most of it *doesn't* go together. That's what makes it so frustrating, spending a lot of time trying to make sense out of things that aren't supposed to make sense. But you never know that when you begin.''

Haydon leaned back in his chair, looking at the groups of papers, at his own scribblings about the series of letters, which might not even be what he thought they were. Suddenly he felt Nina's eyes on him. He turned to her.

"Bob called just before you got here," she said. "They're having the memorial service tomorrow morning. Ten o'clock. Church of the Good Shepherd."

Haydon turned away from her to look outside. "Memorial service," he said.

"He's not going to be buried here. Bob said his brother is taking the body back to Arlington. There's a family plot up there."

Who the hell thought he ought to go to Arlington? Nobody had checked with him about it. They hadn't checked with him. It was presumptuous to think that Mooney would want to go to Arlington. What the hell made them think Mooney wanted that? Mooney would have told them that he didn't, if he could have. It was the farthest thing from Haydon's mind that they would have taken him to Virginia. Christ, Mooney hadn't been to Virginia in fifteen years as far as Haydon knew.

It happened in less than a few seconds. Fleetingly. He pulled back so fast he saw how stupid he was, could see himself being stupid. It was not for him to consider where Mooney would finally come to a stop. It certainly wasn't up to Ed Mooney anymore. Like everyone else surprised by death, he had lost that privilege the instant it happened. But more than that, when Haydon thought about it he was sure that Mooney really wouldn't have cared anyway. You could have asked him about it every day for a year and he would have continued to say he didn't care. After he was dead, he would have said, it wouldn't matter to him if they burned him up, or pickled him, or froze him, or dropped him into the Gulf of Mexico, or tossed him over into the Grand Canyon. What the hell would he care? And he probably wouldn't.

Haydon wondered where the body was now. In the morgue, or a funeral home, or on the way to Arlington, Virginia. He didn't ask, because it seemed he shouldn't want to know. But he did.

"Ten o'clock?" he asked. He hadn't forgotten, but he had been quiet too long.

"Yes." Nina paused a second, then said, "And Bob also wanted to know if you wanted to say something, at the service."

Yes, by God, he did. He wanted to say a lot of things, a book full of words, a dozen books of words, a hundred books. He wanted to say . . . a lot of things.

"No," he said.

~~~~~~~~~~~~~~~~~~~~~~~~~~~~~~ **Chapter 30**

Haydon worked on the code another two and a half hours, guessing, making more trial runs, backing up and repeating approaches with only a minor twist in the technique, running it all in reverse, guessing again, using a small calculator he kept in his desk to doublecheck his formulas.

One of the major difficulties in deciphering codes was not discovering the patterns of the characters, but discovering what was *not* a part of a pattern, identifying characters thrown in arbitrarily with no meaning other than the intent to create the illusion of a pattern where none existed. It was this arbitrary character that Haydon began to look for first. He had a hunch that the best candidates were the double letters that occurred at various places within each series. With the calculator, he began computing the letter-to-number equivalents for each series, making the doubled letters represent, in turn, their own valuations independent of the others in the series.

He filled several pages with combinations of numbers in his peculiar handwriting, a stylized, spare scratch that Nina claimed, with some justification, resembled Assyrian cuneiform more than Arabic numerals. Nothing worked. Next he decided to treat the only occurrence of a pair of consonants— the two F's in the primary position in the second series—as being the only arbitrary descriptors, while the doubled vowels were treated as representing a single-digit numeral, since they fell within the first nine letters of the alphabet. After nearly an hour, he had still made no headway. None of the systems he derived from manipulating the second series produced any success when applied to the other three. He retraced his steps and reexamined his initial assumptions.

Gradually he realized that the first letter in each of the four series of letters had nothing to do with the combinations of numerical equivalents that followed. It was indeed a letter, not a letter representing a number. In fact, it represented itself. All other letters *did* represent numbers. But the key to the cryptogram was the doubling of vowels. The second vowel was the true arbitrary descriptor. When EE appeared in the series it did not represent 55, but simply 5. The second letter in each pair was the red herring.

Working quickly now, Haydon deciphered each series using this method, and discovered that he had four local telephone numbers, each preceded by a single letter: V, F, W, and L. He guessed the letters represented names, and he guessed the first was Valverde. Using a crisscross directory, one of numerous kinds of directories he kept in the library, he checked each of the four numbers. He was not surprised to find they were unlisted.

He looked at his watch. It was two hours before Jack Crowell's shift ended at the telephone company. Crowell answered almost before the first ring stopped. As soon as he heard Haydon's voice, he said how sorry he had been to read about Mooney in the papers. Haydon got away from that as soon as he could without being rude, and told Crowell he had four unlisteds. Crowell jumped at the chance to help and said he would call back as soon as he had them.

Haydon stood, placed his hands in the small of his back, and leaned backward. He had not left his chair for the two and a half hours he was working on the code. Now he faced the possibility of having some real leads, though he had nothing to go on but the fact that they were coded telephone numbers. If it turned out that the V *was* Valverde, then he felt he could be sure of the rest of them.

Then he had an idea. He picked up the telephone and dialed Cordero's number. It rang twice before it was answered by a man. He recognized Ryan Coates's voice, and hung up. He wished he had called earlier, and wondered how long Lapierre's men had been there. He wondered if Cordero had gotten back in time to dispose of the telephone book.

When his own telephone rang, he picked up a pencil immediately.

"Here they are, Stuart," Crowell said. "Ready?" He gave him Valverde's name first; the address was the limousine service, though it was not the company's number. Ferretis, Daniel B., was next. Then Waite, Tucker. And, finally, López, Ireno, H. Haydon thanked Crowell and hung up.

He stared at the list, then he leaned over to his desk and got the Key Map directory of Harris County. The Ferretis address was in Meyerland, an upper-middle-class neighborhood along Braes Bayou just south of Bellaire. He found the street and marked the page with a paperclip. Tucker Waite lived on the other side of the city, in a subdivision called Port Houston, a neighborhood with few amenities across Clinton Drive from the Turning Basin. The ship channel was just across the freeway. Apparently Ireno López lived in some kind of apartment on Lacona just off Sixty-ninth Street, which was also honorarily named Staff Sgt. M. Garcia Drive.

He looked at the list again. There was one big disappointment: no number for a man named Rubio Arizpe. His only hope was that one of these names would be Arizpe's contact. At this point, he still had only the name, the possibility, that Arizpe was indeed involved.

Haydon closed the directory and wrote the three addresses on a clean sheet of paper. He quickly jotted a note to Nina, who had taken Gabriela grocery shopping, telling her where he was going and that he would call her in a couple of hours. He signed it, and made a notation of the time: five-twenty.

It was the hottest part of the day, and at the height of rush hour. Avoiding the expressways, he traveled the oblique streets—there was no direct route—around the southern side of the University of Houston, through MacGregor Park to Old Spanish Trail, where he turned north. At the Gulf Freeway, Old Spanish Trail became Wayside and he was once again in the neighborhoods with the highest Latin population in the city. Just as he crossed Country Club Bayou, he angled to the right onto Sixty-ninth Street, which then ran parallel to Wayside all the way to Buffalo Bayou above the Turning Basin.

He found Lacona, a bleak little street with its pavement almost completely covered with the chalky powder of its caliche shoulders. There was a welding shop on the right near the corner of Lacona and Sixty-ninth. It took up two lots. One lot was given over to a weedy scrap-metal yard with an abandoned welding truck and rusty heaps of twisted steel, the other was occupied by a barnlike corrugated-tin workshop with its greasy wooden doors thrown open to the stagnant afternoon. The rusty tin had collected heat all day, making the inside of the shop a shadowy furnace.

To Haydon's left, directly across the street from the welding shop, was La Concha Courts, a collection of unpainted clapboard cabins on either side of a caliche drive that went through to the next block. They were destitute dwellings occupied mostly by destitute men, merchant-ship sailors from foreign ports who needed a bed and a room for a week or two or three, a place to sleep on whores and sleep off drunks.

Each cabin had an attached carport, and as Haydon turned into the driveway and eased along between the cabins, he noticed the carport of number eight was empty. Not wanting to run the risk of being reported to the police by a suspicious owner, he backed up the Vanden Plas to a cabin near the entrance where a sign leaning against its tattered screen door said "Manager." He got out, went up to the door, and knocked.

"*Qué quiere?*" The voice sounded like years of whiskey and cigarettes, and came from the impenetrable charcoal darkness behind the screen.

Haydon tensed, and held his shield up to the unseen respondent. "Detective Haydon, Houston Police Department. Will you come to the door, please?"

He heard a deep grunting, followed by the unmistakable uncoiling of old sofa springs. There was the ominous moaning of labored breathing, and a fat man appeared on the other side of the screen, his stomach touching the door. He wore a stained undershirt and a pair of gray dress pants that had never been cleaned in their history. He looked at Haydon, chewing something with toothless gums, his lips flibbering obscenely, folding in on themselves to keep whatever it was he was chewing inside his mouth.

"What," he said.

"I want to talk to Ireno López," Haydon said. "Is he in his rooms?"

The manager shoved at the screen door and rolled out onto

the little wooden stoop, squinting down the caliche drive toward cabin number eight. He held a bottle of Lone Star beer by wedging its long amber neck in the crotch of his first two fingers and letting it dangle at his side.

"No está."

"When will he be back?"

The fat man shrugged and looked at Haydon with mindless eyes, masticating.

"How long has he been gone?"

"Two, t'ree day."

"When did you see him last?"

The fat man looked at Haydon blankly, his lips sucked in to form a wrinkled socket, breathing heavily through his nose with a kind of moaning grunt every time he exhaled. He seemed not to have heard the question, to be waiting for Haydon to say something. Haydon started to repeat the question, but the man said, "Mown-day. *Estuvo ahí*, Mown-day." Some of whatever he was chewing escaped from his mouth.

"Morning or afternoon?"

"He lef' in the mornin'."

"Where did he work?"

The fat man shrugged with a grunt.

"How long has he been living here?"

The man shifted on the boards of the porch, still holding the screen door open with his left shoulder, and took a drink from his beer, washing down what he had been chewing. A power drill revved in the welding shop, and somebody banged on steel with a hammer. Hordes of cicadas buzzed in overlapping waves in the still-leafed hackberries that loomed above the squatty units of La Concha Courts.

"He been livin' here, fie, six weeks." The fat man's stomach jumped with an inward belch.

"You need to let me in," Haydon said.

"Momentito." The fat man turned and heaved himself back into the charcoal darkness. When he returned, he did not come out, but stuck his arm around the screen door and handed Haydon a key.

Haydon thanked him, got into the Vanden Plas, and eased along the caliche to number eight.

The door was poorly fitted into its frame, and was only a token of security. The cabin was stifling, and stale from the pent-up heat of several days. It consisted of one room with a double bed, a sofa, an armchair, a clothes chest, and a dinette table with three chrome chairs. One side of the room was recessed for a "kitchen" which contained a single enameled sink, a two-burner gas stove, and a tiny refrigerator. The other half of the setback was the bathroom, with a corner porcelain sink, a commode with a badly warped lid, and a metal shower stall with peeling white paint.

Haydon took a pair of latex surgical gloves out of his suit pocket and slipped them on. The medicine cabinet was almost empty, a flat metal container of aspirin, a disposable plastic razor, a can of Band-Aids, a toothbrush, and some cheap aftershave lotion. He turned, took the lid off the commode tank, looked inside, and replaced the lid. There was one dirty towel on a metal rod. In the shower stall, a well-used bar of Ivory soap—Haydon smelled it—leaned against the rusty shower wall on the floor. The bathroom stank of gypsum-laden water.

It seemed that López rarely used the kitchen. There were no cooking utensils except a coffeepot, which was clean. A small can of coffee sat on the counter beside the sink, along with a box of Fig Newtons. When Haydon tilted the box of cookies to look inside, four or five roaches darted out of the waxed paper. Little beads of roach droppings were scattered along the counter next to the wall. In the refrigerator he found half a quart of milk, two overripe peaches, a shriveled red bell pepper, and three bottles of Dos Equis beer.

Haydon bent down and looked in a small plastic trash basket. Three peach stones, three Dos Equis bottles, a Band-Aid wrapper, all covered with ashes and cigarette butts that had been dumped in on top of them.

The clothes chest was metal, a filthy hospital green, and mostly empty. Except for more roaches. In the top drawer there were a few pairs of dingy jockey shorts, several pairs of dark nylon socks, a single holey undershirt. The other drawers were empty.

A few Spanish-language newspapers and magazines were scattered on the old stained sofa. Haydon lifted the cushion of the armchair and saw a foil condom packet, a quarter, and two pennies. He put the cushion back and kneeled down on the gritty linoleum to look under the bed. A shoe box sat next to the foot of the bed. Haydon dragged it out and found it covered with a gray rag stained with grease smudges. It smelled of light machine oil. He lifted the rag and found three full boxes of Geco-BAT 9mm parabellum cartridges, two extra clips for a .45 caliber Mac-10, and a silencer for a handgun. There was a well-used map of Houston, folded to a size that placed River Oaks at its center. A small square had been drawn with a ballpoint pen on Inverness where Gamboa's address would have been. Charley T's in Greenway Plaza had been circled, and the route down Richmond to the West Loop intersection had been marked. Other routes were traced out from Inverness to other locations where, Haydon assumed, Gamboa often traveled.

There was little else in the box. A few small screwdrivers and a pair of needle-nosed pliers used for cleaning firearms, a few spare screws, a can of oil, and a tube of grease.

Haydon stood quickly, went outside to the car, where he got a folding city map from the glove compartment, and came back inside. Squatting next to the box, he copied onto his map the markings from the other, unfolding it all the way and looking on both sides so as not to miss anything. There were scattered notations which he didn't take the time to reason out.

When he was through, he put the map back into the box and covered it with the rag again. As he bent to shove it back under the bed, he saw a yellowed label, almost unreadable, on the end of the box: "Zapatos Canada, Calle Hidalgo No. 1262, Guadalejara, Jalisco." Mooney had had it all wrong. He would have been disappointed. The idea of a Canadian Mexican had appealed to his sense of vagary.

He had one more task before he left: the bed. He lifted the mattress, holding it up on the sides as he walked around the edges, but found nothing. Next he began going through the folds of the sheet; there was no bedspread. On the bottom sheet he found several dark pubic hairs, one, he thought, lighter than the others. He was tempted to take them and fold them inside the latex gloves, but thought better of it. He would have to ask Vanstraten to run the tests on the sly, and he would taint the scene in the process, as if he hadn't done that already. Still, the hairs were here, and Haydon had a hunch they were going to tie in to something they already had.

Moving to the head of the bed, he looked closely at the flat pillow, under it, and along the edge of the bed. There were several long hairs.

Haydon straightened up and looked around the room one more time. There was a tiny altar set up in one corner on the edge of a nightstand. He looked among the plastic flowers, and behind the picture of an effeminate Jesus sitting on the ground in the garden of Gethsemane, gazing up at an ominous, lowering sky.

He walked over to the telephone, dialed the police station, and asked for Bob Dystal. When Dystal came on, Haydon said, "This is Stuart."

"What's goin' on?" There was an edge of caution in Dystal's voice.

"This is an anonymous tip, Bob."

There was a slight pause. "What is it?"

"You need to send the crime-lab people to La Concha Courts, 802 Lacona Street. That's off of Sixty-ninth. See the manager. He told me the occupant, Ireno López, hadn't been in his place since Monday morning. There are some good hairs on the bed, head and pubic. A cardboard box under the bed contains an interesting map. The shoe box has a Zapatos Canada label. Our John Doe from the Belgrano house was wearing Canada shoes."

"I don't like this," Dystal said.

"López had an unlisted telephone number." Haydon gave him the number and stopped. "Did you pick up Cordero?"

"No. We screwed it up. He's gone," Dystal snapped. From the sound of his voice, Haydon decided Dystal had chewed ass about that. It was a major mistake.

"I found López's number in his office."

"Goddammit."

Haydon wanted to ask if they had found Cordero's little address book, but didn't want to reveal its existence if they hadn't.

"One other thing. You need to watch Lucas Negrete. He was a rogue police officer in Mexico City five or six years ago, and was responsible for a lot of violence. There are six men working for him, and I think they're doing a lot more than standing guard around Gamboa."

"You gonna be at the place when we get there?"

"No. I'll get back to you," Haydon said, and hung up before Dystal had time to ask any more questions.

By the time he backed out the door and locked it, he was sweating through his suit. He returned the key to the fat man, who told him from the darkness just to open the screen door and toss it inside. He thanked the fat man's voice, and got a porcine grunt in response.

chapter 31

When Haydon got back to Wayside, he headed northeast. He wriggled out of his suit coat while he waited at the Navigation stoplight, then picked up the Key Map notebook from the seat and flipped to the next paperclipped page. Tucker Waite. Stang Street.

It was approaching seven o'clock when he turned past the Athens Bar and Grill at the corner of Clinton and McCarty. For a split second he thought about stopping for a cool drink, but he didn't even hesitate as he turned onto McCarty. The sun was low on the horizon behind the city, though it was still nearly two hours before dark. The Port Houston and Pleasantville subdivisions were a collection of scattered streets within a rhomboid formed by the sparsely populated Market Street on the north, Clinton Drive and the Turning Basin on the south, East Loop North Freeway on the east, and the Port Authority North Railyards on the west.

Within these geometric borders were bare stretches of sandy coastal pasturage, brown with tall, dead grass and scrubby bushes. Some of the streets had only a few houses, isolated by vacant lots that had never held anything more useful than scavenger weeds tangled with trash. Abandoned rail spurs sometimes ran out into the weeds, forgotten.

Stang Street was one of the thinly populated ones that ran into a desolate little field with brittle coastal grass, and an occasional chinaberry or mesquite tree. Haydon slowed and checked the numbering system. Waite's house stood off by itself where the pavement stopped and the street continued as a crushed-shell road around a sandy hump of dune grass. As Haydon approached, he was unsure of how to present himself. Then he remembered he had forgotten to call Nina.

The far side of the house was protected from an open expanse that reached toward the freeway loop by a thick house-high hedge of junipers planted so close together they formed a solid green wall. On the near side, a clapboard garage was offset thirty yards from the house, one of its double doors folded open to reveal the rear end of an old pickup sitting on cement blocks. A fishing skiff sat on a rusty boat trailer in the drive. A battered Evinrude outboard mounted on the skiff's stern looked as if it hadn't run in years. One of the trailer's tires was flat.

The yard had no curbing, and the Bermuda grass, looking pale from too much sun and too little water, simply grew in uneven margins out into the crushed shell. A sidewalk ran straight out from the front porch. There was a beaten rut in the grass at the end of the sidewalk where someone habitually parked a truck or car. The house was covered with white asbestos siding, and the green aluminum awnings on its front windows had been bleached pale by years of the southerly angle of the summer sun.

Seeing no vehicles that seemed currently in use, Haydon pulled up to the side near the boat trailer so his car wouldn't be visible from the intersection at the end of Stang. He turned off the motor, opened the glove compartment, and took out a thin leather pouch, which he slipped into his jacket pocket.

The heat had not yet begun to recede, and the traffic coming off the long fall of Sherman Bridge on the Loop glittered like a string of sequins reflecting the last sharp rays of the July sun. Haydon lowered the driver's window on the Vanden Plas and got out. A hot breath moved over the mounds of sand and clumpy dead grass, bringing with it the shuddering rasp of grasshoppers in the fields.

He walked around to the front of the house, stepped up on the prefabricated cement stoop, and knocked on the door. To the right of the porch a spray of oleanders defended the front windows, and the rear end of a sleeping German shepherd peeked out of its shade.

Suddenly Haydon was bathed in the cool, rippling wave of premonition, his eyes locked on the motionless flanks of the reclining dog. He slowly back down the steps, and saw the chain locked to a steel stake at the side of the porch. It snaked around the back of the oleander to the dog. Haydon crouched and pulled the chain, taking up its slack until it stopped. He tugged firmly, and kept it taut as he concentrated on the oleander. The blood was almost perfectly camouflaged until he saw a single splash of it, and then all of it became instantly visible as if he had finally identified the telltale pattern of the leopard's spots in the dappled shadows.

He went ahead and pulled the dog out until he saw the mess of its head. Then he dropped the chain, drew his Beretta, and moved around the side of the house to the junipers.

The Venetian blinds on the front two windows were closed, and the stained shades on the back two were pulled all the way down. In the back it was the same way. There was another dog chained at the back door, its head hidden under the wooden steps. Haydon didn't even bother to look. He went to the side of the house where the boat trailer stood, looked toward the street, then returned to the wooden steps. He mounted the steps over the body of the second dog and opened the back screen. He held it open with his foot as he gently leaned against the door. It was not locked. Slowly he put his ear next to the wood door and listened. Nothing. The muscles on the sides of his neck were tight as he slowly pushed open the door.

It was the kitchen. A thin naked woman in hair curlers and a stocky man in a port authority uniform with the sleeves rolled tightly over bulky muscles sat on opposite sides of a wooden table in the middle of the room. They were gagged, and tied to their chairs. Their hands were flat out in front of them on the table, palms down, a big nail in the center of each hand keeping them in place. Each had been shot in the right ear, and they were covered with as much blood as their hearts could pump in the convulsive seconds that followed the explosions. The woman had suffered a dozen or more cigarette burns around her breasts. Only four of her ten fingernails were painted with a fresh coat of nail polish, but two fingers on each hand still had needles rammed under their nails. Some of the needle points had exited out the flesh behind the nail roots. The man's fingers had been treated differently. They had been twisted at the joints, skewed at impossible angles, the ends pulverized. Haydon recognized the technique, and remembered the John Doe in the morgue. The man and the woman had both vomited on themselves sometime during their ordeal. The surface of the table was horrifying.

Haydon fought light-headedness, but couldn't bring himself to take a deep breath because of the stench. He moved around the table, his eyes suddenly jerking to the door that led to the rest of the house. From the kitchen door he could see into the living room, its furniture in tumbled disarray. He jerked left to a bedroom. A tall, thin young man in jeans and a black T-shirt was sprawled face up on the floor, his shoulders and head in a darkening pool. In the bathroom: a mirror broken with such force that glass was scattered all over the room and into the hallway, commode overflowed, shower curtain ripped off its clips. Another bedroom, empty. A small house.

He returned his Beretta to its holster and took out the latex gloves again. He didn't know what he was looking for, didn't know what they had been looking for, but soon saw they already had been through every drawer in the house. They had looked under every cushion, under every mattress, turned every picture, searched every pocket in every article of clothing in every closet. And, of course, they had talked to these people, and had probably learned something.

Walking back into the kitchen, Haydon stopped inside the doorway near the refrigerator. His peripheral vision caught something at eye level, and he reached on top of the refrigerator beside a Sony radio and took down an open wallet. The picture of the man nailed to the table was on the driver's license: Lawrence Tucker Waite. The wallet had been rifled. There was no money, but the credit cards were still there.

Haydon looked up, thinking, and it was then he noticed the woman was not so much in her chair as out of it, her back awkwardly arched. His eyes followed the line of her naked body to the floor, where he saw the mop head under the table, its handle angling up between her legs. From where he stood, her forward-stretched arms accented the narrowness of her waist and the flared bellows of her rib cage. It didn't matter who she was, they had taken more from her than her life. He moved mechanically around the edge of the kitchen and out the back door, fighting the constriction in his chest.

Standing in a patch of bare ground under a leaning salt cedar at the foot of the wooden steps, he spat and sucked in air, unable to get the odor out of his nostrils, the taste out of his mouth. He wiped at the perspiration pouring off his forehead, recoiled at the touch of the latex, and tore at the gloves, snatching them off in a frantic effort to free his hands. His legs wobbled, and he wondered if he was going to faint. What an absurd picture that would be, him falling away cold in the dirt outside a house full of bodies, a few feet away from a dead dog, all of them lying silently in the day's late heat, only Haydon breathing, and only Haydon eventually to open his eyes to realize how bizarre it all had been.

He moved to the Vanden Plas and leaned on it, his hands on the roof, his arms straight out, his head slumped between his arms until he felt the tendons stretching to the bursting point at the back of his neck.

It was Cordero's list. A *teco* list. Not an intended hit list. Then why had Ireno López—if John Doe was López—and Tucker Waite turned up dead? Had they been *teco* contacts or resources who, once they had served their purposes, were then dispensed with for security reasons? If so, why was López found lying at the gates of their own safe house? It didn't seem to fit together. Nor did it seem like a reasonable scenario in light of the torture evident in all the killings. Why would the *tecos* do that to their own resources?

The people who had done what Haydon had found in the house were looking for answers, and they had been looking for answers from John Doe/Ireno López, too. What Haydon needed to know was: What were the questions, and who was asking them?

He straightened up from the car and turned to face the house. The shadows were long now, spreading, blurring into one another like a growing stain. He had left the back door open, a sinister rectangle in the white cube of the house, a doorway to a despicable scene. There was very little to be learned about the investigation from seeing the two bodies in the kitchen, but if you had the strength, if you had the courage to look at them long enough, you would learn something about the darker corners of human nature.

Haydon walked back to the wooden steps and pulled the kitchen door closed, using the rubber gloves on the doorknob. He walked over to the salt cedar and broke off a leafy branch, which he used to obscure his footprints at the back of the steps. He got into the Vanden Plas and backed away from the garage and onto the pavement. Leaving the motor idling, he got out and made sure none of his tire tracks were left in a dusty pocket of the coarsely crushed shell.

He drove back to Clinton Drive, and decided against using the cubicle telephones at the Athens Bar and Grill. He would look for a booth as he returned on Wayside. The city was beginning to glisten as late afternoon slipped into evening and the light in the barrio faded into blue. Not far from Harrisburg, he saw a booth at a small convenience store near a gas station. He pulled off the street, parked to one side of the store in front of the booth, and got out. A yellow neon sign that ran the length of the front of the store threw a jaundiced glow over the parking area, turning Haydon's linen suit a bright gamboge. He called Nina.

"I was beginning to wonder," she said. "Are you all right?"

"I'm fine. Were there any calls?"

"Celia Moreno, about half an hour ago. She wants to talk to you."

"She didn't say why?"

"No. I told her you were out, but I was expecting you to check in anytime. She said she would call back in an hour. That would be around eight-thirty, I guess."

He looked at his watch. "She didn't leave a number?"

"She wouldn't."

"If she calls again before I get back, try to get a number from her. Ask her if she's at home."

"Are you on your way home?" Nina asked.

"Just about. I've got to make another call. Maybe two."

"Is everything all right? You sound . . . you sound a little tense."

"I'm fine. I'll get back to you."

He hung up and put in another quarter. When information answered, he asked for Celia Moreno. No listing. He asked for C. Moreno. No listing. He hung up. He couldn't think of her mother's name, but he remembered the address. He reached down for the telephone book, knowing it wouldn't be there, and found only the dangling chain.

Cursing, he put another quarter into the telephone. When the dispatcher answered, Haydon identified himself and asked for Lieutenant Dystal. He said he knew Dystal was out on a scene, but it was important that he talk to him. He gave the number at the booth and said he would wait ten minutes. He opened the folding door to ventilate the suffocating air inside and stood looking through the wash of yellow light at the cars on Wayside. A couple of kids on bicycles coasted up to the store from the street and went in. Yellow Chicanos, smiling yellow smiles. A yellow woman in a sagging print dress plodded across the stretch of yellow caliche carrying a paper sack loaded with empty soft drink bottles and holding the hand of a yellow child. The little girl stared at Haydon standing silently in the booth until she disappeared into the white fluorescence of the store. The woman never saw him.

When the telephone rang, Haydon quickly closed the door.

"Well, we found the place," Dystal said. Haydon could hear the static from the radio cars in the background.

"There's something else."

Dystal waited. The strain of his predicament filled the silence between them. Haydon wasn't the only one having to pay for what he was doing, but Dystal was handling it stoically.

"There are three bodies at 1119 Stang Street, over in Port Houston. One white male in the back bedroom. A white woman and a white man named Lawrence Tucker Waite in the kitchen. Waite's driver's license is in a wallet on top of the refrigerator. I don't know who the other two are. It's a bad scene, Bob. They've all been shot, but the two in the kitchen have been tortured."

"God a'mighty."

"Bob, when I was in Cordero's office, I copied an address book I found in his desk. I thought Lapierre's people would find it, but I guess Cordero came back and got it before he disappeared. At the back of the book were four coded names. When I finally deciphered them, they turned out to be the telephone numbers of four people: Valverde, Ireno López, Lawrence Waite, and someone named Daniel Ferretis. I don't know anything about him, but his address is 2855 Dumfries in Meyerland.''

"I'll get people over there right now," Dystal said. "You got any more surprises?"

"No. But I think Celia Moreno knows something. She's been trying to call me, but won't leave her number with Nina. I'll be trying to get in touch with her."

"Stu, you gonna be home later? I gotta talk to you." Dystal's voice was conciliatory, but Haydon knew that he had better make himself available.

"I'll be there," he said.

"It could be late."

"That's fine," Haydon said. "I'll see you later."

Blas and Rubio sat at a window table in a Sand-wich Chef on the corner of Kirby and Norfolk and studied a city map as the streetlights flickered, then came alive along Kirby and on the overpass of the Southwest Freeway two blocks away. It had been two days since they met with Pro-fessor Ferretis, received the money, and were told to either hurry it up or call it off. They had had no contact with him since, though Blas continued to drive by the dead drop in the mornings and at night to see if a signal had been posted.

Because there were only the two of them now, it had taken considerably more planning and an excessive amount of vig-ilance to tail Gamboa. They had stayed with him all day Wednesday, Wednesday night—except for the few hours when they had bought the RDX from Waite on the ship channel—Thursday, and now Thursday evening. They had taken elab-orate precautions, renting no fewer than four cars, each a different color and make, keeping them scattered in parking areas throughout the western part of the city where Gamboa moved in a relatively confined geographic area. They switched cars frequently so that Negrete's men, more vigilant now than before, would be less likely to tag them. Both Blas and Rubio had had a lot of experience at tailing, and they were smooth at it. They used powerful hand-held radios and made clipped, coded transmissions.

Blas knew Negrete, and he was amused at what had been happening during the past two days. He could easily imagine the mercenary's frustration at being employed to protect a man whose ego got in the way of strict, sensible security. Despite Negrete's conscientious attention to detail, he had not been able to overcome the ingrained confidence of a powerful and wealthy man who could not conceive, not *really* believe, that he would be killed by assassins. Gamboa was probably agreeing to adhere to all Negrete's preventive precautions, up to a point. This was only apparent because Blas had the benefit of Ireno's scouting reports, which he had accumulated over a three-week period before Blas and the others had even arrived in Houston. Gamboa did vary his routes of travel, but over a period of weeks it was clear that only a small number of routes were used. He did vary his dining establishments, but he used only a small number of restaurants. He did vary his timetables, but only by an hour at most.

Blas guessed that deep down Gamboa had allowed his belief in his own importance to supersede reality, just as a young man placed his concern about his own fate in the hands of the statistical odds and rarely gave death a thought. Gamboa probably regarded the possibility with a lack of serious credulity. Besides, Negrete, a man with an extraordinary capacity for venality, was being paid extremely well to keep him alive. If nothing else, Gamboa probably felt safe because he knew the mercenary he had hired to protect him would go to great lengths to preserve such a lucrative resource. It was obvious that Gamboa had more arrogance than wisdom, or he would never have remained in the city.

But the assassination attempt had caused a few blips in the record that Ireno López had kept of the limited variability of Gamboa's routine. In the past two days there had been additional bodyguards in the limousine, and now a car of them traveled in front of, as well as behind, Gamboa. Security around the house itself was beefed up. And there had been a deliberately visible increase in patrolling police cars.

The most troublesome change, however, was something else. Twice, both Blas and Rubio had observed cars of bodyguards with binoculars and radios sitting alongside Inverness a block in either direction from Gamboa's home. They were taking license numbers, and there was no doubt the numbers were being spot-checked. Even though Blas and Rubio had rented four different cars from four different agencies to decrease the risk of being spotted, this new effort by Negrete could tap them. If the spot checking identified an increase in the number of rental cars traveling on Inverness, it could trigger an inquiry. So now Blas and Rubio had begun passing by on cross streets, and would loop back and make a run down Inverness only if there was no sign of stake-out cars.

But the waiting was almost over. As Blas hunched over the map and sipped at the dregs of his fourth cup of coffee, he was formulating his final plans after having spent a dozen long hours poring over the notes López had accumulated about Gamboa's travel routes, as well as their own surveillance in the two days after the assassination attempt. It was true that you could not predict where he would be or when, but there were only so many ways for him to get where he was going. Even in a city this size. On the average, the shortest routes were used most often.

Gamboa conducted a lot of business—and pleasure—in the Greenway Plaza area and among the office buildings along Post Oak. Between the River Oaks and the Southwest Freeway, there were only four east-west streets that went straight through to Post Oak: San Felipe, Westheimer, Alabama, and Richmond. There were no back ways, no quiet residential streets to travel unobserved. From Inverness, San Felipe was the nearest route. Sooner or later, in the course of any twenty-four-hour period, Benigo Gamboa's limousine could be seen taking advantage of it.

The exact point along San Felipe at which to make the hit required considerable planning. The RDX would take up roughly the same amount of space as a couple of shoe boxes, though it would have to be kneaded into a shape that would guide and enhance the force of the explosion. And that was a large part of the trouble. To do its best work, the RDX should be directly under the limousine when it was detonated, and there was little way of doing that on a public street as busy as San Felipe. Alternatively, it could be placed in a mailbox, or a trash can beside the street, but more than half the amount of the explosive force would be wasted in a direction away from the car, greatly reducing its effectiveness.

It could be placed in the gutter, disguised as some form of trash—a ragged cardboard box, a torn paper sack—which would get it closer to the passing car and would guide the initial explosion in a ninety-degree radius in the car's direction. An improvement. However, the explosive might have to be left in place for as much as twenty-four hours, and in that length of time it was likely to be picked up by city cleaning crews, or accidentally detonated by a passing vehicle.

Rubio looked at his watch. "I have to go," he lisped. "I want to see if he has any visitors tonight. The old bastard doesn't move much after the sun goes down. He huddles up like a crow after dark."

Blas nodded, and looked at the map they had been studying. "We've got to settle on something," he said.

"That is your problem, huh? I will do my part." Rubio grinned crookedly; his bottom lip did not behave the same on both sides of the deep notch. The nerves had been damaged on the left.

"I'll make a decision tonight," Blas said. "We can't afford to put it off any longer."

"Bueno." Rubio pushed back his chair as he wiped at his mouth one final time with a paper napkin. He stood and walked out of the shop without another word, or even a glance back.

Blas watched him leave. He had never heard Rubio say goodbye to anyone, not even a casually polite "See you later." Blas had decided long ago it was a superstition. When Rubio walked away from you, you could never tell by his attitude whether he would be gone five minutes or a year. And you learned nothing from the Indian's broad, thick back.

Blas signaled for the waitress to bring him a refill, and watched her as she finished writing up the check for the one other customer in the shop. Then she went behind the counter to get the coffeepot off the hotplate. She was a Mexican girl, and when Blas and Rubio had first come in, her friendly, quick smile had not been wasted on him, though he had been unresponsive, and otherwise ignored her. He had his map to study. By the time she had served them their third cup without so much as a glance from either of them, she had gotten the message and didn't even bother to smile anymore.

But now, as she came up to the table and started to refill Rubio's cup, he stopped her with a quick gesture.

"No, he's not coming back."

She shrugged, poured his coffee, put down a plastic container of cream, and started to turn away.

"What is your name?" he asked.

She looked at him, surprised. A tentative smile.

"Yolanda." A savvy city girl. No last names to strangers. She wore her waitress uniform well, and held her long, girlish hair in an upward sweep at her temples with simple white barrettes. Her mouth was large, and pretty. She had one dimple.

He said something to her in Spanish. She grinned, a little embarrassed.

"I don't speak Spanish," she said, cocking one hip as she stood in front of him.

He wasn't surprised, but he was disappointed.

"You were born in Houston?"

She nodded. "Right." She was still smiling, pleased at his attention.

"Have you ever been to Mexico?"

"Just to Matamoros." She seemed to wish she could have told him Acapulco, or Cancún, or Mexico City.

"You have family there?"

"In Brownsville. My grandmother lives there."

He nodded, and smiled back at her, but was already deciding that it wasn't any good. He shouldn't have started it. She was still standing there with the coffeepot, but she could see it slipping too, a little puzzled by it.

"If you need anything else . . ." she said.

"No," he said, opening the plastic container of cream. "Just coffee right now. Thanks, Yolanda."

"Sure," she said with a slight shrug again. His use of her first name seemed to soften a little of the disappointment. Her smile flickered again, faintly sad this time.

Blas was angry with himself, but he didn't dwell on it. He dumped the cream in his cup and stirred, then sipped carefully. The coffee was hot, but strong. When the temperature was in the nineties, hot coffee was not in great demand in sandwich shops. He put down the cup and looked back at the map. He felt tired, very tired. Once again, he traced his pen back and forth along San Felipe. From River Oaks Boulevard to the West Loop there were exactly a dozen points at which side streets intersected San Felipe. Some of them did not cross, but came to a dead end there. He was sure Negrete's men would pay particular attention to these.

Then his pen froze, and he stared hard at something on the map as if he were seeing it for the first time, though it must have been the hundredth. He was amazed he had not recognized its potential long before. It was the perfect site, so perfect that he had a tremendous sense of relief. He had no doubts now that they would be able to pull it off.

chapter 33

After hanging up the telephone, Haydon opened the door so the light would go off and leaned against the glass of the booth. He thought about Mooney. It was so damned unreal. He would have been inside the store now, buying a couple of sweet rolls for a snack, buying something for the little girl with gold earrings as naturally as if she had gone in there with him, and watching out of the corner of his eye to see if the two boys who had left their bikes outside were going to lift a package of gum over in the candy aisle. Instead, he simply didn't exist, didn't play any part at all. Except that he was a part of the puzzle, or rather, his death was. He was a number in a larger equation, an unknown factor. A candidate for an interview with the extraordinary Detective Voyant. Christ. How had he thought of that? It was freakish.

Mooney used to do a little routine in which he satirized the "if-only-the-dead-could-talk" wish of frustrated homicide detectives. He became the famous female Detective Claire Voyant. Detective Voyant tried to solve her cases by interviewing the dead, taking statements from the victims, the only people in ninety-nine cases out of a hundred who knew who had killed them. This would have seemed the answer to a homicide detective's prayers, but as it turned out, the bewildered Detective Voyant invariably discovered that the ghosts of the victims—in Mooney's words—"didn't know Jack shit" about who had killed them. Claire was the supremely frustrated investigator, and in all the years Mooney had been relating her stories, which were drawn larger than life with Mooney's special brand of irreverent humor, she never cleared a single homicide case through her unique ability to interview the victims.

It occurred to Haydon, standing in the telephone booth and staring out through the lemon light, that he had heard the last of Detective Voyant. However, it seemed to him that had she tried her technique in one last case, that of her creator and fellow detective, she would have appreciated the irony in the fact that even Ed Mooney, really, didn't know Jack shit about who had shot him that dark night from the impenetrable wall of black bamboo.

Haydon was burning up in the booth, but stood there, sweating, thinking. He remembered the swell of Mooney's stomach as he lay on his back. He remembered the sound of the gunfire, and his own mental image of what it meant, Mooney's appalling death grunt, the heat and brilliance and roar of the blasts lifting him off his feet and hurling him backward in darkness to the dirty sidewalk where he died staring up to the night sky until one darkness overcame another and he, the profane and contentious and likable and terrified Ed Mooney, stepped across that awesome border into eternity.

Haydon heard his heart in his ears, hammering. He felt perspiration on every inch of his body. He saw himself standing in the dark booth as if he were outside himself looking back from a slightly higher angle. Then he moved back, and saw the booth in front of the convenience store bathed in the hazy nimbus of yellow light, then from higher and farther away he saw the barrio, then the breadth of the encompassing city, itself continuing to recede, becoming smaller and smaller until it hung like a sparkling pendant in the vast expanse of a starless sky, shrinking, diminishing, ultimately lost.

He stepped out of the booth, and went home.

He sat in the library, his coat off, his tie loosened, his sleeves turned back, sipping a gin lime he had made for himself the minute he came home. He had made one for Nina too, and she was sitting across from him in the same white linen dress she had been wearing in the afternoon. She also wore a sober expression, almost strained, as they looked at each other. He had just told her what he had found at La

Concha Courts and Stang Street, and what he had conveyed to Dystal. Then he had fallen silent.

"Celia Moreno never called back?" he asked after a moment.

Nina only shook her head. Haydon looked at her. She had put her drink on the small table beside her chair and was sitting with her arms crossed, almost hugging herself, an attitude she had assumed as she listened to him recount the afternoon's events. Maybe he shouldn't have told her everything. He really hadn't thought about it, about the effect it might have on her, before he started talking. With all the excitement and the tension, he simply had told her everything. It hadn't been prudent. She was already scared for him, and telling her what he had seen at the Stang address didn't help matters. She wasn't used to it. His talking to her about his cases, in this sort of detail at least, was still new to both of them. If it hadn't been for Mooney, it might not have happened at all.

He knew too that she still was wishing he would turn it all over to Dystal, that he would back out of it altogether and let the others take it to the end. But it was something she wasn't going to bring up again.

He sipped his drink, and his mind went back through the day's events. He sifted through the debris of the case, trying to pick out the one item that would point him in the right direction, trying to spot the anomaly.

"Somewhere in all this," he said, "there's got to be a direct connection to Rubio Arizpe. We've yet to come across that one crucial contact. Cordero. He knew something, but it's too late to get anything out of him now."

He leaned forward in his chair, holding his glass in both hands, forearms resting on his knees. "Negrete's played hell with this," he said. "He's caused a lot of confusion." He paused. "It doesn't make sense that the *tecos* would be killing their own people, I mean, López outside that old Belgrano house, and now Waite. It's got to be Negrete. Dystal's going to have to do something about him. I don't know how they'll tie him to it. It's not going to be easy."

"Who's left?" Nina asked. "Of the *tecos?*"

"The only one we know about is Ferretis."

"What did López and Waite do for the *tecos?* What was their role?" She was frowning, intent.

"I don't have any idea," he said.

"Well, who were the other two people in the house with this man Waite? Do you think they were *tecos?*"

Haydon shook his head again.

"It seems to me that if Rubio Arizpe was the other man on the motorcycle, he's certainly cruel enough to have killed those people," Nina said. "It doesn't necessarily have to have been Negrete."

"I thought about that too," Haydon said, pushing his lime down into the ice. "But then I can't think of any reason for the torture. Not only that, but if he's a professional, and I'm betting he is, he wouldn't want to attract that kind of attention. That kind of scene is a red flag to police. It really stirs up things. Arizpe's going to want to be the next thing to invisible . . . until he makes his move for Gamboa."

Nina picked up her drink and sipped it. She ran her fingers through her hair, a gesture that recalled Renata Islas. There was an intercourse with women, Haydon thought, that had nothing to do with sex. At least, not explicitly. It was a communication of gesture and movement that he did not always understand, but observed with invariable appreciation. It was a dialect of gender.

"What makes you so sure this other person is Rubio Arizpe?" Nina asked suddenly. "Maybe you haven't come across a connection to him because there isn't any. Don't you get leads in cases all the time that never develop into anything? Renata Islas only gave you a name and a description. That's all."

"That, and the knowledge that he's operated here before."

"She has no proof of that."

"No. Not the kind of confirmation we'd like to have. Still, I guess it's more of a hope than anything," Haydon said. "Because if it's not him, then there's someone else out there we don't even know about yet. And that's a considerable setback. I'd hate to think we're still at that point."

"Have you told Bob about Arizpe?"

"There really hasn't been time. I'm going to give him everything when he gets over here tonight."

"Maybe your assassin is Cordero or Ferretis."

Haydon smiled at her. "If you'd met Cordero you'd mark him off your list. I don't have any doubt that he was instrumental in putting it together, but he's a hell of a long way from being an assassin."

"And Ferretis?"

"I don't have any idea, but it seems highly unlikely to me that an organization of militant right-wing Mexicans with involvement in death-squad activities throughout Mexico and Central America would use a man who lives in upper middle class Meyerland as an assassin. It's just too improbable."

"I guess that's right," Nina said. She stared at her glass, running her thumb from top to bottom all around it, erasing the beads of sweat. "Do you really think Negrete has any better idea about where he's going with this than you do?"

"Well, he's had some serious 'interviews' with López and Waite." Haydon nodded to himself. "He knows something. I just hope Dystal gets to Ferretis before Negrete does. And I hope Celia Moreno . . ."

Haydon stopped, and looked at Nina. Without saying anything, he stood and walked across the library to his desk. He flipped through a stack of papers until he found the stapled pages of the copies of Cordero's address book. He had been an idiot. Surely he had seen it when he was going through the names before. He turned to the M's. It was there. After Bernardo Montez, C. Moreno.

He dialed the number, and it rang four times before someone picked it up. It was a woman's voice, but it wasn't Celia.

"This is Stuart Haydon," he said. "Is Celia there? I'm returning her call of an hour ago."

"No," the girl said. "She's not here. This is her roommate. She left about half an hour ago."

"Do you know where I can get in touch with her?"

"Uh . . ." The girl hesitated. "She told me that if you called, I should ask you who you talked to at her mother's house today."

Haydon understood. "Besides her, I talked to two young men, I think they were cousins. They didn't think I belonged there."

The girl repeated what he said, as if she were writing it down, and then Celia Moreno came on the telephone.

"Hello?" Her voice was soft, a kind of hesitant half-commitment, as if that provided her with some kind of protection.

"This is Stuart Haydon."

"Oh, God." She recognized his voice. "Listen, I've got to talk to you, but not on the telephone."

"You know you could be in danger, don't you?" he said.

"I think so," she said, her voice cracking.

"I'll come by and get you."

"No, I'm not staying here. I'm leaving, Nikki and I both are leaving."

Good. "Where, then?"

There was a pause, and Haydon could tell she was trying to figure out how to give him directions to a meeting place without also revealing the information to whoever might have tapped her telephone.

He helped her. "Do you know where I saw the girl exercising today . . ."

"What?"

"Do you know the place where I saw the girl exercising today? Cover the mouthpiece and ask Nikki about it."

There was a moment of muffled conversation, and then she came back on. "Yeah, okay. I understand."

"There's a service station near there that stays open all night."

"The closest one?"

"Yes. I'll pick you up there. Just wait inside with the attendants. It's well lighted."

"I'll be there."

"It's going to take me ten or fifteen minutes to get there," he said. "Any problem with that?" He didn't want her to panic, leave before he got there.

"No, no problem. I'll be there."

"I'm on my way," Haydon said, and hung up.

Chapter 34

Memorial Drive split into two main thoroughfares on the western side of Memorial Park. Its southern trunk became Woodway, a sinuous and heavily wooded drive that cut through the affluent section of Tanglewood west of the Loop. Haydon made good progress in the traffic, and by the time he rounded the curve of looming pine trees and saw the blue-white neon lights of the service station, it was closing in on the fifteen minutes he had predicted.

The station driveway was glistening with water as he turned off Woodway and rolled to a stop under the canopy near the front door. Two attendants in rubber boots were working outside, one rolling up the water hoses while the other used a wide rubber squeegee to push the last ripples of foam down the sloping drive toward the street. A third attendant was inside the bright office, but Celia wasn't with him.

Haydon left the Vanden Plas idling, and got out as the attendant inside looked up. He was sitting behind his desk staring at a color television perched on top of a display stack of oil cans. When he saw Haydon, he looked out to the other two men, saw they were busy, and reluctantly got up and walked to the door.

"Yes, sir," he said.

"A woman was supposed to be waiting here for me," Haydon said. "Dark hair, attractive."

"Nope," the man said, shaking his head and rubbing his elbow as he stood in the doorway. "No woman like that been in here tonight, that's for sure."

Haydon hadn't expected this; her condominium was only five blocks from the station. He had started to say something to the man when the attendant's eyes shifted past Haydon's shoulder. He looked around to see Celia riding a bicycle into the station's light, the gears clicking as she approached, gliding on her own shimmering reflection over the wet drive.

She pulled up beside the Vanden Plas and got off the bike.

"I'm sorry," she said, her face a mask of restrained self-possession. "I helped Nikki get some things into her car."

"Fine," Haydon said. This was a different Celia. She wore a long, diaphanous lavender skirt, which she had gathered up from around her ankles by running a purple cord under the hem of the skirt, front to back, and pulling both ends up between her legs to gather the long material into a pair of chic billowing pants. Her blouse was a black satin camisole with lace over the tops of her breasts. She had pulled her dark hair up off her neck because of the evening heat; a few strands were coming loose at the back.

Haydon looked at the attendant, who was looking at Celia.

"Could she leave her bicycle in your office for a while? She'll be going with me."

The man shifted his attention back to Haydon.

"Yeah, I guess so," he said. He politely came around the rear of the car and took the bicycle from Celia. He smiled at her as she thanked him, and told him she appreciated it, and then he gave a different sort of smile to Haydon as Celia untied the cord from her waist and let the skirt hem fall.

"I get off at six o'clock, sport," the attendant said to Haydon. "I don't guarantee anything after that."

"We'll just be a little while," Haydon said. Celia was already walking around to the passenger side, dabbing at the perspiration on her forehead with a tissue she took from the waist of the skirt.

As the attendant walked the bike into the office, Celia and Haydon got into the Vanden Plas. Haydon put the car in gear and drove out of the glare of the neon and into the scattered shadows of the street.

"You're going to find this unbelievable," she said, starting to talk before Haydon had a chance to say anything. She turned the vents of the air conditioner to blow on her face and dabbed the tissue around her neck. She lifted the front of the camisole and fluttered it. *"I* find it unbelievable."

Haydon waited.

She glanced at him, then said, "Where are we going?"

"Nowhere. I'm just going to drive while you talk."

She looked at him, assessing his intentions. The car was filling with her perfume, carried on the cool air that blew over her. Haydon noticed that she hadn't been so preoccupied by fear that she had forgotten that detail of fragrance. Then again, with a girl like her that was no telling observation. She had probably dabbed it on hurriedly, a second-nature habit of grooming, like quickly running a brush through her hair. Then he found himself wondering where she had put it. With Celia, that could have been an erotic thing to watch.

"Okay," she said. "Okay." She looked out her window a moment, her hands playing with the tissue in her lap. Then she turned around, squared her shoulders on the white leather seat, and stared straight out the windshield to the headlights following the winding street.

"Valverde and my brother were *tecos*," she began. "They'd both gone to school in Guadalajara, where they were recruited some years ago. My brother really wasn't college material, and eventually dropped out and came back to Houston. But Valverde stayed, finished college—a degree in business—and lived there for several years. About three years ago he moved back to Houston and started the limousine business. He looked up my brother, and Esteban went to work for him as a driver.

"I went to college here, the University of Houston. Majored in political science. One of my professors there was Dr. Daniel Ferretis."

Haydon hadn't given any thought to where he was going, and when he heard the professor's name he didn't even give any thought to his driving. He let the Jaguar move with the traffic.

"Dr. Ferretis had been known to alter grades for women students in exchange for sexual favors, and during every semester two or three of the girls out of his classes would be invited to his office to see if they wanted to improve a faltering grade point average. They didn't all take him up on his proposition, but enough did so that he kept trying. When my turn came around one day, Ferretis was warming up to his offer with some casual conversation. He mentioned that he frequently did guest teaching stints at the Autonomous University of Guadalajara, and I said that my brother had gone there. He was surprised, curious. He asked a lot of questions, and I told him about my brother and Jimmy Valverde. He was amazed that I knew Valverde, or at least knew who he was.''

She hesitated. "I've thought about that a lot since then. It seems too much of a coincidence, but I can't see how it could have been anything else. I mean, life has got to have some actual coincidences, doesn't it?''

Probably more than we're willing to accept, Haydon thought. We are a reasonable people, and if logic can't explain such things, then our cynicism will. But he didn't say anything. He wanted a cigarette.

"One thing led to another, but not to sex. I had discovered there was something that obsessed Dr. Ferretis even more. I don't remember how the subject of the *tecos* first came up, but Ferretis began recruiting me. I'd heard a lot about them from Esteban, so I already knew much of what Ferretis was telling me. I didn't like it. I thought all that brotherhood business was a crock, and the racial hatred . . . I just couldn't get whipped up for it. But I pretended to be interested. I figured it couldn't hurt my grades.

"I did a pretty good job of being the impressed student, and he came right along with his professor role, too. The more he told me, the more 'impressed' I was. Soon he was telling me he and Valverde, along with a couple of others, formed a kind of 'affiliate' branch of the *tecos* in Houston. They handled money that the *teco* big shots wanted to squirrel away on this side of the border, and were generally a useful support group."

She stopped and looked out her window again as she held a well-manicured hand in front of the vents and turned it in the cool air. Distractedly, her mind absorbed in what she was going to say next, she gathered the thin material of her skirt on one side and pulled it up to just above her knee. She fanned the material, then held it there.

"I was in for a surprise," she said. "After this had been going on for a couple of months, a graduate student I'd been dating quite a bit and had gotten to know fairly well suddenly dropped a bomb on me. One night we were having drinks at my apartment—which at that time was a dumpy little place over by the university—and he came right out and told me he worked for the FBI. I mean, not out of the blue. We had been talking politics a lot. He knew how I felt about things, and that's what we were discussing when he popped this on me. He said he worked for them on the side, that he had been doing it quite a while. He said it wasn't any big deal. He just hung around a lot of different political groups, and made extra money writing these little reports about all that was going on with these people. Just gossipy stuff, who their friends were, what they talked about, where they hung out, what kinds of ideas they were kicking around. Things like that. He asked me if I would be interested in doing the same thing on the *tecos.* He said it was a good way to pick up a little cash.''

She took a deep breath, let it out, said, "Jesus," and went on.

"Well, I'd read all about the sixties, the Kent State business, how the FBI infiltrated those radical groups. I knew what he was asking me to do, and I knew how that was viewed by the students of the seventies when it all came out. But I personally didn't see anything so terrible about it. I can understand that a government needs to do that. What they do with the information is something else. If they use it to abuse our basic freedoms, that's one thing, but if they use it to protect those freedoms, that's something else. I don't think you can write off the entire concept of a government's right to gather intelligence because at some point in history it abused that right.''

She looked around at him, a little sheepishly he thought.

"Anyway, I did it," she said. "I began writing reports on what I heard about the *tecos.* "

"Did you give these reports to your friend?" Haydon asked.

"Initially, yes. Until they were sure I knew what I was doing. Then I started simply mailing them to a post office box.''

"How did you receive your payments?''

"Well, that was a little cloak-and-dagger-ish. At first Rich, my friend, gave them to me. When I finally got a mailbox in the university post office—at Rich's request—I began receiving it there. It just showed up in my box on the fifth of each month. Cash in an envelope. I guess they had someone on the inside there, too. After I graduated and left the university, I got a mailbox in the post office over on Timmons.''

"How did you stay in touch with the *tecos* after you left the university?''

"Things had progressed pretty well by that time, and Dr. Ferretis had gotten me a job with Valverde. Oddly, once I showed an interest in the 'movement,' Ferretis completely turned off the sex thing. Suddenly it was all business. I wasn't so lucky with Valverde. Anyway, as the quality of my information increased, the bureau increased my 'gratuity,' which, I admit, surprised me. Valverde was paying me well, too, so with the combined incomes I was able to move to the condo where I'm living now. Ferretis, Valverde, and eventually Cordero really took me in. I actually became a member, with all the attendant hocus-pocus that involves. I even took a trip to Guadalajara, where Ferretis showed me off.''

She nodded pensively, as if confirming a question in her own mind. "I'll tell you, the more I was around those people, the more I despised them. I learned to detest what they stood for more than you can imagine. Informing on them became an obsession. I would have done it for nothing. Every time I mailed a report I felt better.''

"What about your brother?'' Haydon asked. "How did you reconcile working against him?''

"Oh, Esteban was too wishy-washy to be a real *teco*. He did as little as possible with them. Mainly he was just a chauffeur working for Valverde. Esteban didn't have any ambition. His *teco* days never amounted to anything in the first place.''

Haydon had gone the length of Woodway, and circled back on San Felipe. When he got to Fountainview he cut across to Woodway again, made a jog to the left, and entered the maze of winding and wooded streets along the eastern boundaries of the Houston Country Club. After a few more turns, he pulled into a narrow cove off the street that looked across a large expanse of the golf course. He cut the lights, except for the low glow from the dash, and left the motor running for air conditioning.

Celia stopped talking and looked out to the rolling greens of the course, their farthest edge closed off by the towering pines. For a moment she seemed to lose the thread of her story. She had put her shredded tissue into the trash and was winding and unwinding the purple cord around one of her hands. Her eyes fell to what she was doing, watching but not watching, coiling and uncoiling the cord with a peculiar tension, pulling it tight enough to require some effort.

Haydon looked at her profile, at her bare neck and shoulders, at the lift of her breasts holding up the lace camisole. His eyes fell to her leg where the dress had ridden slightly higher now, revealing the smooth beginnings of her thigh. It was not an artful gesture; she was too absorbed in her thoughts to play that kind of game now. If he wanted to be honest with himself, he would have to admit that he was finding practically everything about her more than a little seductive. He couldn't pretend that it was all a calculation on her part. He would have found her appealing under any circumstances.

He remembered standing in Valverde's office and pulling the long pink stockings out from under the sofa cushion. And he remembered the way she had smiled at him as she walked out of the room. She was awfully young to be playing in this league, but she seemed capable of taking care of herself. Up to now. She obviously was feeling that she had miscalculated some angles, that she had lost control of her situation. Or, more accurately, she was only now realizing that perhaps she had never had control in the first place. In any circumstance that was a sobering apprehension, but even more so in a matter of life and death.

"I learned about the plans to assassinate Gamboa," Celia said. "Although they included me in everything—at least I thought they did—something like that was up to the *tecos de choque,* their death squads, and even Valverde didn't know very much. I couldn't believe I'd uncovered this. I got off a quick note to the Bureau and they called me that night. Elkin did. He said they wanted details. He pressed me, said lives depended on it. Goddam, didn't he think I knew that? I was a nervous wreck. That . . . that was when I started letting

Valverde . . .'' She stopped, waited, and then said, "I found out what little more he knew.''

She was winding the cord furiously now, as if the strength with which she wound it was an exact parallel measurement of her anger and, certainly, fear.

"Esteban knew nothing about it at all,'' she added. "I didn't know the exact time and date, but I was scared for Esteban and had gotten reassurances from Valverde that whenever it came down, nothing would happen to him. I was concerned, because I knew he was Sosa's driver.''

"You knew how it was going to happen?'' Haydon asked. "That it would be a hit on one of the limousines?''

"No. No, I didn't. Only that Valverde had said it could be something like that. He didn't know how. Anyway, he was most reassuring,'' she said, remembering. "Would he do a thing like that to a friend, to *my* brother? He reassured me every time he took my clothes off. After a while the sexual exchange between us underwent a subtle change. I don't know; I guess he noticed it too. Before, I had always used it to manipulate him—though I don't think he ever understood that—but now it was turning out that he was using it to manipulate me. It occurred to me that my body had become Esteban's insurance policy.''

She unwound the cord. "It turned out to be a worthless one,'' she said.

"Why was Gamboa targeted?''

"As the *tecos* see it, and in actual fact, he was one of half a dozen former Mexican politicos from the López Portillo administration who, collectively, took billions of dollars out of Mexico. Actually stole from the Mexican people. The *tecos* wanted to make examples of them, a warning to the de la Madrid administration.''

"You say he was one of half a dozen. Are there plans to assassinate others?''

She turned to him, and he saw that she had been crying. Her wet cheeks glistened in the dash lights. "Yes.''

"Here?''

"No. Other cities. Miami, one in Miami; one in San Diego; Los Angeles. One in Paris.''

"When?''

"As close to the same time as possible. Ideally within the same day or two, for greater impact."

God, Haydon thought. What in the hell had he uncovered?

"And you've passed all this on to the Bureau?"

"Yes." She frowned at him, continued looking at him, waiting to see in his face that he was beginning to understand. "Goddam!" she said. "Don't you see? They're *not* stopping this. The Bureau. I mean, I thought they were on top of this thing. I thought I was really doing something valuable here, but they're not moving on it. They're letting this thing happen!"

"Have you tried to contact them?"

"Of course I have! I can't get any response."

"What about Rich?"

"Hell, he disappeared weeks ago," she said disgustedly.

"Does the name Rubio Arizpe mean anything to you?"

She shook her head. "No."

"How about Ireno López?"

She glowered at him, her eyes portraying suspicion. "What's going on here? How'd you get that name? Do you already know all about this?"

"No, I don't. Who is he?"

She considered her response. "One of the *tecos de choque*."

"He's one of the assassins?"

"He was supposed to be," she said. "But let me explain. He's the only one I know, and only because he was sent up here from Jalisco three weeks in advance of the others to reconnoiter Gamboa's habits, movements, and security setup. Since he was here so long, Valverde couldn't keep his mouth shut, and told me. The FBI know this. I've told them everything. Everything!"

"Who killed him?"

"Lucas Negrete. They think Negrete's boys spotted his surveillance, captured him, and tortured him for information about the plot."

"Do you think López talked?"

She nodded. "That's why everything's coming unglued. That's why I'm afraid of Negrete getting to me. I don't even know if he knows I exist, but I don't want to let that bastard get his hands on me."

Neither of them said anything for a moment, and then she said, "I just really don't understand this." She put one hand across her stomach and sucked in a deep breath. "It's making me sick."

Haydon had looked away from her, through the windshield to the golf greens stretching toward the pines. Garner had been right—these people had to have some prominent connections. You couldn't expect to execute a plan of this scale in the States without a considerable amount of cooperation from somewhere. But he couldn't bring himself to accept the implications of Celia's story.

"What am I supposed to do now?" she snapped at him, her nerves getting the best of her. "I don't know why the Bureau isn't offering me some protection, or something. Where the hell are they?" She started crying, burying her face in her hands, the purple cord dangling down in front of the black satin camisole. She leaned her head against the window and cried until her shoulders shook. She lifted the long folds of her skirt and held it to her face, trying to stop crying as she wiped her eyes. A sob escaped as Haydon handed her his handkerchief. She gained control, wiping under her eyes with the handkerchief, trying to clean up the dark smudges of mascara.

"God," she said finally, her voice thick and scratchy from the crying. "What a mess. I can*not* believe this."

Haydon looked at her. His gut feeling told him she was telling the truth—as she knew it. But he also had a strong suspicion that she had been deceived. He didn't believe she had been dealing with the Federal Bureau of Investigation.

"You're not going to be able to go back home," he said.

"Yeah," she nodded, wiping her nose. "I know."

"Why did you ride your bicycle to the station instead of driving your car?"

"They know the car. I'm afraid of . . . car bombs . . . of, I don't know, being shot to pieces in it, like Esteban. Christ!" She wiped her nose again with Haydon's handkerchief. "I'll wash it," she said, wadding and unwadding it nervously in her lap. She looked at him. "So what am I supposed to do now? You going to be like the FBI, and drop the ball on this?"

SPIRAL

She was talking bravely, but Haydon had been watching her twitchy movements. She was scared to death.

He turned and flipped on the car lights, put the car in gear, and started backing out of the cove, the headlights panning across the pines.

She jerked her head up and looked at him. "Now what?" she asked nervously.

Haydon straightened out the Jaguar in the street and accelerated into the first sharp turn. "I think you'd better come home with me," he said.

Chapter 35

Haydon took Fountainview off Woodway and stopped at the first telephone he saw along the street. He called home first.

"Nina," he said, "I'm bringing Celia Moreno home with me. Would you ask Gabriela to get one of the guest rooms ready?"

"What's the matter?"

"I think she's going to be the key to all this," he said, looking through the glass booth at her sitting in the Jaguar. "But she's got to be tucked away somewhere for a few days."

"Okay."

"I'm at a telephone booth on Fountainview. I'm going to call Bob, and then we'll be coming home."

Nina said fine. She didn't ask any more questions. Haydon hung up and dialed the dispatcher, who took his number. He waited, leaning on the aluminum shelf, watching Celia. She was still wiping at her eyes. She pulled down the car visor and looked at herself in the lighted mirror there, shook her hair, ran her fingers through it, and shook it again. She ran her fingers over her eyebrows. She stared at herself, not blinking, not fussing with her face, then in a frustrated gesture flipped up the visor. She propped her elbow on the windowsill and started chewing on a red thumbnail, looking out at the traffic.

The telephone rang, and Haydon picked it up.

"This is Dystal."

"Bob. Listen, I'm at a telephone booth out on Fountainview. I've got Celia Moreno with me. Did your men get hold of Daniel Ferretis?"

"Not exactly," Dystal said. "They got over there and he wasn't there, but a real worried wife was. She told 'em he'd called from his office at the University of Houston—he's a professor of political science there—earlier this afternoon, and told her he was going to be late tonight. But it's already a lot later than he told her he'd be."

"How about his office? You've checked that?"

"Yeah, sure did. It's been ransacked."

"Damn."

"They're checking with the political science office, and gettin' the names of the other professors teaching this afternoon, gettin' names of the students in his afternoon class to see if anybody noticed anything. That's gonna take a while. What about Moreno? She know anything that's gonna help us?"

"A lot. I'm getting ready to take her home with me. She'll be staying there. You're going to find what she has to say pretty interesting."

"Well, this is purty damn bad over here on Stang, but I think Pete's about got it whipped. I'll be over there as soon as I can."

"There's going to be a lot to sort out."

"Listen," Dystal said. "I hate to bring this up now, but I don't think I can cover you on this anymore. We got too much happening, Stu. You gotta understand that."

"I understand," Haydon said. "I appreciate what you've been doing."

"I'm on my way," Dystal said, and hung up.

Haydon put Dystal's last remarks out of his mind and stepped out of his booth. He went around and got into the car.

As they drove to Richmond and then turned east, Haydon's mind was jumping as far ahead as his imagination would allow with the available facts. He wasn't paying any attention to Celia.

"What's going to happen now?" she asked finally.

"You're going to stay with us until we get some of this sorted out."

In his peripheral vision he could see her looking at him.

"I mean, right now, tonight," she said.

"I've called my superior officer, Lieutenant Dystal. He's going to come over to my house and I want you to go over everything with him. Everything you know from the beginning." He looked over at her. "Did you keep copies of your reports to the FBI?"

"No. There was a strict rule about that."

"Obviously we're going to want to know everything you can tell us."

He could see that she was continuing to stare at him, but she didn't say anything else. After a while she settled back and turned her eyes out the window on her side of the car.

Less than a block from the house, Haydon pushed the remote control on the gates, and they drove through to the brick drive without even stopping. He lowered the windows on the Vanden Plas to let in the fragrance from the damp lawns in the night air, an odor that often brought him outside to the terrace on summer nights despite the oppressive heat. As they followed the curve of the drive to the porte cochere, Celia sat up and bent forward, looking through the windshield at the old limestone home with its Belgian slate roof. When Haydon stopped in front, they could see through the tall front windows into the living room, and from outside, the incandescent lights made the shell-white interior appear fawn.

"Jesus," Celia said, leaning into Haydon and looking through his window at the front of the house. He felt the cushion of her breast against his chest.

In the entranceway Haydon introduced Celia to Gabriela, who, excited to have a guest, had come in as soon as she heard the door open. She asked if Celia would like to freshen up in her room, and the two of them started down the hall.

"We'll be in the library," Haydon said.

He turned and went up the stairs to their bedroom, where Nina was finishing dressing, sitting in front of a mirror combing her hair. She had bathed and changed dresses.

"How did it go?" she asked, stopping and turning to look at him.

He immediately took off his suit coat and flung it on the bed as he walked over and kissed her.

"Better," he said. "I think we're getting somewhere." He loosened his tie, walked into the bathroom, and turned on the cold water, letting it run while he rolled up his sleeves. "If Celia Moreno knows half of what I think she does, she could break it open for us, maybe keep Gamboa from getting blown away. If we have time."

He took off his watch and laid it on the marble vanity while he washed his face, holding it in the cold water cupped in his hands. Taking the soap, he worked up a thick lather and washed his arms to the elbows, then his face, and rinsed in more cold water. Drying with a towel, he walked back into the bedroom.

"Bob's on his way over, too," he said.

"What's the situation with Celia Moreno?"

"In essence she'll be in protective custody here. I was afraid to take her back to her place tonight to get clothes, so she's only got what she's wearing. We'll have to go over there tomorrow and get some of her things for the next few days."

He returned the towel to the bathroom and came back to the dressing table, where Nina was trying to decide whether to put her hair up in a chignon or leave it down.

"Why don't you leave it down?" he said, buckling his watch band. "Would you mind sitting in on this interview? I'd like to get your reaction."

"My reaction to what?" she asked, picking up her brush and running it through her hair a couple of times.

"To Celia Moreno."

The buzzer for the front gate sounded, and Haydon walked over to the wall and pressed the intercom.

"This is Dystal." The lieutenant's drawl sounded tired. Haydon pushed the button to open the gates, and they went downstairs.

Celia was coming down the hall with Gabriela just as Haydon and Nina got to the bottom of the stairs and Dystal rang the doorbell. There was a little disorganization until everyone had been greeted and introduced, and then Haydon asked them into the library. Both Dystal and Celia turned down offers to get them something to eat, but accepted his suggestion for drinks.

When they finally settled down, Celia Moreno was visibly uneasy. Haydon was sympathetic. He didn't know what she might have expected, but this certainly wasn't it. He saw her watching Nina. Even for a savvy young woman who was used to operating in the fast lanes of the Post Oak world, Nina was a class act that definitely had a humbling effect.

Haydon himself was not entirely at ease. He was well aware that Dystal had gone far beyond the jurisdiction of official license in letting him operate in the way he had, and sooner or later was going to have to explain—exactly, or with a considerable strain on the truth—how all this new material had come to him from outside the official investigation being organized by Lapierre. It was possible to attribute a great deal to "tips," but this wasn't going to fit. He and Dystal would have to work it out.

"Celia," Haydon said, "I've told Lieutenant Dystal only a little background regarding your situation, so I want you to start at the beginning, just as you did with me. Try to present as much detail as possible." He glanced at her. "I'm going to record this. It's standard practice. There's simply no way we can remember it all otherwise, and we want to have something to reference when we ask you questions later."

"Fine," she said. "But I've got one question." She looked a little apprehensive, yet determined, as if she were going to ask the question even though it might be inappropriate at this point. "Where does this put me with the FBI? I mean, couldn't this be construed as giving some kind of evidence against them? Can't they prosecute me for this? Where do I stand if there's a federal-state conflict over this?"

Haydon glanced at Dystal again. The lieutenant's eyes were settled on the girl as if the rest of the room did not exist. Celia's reference to the FBI had concentrated his attention. He wasn't going to miss anything about this woman, and when she was through talking to them he would have very strong opinions about her story, and about Celia Moreno.

"I don't think there's any conflict here, Celia," Haydon said. "I'll tell you why later. Right now I'll give you my personal guarantee you're not going to get yourself in legal trouble by talking to us." It was a guarantee that meant nothing. Dystal didn't flinch.

Haydon got up and turned on the recording system. A microphone sat on a small vitrine between them so it could pick up all their voices. He stated the date, the circumstances, and the people present at the interview.

"Okay, Celia. Go ahead."

chapter 36

Blas Medrano drove back to La Colombe d'Or and went up to his suite. It was shortly after eight o'clock when he sat down at the desk in the living area and picked up the telephone book. He looked under railroads, Southern Pacific Transportation Company. There were several numbers listed, so he called the general offices. There was a recording saying the office was closed and giving the hours it was open and numbers that could be called for passenger service, freight service, and the roadmaster's office for reporting repairs.

Before dialing he made a few notes about the questions he needed answered, mentally going through the mechanics of his plan. Then he picked up the telephone.

"Roadmaster's office." The woman sounded like a dispatcher, or a switchboard operator.

"Yeah, I need to speak to somebody about repairin' a track at a street crossin'," he said. He slipped into a heavy Chicano speech pattern, knowing he wasn't going to be able to disguise his Mexican inflections anyway, and that in the subsequent investigations a less distinguished voice would simply be described as Mexican.

"Which crossing is that, sir?"

"Oh, the place where it crosses Richmond," he said, looking at his map.

There was a second's pause. "That'll be Mr. Branard's division. Hold on, I'll connect you."

Another woman answered.

"This is Lisa Welch."

"Yes. I would like to ask some questions about how you repair your street crossin's?"

"How?"

"Yeah. You know, like do you check them crossin's at regular times, or do you just fix them when they need it, or when somebody reports it, or what?"

"You want to report a crossing that needs repairing, sir?" She was a little testy.

"I just wanted to know how you handle it."

"Look, you don't want to report something wrong?"

He could tell she wasn't going to be easy to deal with, so he had to explain.

"Lady, I'm sorry to bother you." He tried to sound contrite. "But if you're not to bissy I would like to ask a few questions." He heard her sigh dramatically, but he went right on. "See, I'm kind of a railroad buff, you know. I been in a wheelchair ever since I was in Vietnam. While I was gettin' over it I used to sit by this window all the time. I was near this railroad track so I started watchin' the trains coming and going and the work crews, and all that. I got some binoculars, and watched those guys all the time. I could tell you everything that went on along those tracks, you know. I memorized the numbers of the engines so I could tell how many times they went east or west, learned the switchin' schedules, the different kinds of things they carried. You know, caliche, oil, cattle. Different kinds of cars. Longest train ever went by there wass one hundred sixty-eight cars. Anyway, see, I just moved here from Laredo and I don't know nothing about your routines here. Man, I knew everything down there. So I was just wonderin' about your work crews. It's just a hobby, you know, 'cause I'm in this wheelchair. I ain't got nothin' else to do."

There was a pause. Blas could imagine what was going through the woman's mind. He would be surprised if she hung up on him now.

"Yeah, well, okay," she said finally. She didn't want to be a bitch to a man who couldn't walk. If his legs had been good she would already have hung up on him. "What is it . . . what do you want to know?"

"You sure you have time right now . . . I mean . . ."

"Oh, yeah. It's okay."

"Thass great. Okay, in Laredo I used to watch them so much I knew everything about the repair crews, too, just like the engineers. How many they had on each shift, the color of their uniforms. One crew had women on it. Worked just like the men, you know. Did all right, too. Drove these big ol' green trucks with the name of the railroad on the side in yellow letters: Santa Fe Railroad Company. Your people drive special trucks, and have uniforms too?"

"Okay, I see. Yeah, the crews drive orange dump trucks. Usually there's three or four on a crew. A couple of patching men, a flagman, the crew chief. No women, though."

"They wear uniforms?"

"No, no uniforms."

"Do you always drive those big trucks? I mean, if they're working there the big truck's there too, huh?"

"Oh, yeah. They have to have them because of the asphalt."

"How many shifts you guys have here?"

"Only one. Seven in the morning until three o'clock in the afternoon."

"No kiddin'? I thought you'd have a night shift."

"No one works on the tracks after three in the afternoon."

"Man, I wouldn't have thought that in a big city like this. I used to see 'em workin' at night in Laredo. It was fun watchin' them through the binoculars at night with their lights. It was like a movie. I was hopin' to see some night crews here, too."

"The only time they work at night here is if it's a real emergency that holds up traffic or something, or the signal crews get called out."

"The signal crews?"

"Yeah, the signal crews work anytime they're called," she said. "If there's something wrong with the signals at those crossings they have to be fixed whenever they break, no matter when it is. You can't have a gate that doesn't go down, or flashers that don't work. Those things break we have to repair them right away. That's a safety thing."

"Yeah, you can't let that happen. How many people on a signal crew?"

"Just two."

"They drive big drump trucks, too?"

"No, they don't have any big equipment. Just electrical stuff, small tools. We've got those S-10 Chevys for those guys. You know, those little pickups."

"Oh, yeah. They have the railroad name on the side, too?"

"No. They don't put any name on those."

"So they just show up at the track and start workin', huh?"

"Well, yeah."

"Do they put up those sawhorses or anything?"

"No, one of the guys just flags the traffic."

"No uniforms either?"

"No. Well, they wear those yellow hard hats and bright orange plastic safety bibs, but that's it."

"That's interestin'." Blas was hurriedly making notes. He glanced over them, trying to see what else he should ask. "Well, I will know what to look for. I really get a kick out of watchin' those guys. I got real strong binoculars. Sometimes I can even see what it is they're doin'."

"That's good," Lisa said. "Anything else?"

"No, I guess not right now. Maybe I'll call back sometime."

"That'll be fine."

"Thanks a lot for takin' the time to talk to me. Have a good evenin'."

"You too," Lisa said. Her voice was a lot cheerier. She had done something that fell into the "good deed" category.

Blas studied his notes, then looked at his watch. He picked up the radio, called Rubio, and told him he would meet him at one of the parking lots near the Medical Center. Hurriedly, he packed the RDX in one side of one of the larger suitcases, placed the switchboard on the other, and put the Futaba radio transmitter in the canvas airline bag. He walked over to the small mahogany table and poured a dash of brandy. It was still burning in his throat when he walked out the door carrying the two bags.

They found a car rental agency on the Southwest Freeway that had the small Chevrolet pickups they needed. Blas transferred his bags to the pickup, and Rubio followed him to Sharpstown, where he stopped at a large discount store. Rubio watched the pickup while Blas went inside and bought hard hats, gray work overalls, flashlights with orange lens cones, battery-operated roadside amber safety flashers, a pick and shovel, a large gray toolbox, an assortment of electrician's tools, and leather electrician's bags to hold them.

The intersection where the Southern Pacific railroad tracks crossed San Felipe seemed at first to be a highly inappropriate location for what Blas wanted to accomplish. First of all, it was only a little more than a block from the eastern edge of the exclusive business complex of Post Oak Park, and the elegant Remington Hotel located in the park's southeastern corner. The West Loop Freeway was a couple of blocks beyond, with apartment buildings on the left and an Exxon service station adjacent to them where San Felipe went under the freeway overpass on its way to intersect Post Oak Boulevard a few blocks farther on. Directly overlooking the crossing from the west side of the Loop was a towering mountain range of office buildings, 3D International, Control Data, West Loop Place, West Loop Tower; and to the right was the looming column of Five Oak Place. In short, it was a high-profile area.

But in addition to its being the most frequently crossed intersection in Benigo Gamboa's weekly itinerary, it was precisely this prominent visibility that attracted Blas. It was an area of assumed security, and assumptions like that were the terrorist's gift from a complacent society.

They passed over the tracks several times, Blas in the truck, Rubio in the rental car, each appraising the crossing from different perspectives. Blas had spent nearly a thousand dollars for his transmitter alone, almost all of that price to acquire a special feature called pulse code modulation which converted the radio signals to a digital, binary code. One of the gravest hazards of remote-control transmitters was that the receivers were highly susceptible to signals from sources other than the intended transmitter. This risk was greatly reduced by the PCM feature which enabled the receiver to reject most "dirty" transmissions on a given frequency, and minimized the loss of control problems caused by adjacent and direct band interference. But it only reduced the risk. It didn't eliminate it. From the moment he set the explosive in place and turned on the receiver, there was the chance it could be inadvertently detonated by an errant, stronger signal.

By ten-thirty, the traffic had slowed considerably, and they drove to the underground parking garage in the Galleria and changed into the clothes Blas had bought earlier. While Rubio drove, Blas began wiring together the bricks of RDX, two in one bundle, three in another. He did not connect the two bundles, deciding to make that final connection after the bundles were in place.

It was almost eleven o'clock when Rubio slowed the pickup at the crossing, pulled off on the shoulder, then turned parallel with the tracks and stopped beside the signals with his left-side wheels on the caliche bedding. Blas got out and quickly used a screwdriver to wrench open the control box. He did not disconnect the wires. They didn't want to be caught by surprise. Rubio got the pick and shovel out of the back of the truck while Blas hung a few dead wires out of the control box for effect.

In his computation of Ireno López's surveillance records, Blas had determined that Gamboa had traveled west over this crossing nearly twice as many times as he had traveled east, usually taking advantage of one of the other east-west arteries to return to Inverness. He had decided, then, to put all of the explosives between the ties in the westbound lane. Rubio placed the amber flashers in the center of the lane, screwed the orange lens over his flashlight, and diverted the occasional car while Blas began digging out the caliche from between the ties.

Only minutes after beginning, his clothes were clinging to him like cellophane. He tried to ignore the idea of suffocating. The caliche bedding had not been replaced in a long time and was packed tight. Blas had to use the pick every inch of the way. Pick, then shovel the loose dirt, then pick again. Luckily, he didn't have to dig far below the surface. The white chalky earth covered the new low-cut street shoes, falling in the gap at his instep until the insides were filled with crumbly clods. His feet kept slipping on the slope of the caliche bed.

Rubio paced back and forth, never saying a word. Sometimes when there were several cars in a row, he would wave them around, get the line of them started, and then walk over to the control box and pretend to work with the wiring, looking back at Blas as if they were coordinating their tasks. The only thing they had to worry about was someone coming along in one of the darkened cars who actually knew how the crossing lights functioned, and might notice that what Blas was doing bore no relationship at all to the flasher control box. There was no need to be digging between the rails and ties.

He did not put the explosive in containers, but dug the holes in the shape of inverted cones and molded the plastic to fit, thereby guiding the direction of the blast. The tightly packed caliche bedding of the track was the perfect repository for the explosive. All the force of the charge would be concentrated within an eighteen-to-twenty-four-inch zone directing the charge upward. It would be as close to the car as possible without actually being attached to the chassis.

By eleven-forty, they were almost through. Blas, drenched in sweat under the hot coveralls and his arms trembling from the hurried digging, covered the explosives with an inch of caliche and ran the wire connecting the two cones under the rail tie to avoid possible accidental severance. He had brought a lot of lead wire, and now began stringing it along under the rail on the east side of the track toward a slope and a stand of brown, sun-parched Johnsongrass. It was the nearest cover large enough to hide the toolbox which would contain the receiver and switch.

The traffic had slowed to only an occasional car now. Blas walked to the pickup, leaned over the sides of the bed, and transferred the receiver and switchboard from the airline bag to the empty toolbox, from which he had already removed the shelving. The rigid toolbox provided excellent protection for the moving parts on the board. When he had the board set as he wanted it, he turned on the receiver and ran two lead wires out of the bottom corner of the box, which he then locked. There was no risk until he connected the lead wires to the wires coming from the explosives. He lifted the box out of the truck and walked off toward the Johnsongrass. In less than three minutes he had connected the lead wires to the RDX with plastic screw caps. The explosives were now live. He made sure the grass completely hid the box before he hurried back to the truck.

Within another ten minutes, they had loaded everything

back into the bed of the pickup, put the crossing signal box back in order, and double-checked the caliche around the plastic explosive. They had left the Southern Pacific Railroad crossing at San Felipe near East Briar Hollow Lane primed with enough explosive to rattle all the windows in the Remington Hotel when it was detonated. They drove off, and never looked back.

Chapter 37

During Celia Moreno's recitation, neither Dystal nor Haydon took notes. They had come to rely on the transcriptions of interview recordings for future reference, and besides, there weren't likely to be many details of any importance that either of them would forget. Several times during the forty minutes she talked, Haydon glanced at Dystal. The bearish lieutenant never once took his eyes off her and had let almost all of the ice melt in his drink before he reached out and took his first sip.

Celia Moreno sat up straight in her chair as she talked, her feet together, with her dress falling over her knees to the floor. She held her drink in her hands, resting on her knees. Her story was more smoothly told this time, and she astutely incorporated answers to all of the questions Haydon had asked earlier. From time to time she would stop talking to sip her drink, or she would cut her eyes at Nina, not apprehensively or defensively, Haydon thought, but rather as one woman looking to another for some kind of tacit feminine alliance under the steady, uninterpretable stares of the two detectives to whom she was talking.

When she finally finished, Dystal, who also had been leaning forward in his red leather wing chair, straightened up and settled back, drinking from his glass with several relished gulps as if it were water, not liquor. His eyes continued to rest on her for a while, and then he turned them to Haydon.

"Well, this clears up a lot of stuff," he said, with a dry wink at Haydon. She had raised as many questions as she had answered. He shook his head, then turned to Celia again. "Miss Moreno, what was the post office box number you mailed your reports to?"

"Box 1821, Main Station."

"Uh-huh. And this Rich Elkin fella was the only contact you ever had with them?"

"Yes."

"Did he ever show you any identification, any proof that he was employed by the Federal Bureau of Investigation?"

It was a moment before she spoke, though the answer required no thought. She obviously had realized the implications of her response long before tonight.

"No," she said. "I'm afraid not."

"Uh-huh. Well, do you happen to have a picture of Mr. Elkin?"

"No," she said again. "I don't."

Dystal smiled kindly. "Well, it's not like it used to be. People don't exchange pictures anymore. Life clips along too fast." He wanted to ease back on her. He had no wish to embarrass her or make her any more uneasy than she already was.

"Tell me," he said then. "After you got on your own, did he ever make any comments on those reports? Do you think he ever saw 'em?"

She thought a minute. "I don't know if he saw them, but after we learned that Ireno López had arrived in Houston, he called me twice on the telephone—he had already 'disappeared' at that time—and told me 'they' were wanting to know if I had any more details since my last report."

"Uh-huh." Dystal nodded thoughtfully.

"You said Elkin dropped out of the sight several weeks ago. Do you have any idea why that was?" Dystal asked.

"No."

"Where's he live?"

"I don't know, now," Celia said, her tone slightly embarrassed again. "I knew when we were dating, but, well, he grew more and more distant after I started doing the reports, and I didn't see him as much. Then one time I tried to call him, and got a recording that the telephone had been disconnected. I called information, but he wasn't listed."

"Uh-huh. You ask him about that next time he called you?"

"Yes. He just said he was going through some 'life changes' and he wanted to be left alone. He pretty well cut me off. I never heard from him anymore except for those telephone calls."

Dystal finished his drink and declined an offer of another.

"Miss Moreno," he said slowly, "when you went down in Old Mexico to visit the *teco* people, you stayed a week or so, is that right?"

"Yes. In fact it was a week."

"And you met a lot of their people?"

"Yes."

"Well, tomorrow we're gonna ask you to write up a little report of that trip for us. A kind of debriefing. Like for you to give us as many names, descriptions, things like that, as you can. It would be a big help to us. Mr. Haydon's got a typewriter and a CRT here that you can use. Okay?"

Celia Moreno nodded.

"Now, your first item in this little project is going to be to give us everything you know about the *tecos de choque*. Right? I mean rumors, hints, maybe-type thoughts, anything that goes through your mind that we might work a wedge into. Know what I mean?"

Celia nodded again.

"We need it as soon as possible."

Another nod.

"That's good. I appreciate your help, Miss Moreno," he said, standing with a restrained grunt. "I'm sure we're going to be talking some more. Stu," he said, turning to Haydon, "you got another telephone around here I can use?"

"Sure. We can go into the living room."

The two men excused themselves, and Dystal walked out into the hall. Haydon paused beside Nina and asked her to make a copy of the tape for Dystal, then followed the lieutenant around to the living room. When they got inside, Dystal squared his huge frame to face Haydon.

"Okay. Now I want to hear *everything*. Don't leave anything out, Stu. Not anymore."

Haydon turned and closed the double doors to the living room. While both men stood, he started talking, beginning with the first half hour after he left Dystal's office the day before when he went to see Mitchell Garner for the first time.

He told him about Renata Islas, his brief encounter with Lucas Negrete, about copying Cordero's address book, talking to Celia Moreno for the first time, working out Cordero's code and going to La Concha Courts, then to Waite's house, to Gamboa's to see Negrete, and then picking up Celia Moreno.

During the course of Haydon's account, Dystal had listened with his arms folded, his head bent down as he looked at the toes of his Nacona boots. Haydon paced, walking to the windows to look out to the lawn lights, to the ebony grand piano where he unconsciously touched some of the picture frames, to a collection of red Conté drawings above the fireplace, and back again.

Dystal had finally sat down on the heavy divan of Haitian cotton by the time Haydon finished. Haydon sat on the piano stool and looked across at him.

"Well, I can't say you didn't make a lot of mileage on your own," Dystal said. "It wouldn't have happened just that way otherwise. That damned little old notebook was the key. We sure as hell missed that."

"Celia Moreno has saved us a lot of time," Haydon said. "We could have spent weeks trying to clear up some of that."

"Yeah, we never would've got anywhere without that gal," Dystal conceded. "This is the biggest mess I've seen in a long time. We got dead people scattered from here to Hondo and this little thing comes in here and tells us all about it like it was office gossip." He narrowed one eye at Haydon. "Who the hell you suppose she's been feeding all this to?"

"Not the FBI."

"No, of course not, but it'll be easy to check out. If this Rich Elkin is for real, I'm gonna raise old Billy Hell. But I think the gal's been taken for a long ride."

"It was a pretty elaborate setup," Haydon said.

"Yeah," Dystal agreed, "it was." Still looking at Haydon, he said, "You got any guesses?"

Haydon shook his head. "I almost wish it was the Bureau. We might not like what we'd find, but at least we'd have a reasonable assurance it could be dealt with. As it is, I don't know. We're dealing with exiles; with foreign radical groups backed by wealthy men with considerable power. We didn't even know something like the *tecos* existed until yesterday.

Who knows what we'll uncover tomorrow, or two days from now? I don't think we're anywhere close to the source of this thing." He stopped. "But when we get to the bottom of it— if we do—I won't be surprised to find some of our own people."

"Our own people?"

"I think what we're seeing here is only a sideshow, but it may be all of the circus we'll ever be allowed to see. I keep asking myself who would want to monitor, but not influence, the impending assassination of a former cabinet minister of the Mexican government. Especially a notoriously corrupt cabinet minister who could easily have been involved in a lot more than we've uncovered so far. And who would have the expertise to do it the way Celia Moreno has been handled? Does that methodology seem familiar to you?"

Dystal stared at Haydon. "What—you mean State Department?"

"It's occurred to me."

"Goddam, Stu. That's a little hard for me to get a grip on."

The two of them were quiet a minute, Dystal thinking, Haydon wondering just how bizarre his suggestion had sounded to the lieutenant.

Then Dystal said, "Okay, listen, maybe that's a little crazy, but maybe it's not so far wrong either. I'm sure as hell not going to turn down the possibility of anything right now. In the meantime we got to get on with the business at hand here. As soon as I give the Bureau people the tip on the other hit targets, they're gonna want to talk to the girl. You sure you don't want to move her to a motel somewhere? I don't know if they're gonna be satisfied with this deal here."

"Let's just wait and see what develops."

"Fine." Dystal fixed his eyes on the toes of his alligator boots. The one thing on which he was willing to spend a lot of money. "You think this Rubio Arizpe's our man?"

"According to Renata Islas he's been to Texas twice for the same reason."

"I'll tell you what we need to do. We need to get this Islas woman's help on this. Get back with her, maybe get her over here to compare notes with Moreno in there. Get back to her people in Old Mexico who told her about this guy in the first place." Thinking, he propped one boot across a beefy thigh and idly traced a stubby finger over the Spanish stitching. "I'll call the Bureau's hand on this one. Them and the CIA's the boys that's got intelligence operations down in there. We'll put the snake in their britches, and see how they like it. They're supposed to be on top of this terrorist shit."

"And what do you want to do about Negrete in the meantime?" Haydon asked.

"I want that son of a bitch," Dystal said, looking at Haydon. "This ain't Beirut, for God's sake. You told him we were going to keep our nose on him, right?"

Haydon nodded.

"Well, we're gonna do just that. And I'll get somebody over there to get that list you told him you wanted of the names of the boys he's got working for him."

Haydon nodded again.

"I'd like to run about half of 'em off, but we don't know which ones were mixed up in that Waite mess, or the López thing for that matter. We're gonna have to keep an eye on all of them. I'll talk to the DA and see what kind of damn order we can get confining every one of them to Gamboa's place. And I'll set up a task force to work full-time on building a case against Negrete. I told the crime-lab people to take that Waite place apart with a microscope. As long as those people were there, they had to leave something behind. Somewhere in that house we're gonna find some evidence."

"Shouldn't we send the explosives dogs over to Gamboa's?"

"Yeah, we'll do that. Once the dogs give his place a clean bill of health, then it's going to be up to them to keep it that way. If we can get that whole bunch confined to that one place, we'd be getting rid of half our lice in one dose."

"I just hope they haven't already gotten their hands on Ferretis."

"Yeah, me too. That was a big mistake, Stu. When you first got those names you should've given them to us and we could've gone after them all at the same time. Right now I don't see any other way of getting to the bottom of this except through that professor." Dystal grimaced, and made a hissing sound between his teeth. "Goddam. What a mess."

Haydon looked at him. The big lieutenant slumped on the divan.

"Bob," Haydon said, "supposedly all of this has come about as a result of Mexican political 'flight' money. What do you think about those figures I quoted you?"

"Too damn much money."

"Do you believe those figures?"

"I don't know," Dystal said, looking at Haydon with weary eyes. "You trust your source?"

"Explicitly."

"Then I guess I accept the figures. It's hard to understand how a nation of people would settle for that kind of crap from their politicians, though."

"Garner says most of the money came here, to the States," Haydon said.

Dystal sighed heavily, then nodded slowly. "That don't surprise me."

"He says it came in cash, huge shipments of it. Larger than the drug cartels. You couldn't get enough Smurfs to peddle it for you. One, two billion."

Dystal was still, gazing out through the tall windows across from him. Slowly he turned his face to Haydon and said, "You wonderin' about the currency transaction reports?"

"That, and simply the mechanics of any bank accepting millions of dollars in cash. Let's suppose the depositor proved the money was not drug-related. Fifty million, five hundred million, nine hundred million. The logistics are staggering. What did Portillo's people *tell* the bankers? What banks? Don't you suppose they had to be told where it came from? How was it explained? Do you think that with all the nervousness caused by the money-laundering scandals of the drug cartels these last few years, a bank is going to accept that kind of cash without checking with federal authorities? What did the Mexicans tell these authorities—'This is Mr. Portillo's nest egg from the Mexican national treasury'?"

"What does Garner say about it?"

"I didn't really start thinking about it until I'd left him."

The telephone rang, and Haydon got up and walked across to a small rosewood chest and answered it.

"It's for you, Bob."

Dystal pulled himself up off the divan, groaning, and slouched over to the table.

"This's Dystal." He stood with his weight shifted to one side, one of his pants legs caught on the top of a boot. He listened, mumbled a reply, a one- or two-word question.

"Okay," he said. "Every time you get a little biddy fact, let me know. Much obliged."

Dystal turned to Haydon. "Waite worked for the port authority. The lady was his wife, Ruby. Other guy was named Don Farrell. A neighbor says Farrell's got a wife named Cissy. They're trying to find her."

Dystal walked over to the windows, one hand in his pants pocket jiggling change. He stood with his back to Haydon, his shoulders slightly humped under a suit coat that had never fit very well in the first place, too tired to attend to his posture. When he finally turned around, his eyes were sagging with lack of sleep.

"All right, Stu. What do you want to do?"

Haydon was expecting it.

"I'll save us both a lot of time, Bob. I don't want to work under the constraints of departmental procedure. Not on this one."

Dystal rattled his change. "Well, I guess I could see that coming. I'll tell you, Stu, I came over here with the full intention of twisting your tail. This is so far outta line it makes my conscience hurt, goes against my grain." He looked up from under his eyebrows a little apologetically. "My grain gets straighter every year, and a lot less limber. I don't much like to admit things can be done right if they're not done by the rules. The older I get, the better I like rules, Stu. By God, you can't have a decent society without decent rules, and decent people who know what the rules are there for."

This last sentence was spoken with some heat, and Dystal stopped himself abruptly as if he had headed off a verbal stampede just before it got out of control.

"I don't like what you're doing, Stu," he continued. "If we were in a voting situation here, I'd vote against you." He took the hand jiggling change out of his pocket and wiped it over his mouth. Haydon heard the rough rasp of his stubble against his hand. "Fact is, though, we'd be hard up if you hadn't done what you did. I know that."

Dystal looked as if he was trying to find the right words, the right way to frame something else he wanted to say, but couldn't. Then he said, "Don't withhold information from me anymore." He was frowning, his voice hard. "Don't do that anymore. It's going too far." His eyes were searching Haydon's, frankly probing. He raised a massive, heavy hand and pointed an index finger at Haydon. "You let Nina know where you are every minute. I want to be able to get to you *any*time." He lowered his hand. "By God, Stu, be careful."

Haydon was barefooted and shirtless, wearing only his white *calzones* when he walked across the terrace and went down the steps and through the cherry laurels to the bathhouse. He carried a few slices of smoked ham left over from the sandwiches he and Nina and Celia had eaten after Dystal left. And he carried half a bottle of Macon Chardonnay. He never worried anymore about what was good or bad for Cinco. At this point he only thought of what the old collie would like.

The ceiling fan behind the trellis never stopped, day or night, always there to stir the air, hot or cool, heavy or light. Haydon paused a moment to let his eyes adjust to the darker space behind the latticework. Standing with his bare feet on the cool bricks, he could hear the faint, rhythmic swishing of the fan, and occasionally the syncopated breathing of Cinco. He finally saw the lighter outline of the old dog on the bricks and went over and knelt down beside him.

To his surprise, Cinco's eyes were open, watching him. Haydon put down the ham, and the dog's tail swished across the bricks. With Haydon's help, he sat up and ate a few pieces of the ham while Haydon scratched him behind the ears. After a minute or two, Haydon reached over for Cinco's bowl and poured it about a quarter full of the white wine. Cinco turned from the ham and looked at the bowl, started to make a move for it, but Haydon slid it over to him. The old dog proceeded to lap it, ignoring the ham. Haydon grinned. A lifelong habit. He remembered the afternoon he had first poured some wine from his glass for the inquisitive, manic little pup playing around his chair on the terrace. The pup drank every drop of it, and Haydon had laughed and poured more. Out of curiosity Haydon had kept it up—going into the house for the bottle—until the pup had had all he could take. Then he had wobbled off and flopped down in the shade next to the house, where he immediately went to sleep with his nose in the leg of a rubber boot Pablo had left on the terrace. He had lapped up five good slugs of Sauvignon Blanc, and Haydon had named him Cinco. A lifelong habit.

As Cinco lapped beside him now, Haydon drank from the bottle. Now that his eyes had adjusted, he could see that he and Cinco sat in a cross-hatch pattern of pale light as the late July moon, full and still rising, slipped through the lattice in powder-blue diamonds.

"Stuart." The voice was soft, and the diamonds rippled in the moving shadow as Nina passed the trellis and came around the side.

"Right here," he said.

She stood at the end of the trellis, as he had done, letting her eyes adjust. The moon backlighted her gown, and he saw that she was naked, the silk a misty aura.

"I can hear Cinco drinking," she said.

"He preferred it to the ham."

"Has he got water over there? That ham's going to make him awfully thirsty when he gets around to eating it."

"Yes."

"I see you now." She came over slowly, an arm out touching the lattice, feeling with her feet almost as if she were wading through black water, careful of sharp stones and the unbalancing force of the current. She reached out a hand and touched his shoulder, and held on as she lowered herself beside him.

"Did you make sure the alarm system is on?"

"It's on."

"I'd hate for her to slip out."

"Why would she do that?"

"I don't know. You want a sip?"

She took it from him and drank a little, then handed it back. They sat side by side, covered in pale diamonds.

"She seems like a nice girl," Nina said.

Instantly Haydon's mind entertained an image of her naked on the sofa with Valverde. Doing whatever Valverde wanted.

"She does, doesn't she."

"It's hard to imagine her mixed up in this the way she is. In an assassination."

"She's not mixed up in the assassination."

"But I mean, knowing about it. She didn't seem even to realize how serious her position was."

Haydon thought of her position on the sofa.

"She knew what she was doing," he said.

"But she seems so demoralized by all that's happened. Her brother being killed like that. She's been through a lot. She doesn't seem all that well prepared to handle it."

"She probably isn't," Haydon said. "I see that kind of thing a lot. People—more people all the time—like the idea of stepping over the line. They like to think of it as 'living on the edge.' They think if life gets boring they're being cheated out of something. They think they owe themselves more than that. When it all finally blows up in their faces they're devastated. They can't believe it's happening to them. It wasn't supposed to ever end."

Nina reached across, took the Macon again, drank from the bottle, and handed it back. She laced her right arm through his, and they sat together, their legs crossed and pulled up in front of them, she leaning against him now.

"Somehow I can't think of her being motivated only by the excitement," Nina said. "Maybe at first, but I think it changed for her."

"Maybe you're right," he said. And he was beginning to think she was. Despite his inclination to be cynical about her, he had to grant that Celia Moreno had been through an ordeal that would have badly shaken even a professional. And she was dealing with it; she hadn't completely fallen apart. She *had* thought she was working within the right system. It hadn't been a thoughtless lark. He didn't have any right to be pompous about her motivations.

They were quiet, and Cinco finished his wine, pushing the bowl away from him as he licked it. Haydon pushed it back to him and poured some more. Cinco didn't begin drinking immediately, but sat still, blinking drowsily. Then after a minute he began lapping again.

"Do you find her attractive?"

Haydon was surprised. "Very much so," he said.

"Well, that's honest," she said, a flatness in her voice. "I apologize for having forced it out of you."

Haydon grinned, and nudged her. "You didn't want me to lie, did you?" He looked at her, and could see her smiling silhouette.

After a minute she said, "What about Bob? What happened there?"

"We left it like it was." He knew she was going to be disappointed to hear that.

"But what about her? Shouldn't she be in official custody?"

"I suspect she is."

"What do you mean?"

"I don't know how Bob's going to handle this, but it's my guess he's done something tricky, like officially putting me back on duty without telling me. That way he can tell the people above him that he's given me a special assignment regarding this case. I don't know, I imagine he and Captain Mercer have cooked up something along those lines. Whatever it is, you can bet he's calculated the risks."

"They seem like they would be pretty big risks, to me."

"The pressure he's feeling from the administration and politicians to have this thing closed out carries a hell of a lot more weight than any reprimand he might receive for letting me work like this. He's taking his best shot. It isn't made any easier by having the FBI breathing down his neck, either."

"That's the part that's bothering me," Nina said, as if she had been waiting for him to get around to it.

"What?"

"Her story about her reports. I don't know where the deception lies, whether someone is lying to her, or whether she's lying to you."

"And the question in either case is, why?"

Cinco had quit drinking again, lain down, and gone back to sleep.

"I don't know how long he can go on like this," Haydon said, looking at the old collie. "I wonder if his days and nights run together, or if he even cares."

"Is he asleep?"

"I don't know. Seems like it."

She took the wine again and lifted it to drink. Haydon looked at her and saw the pallid light coming through the lattice, striking the sloping neck of the bottle and refracting, chasing the curve of the green glass that didn't appear green in the night, but black, the light like liquid pearl scribing the body of the bottle. She gave it back.

They sat amid the soft sounds and small movements of the summer night, not talking now, passing the bottle back and forth between them. Haydon relished this, and thought how grateful he was to her for coming out when she had, and wondered how she had sensed that it would be the right thing to do. He didn't know how long they had sat there, but it was long enough for his mind to have ranged and prowled in places he wanted, and didn't want, to be. He fought off images of Mooney that too often jumped into his thoughts now, like single discontinuous frames spliced into a film where they didn't belong. Mooney might appear at any time, or rather Mooney's corpse, bleeding, suddenly, as Haydon read the paper, or shaved, or stopped at a traffic light, or worse, at awkward times that made him wonder about his sanity.

The angle of the moon had changed.

Nina had the bottle, drinking, then she lowered it and handed it to him.

"You can have the last of it," she said, dabbing a finger at the bottom of her lip where she had spilled some. "I think I can understand why you like it."

He was drinking when she said it, and didn't understand at first, because he was tasting the wine. A drop of sweat from the bottle hit his bare chest, cold, and ran down toward his navel.

"Or rather, I can 'reason' why you like it," she added. "I don't really understand it."

Haydon laid the bottle on its side next to the trellis and looked at her. She was facing straight ahead, her eyes reaching out to the varieties of darkness in the cherry laurels and lime trees, her silhouette broken by the diamonds, a strand of hair at her forehead dodging in the wind currents whipped downward by the blades of the fan.

"I've always thought of you as a private person," she continued. "Holding yourself in, finding it difficult to offer yourself to someone else. But I think I was wrong. In a sense, you *do* give yourself away. I mean when you're working. You leave yourself, and try to crawl into someone else's mind, try to become them, so you can know about them what they don't want you to know. The sad thing—sad to me, at least—is that you're giving yourself to the kind of people who don't want you. They're fugitive spirits, people in emotional flight. You're always trying to get close to people who are constantly pushing you away. It's the nature of the roles you play. You seem to be drawn to that kind of situation, for some reason." She paused. "But I'd never thought of it that way before."

Haydon continued looking at her silhouette, the slope of her forehead, which was almost Indian. "What made you think about that?" he asked.

She didn't say anything.

"Come on," he said. He stood, then pulled her to her feet, and holding hands, they walked out of the arbor of the bathhouse, through the path of cherry laurels, and onto the grass in the moonlight. It was warmer on the lawn than sitting directly under the bathhouse fan. The moon was so bright it threw shadows under the trees, and so large it could not for a moment be forgotten. They skirted the orchard of lime trees, whose heavy fragrance hung in the shadows, scenting the air. Turning out of the trees, they crossed a stretch of rising lawn, to the sprawling canopy of a flamboyana. By a trick of night vision the moonlight had shattered, fallen through the filigree of tropical leaves, and lay on the lawn in pointillistic luminosity, a counterpoint pattern of the flamboyana's shadow.

They stopped, standing on the splinters of light, and Haydon moved the silk off her shoulders and let it fall of its own liquid weight to the grass. They lay there, and he touched her, the long, dusky grace of her, and was grateful to her again for being what she was. Breathing in her smell, he kissed her, saw the pieces of the moon coming up through her from the grass so that in those places she was translucent. It was a blue moon, that rare lunar occurrence of every two or three years, the second full moon in a single month, and they lay on the pieces of it, unafraid of its penetrating light.

Chapter 39

Daniel Ferretis slumped in the driver's seat of the old Volvo so that only his eyes showed above the door and looked out the lowered window to the pale-lighted parking garage. He was sweating profusely, from fear and heat, and his heavy eyeglasses kept sliding down on his small nose. It didn't do any good simply to push them up with a practiced shove of his middle finger, because the bridge was so oily they slid down immediately. He had to take them off and wipe them dry with the tail of his *guayabera*. The tail was the only part of it that was dry. The rest of it was soaked with perspiration and clung to his white, flabby flesh like cellophane. But he wasn't complaining. Considering the afternoon's events that had led to his being here, he was fortunate that he was still around to sweat at all.

By a stroke of bad luck, he was having to teach one course in the second semester of summer school. It was a required sophomore course, and no one was in there because he was interested in it. Like swallowing nasty-tasting medicine, they simply wanted it over with. And so did he; he had other preoccupations. To make matters worse, it was a midafternoon class. A down time of day for him, especially in the heat of the summer. So they agreed to agree, and every day he showed up at class, handed out several sheets of information that they should memorize for the test at the end of the week, and after asking if there were any questions—there never were—he dismissed class.

That was the way it had been until today. He had noticed

the girl the first day, not for what she had, but for what she didn't have. She did not have large, round breasts. She did not have a nice round ass. She did not have blond hair, or black hair, or auburn hair, but weak, lusterless straw hair the color of old newspapers. In short, she was not a candidate for grade-point improvement in private consultation. Today when he had asked if there were any questions, she had timidly but resolutely raised her thin little arm.

It took him twenty minutes to answer her. Not because he was verbose, but she had a follow-up question, and then another, and another. He responded with restrained patience—she *could* have been an administrative spy—and gave her her money's worth, which the little bitch seemed determined to get. Whereas he usually was back in his office fifteen minutes after convening class, today he had gotten back thirty-five minutes later, and just in time to round the corner of the hallway where his office was located and see two men standing at his office door. One was bent over the lock, picking it, and the other was keeping watch, though in the split second it took Ferretis to see and understand what was happening and to jump back, the man on guard was looking down the hall in the opposite direction.

Ferretis ran down the stairs, across the yard separating Erby Hall from the building north of it, and climbed to the second floor, where he searched for an empty classroom on the south side. When he found one, he locked the door behind him and glued himself to the windows, after closing the Venetian blinds to a sliver of visibility, from where he could see both entrances to Erby Hall. His heart was throwing a fit, and his side hurt from running. He hadn't run that much in fifteen years. He probed his potbelly, wishing he had continued his long-abandoned routine of riding the stationary bicycle in the garage.

The two men were in the building half an hour, but it seemed like the rest of the afternoon. It was long enough for him to imagine that these two men might well fit into any number of scenarios that would herald the beginning of the end. He was not an excitable man, but that was not to say that he was incapable of getting excited. Now he was dumbfounded. They knew about him. Really, he had never thought he would be connected to this. He had planned it so carefully.

So cleverly. They? He didn't know who they were. Still, he was surprised *anyone* suspected. But there could be no other explanation. Why else would someone break into his office?

When the men emerged from the east end of the building, he flinched. He got a good look at them, and then rushed to the door, plowing, stumbling through desks, leaving a wake of them behind. He lurched down the stairs and outside onto the mall, which was, luckily, busy. He spotted them immediately, and followed them through the crowds of students from fifty yards back. When they entered one of the parking lots, he took a shortcut across to the exit and was there, crouching and looking at them through the windows of the surrounding cars when they drove out. He noted the license-plate number.

A quick call from a pay telephone in the nearby student union building to the state motor vehicle division told him that the car was registered to a Mr. Ramón Sosa Real.

He didn't return to his office. He didn't do anything for nearly fifteen minutes while he tried to calm down, tried to decide what to do next. If Negrete knew where his office was, then he would know almost everything else too. Where he lived. What kind of car he drove.

This last problem he settled by putting another quarter in the telephone and calling Lucinda Breman, a rangy, long-legged, high-hipped fellow professor whose office was just down the hall from his. He told her his car had had to be hauled to the shop, and he was without wheels for a couple of days. Could he borrow her second one? Lucinda's husband, Cliff, had recently run off with another woman, leaving her with her credit-card accounts run up to the limit, an apartment she couldn't afford on her salary alone, and his 1968 Volvo with a broken air conditioner.

She picked him up at a gas station a block from campus—he told her that's where his car had been towed from—and took him to her apartment. She had started talking about her "situation" on the way, and by the time they got there and he went up with her to get the keys, she was in tears, and astonished him by suddenly and without preamble beginning to undress, weeping and undressing, pleading with him to go to bed with her. He felt as if he were watching a movie, that it was happening to someone else. It was an odd experience, having intercourse with a sobbing woman who nevertheless managed to whip herself up to a surprising frenzy of passion that he wouldn't have expected of her in even the most ideal circumstances. Afterward, she conjured up another kind of passion, screaming for him to get out, standing naked on her bed, throwing his clothes at him, then staggering to a clothes chest and throwing Cliff's clothes at him, too. He dressed in the living room, tying his shoes as he listened to her bawling in the bedroom. Then he took the keys off the dining-room table and left.

The Volvo's gas tank was empty, of course. Cliff really was a bastard. He filled it at the self-serve pumps of an Exxon station, spilling some gasoline on his shoes, soaking one of them, but finally getting the little latch that kept the nozzle running to hold while he walked over to the pay telephone and called home. He told Melva he was going to be late, something about curriculum staff meetings. It didn't matter what he said. He lied to her all the time and she accepted everything.

The next thing he did was to try to get in touch with Blas Medrano. Cordero was gone, so that left only himself and Blas and Rubio. Since he had no idea where Blas was, the dead drop was the only means of communication. He needed to know if Blas knew anything about this latest development. Now he could see that he had been wrong to think Haydon's knowledge of Rubio Arizpe's existence hadn't been important enough to relay to Blas through the dead drop. Now he had twice as much reason to use it. There had been a leak somewhere. He needed to know if Blas himself had been taken.

They had selected one of the parking garages on a quiet street in the area north of Hermann Park. On the northeast corner of the garage there was a landscaped area between the curb and the garage itself in which grew a cluster of palmettos. Next to the palmettos was a cement post, a hexagonal stele left over from the 1940s, which held the street sign, and which was girded with two metal bands to discourage cracking. If there was to be a message in the dead drop, a small piece of paper folded in a triangle would be placed in the higher of the two metal bands. The message itself would be on the second floor of the garage, wedged between the cement pillar and the wall of parking space 28.

Ferretis drove to the designated dead drop and circled the block, the ratty Volvo interior filled with the heavy, resinous odor of gasoline from his soaked shoes. He saw nothing on the cement post, even after circling the block a second time and gazing down at the ground beneath the sign in case the paper triangle had accidentally fallen from its signal perch. But there was nothing. Okay. He then drove to Hermann Park and stopped the Volvo under the shade of a catalpa tree. Looking around in the car he found a steno pad in the back seat and ripped out a sheet of paper. As he reached for the felt-tip pen he always carried in his *guayabera*, he realized with a jolt that he couldn't code the message. The code key was hidden in his garage at home. And he sure as hell couldn't risk going by there to get it. He hesitated. Shit! Well, it couldn't be helped. There wasn't that much time left. He had to take the chance. Christ. Everything was falling apart. He starting scribbling the message to Blas.

C fled to Mexico. Police know A is involved and looking for him. Negrete's men broke into my office and looking for me. Cannot go home. Has there been a leak? Need to know. Be careful. Am floating until I hear from you. F.

It took him only moments to write the message. The sweat from his hands smeared some of the ink as he fumbled with the paper, folding it, but it was perfectly legible. He was so slick with perspiration he began to smell a dank odor overriding that of the gasoline. It was not the stench of body odor—for some reason, chemical he guessed, he had never had that problem—but something like the smell of damp wool.

He jerked his eyes up from the paper. Jesus Christ, he thought suddenly. What a ludicrous idea. Wool was a neglected commodity in Houston, certainly in July. There wasn't any smell besides the gasoline. What in the hell was the matter with him? Was this the way it started, reality and hallucination jumping back and forth across their boundaries, short-circuiting? Was he losing his grip on this? Could he trust himself? Jesus. He couldn't start thinking like that now. He wouldn't let himself.

Looking down at the paper again, he tried to think if there

was anything else he should have said in the message. He decided not. Anything more would have sounded unprofessional. He tore another sheet of paper from Cliff's notebook and folded it into a triangle, reminding him at this moment, but never before, of those little hats his older brother used to make for him out of folded newspapers. Closing the car door, which he had opened to dissipate his collection of odors and, he hoped, to catch a stray wisp of air, he started the car and drove back to the garage. He circled the block clockwise this time, so he would be in the lane next to the landscaping. He stopped and got out, leaving the Volvo running as he stood on his toes and jammed the paper triangle into the metal band.

The only drawback to having a dead drop in a parking garage was that it cost you a minimum of $1.25 every time you delivered or picked up a message. He took his ticket from the machine, waited for the arm to rise, and drove up to the second floor. A car was parked in space 28, so he stopped, left the Volvo idling again, and slipped the folded note behind the pillar, making sure it couldn't be seen from the aisle, making sure it was wedged tightly and wouldn't fall out. When he got back into the car he drove up to the top floor and found an empty parking space facing downtown. He had paid for an hour anyway, and he had nowhere to go. In fact, it was best if he stayed "hidden."

The top floor was almost empty, and he found a parking space with empty spaces on either side so he could open the front doors on the Volvo once again. He stared across the tops of the trees to the stalagmites of downtown. He needed to take stock. What the hell had happened? All of a sudden everything was falling apart. What did he really think were his odds of coming out of this unscathed? Always before, when he had imagined the aftermath of the assassination, he had pictured himself opening the newspaper the next morning and reading about it. Of all the city's inhabitants, only he would know the truth. Smugly, he would follow the investigation in the newspapers and on television, knowing the heady feeling of true, anonymous power. The man behind the scenes. The highest position of real authority.

But now he could more easily imagine something else. Constant fear. Unceasing tension. Sleepless nights. Unrelenting insecurity. Six months ago he had had no doubts that he would get away with it, but now, when he might be only hours away from accomplishing what he had planned, thought about, and desired for so long, it seemed to him that his connection to the affair might be the news on the front page instead of the assassination.

He was ashamed at his sudden pessimism, his—so obvious—fear. It seemed now, at the first sign of trouble, he was turning into a whimperer.

The next question: How much time would he have, after the assassination? That was easy to answer: He would have no way of knowing. Perhaps he had planned it wrong all along. Perhaps he was naive to think he could continue to live as he had always lived, the brains behind the perfect political assassination. It seemed obvious now that he should leave with Blas and Rubio. Only a fool would stay behind. It was smart, cunning, to leave. Strike, and then flight. Isn't that what they were doing? Of course.

Then he thought of the obvious once again. If he had to get in touch with Blas, why leave a note? Why not wait in person? He could talk with Blas when he came to make the pickup. It was stupid to send messages when he could simply talk to him.

He slammed the doors of the Volvo, started the car, and roared to the down ramp, descending to the second level. Finding a spot with a clear view of the dead drop, he backed in—just in case—and cut the motor. He wasn't near the outside here, there was no breeze, and it was gloomy, but he felt safer. He would feel a lot safer after talking to Blas.

Cissy Farrell sat cross-legged in the middle of her bed in Cappy's Cash Motel off the Gulf Freeway, picking at a fever blister at the corner of her mouth with trembling fingers which also held a freshly lighted Salem. Her eyes were puffy from crying and too much beer, and her bleached hair was stiff and sticking out on one side where she had nervously run her sweaty hands through it maybe a thousand times. She wore blue jeans, and one of Donny's plaid western shirts with snap buttons. Staring at a rerun on the black-and-white TV set, she watched Angel trying to lay a scam on Jim Rockford—she guessed, she didn't know because the sound was off. She reached down between her legs and lifted a Coors Light. Draining the last of the warm brew, she tossed the can off the edge of the bed with the others. An advertisement for an anniversary special of Country and Western's Greatest Hits came on after a Rockford fade-out and Cissy thought for a second she was going to throw up. She waited to see if she was and when she didn't she went back to picking the fever blister. Then she started crying again.

She fell back on the bed, unfolding her legs and letting them dangle over the end, her arms flopping out and scattering cigarette ashes. Scared and dead-ass drunk on the Coors, the same damn Coors she had gone to get in Donny's pickup and had come back with when she saw the two cars at Tucky and Ruby's. She didn't know what had made her suspicious, maybe because there was two of them, but she had stopped and sat there and looked at them and just had this feeling. So she turned around and drove back up McCarty. She didn't know what to do but she wanted to look at the cars again to make sure. She drove down Clinton to Mississippi, and got up on the East Loop North and drove in the goddamned traffic in the sun and looked across the sand fields and dried grass at Tucky and Ruby's. A bag of ice melted on the front seat beside her next to the sack of six-packs and she could still see the two cars from the Loop, too. So she kept driving.

Worrying about it all the way to Market, she got off the Loop there and drove to Wayside, where she stopped at a U-totem store. She tried to think whether it would be good or bad to call but after a minute decided what the shit she had to know and called. Nobody answered. It rang nine times before she hung up. Scared now. But she didn't know if it was the police or the Mexicans and she didn't know what to do either way because it just wasn't something she had figured on happening while she was out to get some beer.

She drove back to McCarty and passed by Stang at a good clip, looking down the street as she went by. The two cars were still there. During the next two hours she must of done that a dozen times. She drove out to her and Donny's place in Pasadena but didn't stop even though she didn't see any strange cars around. Maybe the place was staked out or somebody was waiting inside and her by herself she didn't want to get arrested or raped whichever way it was going to be.

After a while she had to pull over at a Texaco and get some gas because the goddam truck only got about ten miles to the gallon the way Donny had it rigged out. She paid for the gas and bought three packages of barbecue-flavored Doritos and crawled back in the truck. She popped the tab on one of the beers and tore into a bag of chips as she headed back to make another pass by Tucky's.

The cars were gone this time, so she turned in and went down to the house.

She wished to God she'd of kept on driving.

God Almighty damn.

Oh, God Almighty.

She ran outside slamming the door behind her and threw up at the pickup but she was so scared she grabbed at the door handle before she was through with it but couldn't get it opened and then did and jumped in and peeled out of there and threw up in her lap while she was driving. She was so crazy she didn't even start crying until she was nearly to Lyons, right at the East Freeway, and when she did start crying it sounded funny like it was a sort of hoot that didn't bring tears for a long time and she thought she wasn't going to be able to get sane again or hold the pickup on the freeway. She got on the Loop and drove around the entire city of Houston trying to get hold of herself and put her mind in gear. She didn't know what else to do and the driving helped keep her mind off the god-awful horror back there.

She drove and drove in the late-day heat until the seat of her blue jeans was all soaked through from the melted ice and she might of even peed her jeans she didn't know and then she thought of checking into Cappy's Cash Motel. She did and paid in advance not even minding that she was still crying and that she had to turn her back on the guy at the desk who was a little leery of her anyway and walk out with him seeing her wet butt. It didn't matter, she just wanted to get the hell in that room and lock the door and lie down and drink until she passed out because she didn't want to think about Tucky and Ruby and . . . She took all the beer and chips and turned on the TV and watched whatever was on and after a while they kept slipping in no matter what she was watching so she turned the sound off and tried to read the lips, concentrating on them so hard her mind didn't have time for the other at all.

Lying on her back, her sunken stomach rolling between her sharp hipbones because she was a skinny lady, Cissy thought sure she was going to throw up again or maybe have diarrhea. She didn't want to because it was nothing but Coors and Doritos which was all she had had since then and it tasted like hell.

Goddamned how many hours now and how many beers? It had been night hours and hours and some of the channels had test patterns. Then she opened her eyes and looked at the square light shade on the ceiling and a dark spot in its middle which was dead bugs in a pile. Well it wasn't the police, so it must of been the Mexicans and if it was the Mexicans they would know Donny's truck and they would find her. She made a face to cry but couldn't she was so weak and dried-out but her body shook like she was.

Then she opened her eyes again because the idea of the gun behind the pickup seat popped into her head. Limp as a washrag she rolled over and hit the floor her face flat down smelling the dirty shag rug and feeling her top lip turned wrong side out against it. She thought she had bit her tongue too. Pulling her arms up to her shoulders she pushed herself up got her top half off the rug and looked at the pickup keys by the telephone on the little table by the bed and looking at them she tasted blood and felt the sting on the side of her tongue. Her arms folded and she hit the floor again but she didn't feel a thing it was as soft as a bed.

If she was lucky she would pass out and they could get her then because it wasn't going to be any good without Donny anyway. Goddam their souls. Despite everything she saw Ruby and Tucky again, like figures in the wax museum at Western World looking pretty real but not real enough because who could look real the way they were it was just too hard to believe. And then she saw Donny who didn't look wax at all but just dead which grieved her and she cried with her nose mashed into the shag rug and the taste of blood on her tongue where she had bit it good. Like the gun the thought of her momma popped into her head and she wasn't sure but she thought she had her hand up in the air going for the telephone, making great big sweeps at it trying to snag it off the table.

"**W**hat do you think?'' Blas asked. They sat back a good way from the railroad crossing on St. Regis Place, a short street that lay parallel and next to the railroad track on its western side. He simply had wanted to look at the crossing awhile, watch cars go over it, which were few and far between this hour of the night.

"It looks good,'' Rubio said. "But I hope we don't have to wait too long.''

Blas nodded in the darkness of the car, and they both stared at the crossing. He wondered what Rubio was thinking. He wondered if, when the time came, now or in the far future, the Indian would have prescience of his own death. If fate had chosen it to be during this operation, had Rubio already glimpsed the finality of that decision? How did such a thing happen?

"Let's get some coffee and go over the maps,'' Blas said.

He started the rental car, drove to San Felipe, and turned left. Passing under the West Loop, he braked a block from Post Oak Boulevard and pulled into a small Steak 'N Egg Kitchen. The place was empty, and they chose a booth with a window that looked out onto the lighted skyscrapers thick as a mountain range toward the Galleria.

After the waitress brought their coffee, they both took out their enlarged copies of the Key Map pages of River Oaks and the Post Oak area. They each took the caps off fine-point felt-tip pens, and Blas began calling the street names followed by a second name. They wrote the second name over the original, renaming each street within the immediate vicinity of the railroad crossing. According to Blas's strategy, Rubio would begin watching Gamboa's movements early in the morning. He would stay with him all day while Blas hovered in the area around the San Felipe crossing. They would not communicate over their radios unless Gamboa entered an area within a certain number of blocks within the vicinity of the crossing. If it looked as if Gamboa might be heading for the crossing, Rubio would begin transmitting one-word coordinates beginning with the direction opposite that in which the limousine was actually moving. That is, if Gamboa was going west on San Felipe and was at Claremont heading toward Larchmont, then Timberlane, then Weslayan; Rubio would say: "East-Smith-Jones . . . Bailey . . . Glenn . . . Sayle," calling out the code name of each cross street as the limousine approached it.

By this method, Blas would have time to position himself in such a way as to see the exact instant when Gamboa's limousine would be directly over the rail crossing, and the twenty-five kilos of RDX.

Over fresh cups of coffee, they rehearsed the routine several times, Rubio calling out with his lisping pronunciation the direction and new street names, executing surprise turns, leaving the designated "alert" vicinity and then returning, while Blas followed him on his own map. After numerous trial runs, they each studied their maps in silence until Blas asked, "Any questions?"

"No."

"All right," Blas said. When Rubio was satisfied, Blas knew there would be no mistakes. Gamboa's men would never break the code. The Indian stayed alive by his intimate understanding of each operation. "Let's go back to our hotels and try to get some sleep. When do you want to be in place?"

Rubio thought. "No later than seven o'clock. Just to be sure."

"Good. Then I'll check with you by radio at seven o'clock."

"*Bueno.*"

Blas got up and walked out of the diner, leaving Rubio to pay. He crossed San Felipe to the parking lots of Post Oak Plaza, where another rental car was waiting. Unlocking the car, he became aware of how the tension of the past several days had sapped his energy. He had not had time for his daily workouts at a gym, and he was feeling small and shrunken from within, his shoulders seeming narrow and tight.

Sitting behind the wheel, he leaned forward and looked at this second city within the city: the complex of banded lights composing the buildings of Post Oak Central, which were separated from one another by emerald sheets of lighted lawns; the office towers and hotels surrounding the core of the Galleria and sparkling like chunks of pyrite; and then beyond them, looming above it all like an awesome mother ship, the inner-lighted monolith of the Transco Tower.

It was beautiful, this second city. Unreal and overpowering. So far away, in geography and in spirit, from the steep, dry gorges of the Barranca de Oblatos and the Río Santiago, so far from the broad night sky of the Jaliscan desert with its smaller lights, more intricate, more delicate, but made large in the mind from their fullness of symbol and myth.

He pushed himself away from the steering wheel and started the car. He had not thought about his route, just making the turns to get to the Southwest Freeway, which would take him back to Montrose. The traffic light caught him, and he recognized the intersection with a numb uneasiness.

Richmond and the West Loop.

He looked out his window and saw, thirty yards away in the garish lights of the underpass, the pavement where Teodoro had won his glory, borne with honor the distinction of being a *teco,* faithful to the Brigade and the most rigorous secret of its existence, where he had flourished his talon and ended his labor with the satisfaction that he had completed it according to his duty, obeying without question the will of the Brigade. Blas could still see the stains that had been the boy, darker than the dark pavement where his body had learned to suffer with a smile on his lips, where he had gained the satisfaction, not of Victory, but of the honor of dying for God and for Mexico so that his soul could live century after century in the presence of a Holiness for whom he had killed and been killed, an honorable end, in obedience to the Brigade.

All this, Teodoro, for letting a limousine run over you.

All this, for mixing your blood with radiator coolant.

It meant nothing. Perhaps even less than nothing.

When the light turned green, he drove up onto the freeway and headed east, watching the city grow larger out of the night as he approached it. Then down on the Montrose exit, but not stopping at Montrose, going beyond it to the smaller streets north of Hermann Park.

He didn't expect anything, but he approached the intersection at the corner of the parking garage with studied caution. Slowing at the stop sign, he looked across at the cement post beneath the street sign and saw the triangle of white paper. He felt as if someone had suddenly risen up out of the darkness of the back seat and lightly touched the point of a blade to the back of his neck. His weariness melted, the dullness that had crept upon him as he anticipated his bed at La Colombe d'Or dissolved, forgotten.

There was no hesitation. A stakeout watching the intersection would have seen nothing to remark on, only a car coming, stopping, going, disappearing into heavier traffic a few blocks farther on.

But Blas would not make the fatal mistake of passing by again, even half an hour later. He had seen that done. If a man failed to believe his eyes the first time, "making sure" could kill him. He had seen the triangle.

He would not make the mistake, either, of entering the garage in a car. It was a good place for a dead drop, under less rigorous circumstances. But now, with the hit only hours away, with Negrete prowling the city, with the police swarming and probing the streets like confused and maddened wasps around a raided nest, he would not accept the safety of the arrangement. The drop was for an emergency, and an emergency might mean that anything and everything had been compromised . . . even the drop. The very fact that there was a message made the site suspect.

Leaving the car several blocks away among the dozens of other cars in one of the parking lots of the Park Plaza Medical Center, he started walking toward the garage in the direction of downtown. The sidewalks were old, sheltered by heavy trees. Blas could hear the traffic on Main Street a few blocks to his left, and glancing back he caught a glimpse of the Museum of Fine Arts. He crossed several streets, keeping to the inside of the sidewalk, protected from the streetlights by the canopy of trees. Only his feet occasionally flashed in the pale light.

He stopped next to a hedge of nandina and looked at the garage at an angle from across the street. It took up half a block, and was surrounded by old brick boardinghouses and apartment buildings from the thirties. The entrance was on the other side, out of his view. He stood still. Sweating. Looking. This was not good, not good at all. They could be in the ribbons of darkness that marked every level, in the shadows of the yards, a darkened window in one of the old houses. There were moments in every operation, he thought again, when you openly subjected yourself to blind risk and you had no right to expect what you hoped you would get.

He stepped out of the shadows and crossed the street, un-hurriedly, casually, in case he was seen. He would not have been surprised to experience that scintilla of knowledge that he always believed existed at the moment of being shot in the head, that you had been killed.

But it didn't happen, and he reentered the shadows as he approached the back of the garage. Without hesitating he crawled over the low wall into the blackness of the first floor. He felt the slight incline and knew he was on the up ramp to the second floor. He moved over until he felt the wall, and then started walking, feeling the ribbed concrete under his shoes. When he reached the second floor, he stopped again, standing flat against the wall and looking at everything visible from his vantage point. There were not that many cars, and all of them had their windows rolled up, locked. A stakeout would not be able to do that without suffocating.

Parking space 28 was around the corner to his left. He stepped sideways, and was on the other side of the ramp wall, looking down the aisle toward space 28. Again not many cars. He examined them as best he could, wishing he had binoculars, straining his eyes to see something out of the ordinary. And then he did. He saw nothing but rows of tail-lights . . . and one pair of headlights. One car, two slots down from the drop and across the aisle, had backed into its space. Because of the angle of the slots, the car was facing away from him, but he knew the rearview mirror would be positioned for a clear view of the aisle in his direction.

He dropped down, took the Heckler from his waistband,

and began crawling under the front ends of the cars, squeezing between the front wheels and the concrete wall. There were six of them between him and the car he was watching. At four, he stopped and got his breath, lying on the garage floor. When he had controlled his breathing, he gradually raised himself until he could look through the windows of the two remaining cars. The target car had its windows down, and he could see someone slumped behind the wheel.

Down on the floor again, he slowly reached into his suit pocket, took out the silencer, and screwed it onto the Heckler barrel. When it was tight, he carefully laid the gun on the garage floor and wiped the sweat from the backs of his hands, his wrists, and his palms. Then he picked up the Heckler, crawled under the two remaining cars, and stopped at the rear end of the Volvo. He looked along its side, and confirmed his assumption that the rearview mirror was trained on the corner of the up ramp. That meant that unless the driver turned around, he would not be able to see someone approaching from the rear of his car on that side. Crouching, Blas worked his way up to the front window opposite the driver and leaned lightly against the door. The man behind the steering wheel shifted restlessly in his seat, and the car creaked on its springs.

Blas rose in one fluid movement, bringing the Heckler out in front of him as his hands stretched through the window and put the barrel of the silencer within inches of Daniel Ferretis's horrified face, his eyes magnified owlishly behind the thick lenses and heavy frames, his mouth dropped open in stupefaction as if he were fatalistically providing a reception for his own *coup de grace*.

chapter 42

They remained frozen in position, mind and body. Blas was unable to persuade himself to lower the end of the Heckler, not yet having worked through the ramifications of Ferretis's presence. He had known men killed by trust, by friends, by compatriots. Survival was more elemental, singular. There was no room for another person. A survivor sacrificed everything and everyone for himself.

Ferretis looked as if he were going to explode. Blas didn't think he was breathing.

"What is this?" Blas asked slowly. He was whispering.

"Trouble," was all Ferretis could say. He sounded as if he were strangling, his neck strained back, and locked at an impossible angle as he tried to keep his face as far away as he could from the barrel end of the Heckler.

"Are you alone?"

Ferretis nodded.

"Is someone after you?"

Ferretis nodded.

Blas burned inside. "Are you being followed?" Even as he asked, his mind populated every dark corner of the garage.

Ferretis shook his head.

"You're sure?"

Ferretis nodded, but Blas thought he had detected an almost imperceptible hesitation.

"Who?"

"Ne . . . Negrete."

Ferretis's strained response made Blas consider his Heckler. He moved the barrel to the side, still crouching at the window, and regarded the professor's glistening face. The heavy frames were low on his nose, and oily strands of his straight, dark hair were plastered over his blanched forehead. Blas looked at him, his mind bouncing off the possibilities.

He reached up with his left hand, jerked the cover off the interior light of the Volvo, unscrewed the bulb, and let it fall. Carefully, he opened the door and crawled into the front seat beside Ferretis. There was a heavy smell of gasoline inside the car.

"Explain," he said, turning toward the professor, his back pressing against the door. He still held the Heckler in his right hand, though the barrel was now pointing roughly at Ferretis's feet. He heard the professor swallow.

"You heard the news? On the radio?" Ferretis pointed to the car radio, as if the gesture were an explanation.

"No."

"Waite's . . . dead . . . two other people, too. Tortured. Jesus, tortured!" Ferretis was still trying to control his voice.

"This was on the news?"

Ferretis nodded, his eyes immobile.

"What happened?"

"It was sketchy. They were just found dead in Waite's home—violent deaths, it said, torture."

"Three of them, it said?"

"Yeah. Waite, another man, and a woman."

"That's why you came here?"

"No—I only heard that after I got here." He gestured at the radio again.

"Well?"

Ferretis told him everything that had happened: Haydon's visit to Cordero, Negrete's men at his office, his decision to wait at the dead drop for Blas to arrive. He talked fast, and fidgeted as he related the sequence of events. When he finally stopped, he peered hard at Blas and added, "Everything's falling apart. They're all over us!"

Blas looked at Ferretis carefully. The great tactician was not bearing up well. It had been unforgivably rash of him to come to the dead drop to wait. It could have been a fatal mistake, an enormous miscalculation. Blas looked at Ferretis's doughy complexion, and the wild stare of his eyes behind his stupid intellectual's glasses. Where was the ruthless theorizer who had been so quick to sacrifice lives for the cause? Where was the man of ideas who burned with an inner fire of conviction? Not here. Not Ferretis. This was no Renaissance man.

"Well, goddammit, Medrano. What the shit's going on?"

"Keep your voice down," Blas said, his own voice low and calm. But inside he was furious at Ferretis. It was all he could do not to lunge across the seat at him and beat him with the Heckler until he had sated an emotion so real he could almost smell it. He moved the gun slightly. "I don't know," he said. "This is the first I've heard any of this."

"We've got a leak," Ferretis said with finality, and in a tone of grim resignation.

"There's no leak."

"Then how the hell did Negrete's men know about me?"

"They had probably beat it out of Ireno," Blas said. "The real question is, how did the detective get Rubio's name? And why wasn't my name mentioned with his?"

Ferretis removed his glasses and worked them over with his shirttail. "At this point it doesn't matter. We've got to salvage what's left."

Blas looked at him. "What do you mean?"

"We've got to formulate a plan," Ferretis said, looking up and putting his glasses on again. "We've got to get out of here. If we stay it's only a matter of time before Negrete, the police, somebody, picks us off."

"We haven't finished our job."

"Fuck the job. You've already blown your chance at Gamboa. We've got to fall back, regroup for future operations. We're not any good to them dead."

Blas looked across the aisle to the cement barrier. In the opening between the barrier and the ceiling, he could see the tops of the neighborhood trees, and the lights of downtown. He looked back at Ferretis. Fall back. Regroup. The man was hiding his fear behind a pseudo strategy. And then there was *we've* got to fall back, *we've* got to get out of here. Was Blas understanding him correctly?

"Yes, I think I see what you mean," Blas said.

"Do you still have the money?" Ferretis asked suddenly.

"Most of it."

"We'll need the money," Ferretis said, calculating, planning. "We'll charter a plane at one of the private airports . . . no, wait, that wouldn't be smart. Rent a car. We rent a car and drive out of here . . . go to Brownsville, like Cordero."

"What about your family?"

"It's a sacrifice . . . a sacrifice I'll have to make. I could send for them later. But I can't stay. No way. Maybe, if this hadn't happened, if Ireno hadn't run off his mouth to Negrete. Maybe. But not now."

The car rocked slightly as Ferretis nervously wagged one foot, beating the side of his shoe against the floor. Blas felt an instant contempt for this adolescent gesture of agitation. He also thought of Ireno, "running off his mouth" as Negrete's men beat his insides to jelly. Ireno knew Negrete as well as Blas did, he had known what was going to happen to him before it happened, while it was happening, until it was over.

"I'll have to finish the job before I can do anything else," Blas said coolly.

"What do you mean? It's too late! Too big a risk."

"It's already set up."

Ferretis gawked at him. "When?"

"Soon."

Ferretis ran a hand through his limp hair. He seemed stunned, confused, as if this new possibility had thrown everything out of perspective.

"You don't need me to help you get out of town," Blas said, watching him. "Do exactly as you instructed Cordero. You'll be all right."

Ferretis looked at Blas with panic in his eyes.

"Wait a minute. You're crazy. This piece of garbage won't make it to Brownsville. I'll never make it."

"Rent a car."

"What if there's a bulletin out on me?"

"What makes you think the police know about you? It's Negrete you were worried about."

"Give me your false ID," Ferretis said desperately. "You've got to do that, by God."

"I can't," Blas said, looking at him. "Drive to Rosenberg. It's on the way—rent a car there."

"Oh, shit." Ferretis's voice was anguished.

Blas did not like seeing this. It was embarrassing. Cowardice was embarrassing. He opened the car door and got out, closing the door again. He bent down and looked at Ferretis through the open window.

"Drive out of here, get on Highway 59, and go to Rosenberg."

"Wait a goddam minute," Ferretis said hoarsely, and he scrambled out of his own door and stood on one leg, the other still inside, looking across the roof of the car at Blas. "You can't walk out on me like this. You've got a responsibility . . ."

Then they both heard them.

Two cars. One, its engine whining and tires squealing, was climbing the entrance ramp on the other side of the wall; the other was screaming up the exit ramp at the opposite end of the aisle. Suddenly its headlights burst along the walls as it shot out of the ramp and into the aisle, sparks flying from under its chassis as it slammed down on the cement.

Blas met Ferretis's disoriented, catatonic stare across the roof of the car, and raised the Heckler to his waist. He fired three shots through the open windows into Ferretis's stomach, three sharp smacks as if he were being hit with fists, staggering him back against the car behind him.

The car coming from the exit ramp at the other end of the garage was already barreling down the aisle, its headlights on bright, as the second car burst out of the up ramp six cars away, its headlights panning the walls and swinging around to meet those from the other direction. Blas fired two shots in each direction as he sprinted across the aisle in front of them, and dove over the second-floor barrier into the darkness.

Haydon swung his legs over the side of the bed and let the telephone ring one more time. He was aware that it was still dark outside as he lifted the receiver and looked at his watch in the light of the bedside lamp Nina had just turned on. It was three-twenty.

"This's Bob, Stu," Dystal said. "That son of a bitch Negrete's gone mad dog on us again."

"What's the matter?" Haydon had to clear his throat.

"You awake?"

"Yes. Go ahead." The bottle of wine Haydon had shared with Nina only hours before was making the top of his head feel as if it were filled with lead.

"Ferretis has been killed. Night guard in a parking garage down near the Warwick heard a coupla cars ripping up and down the ramps and some shouting on the second floor. Cars tore outta there and he went up to have a look-see and found him. Three nine-millimeter slugs high in the stomach."

"Is that all?"

"Yeah, I asked too, but it looks like he was just blown away. Nothin' else except that he didn't have any ID on him. Somebody'd been through his clothes and took everything. They identified him first from a picture they'd gotten from his wife earlier, then she went and made a positive identification later."

"The guard didn't get license numbers?"

"Nope, but we got good descriptions of the cars. Next thing. They've picked up that little ol' Cissy Farrell in a motel on the Gulf Freeway. Drunk as a skunk. She'd knocked her phone off the hook and the night manager went to check, called a blue-and-white unit to haul her off. They hit on her name and took her in. She's sleeping it off down there."

"You're not downtown?"

"Hell, no. I'm sitting here on the edge of my bed in my underwear. I thought you ought to be there when we talk to her."

"Right. I'll be there in half an hour."

Haydon hung up, and massaged the muscles at the back of his neck.

"What's happened?" Nina put a hand on his back.

"Ferretis was killed a few hours ago, and they've got Cissy Farrell downtown." He stood. "I've got to get down there."

He threw his pajama bottoms on the foot of the bed and walked naked into the shower. Turning the water on cold, he sat down on the marble seat built around the walls and let the cold spray beat his head and back. He thought of the scene he had found in Lawrence Waite's kitchen, and wondered how this girl had missed being one of those grotesque victims. Cissy. He tried to imagine what she looked like.

After drying off, he wrapped the towel around his waist and shaved. He splashed Kuros aftershave on his face and selected a charcoal double-breasted pinstripe from his suit closet. If he was right, there wouldn't be any time to change clothes before Mooney's memorial service later in the morning. He sat in one of the armchairs in the dressing area and tied his shoelaces. Nina was watching him from the bed.

"How do you feel?" she asked.

"All right." He stood, took a fresh shirt from his armoire, and put it on, taking cufflinks from one of the drawers. "Listen," he said, fastening the links. "Would you make sure Celia gets started on the *teco* report? Somewhere inside her head she's got a piece of information that could open this up."

"What about Renata Islas?"

"I'm going to try to get over there after we talk to Cissy Farrell." He selected a tie and slipped it under his collar. "It was a good idea to get them together."

He took his Beretta out of an armoire drawer and slipped it on his belt in the small of his back. Taking his suit coat off a hanger, he walked over and kissed her. "Don't let Celia out of your sight."

"Okay," she said. "Be careful."

At almost four o'clock in the morning Houston streets are as empty as they ever get, and Haydon made good time by way of Montrose and Memorial Drive. The night shift still had three hours to run, and some of the detectives on Lapierre's task force were in their offices. Others had gone downtown to the garage where Ferretis had been found.

Haydon walked into his office, where a night-shift detective was tapping away at one of the terminals. The detective turned around, saw who it was, started to speak, then hesitated when he saw that Haydon had stopped in the middle of the room and was staring at Mooney's cubicle.

Mooney's coffee mug, a gift from another detective who had brought it back from a summer vacation in Ireland; his big-breasted pin-ups taped on the side of the cubicle next to the monthly boxing schedules; his caricature on a piece of yellowed notebook paper sketched as a gesture of friendship by a man who had dismembered his wife, but who, Mooney said, was "otherwise a nice guy with talent"; his cartoons cut from a variety of magazines . . . everything . . . was gone. His desk was bare; nothing of Mooney remained but the hand-soiled outlines where the strips of tape had been pulled up.

Haydon had not been ready for this. Mooney was memory.

"Sorry about Ed," the detective said. His name was Harker, a young detective with wavy blond hair and a well-trimmed mustache. "I wish I was on that task force."

Haydon nodded, and turned and walked out of the office.

He was standing at the coffeepot, stirring nondairy creamer into a Styrofoam cup of coffee and thinking of the bare cubicle, when Dystal came up beside him and poured a cup for himself.

"Morning," he said. His voice was early-morning basso. Neither man looked at the other as they stood side by side stirring their coffee. "Okay. The story is this way about your situation. You're doing some sort of undercover stuff. Uh, the details aren't all worked out real clear, but . . . well, you don't have to talk to anybody about it and we've briefed the couple or so that needed to know and they aren't going to be asking you any questions. We had to do some stuff, you know, I mean, Pete's coordinating this thing and we didn't want him to think you were doing any kind of end-run kind of thing. Didn't want to get men crossways on this.''

Haydon didn't have any idea what had been done, and he didn't want to know.

Dystal heaved a weary sigh. ''You can ask any questions you want to when we get her in here.'' He sipped loudly from the Styrofoam cup. ''They're bringing her up now. Pete's been down there where Ferretis was killed. He'll be here in a minute.''

The squad room was quiet. Even with the twenty-four-hour task force in full swing, four o'clock in the morning is slow.

''Did you find out anything about Rich Elkin?''

''I got Moyer out of bed to ask him about it after I left your place. I didn't explain the whole deal to him, but I let him know it was purty damn important and I needed something pronto. He's supposed to get back with me early this morning, and we can get into it about his Mexican connection and what they can do for us.''

Cissy Farrell was waiting in Dystal's office with a jail matron when the three detectives walked in. She sat in a straight-backed metal chair, a skinny, wasted-looking girl in her mid-twenties. After having thrown up her binge of Doritos and Coors, she looked pathetically gaunt, with pasty skin. She was nervously smoking Salems, and drinking a Classic Coke, which she put down on the edge of Dystal's desk, making rings on the top. Her hair was so dirty it looked wet, and the bruised bags under her eyes were painful to look at. She had a thin nose, thin lips, and brown eyes that bulged slightly. She was trembling. The matron stepped outside to wait in the squad room.

Dystal introduced himself, and then Haydon and Lapierre. He went around behind his desk as the other two men took chairs across from the girl.

''Now, Mrs. Farrell,'' Dystal began, leaning toward her and assuming an avuncular tone. ''Do you have any idea why we brought you up here to talk to you?''

She shook her head, which was bent down between rounded shoulders. She had the demeanor of a scolded dog.

"Well, the motel manager called the police because of your drunkenness, and when they picked you up they realized that you were someone we were looking for. Do you know why we were looking for you?"

The girl shrugged and limply lifted the cigarette to her colorless lips.

"Do you know what has happened to your husband, Mrs. Farrell?"

She grew rigid in her slumped position. It seemed that even her heart didn't move for a full two minutes, and then she said, "Goddam." It was not said in anger or fear, but in unmistakable anguish. But she seemed too weak to cry, and her hand went up to her mouth, which was hidden by a stiff hank of hair that had fallen away from her head. As she exhaled the smoke, she nodded.

"Well, hon, I hate to do it," Dystal said kindly, "but I got to ask you about it. You know anything about it at all?"

The girl nodded. She kept her head down slightly and only looked at Dystal from under her eyebrows.

"Now you just relax as best you can," he urged, "and tell us what you know, or think you know."

Cissy dragged on her cigarette. "I want immunity," she said.

"Immunity?" Dystal frowned and sat up a little.

"Uh-huh."

"From what, hon? You're not any kind of suspect in this thing."

"But I know some thangs."

"Well, you don't need immunity because you know some things."

"About criminal activity, though," she said, sucking at the cigarette again.

"What criminal activity is that?"

"Guns an' . . ." She stopped and reached for her Coke. She took a few swallows and went back to the cigarette.

"Guns and what?"

Her voice was weak. "Explosives."

Dystal didn't even flinch, but kept his easygoing comportment as if she had said candy bars. "Well, hon, we don't know anything about anything. All we know is we found your man and your friends dead in that house and we don't know why, or when, or who, or how. If we're gonna do any good on this, you're gonna have to straighten us out. We sure do need your help."

"I want protection."

Dystal cut his eyes up at Haydon and Lapierre. The one thing they didn't want to hear her say now was that she wanted to see her lawyer. Dystal leaned toward her again.

"Listen, hon, we're not gonna let anything happen to you, but you gotta tell us what it is you're talking about."

Cissy leaned forward and mashed her cigarette out in Dystal's Texas-shaped ashtray, grinding the butt out on the amber-stained rattlesnake rattles. She dug in her purse, found her pack of Salems, and took out another one and lighted it.

"Me an' Donny, we met Ruby and Tucky a coupla years ago," she said, clearing her throat. "At a gun show. Donny, he likes pistols, six-guns. Western revolvers. He had an Hombre, a Dakota, a Texas Ranger, like that. Shot 'em out on his daddy's place out past Galena Park. Just at cans 'n' thangs. Tucky had a table at this show, an' we stopped to look at his stuff. We got to be friends, 'cause Ruby was there too and I kinda hit it off with her while the boys was talkin'. We both was Waylon Jennings fans."

Cissy crossed her legs and leaned forward a little as if she were trying to ease a cramp.

"Tucky's a real heavy-duty gun hog. A dealer at these gun 'n' knife shows an' stuff. His big thang is survival warfare. We went to this survivalist camp around Conroe with him an' Ruby two or three times, and Donny really got off on it. Those people was really military. Assault weapons, camo outfits, the whole bit. All the women knew how to shoot as good as the men. I learned how, an' we painted our faces an' played war games an' had some good times. Anyway, we got to be real close friends with those people, an' after several months, Tucky, he let Donny in on his side business. His job was at the ship channel. Night watchman, but he moonlighted buyin' an' sellin' illegal guns. Machine guns. Full-automatic stuff. And then he got into explosives. RDX. C-4. Donny got into it with him."

When she stopped to pull on her cigarette, Dystal asked, "Where'd they get these firearms and explosives from?"

"I don't know. Somethin' to do with the ship channel,

came in on ships or somethin'. It was Tucky's deal. Me and Ruby, we stayed out of it, at first.''

Cissy's voice cracked a little at this point, and she ground out another cigarette in the ashtray. She drank from the Coke again, and when she put it back on the desk she knocked it over.

''Oh, goddam.'' She grabbed for it and stood. ''I'm sorry, I'm sorry,'' she said, hovering over the spilled cola, her arms trembling. But Dystal was already reaching in a desk drawer for some paper napkins he kept there.

''That's all right, that's all right, hon,'' he said. ''Don't mind it. Just sit down. No harm done.''

But Cissy had already collapsed in her chair, and was crying, ducking her head and holding it in one hand and crying. Dystal mopped up the spilled Coke, put the napkins in his trash can, placed a fresh napkin under the can, and pushed it back to her.

''Mrs. Farrell, I know you're upset, but just hang in there. There's no need for you to be jittery with us. Okay? Come on, now,'' he said, pushing the Coke toward her a little more. ''Take a sip, and go ahead on.'' He gave her a paper napkin to blow her nose.

After a minute she continued.

''I don't know nothin' about who Tucky sold to. Donny was just learnin' the ropes, so he didn't really know a lot, I don't thank, and he didn't tell me much about what he knowed. He's the quiet type, anyway. But about a month ago Tucky and Ruby asked us over to their place one night an' we all sat down in the . . . kitchen . . . and Tucky was real excited. He said he had got a feeler from a Mexcun that could maybe turn into somethin' real big. He said the Mexcun was wantin' a bunch of RDX, like twenty-five kilos. He said it was gonna be a lot of money, but it was gonna take all of us to pull it off because he couldn't trust the Mexcuns at the payoff.''

''Excuse me,'' Haydon interrupted her. ''Do you remember if he mentioned the Mexican's name?''

''Mostly he just called him the Mexcun,'' Cissy said, lighting another Salem. ''But I remember his name was something like a girl's. Uh . . .'' She tilted her head back and looked at the ceiling. ''Irene. Yeah, like Irene-o.''

"Fine. Go ahead."

"Well, after a couple of weeks when it was all firmed up, an' the delivery date an' place was set with this Mexcun, Tucky made us plan out this operation like it was some kind of military thang. We all wore these little mikes so we could all hear each other and talk to each other. He was to square the deal down on the channel. Me and Ruby was posted on top of some oil storage tanks with these little Weatherbys with night scopes, an' we were gonna cover the boys. But it went off without a hitch."

"Who did Mr. Waite deal with on the channel?" Lapierre asked. "Was it with the same man?"

"Oh, no sir. It was two other guys, but we knowed that might be. The Mexcun and Tucky had arranged some passwords, and these two guys knowed the words."

"Do you know their names?"

"Just their first names, which I heard on the earpiece. One was Rubio. Ruby, she laughed at that 'cause it was sorta like hers, another girl's name, too, like the first one. An' the other was somethin' like Blahs. I don't know for sure. I don't know Mexcun."

"And they bought twenty-five kilos of this RDX?" Dystal asked.

Cissy nodded.

"Well, do you know anything else about these boys?"

Cissy shook her head.

"Did you get a good look at these men?" Haydon asked.

"Not really. That night scope don't give great detail, an' they were movin' around an' talkin' with their backs to us an' stuff. Naw, I couldn't tell much about 'em."

"Are these the boys you wanted protection from?" Dystal asked.

"Yeah," she said hoarsely.

"Why would they want to kill you?"

"Shut me up, I guess."

"You think that's why the others got killed?"

"I guess."

"Where were you when this happened?"

"I'd gone down to get some beer. When I came back I saw these two cars at Tucky's and I got leery and drove aroun'

until they was gone and then . . . I went . . . and found
'em.''

Her voice squeezed off and she started crying again.

"And so you went to the motel to hide?" Dystal asked.

Cissy nodded, and continued crying. Haydon could see her
shoulder blades through the western shirt, and it reminded
him of the pale back of Ruby Waite as she slumped over the
kitchen table.

"Can you describe the cars for us?" he asked.

She sniffed, cleared her throat, and coughed. "I don't
know. They was light-colored. I don't know. I can't tell anymore about cars. I get 'em all confused. And they was down
the road a bit." She shook her head, "I don't know."

"Mrs. Farrell," Lapierre said. "Do you have any idea
what the men planned to do with the explosives they purchased from Mr. Waite?"

"No, not at all."

"You never heard Mr. Waite or anyone else use any other
Latin names in regard to this or any other transaction?"

She shook her head.

"Were these men from Houston?"

"I don't know."

"Do you know how Mr. Waite got in touch with them?"

"No, sir. Only that it was all arranged through that Irene-o
and then the other two Mexcuns showed up an' took delivery."

"When did this exchange take place?" Haydon asked.

"Uh . . ." Cissy studied the end of her cigarette, which
was shaking in her bony fingers. "Uh, this is Friday? That
woulda been, uh, Wednesday night."

All three men looked at the girl in silence, and then Dystal
said, "Okay, hon. We appreciate your help. Right now we
gotta get some things lined out here. I'll get the lady out there
to take you to a nicer room than that tank, and then we'll talk
some more a little later. You want some breakfast?"

Cissy nodded. "I better get somethin' in my stomach,"
she said.

Chapter 44

By eight-thirty, Dystal and Captain Mercer had already had their briefing meeting with the HPD brass and public-relations people. The mayor had already checked in, as well as several councilmen. Everybody wanted to get "this thing" cleared up as soon as possible. Downstairs the headquarters lobby was crowded with reporters and television cameras, and more than just a few people were hanging around waiting to see the news people go into action. The discovery of the bodies at Waite's house in Port Houston the evening before and the shooting in the garage early in the morning hours had all been reported on the morning television news. The news teams were getting as little sleep as the police, and since the police department itself had few clues as to what was going on, the reporters were doing more than their share of speculation. And the excitement seemed justified. Within the space of three days a full-scale Latin underworld slaughter had taken place, and six U.S. citizens had been killed in its wake. One of them a policeman. In light of that, the public, and the law-and-order politicians, did not feel they were getting satisfactory information. Most assumed the entire Miami drug business had moved to Houston.

The FBI special agent in charge of the Houston field office had been there since seven-thirty, and had already established that Richard Elkin was not one of their agents or employees or contacts, nor did any of their computer indices checks come up with *any* hit on a Richard Elkin. Not even in Mexico. The Drug Enforcement Administration agents in Mexico

City and Guadalajara were in the process of running through their computer checks, not only on their Elkins, but also on their Rubios and Blases. The Bureau of Alcohol, Tobacco, and Firearms was doing the same.

The U.S. embassy in Mexico City was on overtime too. Mexico was the only place in the world where the FBI and its State Department counterpart, the Central Intelligence Agency, worked in uneasy tandem. The number of FBI agents, known as "legal attachés," attached to embassies around the world rarely exceeded one or two, and frequently were positions of mere formality. But in Mexico City, the FBI personnel numbered in the high twenties, and the agents were active. As for the CIA, Mexico City was one of its most important stations in the world. Not only did Mexico stand as a physical buffer between the United States and the sometimes unstable and communist-prone countries of Latin America, but it was also, for the same reason, crawling with KGB activity. With well over three hundred people attached to it, the Soviet embassy on Calzada de Tacubaya in Mexico City was the largest diplomatic mission in the world. It also bristled with the most sophisticated electronic equipment available to the KGB. Mexico City was a circus of East-West espionage activity.

Representatives of both the FBI and the CIA in Mexico City would have extensive files on extremist groups operating there, but Haydon and Dystal were practical, and held little hope of learning anything from those sources soon enough to help them, if they learned anything substantive at all. In the meantime, they had to go with what they had.

Lapierre had been brought up to date on everything Haydon had discussed with Dystal the previous night, and the three men sat together in Dystal's office to reevaluate their position.

"There were three nine-millimeter casings in the passenger side of the Volvo," Lapierre said. Though always precise and pleasant in a subdued manner, Pete Lapierre was beginning to show the strain of being in command of a task force that was receiving a great deal of political heat. He reacted by being excessively methodical. Haydon felt distinctly uneasy for ducking the official responsibility.

"Two in the floor, one in the passenger seat, which would

seem to indicate that the gun was fired inside the automobile. The passenger door was closed, but Ferretis's door was standing open." Lapierre referred to his notebook, though he probably had all the details in his head. "Ferretis seems to have been standing outside the car with the door open when he was shot. In the aisle in front of the car, there were skid marks from both directions in front of the Volvo, up to within fifteen feet of each other. It appears that they closed in on the car and skidded to a stop almost bumper to bumper. The skid marks of the car that came from the direction of the exit ramp are overlapped, indicating that that car seems to have been thrown into reverse after coming to a stop, and then peeled backward, turning in an open space and going down the ramp forward followed by the other car. The guard said they came out fast, one after the other."

Lapierre stopped and carefully sipped from his coffee mug, then continued, "Four more nine-millimeter casings were found in the aisle. Two in the aisle itself, one of them mashed by one of the cars, and two near the outside barrier. At the barrier, we also found seventy-three forty-five casings. Directly under the barrier, on the ground, we found an additional twenty-eight forty-five casings around some crushed shrubbery."

"Goddam," Dystal said. "Those MAC-10s again."

"I'm sure they were," Lapierre agreed. "Converted, a couple of men could pump out that many casings in a second."

"So you think they fired at somebody who jumped over the barrier," Dystal said. He, too, was beginning to show a grim tenseness. Despite his ability to display elaborate courtesy to Cissy Farrell, Dystal was quietly doing a slow burn. Aside from the real anguish he felt at Mooney's death, the burly lieutenant felt personally sinned against by the storm of turmoil that the killings had unleashed in Houston. He was furious at the sudden disorder, at the reckless way in which Gamboa and his henchman Negrete had brought flagrant death in their wake. Dystal put no man above the law, and was the sworn enemy of those who considered themselves to be so.

"Right."

"But the guard didn't hear any shooting," Dystal said sourly.

Lapierre shook his head.

"You know, this business is changing fast." Dystal's expression was sarcastic. "I went to one of those gun shows myself a couple of months ago. Out in Pasadena. Guy at one booth was selling components for a MAC-10 silencer for ninety bucks. Ten yards away another guy was selling the container tube for thirty-nine ninety-five. Put those pieces together, and you could get twenty years for manufacture and possession. But there they were, for sale."

He raised his heavy eyebrows and impatiently wriggled his booted foot where it rested on a drawer he had pulled out of his desk.

"So that would be Negrete's boys in the cars," he postulated, looking at Lapierre and Haydon. "Thinking they'd trapped these other boys, except one of them gets away." He squinted at Lapierre. "That's a purty good drop from the second floor. Maybe he broke his butt. Why don't we put some checks on emergency rooms."

Lapierre made a note.

"Now," Dystal said. "Who shot Ferretis?"

"After listening to Cissy Farrell's account of the explosives sale," Haydon said, "we now know there is yet another *teco:* Blas. I think we have to consider him a new actor. If Cissy had named two names we had never heard before, then I might have been inclined to think the *teco* buyers were using fictitious names. Yet she named not only Rubio, but also Ireno, as being involved. So I think we have to take Blas as a real name too."

He paused, thinking through what he was going to say.

"Since Rubio and Blas were the ones purchasing the explosives, we can hypothesize that they're the hit team, and for some reason one—or both—of them met with Ferretis. The circumstances could have been similar to that at the limousine shooting. Surprised by Negrete's sudden arrival, Rubio or Blas, or both, shot Ferretis to prevent him from being taken alive, and possibly tortured to talk."

Lapierre nodded. "That's the way I would read it, too. We should have something from ballistics this afternoon to indicate whether the three nine-millimeter casings inside the Volvo were fired from the same weapon that fired the nine-millimeter casings found on the garage floor. And the same distinctions for the forty-five casings.''

"God a'mighty," Dystal said. "There's a lotta high-powered law looking for those two Mexicans.''

"That's only one scenario," Lapierre put in cautiously.

"True," Dystal said. "True. You see another story?"

Lapierre shook his head. "I guess I don't understand enough of what's going on to lay one out."

"What do you suppose they were doing in the garage?" Dystal said. "And how the hell did Negrete know they were there?''

"Maybe he learned about Ferretis's part in this from Waite," Haydon said. "And instead of going through another 'interrogation,' he could have decided to tail Ferretis, hoping the professor would lead him to the other two.''

Dystal looked at Lapierre. "You people didn't find any blood in that shrubbery, did you? One of them could have been hit.''

"Nothing.''

"Regardless," Haydon said, "we need to remove Negrete. So far we haven't been able even to get close to these people because he's gotten to them first.''

Dystal dropped his leg heavily to the floor. He leaned his elbows on his desk in his familiar discursive posture, and looked at Haydon and Lapierre.

"Number one." He held up a thick index finger. "It's gonna take some time to get enough court-admissible evidence for the DA to agree to let us arrest Negrete. It's as plain as day what's happening, but it's all circumstantial.

"Number two." A second stubby finger went up. "The son of a bitch is running his own goddam little army out there on the streets. Him and his boys have dusted this Ireno fella, the two Waites, and Farrell. Stu's right, we gotta stop him, plain and simple.

"Number three." Dystal held three fingers up to Haydon and Lapierre and slowly shook his head. "We don't have one goddam ounce of a lead as to how to get to these asshole madmen who want to blow up Benigo Gamboa with the twenty-five kilos of RDX. Here it is Friday morning, and ever since Tuesday afternoon when the limousine got shot up, we've just been going around picking up Negrete's turd droppings, a day late and a dollar short.''

There was a brief silence as Dystal sat with his elbow propped on the desk, his three fingers up in the air, looking at the other two men.

"So what do we do?" Dystal asked suddenly and rhetorically, letting his hand fall to the desk with a thunk. "We're gonna pick them up. All of them. Mercer's talking to the DA right now to see how we can make it tight. We're gonna bring Negrete in and explain to him how he can cooperate, or he can get his ass deported. We're gonna bring all his boys in. We've got that list Stu snookered outta Negrete, and the DEA down there in Guadalajara is checking it out for us. Anybody's got a sheet down there can cooperate with us, or be extradited. If they don't have a sheet, then they can cooperate or be deported. And we're not going to just haul them across the border and turn them loose like wets, we're gonna do a bunch of fancy paperwork, make a big deal out of it. Kick up some dust. We're gonna drag Gamboa into it, get him some nasty publicity.''

Dystal had started to say something else when his telephone rang. He said, "Shit," and answered it.

"This's Dystal." He listened, looked at Lapierre, and said, "Well, I'll be damned. Sure I do, just a sec." He cradled the telephone between his beefy neck and shoulder and grabbed a pencil and note pad. "Okay," he said, and began taking notes, saying, "Uh-huh," "Wait," and "Uh-huh," as he copied down what he was being told. Finally he said, "Much obliged, Robert. We'll be getting back to you."

He stared down at what he had written, shook his head, and looked up.

"That was Nunn down there at that garage," he said. "They were prowling around in all the crannies around the Volvo and one of the boys saw a piece of paper stuck in a crack by a cement pillar, right where whoever it was jumped over the barrier. It was a note.''

Looking down at his paper, he read what Nunn had dictated:

C fled to Mexico. Police know A is involved and looking for him. Negrete's men broke into my office and looking for me. Cannot go home. Has there been a leak? Need to know. Be careful. Am floating until I hear from you.

F.

"He was writing to Blas," Haydon said immediately.

Dystal nodded, his mind already working.

" 'C' is Cordero," Lapierre said. " 'A' is Rubio Arizpe. 'F' is Ferretis." He had taken his own notes in shorthand, and was studying them on his pocket notepad.

"Then maybe it's this Blas, not Rubio, who's heading this thing up," Dystal said, more to himself than to the others. He was looking at the message and tapping the end of his pencil on the piece of paper. "A damn mess," he added.

"The garage was a dead drop," Haydon said. "Negrete knew it was there."

Dystal nodded. "Yeah, that's right. Negrete seems to know a hell of a lot more than he ought to." He looked at Lapierre. "Pete, put together however many men you need to go get them. Every last one of them. If Mercer doesn't have something trumped up with the DA by the time you bring them back, we'll think of something ourselves."

He looked at Haydon. "Stu, you get that Islas woman over to your place with Moreno, and pick their brains. We've gotta get *something* on the boys with the explosives."

Dystal stood. "I'm going to stomp and cut up rough with these other agencies. These *tecos* didn't just drop out of thin air—somebody down there's got names—" He stopped in midsentence and snapped his fingers. "Stu. Get back with Mitchell Garner."

"One more thing," Haydon said. "Why don't we distribute a description of Rubio Arizpe to the media? We've only got Islas's secondhand description, but it's distinctive: the deep notch in the center of his lower lip, Indian, very dark, below medium height. A description of the notch alone could do it. We might be able to have a sketch ready by the time the evening papers go to press, certainly in time for the six-o'clock news."

"Do it," Dystal said.

It was a clear, hot July morning, and inside the chapel of the Church of the Good Shepherd there was standing room only. The morning sun set fire to the colors in the stained-glass windows, washing the white walls of the high-ceilinged chantry and the silent crowd in a haze of rich hues. Haydon found the service stoic, far removed from the reality and emotion of Mooney's death. Mooney's brother and sister had already taken his body back to Arlington, so there was no family there. Nina had had to stay home with Celia Moreno. There were only Mooney's professional associates, a fifteen-year accumulation of friends and enemies, mostly men, and a scattering of older and retired prostitutes who had known him from his years in vice and who were possibly the only persons on earth toward whom Mooney had been known to exhibit an unguarded tenderness.

The chief spoke. A brief, generic essay on fraternity, honor, service, and duty. Captain Mercer gave the eulogy. Gray-headed and somber, he outlined Mooney's career, talked briefly in a personal way of Ed Mooney's life. To Mercer's credit, in addition to straining memory with the traditional retrospective of the dead that had more to do with euphemism than with accurate remembrance, he honestly, but kindly, mentioned the irascible side of Mooney's nature. Mooney had good friends, and close friends, but he had come by them the hard way. He had not been an easy man to endear, but the value of his friendship was not in its facility. He was a man wary of tranquillity, and suspicious of people and circumstances that wanted to be accepted at face value. He professed to have few misconceptions, and met life head on, never blinking. Only death deceived him, taking him by surprise.

Haydon did not sit in the front pews with the department and city officials as he had been invited to do in deference to his relationship with Mooney. Instead, he took a place three-quarters of the way toward the back, next to one of the large stone pillars that reached to the vaulted ceiling. He sat behind a middle-aged woman in a navy dress that fit her a little too snugly across her back so that he could see her bra strap cutting into her flesh. She wore the dress with a bit of a flair, and her silky blond hair was in a style many would have considered a little young for her. One of Mooney's girls. Haydon watched her, and when she bent her head from time to time, a splash of wine light bathed her hair from high above. Symbol within a symbol. What had she ever meant to Mooney? What had he ever meant to her that she should come to this place that she knew was alien to him and alien to her, and sit among strangers speaking strangely of him she knew to be so different from his memorial? Exiles, the two of them, and content to be so. Haydon suddenly felt a great compassion for her, for whatever it was they had shared, however unsentimental it might have appeared to the rest of the world, it had been a binding affection, truer than ceremonies and words.

The circumstances of Mooney's death had robbed him of the kind of funeral he would have liked to have. A big dinner afterward, or barring that, at least a casual leave-taking with time to stand around and visit with old friends, and tell time-worn stories that you had had plenty of time to polish. But that wasn't to be. After the last prayer, the chapel emptied without the delay of lingering conversations. Practically every man in attendance had only stolen the time to be there, and the moment the service was concluded they immediately turned their attentions in other directions. Mooney's death had initiated an investigation the urgency of which quickly superseded any tranquil consideration of his life.

Haydon stopped on the far side of the courtyard arcade that separated one side of the chapel from the church's business offices and put a quarter in a telephone located in a covered walkway that led to the front of the building. It was ten-thirty.

It took a minute to get from the receptionist to Garner's secretary, and then to Garner himself.

"It's me again," Haydon said. "I need some more help."

"Sure," Garner said.

Haydon brought him up to date, explaining in as much detail as he thought he could under the circumstances.

"I'm getting ready to call Renata Islas right now, and ask her if she'll let me pick her up and take her to my house to compare notes with Moreno. If you think you could contribute anything to this, I'd like you to come over too. Or if you thought you could contact anyone in Mexico . . . we're at the bottom of the barrel, Mitchell. We don't have anything."

"I'm afraid you're not going to get a great deal of help from the agencies," Mitchell said. "They've got informants all over the place down there, but they're competitive and the connections are so convoluted . . . but, yeah, I'll be there. I'd like to hear what Moreno's got to say, too. What time?"

"Let's make it eleven-thirty. We'll have sandwiches while we talk."

Renata Islas listened to Haydon's synopsis of the events that had taken place since he had first spoken with her. He expected some equivocation, but she agreed immediately. With a third quarter he called Nina and told her of his plans, and asked her if she would get Gabriela to make sandwiches for all of them.

It was noon by the time everyone had met, settled around the refectory table in the library. While they ate a variety of sandwiches, cold cuts, and sliced fresh vegetables from platters in the center of the table, Haydon explained what Celia Moreno had been doing during the morning and suggested they begin by reading her notes, using them as a starting point for comparing information.

Celia had spent her time well. She had typed out seven double-spaced pages of names whose relationships and duties within the *tecos* she explicated with two or three sentences. There were names of businesses and organizations as well as individuals. But very little of it dealt with the *tecos de choque*. Most of the information pertained to the part of the organization that showed its face to the public as a kind of nationalistic fraternity, housed and sponsored by the Autonomous University of Guadalajara. This was the face Dr. Ferretis had wanted her to see. His own involvement with the "enforcing" arm of the secret society had been off-limits to her.

As they ate with one hand and passed the pages around the table with the other, Celia sat with her back to the terrace doors and watched them. She was subdued; the news of Ferretis's death coming on top of all the rest that had happened had disturbed her considerably. Haydon also suspected she had begun to draw some obvious conclusions about her own vulnerability.

He sat at the end of the old table near his desk and watched her. There had been no time, nor had Haydon thought it safe, for her to return to her apartment for clothes, so she wore one of Nina's cream silk blouses and a cocoa-brown linen skirt. Celia was a little smaller than Nina, but she wore the slightly oversized clothes as if they were designed to be coolly loose-fitting. Most of the time her eyes were on Renata Islas.

Renata sat directly across from Celia, reading the pages somberly, slowly, her dark Indian eyes floating along the lines. She excluded everyone from this process, and Haydon had the impression that the names of the people and the streets in Guadalajara recreated a world for her that none of them could imagine, and that she must have found painful to relive. He remembered what she had said about hate, and wondered how that philosophy was affecting what she must be feeling.

Mitchell Garner sat next to Renata, leaning forward over the table. He had removed his ballpoint pen from his pocket and was fiddling with it in his right hand, occasionally using it to put a check mark by something he had read. He read quickly, always finishing before Renata passed him another page. As he waited, he ate his sandwich like a man familiar with having to juggle food and paperwork, eating, drinking, and wiping his hands and mouth with his napkin without ever taking his eyes off the pages.

Nina sat across from him, beside Celia. Haydon occasionally could feel her eyes studying him.

Finally everyone finished, and Celia shifted uneasily in her chair.

"All right," Haydon said. "We have to come up with leads, or even one lead, no matter how remote."

"I have a question," Renata said immediately, looking at Haydon.

He nodded. "Go ahead."

"If you are correct," Renata said, looking across at Celia, "you have confirmed our group's suspicions regarding the involvement of some of these businessmen. I was glad to see their names here. Can you tell me exactly how were they involved? This man, for instance," she said, turning the page around and pointing to one of the names.

Celia nodded. "Well, do you know anything about the *teco* organizational structure?"

"Only a little," Renata answered. "But assume I know nothing. Explain everything."

Celia looked at her. "Okay. The, uh, Brigade's also known in Guadalajara as the Organization or the Movement, and it has a close association with the university there. Most of the professors, administrators, and university officials are members, which is why the Movement is able to exist without restraint within the university system. There are roughly three levels in the Movement—the university staff I've just mentioned; the students, who really amount to little more than spies on other students, other professors, anyone and everyone; and the *tecos de choque,* who are the disciplinary arm of the Brigade. The university affiliation is only a legitimizing cover for them. On the university level, the Brigade operates kind of like an ROTC without uniforms, a secret organization everyone knows exists, but only those within it know anything about it.

"When the Organization targets a student they want to recruit, he's approached. If he shows an interest, he's asked to fill out an 'application' for admission. This thing is incredible, a sixty-question document which warns the applicant at the beginning that he must answer all the questions honestly. If it's determined that he's answered falsely, or with duplicity, he must accept"—she made quotation marks in the air with her fingers— " 'the condemnation of God and the punishment that spies and traitors deserve.' "

She paused and looked around the table. "I'm probably repeating some things you already know."

Islas nodded, with a patient smile. "Yes, but please continue. In small ways, every story is different."

Celia looked at her curiously, glanced at Haydon, and then went on. "The questions are detailed, about the ideological and personal lives of the student's parents, brothers and sisters, friends, girlfriend or wife, teachers, employer, neighbors. Everybody he knows. He's asked to provide these people's full names, addresses, telephone numbers, political orientation, all kinds of information. But above all, he's impressed with the idea that the interests of the Movement, the Brigade, are to become first in his life, even 'before filial respect and the unity of the family.'

"In the weeks after the application is completed, the student undergoes two pretty extensive inquisitions directed by an 'examiner/investigator.' They involve surprise visits to the student's home to talk to him and his family, who, in most cases, don't even know what's going on. They're checked out until the Brigade has this huge file on them, and that file is always available to the *tecos*. This man," she said, nodding to the name Renata had asked about, "and the ones listed above him and below him are examiner/investigators.

"Often these men are themselves alumni of the university, and were student *tecos*. The *teco* alumni group is strong, and their loyalty to each other carries over into the business world as well as into politics. After nearly five decades, you can imagine how they've managed to permeate every facet of the society there."

"What's the point in all their data gathering?" Garner asked.

"Leverage," Celia said. "See, this is a Gestapo-type mentality. In their battle against communism, everyone who is not a *teco* is suspect. If they ever want to pressure someone, or use them in any way, they've got the information that could help them to determine the best way to do that. Think of all the interconnections between families and individuals you could come across with this kind of data bank."

"One of these men is in the insurance business," Renata said. "Another is a hospital administrator, another is in the trucking business."

"That's right. Most of them are professionals, at this level anyway. When you get down to the *tecos de choque*, I get the impression they're not so picky about who they use. That part of the organization is made up of gangsters and paramilitary types. The other two facets of the Brigade claim to know nothing of its existence. They shrug it off."

Garner turned to Haydon. "Stuart, have you got that list of board members of the corporation available?"

Haydon reached around to his desk and got a piece of paper, which he handed to Garner.

"When I saw this the other day, I recognized only two names," he said, looking at the list again. "It occurred to me that both of them were Mexico City residents, and both of them were lawyers."

"May I see that, please?" Islas asked, leaning toward Garner. "These men formed this Teco Corporation?" she asked after a minute.

"Right," Garner said. "Do you know any of them?"

She looked at the list a little longer and then said, "Three."

Garner was surprised. Haydon watched her.

"The two with addresses in Guadalajara: one I know, one I've heard about. I've also heard about one of the men from Colima. They also are lawyers." She shook her head slowly, staring at one of the names with an expression of disgust. "This one, I cannot believe it, was retained in 1982 by a man and woman who are members of our group. He represented them in an investigation into the disappearance of their son. He was never able to resolve even the most elementary questions in their case. Now I can see why."

Garner looked at Moreno. "While you were down there, did you notice if lawyers were involved in the activities of the Brigade any more than any other profession?"

"No, not particularly. In fact, I can only remember meeting one. At least, he was the only one introduced to me as a lawyer."

"I've got a hunch," Garner said, "that these board members are 'cutouts'—lawyers hired to represent the interests of other men so their clients' names will not have to appear on a public document."

"Mrs. Islas," Haydon said, "can you associate any names with those lawyers whose names you recognize? Have you ever heard of any of their clients, or businesses they represent? Any names connected with them in any way?"

There was silence as Garner and Islas again studied the list of Teco Corporation officers.

SPIRAL

"Mitchell," Haydon said after a minute, "will you have information about them in your files? Is there some way you can look into these men's clients?"

"I've never dealt with any of them," Garner said, "so I'd have to make some calls to acquaintances down there. But knowing how this group infiltrates Jaliscan society, I'm not sure I'd get any straight answers inquiring about the *tecos* themselves. If I could—"

"Here!" Renata Islas suddenly put her finger on one of the names. "Here. This man . . . there is a connection here." She looked up at Haydon with an expression of triumph. "There *is* a connection here." She tapped her finger on the name and looked down at it. "This man, Mauricio Luquin Spota, is a lawyer with a firm that is very well known in Guadalajara. Hernán and Ramón Rivas. The Rivas brothers are society friends with a very large and old *tapatio* family headed by an elderly man named Apolinar Medrano Mallen. This Apolinar is an elegant old man with a very interesting history. He has three sons and three daughters. The middle son . . . yes, the middle one . . . his name is Blas."

Renata herself seemed surprised to have made this connection. They all had their eyes on her, waiting for her to elaborate, explain, but she only sat looking at the name, her mouth set firmly.

"Apolinar Medrano Mallen," she said finally, as if introducing him, "can trace his family history to the first settlers in the state of Jalisco in the middle of the sixteenth century. He is *criollo*, with not a single drop of Indian blood in the whole line of his family's Spanish heritage. That gives him a tremendous sense of station. The word *tapatio*, which is a nickname for Guadalajarans, comes from an old Indian expression which means 'three times as worthy.' No group believe that of themselves more sincerely than the wealthy elite of Guadalajara, and none of them believe it more fervently than Apolinar Medrano. He is proud with the pride of a man who looks to the history of his lineage and sees men of wealth and influence and power; and he is proud with his belief in the strength of his own destiny, and that of his heirs. His Catholicism is every bit as fierce as the fanaticism we see in the Islamic world today. In every generation a Medrano daughter has denied herself and become a bride of Christ.

"Apolinar's father, Blas's grandfather, was one of the founders of the Autonomous University of Guadalajara in the late 1930s, and as a young man Apolinar himself helped found the National Action Party, known as PAN, in opposition to the Institutional Revolutionary Party. As the years went by and PAN adapted itself to the political winds, Apolinar always came down on the extreme right. He was a founder of MURO, a fascist clique within the university. And, of course, he was one of the founders of *los tecos*. He is a political and financial power who must be reckoned with by anyone who wants to deal with right-wing politics in Mexico."

Renata stopped and took a drink of her iced tea.

"What do you know about Blas himself?" Haydon asked.

"Very little, but I know a woman who went to the university with him. These Medranos, they are like the Kennedy family used to be in the States. What they do and don't do is always a favorite topic of conversation. For instance, even though I don't know them personally myself, I know that the older brother is a lawyer in Mexico City, and that the younger brother operates one of the family businesses in Guadalajara. His two sisters are married to men who are also employed in the family empire. One in Mexico City, one in Colima. Their comings and goings are always in the papers. But about this Blas, I know nothing. Why is that? It makes me suspicious."

"What's his full name?"

"Blas Medrano Banda. His mother, Solana Banda, is also from a wealthy *tapatío* family. That is very important to them. Power begets power."

Haydon pushed aside his plate, glanced at Garner, and addressed Renata.

"You say you know a woman who was his classmate. Would she know any more about him than you? Could you trust her information?"

"Yes, to both questions. She doesn't know the family well, but is close to people who do. She and Blas were in some of the same clubs in the university, and she had a couple of classes with him."

"How old is he?" Garner asked.

Renata thought a moment. "This woman is in her early thirties."

"Can you call her?" Haydon asked. "Would you be able to get information from her?"

"I think she would talk, yes. She has been quietly helpful to our group."

Haydon stood, and walked around to Renata's chair. "Would you call her now?" he asked, pulling her chair out for her. "There's a telephone over here on the other side of the room. Handle your questions any way you wish. Use your own instincts. Find out as much about him as you can—his likes, dislikes, habits, appearance, history since leaving the university, his travels.''

"I understand," Renata said.

"And a photograph. Would she have a photograph?"

"I'll ask." Renata bent down beside her chair and picked up a briefcase. "I brought a Guadalajara telephone book. I thought we might need it."

Haydon walked with her to the far side of the room, spoke with her a few minutes, and then came back to the table.

"Stuart, how are you going to decide if this is the right man?" Nina asked, her voice lowered. "You can't publish his photograph in the media on a hunch."

Haydon shook his head as he sat down. "I don't know. We'll see what she says." Haydon looked at Renata, who was already talking to someone in Spanish. He turned to Celia.

"We're still not any closer than we were before. Did Valverde ever mention any other safe houses, any other addresses or locations besides the Belgrano on Chicon?"

"No," she said. "Nothing. He said these men were professionals, that they'd come in here, do the job, and get out without ever leaving a trace."

"Well, they haven't quite done that," Haydon snapped. "Are you *damn* sure you're telling me everything?"

Suddenly he was surprised to hear the strained, edgy tone of his own voice as if he were abruptly projected outside of his body, observing himself as if he were another person. He saw his forehead twisted in a censuring scowl, his upper body leaning into the table, his doubled fist resting beside the plate with the half-eaten sandwich. Celia stared back at him with a quivering chin, blinking quickly a couple of times. He cut his eyes at Nina, who was looking at him as if she were watching a pot about to boil over and hoping it wouldn't. Celia didn't answer him, perhaps she couldn't, and he said nothing else. He sat back in his chair and looked past Nina, outside beyond the French doors. The terrace was now catching the full glare of the midday sun, its stones seeming to drain of their color as they baked in the bleached light. Quickly absorbed in his own thoughts, he lost track of time.

SPIRAL

"Bueno," Renata said loudly, jolting Haydon back to the present. He turned around to find the others looking at her as she stood by the telephone, concentrating on jotting down a last-minute note.

"We are in luck," she said firmly, walking over to them and pulling her chair away from the table to sit down. When she continued, she addressed Haydon.

"My friend says that Blas was, indeed, a *teco* during his university days. In fact, by the time he had entered graduate school, his own abilities and his father's influence had enabled him to rise above the Brigade's rowdy campus politics into a quieter, more influential role. She said that she had heard that while he was still in graduate school he began to travel to Mexico City quite frequently, and that he eventually married a girl from there. But the girl died shortly afterward, within a year. Sometime after that he was somewhere in the States for a while, a year or more, but she was not sure about this. Then there were rumors that he had become a mercenary in Central America, but none of the people who really knew him well believed there was any substance to that. During the last five or six years, though, she knows of no one who has seen or heard from him directly. Some believe he is again involved with the *tecos* and travels extensively for them. One person claims to know for sure that he was in France during the early eighties, and then more recently, in the last couple of years, they saw him in Tegucigalpa and Guatemala City."

She looked at her notes, which she had taken in a stenographer's notebook, writing on both sides of each sheet. She turned several of these.

"Let's see, . . . before the University of Guadalajara, he attended a Jesuit private school, and was very serious about his religious studies. Evidently he had wanted to go to a Catholic university too, but Apolinar was afraid he was going to ask to enter the priesthood and made him go to the state university."

"What about his personality?" Haydon interrupted.

"All right, uh, what is he like? Handsome, very handsome. Well read, intelligent. Not boisterous, but not a quiet person either. Very pleasant, very polite. She remembered he liked clothes. He dressed very well. About five feet nine or ten. He was well built, but was not an athlete. He was close to his mother, but had a very 'correct' relationship with his father. Apolinar tried to dominate all the sons, but Blas seems to have rebelled the least at his heavy-handedness. He was the one who tried most to conform to what his father wanted.''

Renata stopped. ''I'm sorry, I just took down everything she said. I know some of this is not the kind of thing to help us now.''

''No,'' Haydon said quickly. ''It's all important, every bit of it. Go on. What else?''

''Well, I think that is most of it,'' she said, flipping through her pages. ''She wanted to know why all the questions.''

''What did you tell her?''

''That I would explain when I returned.''

''What about a photograph?''

''Oh, yes. She has several.''

''What's the most recent?''

''1980.''

''Did you ask her if it was clear, in good shape?''

''Yes, I did. They're family pictures that one of his sisters gave a friend, who then gave them to Consuela.''

''Fine, excellent,'' Haydon said. He thought a moment. ''Okay, I want to check something before we go any further. Can you find the Medranos' residence number in the Guadalajara telephone directory?''

''I've looked for it already, but it must be unlisted.''

''We've got to try to locate Blas before we go ahead with this,'' Haydon explained. ''It would be an unforgivable blunder to run his picture only to find out later that he's walking around down there minding his own business, and could have been reached with a simple telephone call.''

''Then the best way to be sure of that is to call one of the Rivas brothers,'' Renata said. ''We would never be able to reach any of the family—there are too many intermediaries whose business is to keep people away. Hernán Rivas would know what to do about your call,'' she said, opening the telephone book. ''Here.'' She circled a number, and handed the book to Haydon.

Haydon took the book and turned around to his desk. The Mexican secretaries were as difficult to get past as Garner's.

He spoke to two of them, identified himself, waited, spoke to another, assured her it was extremely important and confidential. When Rivas finally came on the line, he did not disguise his suspicion. Haydon explained who he was, and said that it was urgent that he speak to Blas Medrano. When Rivas asked why, Haydon explained that the HPD had reason to believe that Blas had been involved in a homicide in Houston the previous night, but if he was there, perhaps he could clarify the mistake. Rivas said that that was a preposterous story because he personally knew that Blas was in Costa Rica on family business. Haydon asked how he could get in touch with Blas in Costa Rica, but Rivas said he was in the countryside there and could not be reached. Haydon said that he was sorry, then, but he would have to go ahead with the warrant. Rivas, very excited, said that would be a grave mistake, and asked for the name of Haydon's superiors. Haydon gave the names to him and said that he would withhold the warrant until six o'clock that evening. If Rivas could provide him with good reasons why he should not issue the warrant, then he could contact Haydon before that time. He gave Rivas both his home number and the number at the homicide division, thanked him for his help, and hung up.

Haydon turned around and stood. "Mitchell, let me ask you a couple of questions," he said, starting toward the library door. Outside in the hall he walked halfway to the foyer before he stopped and turned to face Garner.

"I want to charter a business jet and send her down there for the pictures." He looked at his watch. "It's almost one-thirty. She'd be able to leave Hobby airport by two-thirty. I think it's about a two-hour flight. If her friend would meet her at the airport there, she could be in the air again by five, and be back here in time to have the picture on the ten-o'clock evening news, and before tomorrow's papers go to press."

"Is that the only way you can get them here? Doesn't the DEA have some kind of wire or satellite transmission hookup to the States?"

"No. Everything like this is handled by diplomatic courier, or simply the mails. Mitchell, I need you to go with her. She can't be allowed to do it by herself. You can get in a cab right now, and I'll have all the arrangements made by the time you get to the airport. Richland Charter Flights. I've used them before on Mexican flights.''

"Okay," Garner said. "I'll have to make a few calls first and cancel some appointments.''

"I'd appreciate it," Haydon said. "You can use the telephone in the living room if you want some privacy. It's also a separate line.''

"Give me five or ten minutes," Garner said, turning toward the double doors of the living room.

Haydon walked back to the library and explained to Renata what he wanted to do. She readily agreed.

"I'll call the charter service right now," he said. "I'll make the arrangements and get an arrival time in Guadalajara. Then you'll have to call your friend and tell her when to meet you at the airport. We don't want to waste time having you going into the city.''

As soon as Haydon had confirmed the charter and the arrival time in Guadalajara and called a cab, Renata placed her call. At one forty-five a cab pulled into the drive, Haydon slipped Garner a couple of hundred dollars in case they incurred any out-of-pocket expenses, and they were gone. Haydon went back into the house and called Dystal.

$\mathbf{A}$s he sat at the traffic light, Blas lifted the icepack off his left wrist, which rested in his lap, and checked the swelling. He had tried to keep ice on it from the time he got back to his rooms in the early morning hours. While it wasn't as bruised as he had expected, it was too painful and the swelling still too extensive for him to do enough probing to determine if it was broken. But despite the throbbing, his wrist was not his main concern.

He had been extraordinarily lucky. When he had jumped over the barrier into the dark he had had no idea what lay below, and assumed he would land on cement. But it was dwarf juniper, which afforded a softer landing and had probably saved his life. Had it been cement, he might not have recovered from the impact as agilely as he had, rolling against the wall of the building before the men above him reached the barrier and started firing into the shrubbery. Pressed against the wall, he had listened to the sputtering machine pistols, the oddly muted ripping of the shrubbery and the empty casings plinking into the shredded bushes. He heard cursing in Spanish, car doors slamming, but he didn't begin running until he heard the car engines racing and the screaming tires.

Since the police didn't normally carry fully automatic machine pistols, he knew it was Negrete. While he lay on his stomach in the dark bank of oleanders where he had gone to ground again only a block away, his wrist throbbing and his clothes soaking up the sweat that poured off him in the still, humid night, Negrete's cars circled the neighborhood in the vicinity around the garage. If he had parked the rental car somewhere along the street instead of in a parking lot, they would eventually have discovered it. When they finally disappeared at the first distant wailing of the police sirens, Blas got to his feet and walked with disciplined unconcern back to his car in the hospital parking lot.

He had immediately signaled Arizpe on the radio, and they met at a late-night diner on Richmond. Blas told Arizpe what had happened, that the police knew about him, that apparently Negrete had gotten to Waite, had picked up on Ferretis, and had followed him to the dead drop. After some discussion they decided that whatever Negrete had gotten out of Waite it wouldn't have been enough to threaten them. They decided not to change any plans. They could not determine how the police had gotten Arizpe's name, but believed the authorities had little information beyond that or they never would have let Cordero leave the city. Except for Negrete knowing they had purchased RDX, they were the only two who knew where the explosives had been placed, and they could see no point at which they might have left a trail for the police, or even Negrete, to pick up. The greatest liabilities in this operation always had been the contacts in Houston, and by one means or another, all of them were now dead, except for the escaped Cordero. The only remaining significant dangers were that Arizpe's surveillance might be spotted, and that by some freak change of routine Gamboa would not cross the San Felipe rail crossing for several days. They agreed to go back to their bases, get some sleep, and follow the procedures they had already initiated.

Blas returned to La Colombe d'Or. No one knew he was staying there, not even Rubio. Nor did he know Rubio's base, an arrangement that was a long-standing method of security they routinely initiated in the final forty-eight hours before a hit. It freed both of them from the tension created by the nagging fear that one might be caught without the other's knowledge, and be tortured into betraying his location.

He was in the car by seven o'clock, and drove to the Steak 'N Egg diner near Post Oak Boulevard where he and Rubio had talked the evening before. He bought the morning papers and ate breakfast as he read the articles on Ferretis and the Waite killings. The police, who were still withholding information about the details of the investigation, confirmed that they were utilizing the resources of the FBI and the DEA. An energetic reporter had finally determined that the limousine, though it had been leased in Sosa Real's name, was in the employ of Benigo Gamboa Parra, whose home appeared to be under heavy guard. Though the headlines were big, the articles about the killings were indeed sketchy, just as Ferretis had said, including, now, his own.

Blas left the newspaper behind when he left the diner, making a mental note not to go there again. If he had not been preoccupied he would not have returned there for breakfast. Luckily, a shift change had provided different waitresses. His second appearance there in less than eight hours wouldn't have attracted the attention of any one waitress.

During the next three hours, Blas cruised the streets in a rough rectangle that lay within an area from Post Oak Boulevard to Shepherd on the west and east, and between the Southwest Freeway and San Felipe on the south and north. He stopped for coffee twice, pulled into a service station and filled his half-full tank with gasoline, parked in parking lots and watched shoppers until the heat forced him to begin driving again so he could run the air conditioner. He had had two "nothing happening" signals from Rubio.

Then, while he was examining his swollen wrist at the traffic light, Rubio signaled him to go to a telephone booth on Kirby. When he got there, he called a booth on Buffalo Speedway, and Rubio answered.

"Somethin's happenin'," Rubio said in a flat voice. "About twenty minutes ago, a little after eleven, I saw three or four police cars pulling onto Inverness. I made a pass by Gamboa's, and it looks like they were picking up Negrete's boys. They got the stakeout down the street, too. I don't know how many they took away, but I saw four at least."

"They left policemen around the house?"

"No."

"There are *no* guards at the house?"

"I didn't see nobody."

Blas felt a sudden tingle of warning. "Gamboa's still there?"

"I didn't see him leave."

"What do you think?"

"I don't know. Maybe they tied them to the Waite thing. I don't know."

"It's too soon," Blas said. He was looking through the dirty booth glass, out into the sunlight. "But maybe they suspect them, maybe it's a shakedown. You didn't see them take Negrete?"

"No." After a pause Rubio said, "I don't like this."

Blas thought of Rubio's dark face, the glimpse of a white tooth in the cleft of his lower lip. Then he thought of Negrete's face. His lovely, oily eyes, the broad forehead and narrow face that so much resembled the head of an ant. Like the proverbial master who had grown to resemble his dog, Negrete brought to mind the insect for which he had been nicknamed. Or maybe it was his appearance and his reputation that first had suggested the insect. He was, after all, dark and small . . . and had the sting of death. *El Hormiga Negro.* The Black Ant. Blas remembered seeing Ireno's face through the binoculars, remembered the nail and the ant. In certain parts of Mexico this signature of Negrete's was infamous. Blas had seen his work before, and he had seen the fear it inspired. And now, for an instant, he saw Rubio's forehead . . . the nail . . . and the ant, dancing on the end of the string like a tiny marionette. "Do you think it's too risky to continue the surveillance?"

"I don't know. That doesn't bother me. It could be easier this way, maybe. What I don't like is, where is Negrete?"

"Maybe the police have people in the houses in the neighborhood. Maybe they're trying to draw us out." Blas thought a moment. "Rubio, don't make any more passes by the house."

"What do you mean? What do you want me to do?"

"Let me think."

The telephone booth was like a glass oven. The goddam thing wasn't even in the shade. He stood there holding the telephone, knowing that every minute Rubio was away from Inverness increased Gamboa's chances of slipping through. But he had to assess the removal of Negrete's men. If something happened to Rubio, he would have to call it off. It would be insane to try to monitor Gamboa's movements himself. He drew the line at that. Every assignment boiled down to two ultimate priorities: take out the target; and preserve his own life. He would sacrifice everything and everyone to achieve the former, except the latter. At one time, at some point in the gray, far past that was not so long ago in years, but a vast distance in the mind, he must have thought like Teodoro Anica. He must have held convictions, believed philosophies, adhered to truths. Now such motivations were cold flames. He could imagine nothing in the ideologies of men for which he would give his life; sacrifice had become for him an alien concept.

"With all this going on, the old man might move," Rubio said.

"It's risky."

"You want to call it off?"

"Not yet."

"Okay, then I got to get back over there."

Rubio's matter-of-fact statement resolved Blas's hesitation. The Indian was right. It was his turn with blind risk . . .

"Signal more frequently," Blas said. "Every half hour."

"Bueno," Rubio said, and hung up.

. . . and he had no right to expect what he hoped he would get.

Haydon told Dystal about Renata Islas hitting on Blas Medrano's name and what he had done about it, and asked what had happened at the lieutenant's end of the operation. He was standing at his desk, and while he listened to Dystal's Texas-accented basso, he watched Nina and Celia taking away the plates and glasses from the refectory table.

". . . didn't let them know they were coming, so it was pretty confusing. Lapierre said some of the boys didn't want to give up their firearms and it was a little tense there for a bit. But Gamboa's boy, Efren, came outside and got them all calmed down. And that's where we had some good luck. Three of those boys were carrying Mac-10s—converted to full automatic. So they made three arrests right on the spot. Thing is, they only got four of them. Negrete wasn't anywhere around. If the son of a bitch was telling the truth in the first place, there's two more gone with him."

As he watched the two women, it occurred to Haydon that something unexpected had happened. Nina and Celia had somehow exchanged a sisterly understanding of one another, and seemed very much at ease together.

"They went through the whole compound?" Haydon asked, but his mind went back to Nina and Celia. In a way, he wasn't surprised at their affinity. Not because of what he knew about Celia, but because of what he knew about Nina. The facade of nearly theatrical self-confidence Celia had displayed when Haydon had first met her at Valverde's, the anger she had shown at her mother's, the fear she tried unsuccessfully to hide behind a willful stubbornness in the car when she was telling him about the *tecos*, all had evolved now into an unabashed vulnerability. Not only had she lost a brother, but she had finally realized that a project to which she had dedicated herself with some passion for the past six months had turned out to be only a trick of mirrors. She didn't know *what* she had been doing. Being the victim of such a grand deception was demoralizing, and it was typical of Nina to sense how shattering this sudden vulnerability had been for the girl. It was typical of her too to show in her uncalculating and straightforward manner that she sympathized. That kind of sincerity was seldom wasted on people who truly yearned for it.

"Yeah, they did," Dystal said, "and they found another converted Mac-10 out in that little shack of Negrete's. I don't know what the DA's gonna let us do about that, but I want to charge Gamboa with constructive possession on all four of those Macs, and that'll give us sufficient reason for deportation." Dystal's voice lowered a little, and Haydon had to strain to hear him. "That may be kinda thin soup, but I think the wind's changing a little bit down here. We got some city officials and a senator in here stirring up the water, and, uh, I think the general feeling is that if there isn't any target, then there won't be any shooters. It's gotten to that point. You know, just get the hell rid of this thing, quickest way possible."

Haydon had been afraid of that. The killings had made the network television news again that morning, and the city politicians were eager to avoid being tagged in the national media as a Little Mexico, a haven for plotters of Latin political intrigues. They would be able to explain their way out of that kind of association if they could say that Benigo Gamboa Parra was the object of grievances by an unknown group of radicals in Mexico, and that he simply happened to be living temporarily in Houston when they decided to pursue him. It was just one of those things. If he had lived in Happy Valley, Texas, then the violence would have followed him there, too. It had nothing at all to do with Houston's geography or demographics. Just bad luck.

Benigo Gamboa had cut his teeth on political intrigue in

Mexico, and now he was about to experience the full force of political maneuvering on this side of the border as well.

"So they're going to run him off?"

"That's right. And the sooner the better. They don't want him bombed to jelly in this city."

"And what is Gamboa's reaction so far?"

"The man's pissed we took away his militia. Pete told him we'd leave him plenty of uniformed officers to take their place, but he said hell no he didn't want them. He said he was going to make some calls, straighten this business out."

"So you didn't leave anyone?"

"Nobody showing. We've got stakeouts in the upper floors of residences on both sides of the street in both directions, and there's men in unmarked cars in driveways. He's covered, but he doesn't know it. I imagine he's doing some heavy sweating."

"What did he say about Negrete?" Behind Haydon, Nina finished removing the last place mats from the refectory table. He turned around and watched her as she walked out of the library and closed the door after her.

"Nobody knew where he was. He just happened to be out. In fact, Gamboa asked Pete where he was."

"I'd like to know who Gamboa was going to call."

"Well, if it's anybody with real clout, we'll learn soon enough."

"Has the crime lab made any headway?"

"A little," Dystal said. "Some of the pubic hair and the head hair on the bed at La Concha Courts was Ireno López's, so we got a positive ID there. There was also both kinds of hair from somebody else, too. At the Waite house, well, they've got prints all over the place. They've got a few that don't belong to either the Waites or the Ferrells, but no IDs on them yet. We're taking prints from the boys we brought in, and ballistics is checking to see if their Mac-10s fired any of those shells we found at the garage. So far all the blood's typing out like the Waites', or Donny Ferrell's."

There was a moment when neither of them spoke, and then Haydon said, "This has been a tough one. I can't remember when we've had this many people working so intensively with such little progress."

"We've never had a foreign assassin come strolling in here

either, Stu,'' Dystal said. ''When they come outta nowhere with no domestic background, no domestic ties, and going after people who aren't American citizens, there's not a hell of a lot we *can* do.''

''If those pictures don't work,'' Haydon said, ''it's going to be too late to do anything else. Either Gamboa will have fled, or they will have gotten him. I can't see this going on another twenty-four hours, either way.''

''No, me neither. I think you're right.''

''There are two questions I'm afraid we'll never get answers for,'' Haydon said. ''Who were Celia Moreno's anonymous handlers and why were they gathering intelligence on the *tecos?* And who helped Gamboa and other corrupt politicians and businessmen get their hundreds of millions of plundered funds out of Mexico?''

Dystal snorted. ''You been in this business long enough to know you don't often get answers to those kinds of questions.''

Haydon knew what Dystal was getting at. Both men had come to realize there was more here than the HPD had the power, or the capacity, to deal with. As homicide detectives, they were too far down the pecking order to be able to expect the real story behind the events. No one was going to let them in on the larger picture. They were simply street sweepers; no one was asking them to find out who was leaving the dirt. In fact, no one wanted them to.

Lucas Negrete sat in the backseat of the new rental car as it traveled inbound on the Southwest Freeway. He was angry, frustrated, and running out of time. The three men had parked the car registered in Ramón Sosa Real's name in a Greenway Plaza parking lot, taken a cab to a nearby car rental agency, and rented a Lincoln, using a false ID. Now they were heading downtown to rent two motel rooms. Negrete knew the exact motel he wanted, on South Main, so close to the freeway that the rooms on its south-side third floor sounded as if they were *on* the overpass, a stationary vehicle in a never-ending roar of never-ending traffic. The noisiest rooms in the city.

As the driver, a muscular young man named Siseno with ringlets and oriental eyes, tended to the traffic, Negrete pored over a maze of papers. He held a clipboard in his lap as he recorded a list of numbers, some of which he occasionally called out to Luis, whose bespectacled face and phlegmatic manner disguised a brutish personality. Luis answered yes or no, and sometimes called out a number of his own.

When they arrived at the motel, Siseno got out and went inside to register for the two rooms. Negrete and Luis continued to work. They didn't even look up. When the driver returned, he got into the car without speaking and pulled through the entrance into the motel compound.

The L-shaped motel was six floors high, and was situated so that the blunt end of the bottom arm almost butted up against the expressway. The bottom rooms looked out onto the street underneath the expressway, the ever-shadowy stomach of the elevated highway with its grimy ribs of cement columns and diesel-stained girders, derelict chain-link fence, winos, garbage, and scavenging pigeons. The second floor looked into the silver-painted freeway railings, and the third floor was on the level with the cars. This was the room that was rarely rented. The management actually used to try, but so many people returned the key and asked for a new room or their money back that they gave it out now only when it was absolutely the last room left in the motel. Still, most people passed it up.

The men had only small bags, which they carried through a breezeway from the parking area, past the Coke and 7-Up machines and the out-of-order elevator, and up the metal stairs near the gate to the swimming pool in the courtyard. In the suffocating heat of midday, there were only two people in the pool, or rather, in the pool chairs: a large young Mexican woman whose dark flesh lolled out of the openings of her lavender bikini in glistening, sea-lion proportions, and her smaller, Anglo male companion, whose fair skin had broiled to the startling color of brilliant flamingo. They held hands, their arms draped between the two pool chairs.

The three men entered the first of the two rooms they had checked into. They put down their briefcases and bags and went next door to the last room on the third-floor landing. The roar of traffic booming by thirty feet away at seventy miles an hour was accompanied by gusts of stinging grit whipped off the asphalt in hot blasts that stank of superheated oil and rubber. Inside, Negrete liked what he saw, and liked even better what he heard . . . and couldn't hear.

They locked the door behind them and walked back to the first room. Negrete and Luis sat down at a small round table, pulled out their papers, and resumed working. Siseno took the keys and went back down the stairs to the car. He had seen a liquor store several blocks away.

The same examination of the license-plate numbers continued. For the past week, the plate of every car that had entered Inverness within two blocks of Benigo Gamboa's house had been recorded by Negrete's stakeouts. It was a tedious job checking each day's entries against the others, but Negrete hoped it would pay off. Anyone wanting to kill Gamboa would have to monitor his comings and goings, and to do that would have to approach the house. Somewhere in that pile of numbers were recurrences, and one of those recurring license numbers belonged to the car of an assassin.

By midafternoon they had found nine cars that had appeared on the street more than twice on each of the given days. Five of those cars had "R" written beside them, which meant they had been identified as belonging to street residents. The other four had to be checked out. Negrete moved over and sat on the edge of the bed. From his wallet he took a piece of paper with several numbers on it, and dialed the one for the state office of motor vehicle registrations. Within minutes, he had learned what he had suspected, that all four cars were registered in the name of four different car-leasing agencies.

The mild-faced Luis, equipped with one of the dozens of Mexican police identification cards and badges with which Negrete was supplied, left to call on the agencies. If Negrete's hunch was right again, Luis would be able to obtain not only the name—and possibly the description—of the person who rented the car, but also the car's color, make, and model. They would rent two more cars for themselves, and the three of them would begin stalking the stalker, a delicate and dangerous maneuver, but one that Negrete had negotiated successfully many times before.

Chapter 49

After he had finished talking to Dystal, Haydon paced around the library for twenty minutes, going over and over the events of the past several days. Finally, unable to stay in one place any longer, he walked outside and went down to the bathhouse to check on Cinco. The old collie was asleep, of course, and Haydon, too restless to sit down with him, didn't walk over and pet him for fear of waking him. He continued along the walkway through the cherry laurels to the greenhouse and went inside. Walking aimlessly along its paths, his vision registered only the most brilliant colors among the hundreds of bromeliads. The more subtle shades and tints, which he normally enjoyed seeking out, went unappreciated now. His mind wasn't able to slow down for them. He returned to the house, his hands in his pockets as he climbed the terrace steps and went through the French doors into the library.

He had never felt more useless. Lapierre and the task force had their hands full with the paperwork and evidence gathering in constructing the case against Negrete in the killings of Ireno López, the Waites, Donny Ferrell, and Daniel Ferretis. Bob Dystal was trying to do end runs around the political obstacles that kept cropping up in his effort to get the DEA and the FBI to cooperate with each other to the extent that they could provide the HPD with useful information on Blas Medrano, whose name, now that it was known, was being fed into the computers and distributed to the field agents of both agencies. Renata Islas and Mitchell Garner were now about half an hour out from Guadalajara's Miguel Hidalgo International Airport.

Haydon walked to his desk, opened the rosewood humidor, and took out an Allones corona maduro. He clipped the end, struck a match, and lighted it. The walk had made him perspire. He loosened his tie, removed his cufflinks and laid them on his desk, and turned back his sleeves. Taking the cigar out of his mouth, he stepped over to the bookshelves and looked at the titles. He was tempted to take one down, perhaps a collection of essays, or poetry—nothing protracted—but he couldn't even settle between the two, his mind already trying to see the face of Blas Medrano Banda.

He sensed someone behind him, and turned toward Nina standing in the doorway looking at him.

"What's on your mind, Stuart?" she asked. Her arms were folded and she was leaning against the doorframe.

"Where's Celia?" he asked.

"We were in the living room talking. She's exhausted. She went to sleep on the divan."

Haydon nodded, and went around to one of the wing chairs and sat down. Nina came over and sat on the small sofa.

"What do you think about her now?" Haydon asked.

"What do you mean, 'now'?"

"Now that you've been around her a little more."

Nina looked at him a moment. He thought he saw a touch of wariness in her eyes, a little skepticism.

"I guess I understand her better than I did before," Nina said, going ahead despite her reservations. "What she did doesn't seem so outrageous now, so improbable. I can see how it might have happened, how it might have come about."

Haydon nodded, looking at her.

"She's young, Stuart. Have you lost the ability to know when you ought to be giving someone the benefit of the doubt?"

He didn't know what he had expected from her, but he hadn't expected that. Yes, he thought, he guessed he had forgotten how to do that. "I don't know," he said.

But with Celia Moreno he did know. It wasn't that he didn't

realize she deserved the benefit of the doubt, it was rather that he was too inclined to give it. In fact, he was too inclined toward her altogether, and realizing that had made him wary of every judgment he made regarding her. Recognizing the attraction, he had kept a greater distance than he otherwise would have. He felt a little foolish about it. That, in addition to everything else that had happened during the last four days, had made him guarded and analytic about every nuance of his emotions.

Nina didn't say anything for a moment, and then, "You didn't answer my question."

"I said I didn't know."

"No, the other one."

"What was I thinking?"

She smiled.

"I was thinking about Blas Medrano." Haydon pulled on the cigar a couple of times, tasting the aroma of the dark tobacco. "Renata said he was well read, intelligent, had a Jesuit education. A young widower. A traveler. Compliant son of a bullying father. Handsome. Wealthy. Polite." He looked at the cigar as he rolled it in his fingers. "I would like to talk with him," he said.

"Talk with him?"

"He sounds like an interesting man."

"Good Lord, Stuart. His politics are despicable."

"So are the politics of the man he wants to kill, and I can assure you, if you were to meet him you would find him charming. Besides, we don't really know about Medrano's politics. We know only the politics of the *tecos.*"

"Don't you think he might agree with them?" Nina asked dryly. "And whose father was it that was one of the organization's founders?"

"The bullying father," Haydon reminded her. "All right. But I would wager that the man who fits the profile we got from Renata would have a difficult time living the politics of a *teco*. It can't be easy for him. Not inside, I mean."

"It can't be easy being an assassin, either," Nina said pointedly. Then, "What are you getting at?"

"I'm not getting at anything. I was only thinking about this man we're going after. Wondering about him."

"You spend a lot of time wondering about people," Nina

said. The expression on her face clearly said that it was a suspect preoccupation.

He smiled. "I do, don't I." He looked at his watch. "They should be at the airport now. Renata will be talking to her friend, Consuelo. They were supposed to call me when they were ready to start back."

"Do you think the pictures will work?"

"They're the only thing that will work in time." He crossed his legs the other way and touched the end of his cigar in the ashtray. A cylindrical ash remained in the crystal dish. Haydon sighed. "Jesus," he said, gazing at the ash. "What an incredible chain of events. You get caught up in something like this and you can't believe it, and the moment you finally realize it's really happening to you your perspective changes instantly. It's as if there were a slight shift in the magnetic poles. Bewildering, mildly disorienting, but you recover, you adjust. And then suddenly, you're aware that nothing will ever be quite the same again."

Blas stepped out of the telephone booth and got into the car. Rubio was right in thinking it was a crucial time for Gamboa. Blas doubted that the Houston Police Department would actually leave Gamboa unprotected, but they would surely use a more subtle means of guarding him than did Negrete. It was Negrete's style, the Mexican way, to show your arms, to strut back and forth across your barnyard. Not only did he want to win, he wanted to look good doing it. But not the Anglos. They would hide. They would win first and strut later. Blas trusted Rubio to know this, too.

He went straight back to La Colombe d'Or and began packing his things. If it was going to happen, it would happen within the next twenty-four hours. He could live that long out of a car. It was an acquired occupational talent.

It would take him a while to pack. Not only did he want to avoid leaving behind even a single strand of copper wire, but his wrist was acutely painful now, rendering his left hand practically useless. He poured himself another glass of the brandy and got busy. After packing all his clothes in the suitcases, he emptied the bathroom of his toilet articles, taking all the complimentary soaps and colognes. The small packages would come in handy the way he was going to be traveling. He took a washcloth, soaked it in alcohol, and began a meticulous room-by-room cleaning of fingerprints. He always did this. If you were careful and aware, it was amazing how few places you could leave fingerprints, and how thoroughly you could clean up the ones you did leave. It was tedious, but it was necessary. He didn't like to make it easy for them.

He kept a close watch on the time. Rubio made an all-clear call when Blas was almost through cleaning. He would have to hurry and finish so that he would not be in the process of checking out when the next call came half an hour later.

When he was through, the two large suitcases packed with clothes sat in front of the suite door along with the two briefcases, one containing the cash he hadn't yet spent, and the other containing the radio transmitter. On the brandy table in a plain white envelope he left a liberal gratuity for the man and woman who had been assigned to him during his stay. Then he called for a porter.

As he checked out, he paid his bill with one of his credit cards, necessary equipage for the modern traveler, especially one such as he who dreaded more than anything else to attract attention. He had always thought that one of the most peculiar absurdities about traveling in the United States was that cash was looked upon with suspicion almost everywhere.

He got on the streets in the very middle of rush hour. Risky timing. He had planned to be closer to the San Felipe crossing, in the event Gamboa decided to move while the streets were congested. Although it seemed improbable from Gamboa's point of view (it would have been practically impossible for him to escape an attack in such traffic), under the circumstances it would have been his most fortuitous decision, because Blas would not have been able to make it to the intersection in time. He needed to get closer to the crossing, and stay there.

It was happy hour, although the management would never have used so gross a phrase. You simply received a complimentary drink. He was eating an early dinner at Latouche's, a restaurant that seemed to cater to the young and affluent. For Blas it was in a perfect location, close to the Loop on

Westheimer and only a few blocks from a small street that cut straight across to San Felipe just west of the rail crossing. He told the maître d' that he was a doctor, that he needed the clumsy radio instead of the customary unobtrusive beeper because he had to be available for communication with the Life Flight helicopters. Would they mind seating him at an inconspicuous table so the periodic static would not disrupt their other guests? The maître d' loved the idea, and seated him in a private cove under a canopy of smoked glass with a western view.

He played the game. Himself against himself. To forestall the tension of the waiting, he pretended to have no expectations of interruptions. With his two glasses of Dewar's and water, he ordered oysters Rockefeller to be followed by small portions of red snapper grenobloise and fresh artichokes stuffed with crabmeat. It would be a leisurely meal, eaten while he watched the falling sun descend behind the sparkling towers of the West Loop District, fire into diamonds.

Halfway through the oysters Rockefeller, Rubio signaled again. There was no code to indicate any need for communication, so Blas continued eating. He concentrated on the food, though it was awkward with only one hand. His left wrist was too sensitive even to use a fork. He tried to remember a similar meal eaten under more pleasant circumstances. He remembered a similar fish, not red snapper, but something like it, in a beautiful little restaurant along the *malecón* in Montevideo. And the shrimp? There were memorable shrimp in Veracruz and, oddly, in a tiny fishing village called Monkey River Town in Belize, or at that time British Honduras. But it was also the place where he had tasted the worst liquor he had ever swallowed. Remembering, he sipped the Dewar's with greater pleasure.

He must have played the game extremely well, for he did not know if he had missed an all-clear signal or if the one coming across now was simply late, but when the static of the new transmission broke over the radio, a cold stream flowed down his neck and back before he even comprehended the meaning. The fish stuck in his throat. He felt hot, stunned. Rubio was screaming: Negrete! Negrete! Blas grabbed the radio and bolted outside, stood beside the palms yard, panting, staring at the radio as if he would be able to see what was happening too. Rubio screaming: Negrete! The single word over and over, almost drowned out by the roar of the car engine, the gunfire, the screeching tires, and the collision. Then men shouting, followed by the piercing, unwavering electronic squeal of a smashed radio. It all had happened in seconds. Only seconds.

Haydon had already gone by the office of Richland
Charter Flights to take care of the charges and was waiting
at the side of the tarmac when the small Learjet touched down.
He watched as it turned in the late-afternoon light and taxied
back toward him, its lights blinking and the falling sun throwing a fiery streak the length of its polished aluminum fuse-
lage. Haydon had parked the Vanden Plas on the aircraft's
approach to its hangar, and he waited with the sedan's emergency lights pulsing. The pilot pulled the sleek jet around
until its wingtip almost touched the Jaguar's left front fender,
and settled its engines. Haydon could see people moving behind the portholes, and then the side door lowered onto the
asphalt. Renata Islas emerged first, carrying her briefcase,
followed closely by Garner.

"Good flight?" Haydon asked, taking her arm and opening the rear car door for her.

"Beautiful," she said.

Garner went around to the passenger side of the front seat
as Haydon closed Renata's door and waved his thanks to the
pilot. Haydon got in the car, started the motor, and drove
across the tarmac to the exit gates. Turning onto Telephone
Road, they headed for the Gulf Freeway that would take them
straight into downtown.

"Any problems at all?" Haydon asked, lowering his sun
visor as he merged with the traffic on the freeway.

"None," Renata said, opening her briefcase and taking

out a manila envelope. "Consuelo was waiting for us. Look at these."

Garner took the photographs from her and handed them to Haydon one at a time. There were four of them. Renata sat forward in her seat and looked around Haydon's shoulder, commenting on each photograph as Haydon looked at it.

"This first one is the oldest. His senior-year picture at the Autonomous University of Guadalajara. Very handsome," she affirmed, and he was. He had a strong, firm-jawed face with a fairly low hairline and thick dark hair. He smiled easily at the camera, his teeth as white and straight as a film star's. His upper lip was long and almost full, with clean, delineated margins like those of a marble sculpture. His nose was a little broader than Haydon had imagined it, and his eyes were soft.

"This one," Renata said, as Garner handed him the second one, "is about the same time. Consuelo had a seminar with him their first year in graduate school. This was taken on the terrace of one of the buildings at the university. The four other people are friends, of no importance here. Consuelo took the picture."

The friends were having lunch around a wrought-iron table with a tile top. It was in the fall, perhaps, for they were all wearing light sweaters. The five students had lined up behind the table and had linked their arms together. Blas was on the end next to the balustrade that overlooked a campus mall with trees. Everyone was smiling. Blas was not as amused as the others.

"This next was taken at a family gathering at the Medrano home in Guadalajara. This is Tico, Blas's older brother, and Jorge, the younger one. His two sisters with their husbands, his mother, and Apolinar. The others are cousins, aunts, uncles."

The setting seemed to be in a garden or courtyard of the home. There were colonial arches of a colonnade in the background, a portion of a sloping tiled roof. The family had arranged themselves in several rows for the photograph, and though it was a relaxed occasion, Haydon thought the grouping of persons was interestingly formal. In the center was the unmistakable presence of Apolinar and his wife, Solana. The two daughters sat cross-legged on the grass in front of their parents with their husbands kneeling behind. Tico and Jorge stood on either side of their mother, each with an arm around her shoulders. Blas stood beside his father, both men with their hands clasped correctly behind their backs. The rest of the people seemed to be arranged in their own family groups around the Medranos. Haydon looked at Blas. Although his brothers and sisters were dressed in casual clothes, Blas and his father wore suits and ties. Apolinar also wore a stern expression, as if he was well aware of his burdensome position as patriarch of all those around him. Blas's expression was not so easily interpreted. The eyes which had seemed soft in the earlier picture now seemed to bear a look more akin to melancholy. His posture seemed to indicate that he was a part of the picture only reluctantly. Every person in the photograph was smiling, except the bullying father and his compliant son.

"This one I did not expect to get," Renata said. "It is the most recent. His wedding picture, 1980."

That was all she said, as if the picture spoke for itself. There were only the two of them in the photograph, Blas and his new wife, standing on the flight of steps of a church with its gothic arched doors vaguely visible in the background. Blas was dressed very formally in gray striped trousers and black cutaway. His bride's wedding dress was traditionally long-trained and veiled, the veil pushed up and back for the photograph. She was a handsome girl, blond and rather tall, at least as tall as he was. Both of them were smiling, of course, but Blas's smile was not genuine. His eyes, which in the past had been first soft, then melancholy, now were blank, devoid of any kind of expression at all. They could have been glass.

"How old was he in this picture?" Haydon asked.

"Twenty-six," Renata said. "What do you think?" she asked as Haydon handed the wedding picture back to her over his shoulder.

"Maybe we should use two of them," he said.

"Which two?" she asked. She seemed to be curious about more than just his choice of selection.

"I'd say the one on the terrace, and the wedding picture."

"Yes," she said quickly. "I think those are the ones."

"The school picture is too old," Haydon explained, "and I'm afraid the one with the family is too small. By the time his face was blown up to a useful size, it would be too grainy.''

"Yes," Renata said, sitting back. "Yes, I think so."

"What's your opinion, Mitchell?" Haydon asked, looking over at Garner. He had been unusually quiet since they had arrived at the airport.

"I agree," Garner said. "I think he could be recognized from those unless he's undergone a dramatic change."

"Good. Then we'll go with those," Haydon said, and he glanced once more at Garner, who was looking straight ahead into the approaching columns of city lights.

There wasn't time for Haydon to drop Garner and Renata Islas at his house before he delivered the pictures to the photography lab at police headquarters on Riesner Street. Haydon asked them if they wanted to wait for him in the homicide division offices, but they chose to wait in the lobby instead. Haydon delivered the pictures, and made sure copies would be taken immediately to the newspapers and television stations along with the artist's sketches of Rubio Arizpe. The sketches and photographs were to be accompanied by a press release and a formal HPD request that the pictures be considered urgent public-service items. This request was hardly necessary. The media were starving for information about the investigation.

Haydon made a quick pass by Dystal's office and learned that ballistics had determined that the casings in the garage where Ferretis's body had been found had not been fired by the Mac-10s that had been in the possession of the Gamboa guards they now held in custody. A further indication to Dystal that the missing Negrete and his two companions were indeed the strong-arms within the group. Fingerprinting had no success in matching the few prints found at the Waites' with the men in custody.

The DEA and FBI were still responding negatively. They were aware of the existence of *los tecos*, but they had nothing in their files definitely tying them to specific death-squad activities. There were plenty of rumors of *teco* involvement in all kinds of political intrigue, including narcotics trafficking by wealthy politicians, but very little of it had actually been confirmed. Basically, it was the same kind of information Haydon had gotten first from Mitchell Garner. And there was nothing in their files about Blas Medrano, Rubio Arizpe, or Ireno López.

"Fact is," Dystal said, looking up at Haydon from his creaking office chair behind his desk, "when they see these pictures, they're not gonna be satisfied with just taking information we pass on to them. They're gonna want to know your sources."

"I won't do that," Haydon said.

"Well, I didn't think you would," Dystal said. "But I thought you ought to be looking for it. They're gonna be all over you, like chickens on a June bug."

"Have you heard anything from Gamboa?" Haydon asked, changing the subject.

"Not a peep, but I imagine they're walking around the house with their guns cocked."

"They did check the house and grounds for explosives?"

Dystal nodded. "When they picked up Negrete's boys they took dogs and electronics through. Nothing."

"How do you think they're going to use it?" Haydon said, turning around and looking out the plate-glass window in Dystal's office. The squad room seemed no more busy than normal. The investigation had gotten organized. The work was being done, but it didn't show anymore.

"I don't see how they could," Dystal said. "I think they know they've screwed up and they've pulled out. They may get him sooner or later, but it's not going to be here. Not now."

"I'm not quite that sure," Haydon said. "But it seems they would be running a tremendous risk to go ahead with it after those pictures hit the news tonight."

"You'll get me something in writing on Blas's background?" Dystal reminded him.

"In the morning."

"Along with Miss Moreno's stuff," Dystal said.

Haydon, already walking out the door, nodded, waved, and kept going.

On the way to her house with Haydon and Mitchell, Renata Islas assured Haydon that she was not in the least afraid to go back to her bungalow in the little compound off Canal Street. She was in a good humor, saying that she felt better than she had in years because she felt she had made some real progress in striking a blow at the *tecos*. Haydon assured her he would keep her apprised of what was happening, and thanked her for making the hurried and tiresome round-trip flight to Guadalajara. He went into her house with her and insisted on waiting in her living room while she checked the rest of the house. She laughed at him, saying that she had been going into her house alone for five years, and that tonight was no different. But when she came back into the living room from checking the rest of the house, her smile seemed somehow sad. Haydon did not think it was the dim lighting that made her eyes sparkle as she thanked him and said that it was good to have a man care in that way again.

Haydon walked back to the Vanden Plas, got in, and started the motor. "All right," he said, turning on the headlights and pulling away from the curb. "You've been incredibly patient, Mitchell. What's the matter?"

Garner turned to him and said, "How many people knew we were going to Guadalajara, Stuart?"

Haydon felt immediately uneasy. "Just us, and Dystal. I had to let him know. Why?"

"We picked up tails at the Guadalajara airport," Garner said. "You know I'm no expert on this sort of thing, but I spotted these two guys on a fluke. When we got to the airport there were no flights coming in or leaving. The place was relatively deserted. In fact, I probably wouldn't have spotted them if Renata and her friend hadn't decided to go to the rest room as soon as we got there. I let them walk off, wanting to stretch my legs a little, and then I immediately thought better of letting them go off alone, so I started after them. They were just on the other side of the concourse, and I saw which corridor they were heading for. I was so far behind them there were several people in between us.

"It just so happened that everyone turned off before the women got to the rest rooms except this one guy who thought, I'm sure, that they were heading for the exit at the far end of the corridor. He was closing the gap behind them when they suddenly turned into the rest room. He walked on by, then made a U-turn and stopped. I realized he'd been following them, and was a little flustered that he had seen me make him. I stopped too, and looked behind me in time to see a second man stop and turn back to a water fountain a few steps away. There were only the three of us in the corridor. The man who had been following the women simply looked at me, and the one at the water fountain finished his drink and then headed back to the concourse. The other guy and I stayed where we were until Renata and Consuela came out. They were so busy talking they didn't even notice him, and the three of us walked back to the concourse. The man in the corridor didn't follow us directly, but let the second one pick us up as we entered the larger part of the airport. It was an accident that I made them, but I'm sure of what I saw.''

"They were Mexicans?"

"One was. The other was Anglo."

"How old was the Anglo?"

Garner hesitated, thinking. "I don't know. I guess . . ."

"Young enough to have been Elkin?"

"No," Garner said quickly. "No. He was early forties. He couldn't have been."

"That's all that happened, just what you've told me?"

"That's it."

Haydon drove in silence a little way. "I don't know what to think," he said. "But as soon as we get home I'm going to have a stakeout put on Islas's house. I don't know how to figure this. I have a feeling we're just on the edges of this thing. And I think that's where we're going to stay."

Chapter 51

Blas drove. It was the only thing he knew he could do and still feel as if he were in control. If he sat still, he would have the tendency to think they knew precisely where he was. He knew that, because it had happened to him before. More than once. So he drove, his swollen wrist throbbing in his lap.

He was sweating profusely, but it had nothing to do with the temperature. The new rental car had a superb air conditioner, which he turned on high. But it wasn't the heat. It was a cold sweat and it began as he stood by the palms at Latouche's, listening to Rubio screaming Negrete! Negrete! Negrete! and then the car crash, and the scream of the radio. He felt as if he were being lowered into the Pacific, into the green waters off Cabo Corrientes, down, down to thirty-three feet, where the pressure was twice what it was on the surface, down to sixty-six feet, where the pressure was three times what it was on the surface, down, down . . .

He was not sure that it wouldn't actually kill him someday. It wasn't the confrontation he feared, for he had never panicked in a firefight, or even when it had been worse than that, as in the gritty back streets of Cartagena or the jungles beyond Monkey River Town. The great fear was the squeezing pressure of waiting. When he had heard Rubio screaming he had not felt afraid for Rubio, nor for himself. He had begun to sweat because the scream had announced the beginning of the waiting.

The waiting was a fearful thing because Death hid behind

it, and Death hiding was a fearful thing. He had seen Death *mano a mano*, and it no longer horrified him. Horror, up close, loses its meaning, because you believe yourself to be, at that point, lost, and your mind provides you a state of grace. He had gone that far before, twice, but he had come back. Death had not taken him, and once he had regained his distance, his mind took away the grace and reinstated the horror. So he did not fear Death itself, but he feared the lurking approach of Death, where the horror lay in the waiting.

With darkness came anonymity. The headlights of his car were identical to the headlights of the cars in front and back of him. He became lost in the night streets.

Fixing his eyes on the taillights of the car in front of him, he tried to assess his chances of still succeeding. To be honest with himself, he had to admit it appeared impossible. What were the odds now that of all the square feet in the city, Gamboa would cross the nine square feet where Blas had buried the explosives? Could he surveil Gamboa's house closely enough to anticipate his use of San Felipe, and still remain unknown to the police who, he had assured himself, were watching the Gamboa residence? Only by chance. How long would he have before Rubio talked? Yes, Rubio would talk. If the technician is knowledgeable, and Negrete certainly was, it is almost impossible for the subject not to talk. Hadn't Ireno talked, Rubio's fellow Indian, his fellow coyote? Only once in his life had Blas seen someone actually refuse to be broken. A woman, no, a girl really, and she would not speak in spite of the vast and ingenious cruelty that took hold of her body. He had watched them break and tear and burst her, turn her wrong side out, and disassemble her. The beautiful girl would not talk. She had not been beautiful to the eye, not really. But when it was over, Blas knew she was beautiful to the heart.

Although her death had not occurred in an operation for which he was responsible, it was the last torture Blas had ever seen. He would not allow them under his command, nor would he witness them in the command of another. He would execute, but he would not torture.

Rubio would talk. Negrete already knew about the RDX; all he needed from Rubio was where and when. Where and when. How long could Rubio hold on to where and when? Maybe a better question would be, what would Negrete do when he found out? He would not risk digging it up himself. He wouldn't call the police. Blas assumed from today's actions by the police that Negrete was just as much a fugitive as he was. No, Negrete would simply alert Gamboa in the hope that by doing so Gamboa would consider that he had saved his life, and Negrete would have ingratiated himself enough to be rewarded for it sometime in the future. Then he would disappear into Mexico. That is all that was left in it for him, hope of ingratiation. It was typical of Negrete that he would kill, and risk his own life, for so base a reason.

Blas made a decision, quickly and firmly. At the next traffic light he turned right, continued around the block, and headed back to the Loop. He would commit himself through noon the next day, although he believed it would happen before then, because he expected Gamboa to use the cover of darkness to leave the city. The next six hours, he thought, would be the crucial ones.

Logistically, the Remington Hotel would have been the ideal place, but he did not want to go through the process and hassle of checking in, or to draw attention to himself in a place less than three hundred yards from where he hoped to detonate the explosives within the next several hours. That would be cutting it too close, especially since the explosion would cause a tremendous sensation within the hotel, and anyone leaving the hotel immediately afterward might be remembered later.

During the past days' planning, he had not made a detailed reconnaissance of the buildings along the Loop near the San Felipe intersection, but he had taken note of the several buildings that would have a clear view of the railroad crossing from the west side of the expressway. The difficulty, in fact, was not getting a clear view, for there were a number of those. The greatest problem would be to find a building that would allow him not only a good view but also access to a balcony. Commercial architects planning workplace buildings for Houston's equatorial heat and humidity were pretty well locked into fixed-window designs. Unfortunately, Blas could not trust the Futaba transmitter to work correctly from the inside of the building.

Still driving with one hand, he approached the Post Oak area from the south, looking at the buildings to his left for alignment with San Felipe as he dropped down on the exit. The custodial crews had been in the buildings since before dusk and would work on into the early-morning hours. As he turned under the expressway, he decided there were three possibilities: a long, wide building with silver bands that seemed to be about twenty stories high, on the north; a white rectangular building just south of the first and approximately the same height with its narrow end presenting row upon row of square windows to the expressway; and a third building with black trim and a slightly faceted three-part front with gold louvers running perpendicular in each facet from the ground to the roof.

Blas followed San Felipe toward Post Oak Boulevard, and at the last moment turned into the same Steak 'N Egg diner he had already been in twice before. Though he had considered his last visit a risk he should have avoided, now the diner was the only place he saw open in the vicinity where he could easily walk in and have his thermos filled with coffee. In the interest of time, he would go in once more. He took the thermos from the seat and went in. The woman who had waited on him earlier was busy making hamburgers for a couple of lime-haired punkers, the only other people there. Blas paid and left. He had now been seen in the diner by three different waitresses. He didn't like that, but it was better than being seen by one of them three different times.

He pulled out onto San Felipe again and turned left through the corridor of buildings composing the West Loop District. When he came to Ambassador Way he turned left again and approached the rear of the three buildings he had seen from the expressway. What he had not seen from the other side was that each building had adjoining parking garages, the tallest of which was that of the last building on the south, Tri-Corp Plaza. Not only was it the tallest garage, but it did not totally conform with the lines of the building itself, protruding on both sides in two set-back sections.

He negotiated the lanes and driveways, his headlights raking hedges and landscaping shrubs, until he came to the garage's entrance. A wooden arm operated by a magnetic card blocked the drive. Blas pulled the car over to the right, jumping the curb and squeezing next to the building, and eased forward until the arm touched the windshield. Carefully cradling his throbbing left wrist, he stretched across with his right arm and pushed on the wooden arm, finding a little play in the mechanism, enough to catch the end of the arm on the roof as he let the car inch forward. Then he let go, and drove through with the arm scraping along the roof of the car until it dropped off the rear window.

Wanting to avoid being seen from the offices above, Blas did not go to the top floor but to the one just beneath it, and drove to its northwest corner. He pulled the car right up to the low wall and stopped. He had a clear view of the San Felipe railroad crossing. He killed the motor, reached under the front seat, and took out a pair of powerful night-vision binoculars. He focused on the crossing and the street beyond it. There wasn't going to be a lot of lead time. While the crossing itself was in the clear, the street approaching it was obscured by trees to within a couple of hundred yards of the crossing. Blas could see headlights flickering through the trees, but could not identify the vehicles until they emerged. It would be close.

Still afraid he could be seen from some of the neighboring buildings, he got in the car and backed down the aisle to the first fluorescent light mounted in the ceiling. He stopped the car and, balancing awkwardly with his one good hand, climbed onto the hood, then onto the roof. Reaching above his head, he loosened the long fluorescent bulb until it flickered out. He jumped down, got in the car, and pulled over to a neighboring aisle, where he repeated the same process, and then again in the ramp lane closest to him. When he got back to the spot he had chosen, he was alone in the shadows.

He got out of the car, taking the briefcase and his suit coat with him. He sat the briefcase on the fender and took out the transmitter. Laying his suit coat on top of the cement barrier, he put the transmitter down on it and sat on the car's front bumper. He looped the binoculars around his neck and focused them on the rail crossing by propping his elbows on the low wall, using the suit coat for padding. He practiced holding the binoculars with his right hand while he pretended to flip the toggle switch with his left, an action which required no movement of his wrist. After several tries, sitting, crouching, standing, he was satisfied that he could do it quickly enough from any position if he was caught off guard.

Sitting back, he rested the spot just below his shoulder blades against the grill between the headlight and the hood ornament. He would not have until noon now, only until early morning. Or more realistically, until the black, still hours after midnight. If Gamboa was going to run, Blas could not feature him leaving after that. But it didn't matter. At dawn he was going home, whether Benigo Gamboa Parra was still breathing or not. He wanted to smoke, but he was afraid of being seen. A cup of coffee would have been good, too, but he didn't allow himself that either. He would need the caffeine later.

The waiting began again. He wondered if the toolbox was still safe in the stand of Johnsongrass. He wondered, too, what was happening to Rubio at that moment. It was a fleeting idea; he didn't dwell on it. He thought of going home, back to Mexico. Alone. That had happened to him twice before. This would be the third time he had returned from an assignment as the sole survivor. It was the sort of trip that prompted morose thoughts, or could, if you didn't discipline yourself.

Lucas Negrete knew all about the theories of torture. He had cut his teeth fighting the rural guerrillas in Mexico during the 1970s, and had served with the government-formed secret unit of counterinsurgency police known as the White Brigade which was largely responsible for the hundreds of "disappearances" of political dissidents during that time. He also had learned a few things at the infamous First Military Camp in the heart of Mexico City. Captain Negrete understood the fictions, and the facts, of torture.

He knew, for instance, that given time, torture was invariably successful. Sooner or later, everyone broke. Well, of course, there were stories—he considered them apocryphal—of a man or woman who had not responded, but he himself had never witnessed that. He knew that torture was more trustworthy as a means of gaining information than for eliciting confessions. Some people had pain thresholds so low they would confess to anything under certain degrees of pain. Obtaining confessions by means of physical coercion was a stupid business. He did not respect the validity of coercive confession. But to use pain as a means of obtaining information was a different story. After specific amounts of specific kinds of torture, an intelligent interrogator could obtain reliable information—if it was there. Time and technique were the crucial factors in this endeavor, however, and neither of them were working in Lucas Negrete's favor in the matter of Rubio Arizpe.

There was very little time, perhaps only a couple of hours.

And the techniques best suited to this circumstance required a professional setting. Negrete had only the motel room, no instruments to allow him the precise application of pain. But he was not totally unprepared. He had brought certain articles with him that, though he had not administered them himself, he had seen work with remarkable speed and effectiveness when applied by others.

Negrete walked to the foot of the bed so that Rubio, who was just beginning to come around, would have to look at him over the top of his naked stomach. All of his clothes had been removed, a routine preliminary in any torture, and he had been tied to the bed with his arms and legs spread apart. Urbano held a tiny bottle of ammonium carbonate under Rubio's nose, and he jerked awake, gasping.

"I'm down here, Rubio," Negrete said. He waited a moment until he knew the Indian had gotten his bearings. As he looked at Rubio, he listened with approval to the roar of traffic on the expressway. "In the interest of time I will tell you from the start that we want to know where and when Blas is going to detonate the RDX. Since I do not expect you to tell me voluntarily, I am going to torture you."

Negrete motioned to Siseno, and moved around to the side of the bed to let the other man take up his position between Rubio's legs.

"I know you are familiar with such methods of questioning, and are already preparing yourself psychologically to endure them. But I must tell you, coyote, that your Indian mind is no good to you this time."

Again he motioned to Siseno, who took two thick rubber bands from around his wrist and bent down. He double-wrapped one of them around Rubio's scrotum above the testicles, and the other around his penis.

"As you can see, Rubio, we are not in the proper setting for this. We do not have the instruments. So I am sure you are expecting something rather primitive, and messy."

Negrete nodded to Luis, who removed a large roll of surgical hose from a flight bag and began uncoiling it as he went into the bathroom. Negrete saw Rubio's eyes following him.

"Not so," Negrete said. "You are going to suffer intensely, but relatively neatly.'' He pulled a chair over to the bed and picked up the end of the hose lying on the floor. He reached into the flight bag, took out a piece of rigid rubber shaped like the end of enema tube, and began affixing it to the end of the surgical hose. While he did this he continued talking.

"I have received some recent education, Rubio, which I will happily pass on to you. A doctor taught me these things, so you can rely on what I say. You will learn some new words, and maybe in the ecstasy of your pain, I will give you wisdom, too.

"As even you know, everyone has his own individual level of tolerance to pain. Yes. But the physiological process by which that pain is experienced is the same in everyone. If I put a needle under your fingernail, I will stimulate nerve endings that set off complicated sets of chemical chain reactions in little things called . . . well, let me use the proper name: receptors.'' He gave the hose a quick twist, ramming it up on the shank of the tube.

"These receptors will cause you to sweat. They will speed up your blood flow, and they will start processing the chemicals that cause you to experience pain: histamine, serotonin, large peptides like bradykinin, and the prostaglandins.'' He stopped. "Those are the correct names, Rubio,'' he said precisely. "I memorized them.''

He stopped again, the tube and surgical hose hanging from his hand, and then he stood looking at the Indian's dark body spread helplessly upon the musty bedcovers. Listlessly using the black rubber nozzle as a pointer, Negrete continued, dragging the nozzle down Rubio's arm. "These chemicals, they send the message of pain along nerve fibers to the spinal cord, up the spinal cord''—the nozzle traveled over Rubio's shoulder to the back of his neck—"to the thalamus in the brain, and finally to the cerebral cortex—a place you wouldn't know about, Rubio—'' the nozzle circled around and around the Indian's forehead—"which tells the body where it ought to feel the pain. In the example of the needle, under your fingernails.'' Negrete slapped Rubio's left hand with the rubber nozzle.

Negrete tossed the hose onto the floor and lighted a cigarette. His long narrow face seemed even longer because of his unmistakable fatigue. In the stale light of the motel room the beaked aspect of his nose was exaggerated, as if he were wearing a Venetian carnival mask. His beautiful almond eyes swam in oil.

"Now if this goes on long enough," he said, exhaling, "the body tries to protect itself in that place of pain, and begins producing some different chemicals known as 'pain inhibitors.' These chemicals rush to the place of pain and somehow make it possible for you to endure it. So, then, I have to produce another kind of pain in a different part of your body so you can once again feel the full intensity of it, until your chemistry produces more inhibitors, forcing me to move along to something else again. That is why effective torture, coyote, requires time."

From the bathroom came the sound of wrenches and snapping pliers as Luis hooked the rubber hose to the shower faucet.

Negrete smoked his cigarette, one hand in his pocket.

"But there is a psychological factor. Some people say that the experience of having someone deliberately hurt you takes its psychological toll as well, and may even trigger other chemicals which block the inhibitors so that a man being tortured feels the pain even more acutely than if he suffered the same degree of pain as the result of, say, an accident or an illness."

He shrugged, as if it was anybody's guess as to whether any of this was true.

"How do you feel down there?" he asked, tilting his head toward Rubio's crotch as he blew a stream of smoke out both nostrils. "That wasn't done to cause you pain, although I suppose it does. It was done to stop you from pissing." He looked toward the bathroom, then back at Rubio. The cigarette had burned down almost to the filter, and Negrete was holding it delicately.

"This doctor tells me, Rubio, that perhaps the worst pain the human body can experience comes not from the outside, but from the *inside*. From the 'visceral tissues.' That's the guts. Now, I could stab your guts or cut them, and it would certainly hurt, but this doctor, he says that worse than that is the pain of 'distension.' That means when your guts swell up. That is the very worst pain of all. Not only does it cause you to suffocate, but the pressure causes the guts to feel a special kind of pain that only the guts can feel.''

He nodded, affirming the truth of this observation, and lighted a fresh cigarette off the old one, which he dropped on the carpet and ground out with his shoe. Neither his facial expression nor his tone of voice changed throughout his monologue, but remained conversational without any particular lack or investment of emotion. Turning around once again to the table behind him, he took a syringe and a vial from a plastic bag. Holding the cigarette between his lips, he began filling the syringe from the vial. He talked around his cigarette.

"One more point, and then we can get to it. They say that some of the pain-producing chemicals the body generates when its nervous system is stimulated are things called histamines. They are found in all body tissues—you are full of histamines, coyote—but the largest concentration of these little things is in the lungs. Histamines are the strongest pain-producing chemicals known.'' He eased the needle from the vial and expelled the air, causing some of the fluid to squirt onto his shirt sleeve. He held the syringe up for Rubio to see. ''Histamines.''

He turned to yet another bag and took out a stethoscope, which he hooked around his neck. Then he produced a blood-pressure sleeve and fastened it around Rubio's right arm. He pumped it up and read the gauge. He looked at the Indian. ''Very admirable, Rubio. I would have thought your heart would already be pounding.'' The corners of his mouth turned down in a facial shrug. He looked at Luis in the bathroom doorway, then at Siseno between Rubio's legs, and finally back at Rubio.

''Now this is what we are going to do. Siseno will put this tube down here by my foot into your mouth, down your throat, and into your stomach. Luis will turn on the faucet in the bathroom. Very slowly you will begin to fill up like a rutting frog. Several things will happen simultaneously.'' He leaned forward and interpreted: ''That means 'at the same time.' I will inject your nipples with histamines right away, because histamines cause the blood vessels to open up, and this will help you soak up the water more quickly. This will begin a slow process causing edema—that is, fluid will begin to collect between all the cells in your body tissue. In your skin. If that goes on long enough you will puff up like a corpse."

He took the cigarette out of his mouth and looked at Rubio, letting him think about that last illustration.

"Do you know what speeds up the production of histamines by your body, coyote?" He nodded affirmatively as if Rubio had answered. "Yes. This edema. Your body will begin a terrible cycle. At the same time, the water we are pumping into you will swell your stomach against your other organs, especially your lungs, causing them to dump even more histamines into your system. *I* will inject histamines into your navel, and you will experience immediate hypersensitivity as you begin to suffocate. The pressure against your guts will cause the worst pain you have ever felt, and the rapid production of histamines will make you supersensitive to sensations few people have ever felt."

Negrete regarded Rubio's passive face. "But do not worry, Indian. I will be listening to your heart, and watching your blood pressure." He dropped the cigarette on the floor and put his shoe on it. "Whatever else might happen, you won't die. I think, however, that you will be begging for it before we finish."

He wiped his forehead in the crook of his arm. "Oh, yes. If you decide to tell me what I want to know, simply nod, and this is what I will do . . . if I believe you. I will relieve your pain so that you will be in no danger while we go and see if what you say is true. If it is true, I will call an ambulance to come get you. If it is not true, *I* will come get you. Very simple, huh?"

Siseno moved around to the side of the bed beside Negrete and picked up the rubber hose. As he bent over Rubio, the Indian suddenly spat without warning, and a huge gob of mucus looped across Siseno's face.

"*Puta!*" Siseno screamed, and struck instantly with all his might. His fist was doubled expertly, and a protruding middle knuckle caught Rubio on the outside corner of his left eye, punching it out of its socket so that it sat high and white on the bridge of his nose, but still attached.

SPIRAL

Furious, Siseno jumped on the bed, straddled Rubio, and wrenched open his jaws as he rammed the end of the tube into the Indian's throat with such force that it tore his esophagus. He was already bleeding from his mouth when Negrete, standing with the readied syringe, gave the signal to Luis, and the water began to flow.

vvvvvvvvvvvvvvvvvvvvvvvvvvvvvv **Chapter 53**

At *the top of the news this hour Houston police and the FBI are looking for two suspects believed to be involved in the shooting here last Tuesday afternoon in which six people were killed in an assassination-type attack on a limousine at the intersection of West Loop and Richmond Avenue.*

The two pictures of Blas Medrano and then the sketch of Rubio Arizpe flashed on the screen, and stayed there while the woman newscaster continued with her story. She said it was not yet known if the two men were tied to the killing of three people in Port Houston on Thursday, or the murder of a University of Houston professor in the early-morning hours today. After recapping the unprecedented series of killings during the last four days, the newscaster said the police and the FBI were urging anyone who might have seen the two men whose pictures were still on the screen to please call the Crime Stoppers number immediately, which was then flashed on the screen below the pictures.

The story was over in less than five minutes, followed by a story about a tanker truck that had overturned on the Gulf Freeway.

Haydon punched the mute button on the remote control and looked at Nina and Celia, who were sitting on the library sofa across from him.

"That's it?" Celia asked, her voice rising.

Haydon nodded. "Their pictures were on the screen for about two minutes. That's a long time. Long enough."

"Well, what happens now?" she persisted. "I mean, is that it? Can't they do something else?"

"We wait. Anything else that can be done is being done," Haydon said. "The paperwork, searching files, running down addresses, questioning people, tracing guns. This will go on a long time."

"But what if the people who've seen them aren't watching tonight?"

"It's supposed to run again in the morning."

Celia pulled her legs up on the sofa and folded her dress over them. She was still wearing Nina's skirt and blouse. Her eyebrows contorted in a frown. She seemed always on the verge of tears now.

"If anyone's going to call in, it should be within the next half hour or so," Haydon said. "That is, people who might have seen them, but who have no other knowledge of them. Like a gas-station attendant, or a store clerk. Those who might have knowledge of them beyond that may wait days or weeks to respond while they weigh the consequences. Or they might not call in at all."

Haydon was drinking French dark-roast coffee. It was strong, and he had already had too much, but he wasn't planning on trying to sleep anytime soon. He was still wearing the suit he had worn to Mooney's memorial service at ten o'clock that morning, exactly twelve hours earlier. He looked at the girl moving her mouth on the screen, and then the camera shifted to a different angle and picked up her co-announcer, a man, who was taking the next story. Back and forth, back and forth. They would do this for half an hour, bringing a third person for the weather and a fourth person for sports. This was the way they had done it when they announced Mooney's death, the same way they would do it to announce chili cook-offs and wars, high school football scores and earthquakes, clear to partly cloudy weather and terrorist bombings. Back and forth, back and forth, with something light and frothy at the end of the half hour.

"Why don't we turn it off, Stuart?" Nina said. "Either that, or turn the volume on so we can hear it."

Haydon didn't hear her. His eyes remained fixed on the voiceless automatons as they swiveled from side to side with choreographed precision to catch the alternating camera an-

SPIRAL

gles. He, on the other hand, was motionless, sitting upright in his wing chair with his legs crossed at the knees. He didn't blink. He wasn't even in the room.

Celia looked quizzically at Nina, who kept her eyes on Haydon. When the telephone rang, the two women jumped. Haydon looked at his watch—it was ten twenty-one—laid down the remote-control device, and walked back to his desk.

"Hello," he said.

"Stu," Dystal said. "We got *action* off that news item." Haydon pulled over a notepad and picked up a pencil.

"Phones haven't stopped ringing," Dystal continued. "Some nut stuff, but some good solid ones too. All right: Two guys in different clothing stores in the Galleria said Medrano was in their places Tuesday night, getting what looked like whole new outfits. Paid in cash, paid extra for rush alterations.

"Calls from agents in five different car rental agencies. Arizpe got one car from each of two; Medrano got one car from each of two and a little S-10 Chevy pickup from a third one. Used credit cards, but the names weren't Arizpe and Medrano.

"Call from a waitress in a little sandwich shop over on Norfolk at Kirby, said both of them were in there Thursday evening about dark. Drinking coffee and looking at a map for about half an hour, forty-five minutes. She said she visited with Medrano some and he was a real nice fella, polite, well-mannered.

"Call from management at that ritzy La Colombe d'Or over on Montrose said a guy who fits Medrano's description but using a credit card with another name checked in there around eleven p.m. Tuesday night, and checked out at six thirty-five *this afternoon.*

"Call from a waitress at a Steak 'N Egg Kitchen on San Felipe near Post Oak Boulevard said Medrano was in there at eight forty-five *tonight.* And the gal who works that shift with her said *she* had seen him in there Thursday night with Arizpe. They were going over some maps together. Then we got another call from *another* waitress who works the morning shift there—she was at home when she called—and she said she had seen Medrano in there by himself about seven-thirty this morning for breakfast.

"We're still getting calls, but this is a damn good start."

"You've put a general broadcast on all the cars?"

"Sure have."

"What are you going to do about the diner?"

"We're sending somebody over there in an unmarked car to have a sandwich and drill those two gals. We're gonna stake it out—it's in a good location, easy to do—and if he shows up we're gonna send a man in there dressed like a cabby to check it out. We'll see what happens from there."

Haydon had a map spread out on his desk and was circling the addresses. "He's staying in the neighborhood, isn't he?"

"Yeah, he is. Looks like I was wrong, doesn't it? I mean, goddam, he was still hanging around an hour and a half ago."

"Did he eat a meal at the diner?"

"No. Gal said she filled his thermos with coffee. Maybe he was leaving town then. Gonna drive all night."

"Or he was going to spend all night staked out somewhere."

"You think he's just waiting till he catches Gamboa out on the streets so he can bushwhack him?"

"I think that's probable. He and Arizpe were studying maps for some reason. But what about the RDX? How would he use that if he was planning another hit and run?"

"Goddam, who knows where that stuff is? Maybe he's gonna ram the damn limo Middle East–style."

"Why all the rented cars? And why was one a pickup?"

"I don't know," Dystal said. "We're trying to find out the timetable on that, see what was rented when. Maybe that'll suggest something."

"Your people on Inverness haven't seen anything?"

"Not a thing. Some kids were skateboarding up and down there under the streetlights a while ago . . ." Dystal spoke to someone, said "Wait" to them, and then said to Haydon, "I got something coming in here. Get right back to you."

Haydon put down the telephone and stared down at the map on his desk, his eyes going over and over the locations mentioned by Dystal as he tried to envision a pattern, tried to see beyond the known facts to their implications, and to the numerous possibilities.

"Stuart!" Nina's voice was impatient, and Haydon looked

up to see both women standing, looking at him. "What was it?"

He started to answer, but the telephone rang again, and he picked it up immediately, hoping Dystal had a breakthrough.

"Mr. Haydon, listen carefully." It was not Dystal, or anyone else he recognized. "Lucas Negrete is about to beat you to Medrano."

Haydon was speechless. He could only listen.

"Negrete has Rubio Arizpe." The voice was calm, deliberate. "They are in room 326 of the Golden Way Motel at Main and the Southwest Freeway, Highway 59. There are two men with Negrete." There was a pause. "Have you got that? Would you like me to repeat anything?"

"No, I've got it," Haydon said, and the other end of the line went dead.

"Nina!" Haydon jerked open the desk drawer and took out his Beretta. Nina had been watching his face and was already on her way over to him as he checked the clip, took an extra clip out of the drawer, made sure it was full, and dropped it in a pocket of his suit coat hanging over the back of the chair.

"Listen," he said, looking at her. "That was an anonymous tip that Negrete is holding Arizpe in the Golden Way Motel. You know it, at Main and the freeway. Room 326." He fixed the Beretta in the small of his back, picked up the telephone, and dialed *66, which automatically called the number that had just called him. "I'm going into the living room to the other line and call Dystal, and have him get someone over there right away. I'm going to try to get a tracer on this call here, so don't hang up the phone until you get a call on the other line saying you can. Okay?"

"Yes, I understand." She also understood where he was going. She followed him into the living room, bringing his suit coat off the chair. He called Dystal, but his number was busy, so he hung up and dialed 911. When the dispatcher finally got through, Haydon didn't give Dystal time to say anything but hurriedly told him what had happened, told him to get someone over to the motel, told him to get a tracer on the telephone and that he was on his way to the motel himself.

Dystal swore. "Wait a second! All hell's breaking loose.

That was Gamboa on the line just then. He's chartered a flight out of the country. It leaves from the Intercontinental Airport in an hour. He's got a helicopter's gonna pick him up and take him out there, and he wants us to escort him to the heliport.''

"Which one?"

"The one closest to him, at Post Oak Park over behind the Remington Hotel off San Felipe . . . right across the Loop from that goddam Steak 'N Egg place.''

"Stall him.''

"No way. I tried; he won't listen. He's scared to death, and what I told him just put gas on his fire. He thinks he's doing what he's got to do to save his life. Got his boy all armed, his driver all armed, and his goddam butler or whatever he calls him.''

"Stall him,'' Haydon said again. "This motel thing could be our break. I'll call from there,'' Haydon said, and slammed down the telephone. He took his coat from Nina and slipped it on. "When I get out those gates, lock it up, turn on all the outside lights, and turn on the alarm system.''

He was out the front door immediately, leaving Nina alone in the lighted doorway.

Haydon drove the distance to the Golden Way Motel ignoring everything but his reflexes, taking the tight-steering Jaguar to its handling limits shaving corners, accelerating flat out when he could and breaking into turns, running lights, making the best time traveling the wrong way on one-way streets where the other cars could see him coming and pull over to give him a clean shot.

His mind was working as fast at asking questions as it was at maneuvering the Vanden Plas.

Was the tip genuine?

There didn't seem to be any possibility that he was being set up. The investigation had gone so poorly from the point of view of the police that he certainly was no threat to Negrete's objective, or to Medrano's.

Who was it? And why? And how did he get his information?

Haydon peered into the streaming headlights of the oncoming traffic and realized he had made a mistake. He should have specified a quiet approach. Dystal had his hands full, and wasn't going to think of it. The backup units would come in with sirens blaring—no chance of catching Negrete off guard. If he and his men didn't try to shoot their way out, then they would turn it into a siege. Either way, it wouldn't work to the advantage of what they wanted to achieve: a quick resolution that might gain them information to forestall the assassination. Haydon's only chance of getting that now would be to get to Negrete before he realized that the distant sirens were headed for him.

Braking hard, then jamming the accelerator, Haydon cut in front of traffic and flew into a cross street, then into a one-way street going the right direction for one block, then into another one-way street going the wrong way. He made the block, and entered Main Street one block from the entrance of the Golden Way Motel. Merging with the traffic flow, he went past the motel entrance and turned under the belly of the expressway, cutting his headlamps to parking lights as he jumped the curb and drove along between the cement columns toward the motel on the other side of the derelict chain-link fence.

He cut the parking lights, and the black Vanden Plas melted into the larger darkness as he rolled to a stop. For five seconds he sat in the pitch shadows and listened to the traffic booming overhead as he looked at the end of the motel. He knew the place, knew the numbering system, knew that he was looking at the brick wall of Room 326 through the windshield.

He flipped the central locking system as he got out of the car, slammed the door, and started running toward the twisted chain-link fence, which resembled the barbed concertina wire of a war zone. He cursed as he accidentally kicked a bottle and sent it spinning across the cement, shattering into an expressway pillar. Crouching down to his hands, he scrambled onto the wire, catching a shoe heel in the twisted mesh, finally getting to the other side at the end of the near wing of the motel. He looked up at the walkway of the third floor, where half the lights outside the room doors were burned out, including the one at 326.

Running down the sidewalk, he cut across the grass between the pool and a hedge and barged into the motel office, where a startled night manager held the newspaper-covered bottom of a bird cage in his hands and gaped at Haydon over the counter.

"Police," Haydon snapped, holding up his shield. "I need a passkey."

The clerk continued to gape, frowning myopically at the shield shaking in front of his face, starting to set down the tray. Haydon yelled, "Passkey, dammit!" The manager flinched, dropping the tray and flipping bird lime and seed hulls into the air, but he was already going after the key.

"Patrol cars are on the way," Haydon said, as the manager fumbled open a drawer under the counter and slapped the key down on a copy of a city map covered with plastic. "Stay down, stay out of the way," he said, grabbing the key.

He cut across the grass the way he had come, sweat suddenly popping out of his pores. Reaching the bottom of the stairs at the soft-drink machines, Haydon pulled his Beretta and started up. He was making the turn on the second-floor landing when he heard the first distant sirens and quickened his pace. When he came up on the third-floor walkway, he paused briefly to get his bearings.

Behind him lay the rest of the walkway that formed the shorter, bottom branch of the L-shaped complex; then a corner, and the rest of the L running out past the pool. To his immediate right was a small alcove with an ice machine and two doors on either side, probably supply rooms.

The walkway railing, and the courtyard three floors down, were on his left as he looked toward the doorway of room 326, the last room on the end, three doors away. About twenty feet on the other side of 326 was the steel railing of the expressway, with cars and trucks roaring by at eye level. It occurred to him that anyone driving by could look out his window and see him crouching on the landing with his gun drawn.

But he had more immediate problems:

Would all three of them be in the same room with Arizpe?

Or would they have another room?

Had they posted a lookout?

If so, had he already been spotted?

If he was able to catch them by surprise, what were the odds they would not have their firearms in hand? His mind didn't stay on the Mac-10s.

The sirens grew louder. He could only blame himself for that.

He moved on until he was standing beside the door of 325. He put his ear to the door, a stupid gesture, with the expressway rumbling like a train twenty feet away. Standing back against the brick wall, he tried the door handle, which didn't budge. He moved closer to 326, stopping next to its sliding glass window to see if there were any cracks in the edge of the curtains. There weren't.

Stepping across in front of the door, he stood with his back to the expressway, his shoulder against the brick wall on the left side of the door. A diesel trailer truck whined past, and a blast of wind and grit whipped his suit and the oily stink of diesel filled his lungs as he touched the door-knob. This time the expressway noise was in his favor, making it difficult, if possible at all, for anyone inside the room to hear the tiny clicking of the turning knob. But it was locked. Staying clear of the door, he used his left hand to slip the passkey into the keyhole, the Beretta upright beside his head. He could expect the chain to be latched. He turned the key.

What were the odds that they would be looking at the knob, that they would see the movement?

He was afraid to open it enough to see if the chain was in place. That they would see.

The sirens were on Main, maybe three blocks away.

He stepped in front of the door and kicked it open, the chain snapping like a gunshot, but flying apart as Haydon crouched in the opened doorway and yelled, "Police!"

The man sitting in the chair on the other side of the naked, bloated figure was already turning, stretching for the machine pistol on the round table, had his hands on it when Haydon's first two shots caught him behind his right ear and the back of the neck, blowing his glasses through the air and hurling him across the top of the table, arms flying out against the blast. Two steps inside, Haydon's eyes locked on the open bathroom door. The stench of feces and something medicinal. Expecting something from the bathroom. Then the cold shock of gunfire from the room next door, someone running on the walkway. He whirled around even as he feared shots in the back from the bathroom, lunged to the door and saw the first police car screaming, sliding, bouncing into the drive from the street, his eyes still on it when the Mac-10s opened up from somewhere on the stairs, turning the windshield white as it kept coming, crashing across the hedge, the sidewalk, into the Coke and 7-Up machines at the bottom of the stairs, the booming impact and the walkway shuddering, the unit's flashers still turning, splashing colors in the courtyard.

As the second car careened into the drive, Haydon ran the length of the balcony to the corner of the L, sprinted through the breezeway to the railing that looked out over the back of the motel into a descending spur of the freeway, saw Negrete already on the fence and the second man turning to cover him, the muzzle bursts of the Mac-10 looking brighter than he would have imagined as he fell back against the wall. Instantly he was up again to see the second man scaling the fence, but Negrete didn't stop to cover him. He kept running, through the dead and brittle weeds, to the cover of the long slope of the descending spur. Haydon steadied the Beretta for the long shot at the man on the fence, who, suddenly realizing he was exposed, tried to fire the Mac-10 as he straddled the fence. Haydon fired four times, five, and the man was kicked backward, one foot catching in the top wire, hanging him upside down. Freakishly, the Mac-10 fired somehow, the recoil whipping his limp arm like a loose water hose spraying .45s. Then it stopped.

Negrete had disappeared into Montrose.

Haydon ran back to the front of the motel courtyard to the walkway railing. There were two more units in the drive now, another one coming in, and more sirens. There were policemen running along the walkways, two coming at him.

"There's one man down on the fence behind the motel," Haydon yelled. "He's got a Mac-10, but I think he's dead. Another one, also armed with a Mac-10, is on foot heading into Montrose, maybe Brandt, Flora, Westmoreland, those streets. Get every available unit out in there. He's extremely dangerous. They've got to be *careful*. If there are any questions I'll be in room 326. Send the medics up when they get here."

"You Detective Haydon?" the officer shouted. "We're supposed to see Detective Haydon."

"Yes, hurry." He stopped. "What about those guys in the car down there?"

"They're dead, sir."

"Okay, hurry," Haydon repeated, and headed toward the last room on the end.

There were three patrolmen in the room, one on the other

side of the bed squatting down, checking the man Haydon had shot, the other two staring unbelievingly at the grossly protuberant Arizpe, not sure what to do.

"Is he alive?" Haydon asked, pushing between them.

"I . . ." One of the patrolmen turned and rushed out of the room.

Rubio's dark body had taken on an appearance that bordered on the abstract. His splayed figure alone was psychologically disturbing, bringing to mind the carcass of an animal slaughtered and dressed. Bloated out of proportion, he did not so much lie on the bed as quiver at points upon it, the torture having caused every muscle and sinew to contract in a rigid, unyielding spasm that arched his back to the point of snapping, and thrust his bulging stomach in the air so that his torso touched the bed only across the tops of his shoulders and where his heels dug into the mattress. His head was thrown back and his mouth was locked open with a rubber hose snaking from it, leading into the bathroom. The bed was soaked, some of it was water, some of it wasn't, and Arizpe glistened with an oily perspiration. The stench was unbearable.

"Jesus Christ." The patrolman who had been examining the dead man had stood up, and turned to Rubio. He looked like a veteran patrolman, his dark hair going gray, his body a little chunky. His name was Aledo, and his eyes followed the hose into the bathroom. "Shit, damn!"

Haydon saw the stethoscope twisted under the leg of the dead man on the overturned table, hurried over, and pulled it out. He bent down as he put it on, and placed the stainless-steel disk on Arizpe's chest. There was a heartbeat, erratic, but it was there. He turned to Aledo. "Make sure the water's off."

"What the hell *was* this?" Aledo asked, but he didn't wait for an answer.

Haydon pulled off his coat and flung it over a lamp as he looked at the second patrolman's nameplate. "Thomas, give me a hand. We've got to get the hose out of him."

The young patrolman, who was thin and fair, almost frail in appearance, started rolling up his sleeves as he looked at Arizpe's dislocated eye.

"Water's off," Aledo shouted.

"What about untying him?" Thomas asked.

"Not yet," Haydon said.

"Son of a bitch!" Aledo gasped. He had come back to the bed. "Look what they did to his dick, will ya?"

The young patrolman put one knee on the bed and held Arizpe's head as Haydon grasped the hose. It didn't want to come out.

"Maybe we'd better leave it." Thomas sounded as if he was holding his breath.

"He'll die," Haydon said, working with the hose.

"You gotta cut him loose," Aledo said.

"Yeah, okay," Haydon said, pulling more firmly on the hose until it began to give. A lather of dirty pink foam started boiling from Arizpe's mouth.

"That's from his lungs." Thomas spoke rapidly. "Something's wrong with his lungs."

Aledo had his pocket knife out, cutting the nylon cord at Arizpe's ankles, then moving up to the wrists, which he finished cutting just as the end of the surgical hose came out of Arizpe's mouth, bringing a gush of grumey fluid with it. Freed, Arizpe began to tremble, then shudder, as if someone were shaking the bed.

"Oh, damn," Thomas said, pushing off the bed and backing away, knocking over the television as he retreated. Haydon backed too, stumbling on the man he had shot, grabbing his coat from the lamp as he moved around the foot of the bed with Aledo, who was stunned by what was happening.

Arizpe's shuddering became violent, his monstrously enlarged stomach with its distended navel heaving convulsively. Suddenly the Indian's good eye opened wide and rolled upward. His arms began to flail uncontrollably as he appeared to try to sit up, his head jutting forward with the effort, an awkward wallowing man-frog. Then his mouth yawned open and he disgorged, almost spewed, a thick, arching torrent that splattered the length of the bed, nearly to the wall.

"Oh, my God," Aledo yelled, as Haydon shoved him toward the door, where the three of them stood dumbfounded, horrified. Arizpe, no longer a man but a bloated thing bucking in a broth of its own fluids, ejaculated again and again the remnants of his own tormented viscera.

SPIRAL

Haydon's senses miscarried. In a momentary failure of synapse, his brain simply refused to process what he was witnessing. When he recovered, he was in the room alone, and the unreal spectacle, the desolation of Rubio Arizpe's suffering and death, filled the room. The assault on his returning senses was intolerable.

He backed out and closed the door.

Chapter 55

There were half a dozen or more units in the courtyard of the Golden Way Motel, as well as several ambu-
lances, and the arriving television trucks. Haydon stood a
minute in front of the door he had just closed, then looked
to his right, where the rows of balconies were lined with
motel guests in various stages of undress. The flashers from
the police units flickered off their faces, all of which seemed
to be turned toward him, their blank stares jumping off and
on like neon lights.

Haydon looked around at Aledo and Thomas, who were
leaning against the railing with the freeway at their backs,
looking at him as if they had had their breath knocked out of
them.

"Jesus," Aledo said. "What a . . . what a deal." The old
veteran had to say something.

The walkway of the cheaply constructed motel shook as
other police officers ran up and down the stairs shouting at
each other and at the ambulance attendants, herding people
out of the way.

"Don't let anyone in there until a team of homicide detectives gets here," Haydon said to Aledo. He looked at the
opened door of 325. "Or in here, either."

Aledo had to clear his throat. "Right," he said.

Haydon stepped into 325 and picked up the telephone, using his handkerchief. He stared at the night table, waiting for
Dystal to answer. Outside the radios were bouncing off the
motel walls and the pillars of the freeway.

"Lieutenant Dystal's office."

Haydon recognized Nunn's voice. "Robert, where's Dystal?"

"On his way over to Gamboa's. You at the motel? What in the hell's happening over there?"

Haydon told him briefly, then asked, "Who's coming out here?"

"Pete and Marshall, Singleton and Watts."

"And what's the situation at Gamboa's?"

"The old man's agreed to wait for Dystal, but he's going for sure. I don't know any of the details about how they're going to do it, but I know the lieutenant was going to have cars all around him."

"Okay, thanks," Haydon said, and hung up the telephone. He went outside onto the walkway and saw Lapierre and John Marshall working their way through the police cars in the courtyard, heading for the stairs. He turned to Thomas. "Let me borrow your radio," he said. The young patrolman unclipped the radio from his belt and handed it over. He still hadn't regained his emotional equilibrium. Neither had Aledo, but his experience had taught him to hide at least the appearance of vulnerability; he was lighting a cigarette with an unsteady flame. "Thanks for your help in there," Haydon said to Thomas. He paused a second, wanting to ask the kid if he was all right, but then thought better of it. "I'll get this back to you."

He started down the walkway and met Lapierre at the stairs. They talked briefly, Haydon telling the two detectives what had happened, that Negrete was somewhere across the spur with a Mac-10, and that he would use it at the slightest provocation.

Haydon had already accepted the fact that he had made the wrong decision after shooting the man on the fence. Not knowing that Arizpe was already near death, he had bet that the Indian would be the quickest source of information about Medrano and had not pursued Negrete. Now that Arizpe was dead, as well as the other two men, he was once again in the position of having lost Negrete *and* the most recent information about Medrano. Assuming, of course, that Negrete's methods had succeeded in getting the information out of Arizpe in the first place. He didn't know what significance, if any, lay in the fact that Negrete and the other man had not been in the room with Arizpe.

"I guess nothing new has come in from the tips," Haydon said.

"No," Lapierre said tersely, looking past Haydon to Aledo and Thomas standing outside the doors at the end of the walkway.

"Okay. I'm going to try to meet Dystal and Gamboa at the heliport," Haydon said. "I'll be back over here after he's gone and help you finish it up."

Racing down the stairs, Haydon considered what this past week must have looked like through Lapierre's eyes. There was no doubt that he totally disapproved of the way Dystal had handled Haydon throughout. Haydon really couldn't blame him. The week had been a bloodbath, and Haydon had been bouncing around the edges of it the whole time. If you followed the rulebook, you wouldn't think the week's events had been a tidy way to handle things.

Instead of crawling over the fence again, Haydon walked through the jumble of patrol cars in the motel courtyard, past the office, where he chose not to look toward the people pressed against the plate glass of the lobby windows, and out the drive. He hurried along the edge of the street to the cement pavement that ran under the expressway, and turned into the shadows. It was not so dark now with the lights on the patrol cars throwing splinters of ruby and sapphire through the mangy hedge separating the underside of the expressway from the motel. He unlocked the car, got in, and backed between the rows of columns to the low curb at the street. In a few seconds he was ascending the first ramp to the Southwest Freeway, heading toward the West Loop.

For a split second he was over the Richmond intersection where it had all begun three days before, in the blistering afternoon sun. Then immediately he was in another city, the Post Oak district, where the Transco Tower loomed over everything, skewing the perspective as if to say that *it* was real, and all the rest was miniature.

He continued into the sparkling heart of the district and dropped down onto the San Felipe exit. He could see Post Oak Park where the heliport was located just ahead on his right, but he turned left on San Felipe and followed the gentle curve of the street, past the Steak 'N Egg Kitchen. It tantalized him that only a few hours earlier Medrano had walked in there for a thermos of coffee. Why had he been in this area so recently, and why had he been in that diner so often? Was the obedient son indeed capable of driving a suicide car packed with explosives? Haydon thought not. It would be an unheard-of act by a Latin group, a right-wing group at that, if only because the technique had become so thoroughly identified with Middle Eastern fanaticism.

Then why was Medrano constantly circulating in this area? He couldn't possibly have known Gamboa would decide to go to the heliport tonight. Gamboa probably hadn't even known it himself until maybe an hour ago, and yet even before that Medrano was in the area. Waiting.

Haydon pulled into the parking lot in Post Oak Plaza and parked among the cars of people dining at Tony's. To his right was Sak's across Post Oak Boulevard, and to his left at the end of Ambassador Way was 3D International, Tri-Corp Plaza, Con-Tex Tower, and dozens of other buildings lining the west side of the Loop. He turned on Thomas's radio and called Dystal. A patrolman came on and said Dystal was outside the car on the front portico of Gamboa's house, that they were just about ready to leave. There was static as Haydon waited, then he heard Dystal.

"Stu. Heard what happened over there. You all right, I guess."

"I'm fine."

"God a'mighty. I wonder how much the hell else can happen before we get this man outta here."

"How are you going to do it?"

"Hell, I couldn't make up my mind whether to sorta sneak him out or to go with all my parade lights on. I finally decided to do the parade. I'll have a coupla cars in front, couple in back, and every time we come to a cross street I'll run a car up ahead to block it in case they try to get at him from the side. We won't be wasting any time. Where're you at?"

Haydon told him. "I just couldn't get over the idea of him hanging around here."

"Yeah, I know," Dystal said. "Okay, they're coming down the stairs now. We're gonna be pulling outta here purty soon."

"Who's with him?" Haydon asked quickly.

"Uh, looks like his boy and some other guy carryin' a briefcase. Just the three of 'em.''

Haydon visualized the long portico with softly lighted columns, and the distinguished Gamboa coming rapidly down the flight of illuminated steps with the two other men. Policemen milling around the lawn, the squad cars idling, the limousine sparkling black in the drive, its doors open until Gamboa gets in and then they'd close, solid and dark, like a coffin.

"I'll meet you at the heliport," Haydon said.

"Good enough," Dystal answered, and then he was off.

Haydon wondered where Medrano was sitting at that very moment, and whether or not Gamboa would still be alive in twenty minutes. Suddenly he was aware of the edgy energy of anticipation, a gradual realization of a change in the tempo of his emotions. He started the Vanden Plas and drove out of the lot onto Post Oak Boulevard.

It would be twenty minutes, or less, more like fifteen, before Gamboa would be airborne. Medrano didn't have much time.

After learning about the RDX from Cissy Farrell that morning, after all the speculation about how it might be used, it seemed to Haydon the only feasible method was remote-control detonation. It was the only way to get to Gamboa without approaching him. And since twenty-five kilos of anything was not easily carried around, the explosive itself would have to be stationary, detonated from a distance.

But how would Medrano bring together Gamboa and the RDX? Haydon thought back to the beginning, Tuesday morning, Ireno López. He had been in Houston three weeks observing Gamboa's movements, and would have gathered information about where, when, and how Gamboa traveled. That was the kind of intelligence that had enabled them to hit the limousine only minutes after it left a restaurant where Gamboa often dined. Only Negrete's cunning had saved the older Mexican. Would that data gathered by López be useless after a failed attempt? Not unless Gamboa completely changed travel patterns and habits, which he had not done. In fact, unless he changed residences, Gamboa was like every other person in the city, he had to travel certain streets to get to certain places. That could not be avoided. Since he went often to the Post Oak area, what were his route choices? Without going ridiculously out of the way, there was only San Felipe, Westheimer, Richmond, Southwest Freeway. Actually, once he passed up San Felipe, he was going out of the way. San Felipe was the closest, most direct route from Inverness to the Post Oak District. It was also the closest, most direct route to the heliport, which was why Gamboa had chosen it. The less time he was exposed, the less risk of being ambushed.

San Felipe. Haydon reached its intersection with Post Oak Boulevard and looked to his right at the Steak 'N Egg diner where Medrano had appeared only a couple of hours earlier. How would he know when to detonate the RDX? Unless the *tecos* had managed to attach a directional beeper to the limousine—which was highly unlikely, since Gamboa was no longer using Valverde limousines—Medrano would only know when to detonate by visual confirmation that the limousine was in close proximity to the explosive. The RDX would have to be planted somewhere along San Felipe, somewhere in the area of the West Loop intersection with San Felipe. And Medrano could be in any of the dozens of buildings.

Haydon wheeled onto San Felipe. He headed toward the Loop underpass, scanning the street for trash bins, mailboxes, traffic signal junction boxes, anything situated close to the street and large enough to conceal the explosive, before he realized he didn't have to. The heliport sat in a park area just off the access road on the *other* side, the east side, of the freeway. Gamboa wouldn't even come as far as the freeway itself. In fact, it was more than likely Gamboa's chauffeur would turn off on Park Drive, which formed the eastern boundary of the park, a couple of blocks before reaching the freeway.

Gunning the Jaguar, Haydon flew into the curve and shot under the freeway as the amber light turned red. At this point the street formed a boulevard divided by a grassy median. If the explosive was to be effective against Gamboa within the next few minutes, it would have to be located on the other side of the median, in the westbound lane.

Braking, slowing the Jaguar, Haydon stared across the median. Even under the dim lighting of the streetlamps, he could see it was the cleanest strip for a dozen blocks in either direction. He must have passed here a million times, but never really noticed the details of the layout. The trees from the park were set back a hundred yards or so. A block farther on there was a traffic light, and then the street shrank to two lanes as it crossed the railroad tracks and entered the narrow and heavily wooded section of San Felipe that went into River Oaks. Hearing the faint thumping of helicopter rotors, Haydon looked back and saw the blinking lights of the helicopter approaching from the north. The ship came in low over the expressway and hovered a moment over the park trees before it settled into them, out of sight.

Haydon couldn't understand it. It wasn't what he had expected. Maybe the explosives *were* behind him, on the other side of the freeway. Maybe Medrano was going to miss his target by a matter of a few blocks. Maybe the witless Gamboa had been lucky once again. He looked through the windshield and saw the patrol-unit flashers emerging from the tree-covered stretch of San Felipe approaching the railroad crossing. Dystal hadn't been exaggerating about the protection. They were practically commandeering the entire street. The headlights of the first two patrol cars tilted upward as they crossed the slightly raised tracks side by side, and then separated to opposite sides to block the intersecting streets of Briar Hollow on the right and St. Regis on the left. The third patrol car bounced onto the tracks, followed by the limousine.

In the first instant of the explosion, the limousine did not move, but glowed a phosphorescent white. An orange, solar brilliance lighted its windows from the inside so that Haydon saw into the car, saw the silhouetted figures sitting perfectly upright as if nothing were happening to them at all, saw the solar fire come out the windows. And then there was the explosion. That infinitesimal space of time in which Haydon's brain registered what he saw was already long past, even as it happened.

Chapter 56

The aftershock was political, conspicuous, and ultimately inconsequential. News of the assassination survived the weekend media doldrums and was the lead story on the network news programs through all of Monday, and for three days running, making the front pages of newspapers across the country. In the following week, it received major coverage in *Newsweek, Time,* and *U.S. News & World Report.* Political assassination is always a big story, but this particular killing was immediately recognized as having broader implications.

Within twenty-four hours a special federal commission was established to direct an independent investigation. It seemed that Benigo Gamboa Parra did, in fact, have friends in powerful places. His death caused a flurry of righteous indignation from members of Congress whose somber, measured statements were duly recorded by news cameras and set down for posterity in the *Federal Register.*

Pressed by reporters for a comment, a Reagan administration spokesman demurred, saying he did not want to make any premature judgments, but he thought the assassination clearly proved the administration's claim that Central America and Mexico were fertile points of origin from which communist terrorists could launch acts of violent depredation against the United States.

However, it quickly became apparent to the new commission that the carnage of those four hectic days had been plotted and executed not by communists, but by the radical right, and had its sources within the impenetrable labyrinth-world of Mexican politics and society where the laws of logic and reason did not always govern. The commission's enthusiasm cooled rapidly. The Drug Enforcement Administration's recent Sisyphean efforts to establish cooperative law enforcement operations with Mexico had proved how maddening and futile an investigation in that country could be.

Nevertheless, the commission made polite diplomatic inquiries and proposed the formation of a bilateral task force. In the coming weeks, commission spokesmen publicly praised Mexican law enforcement officials for their "willingness to cooperate," while privately they watched the investigation bog down in a quagmire of vague communiqués and polite but unproductive meetings. Requests to the Mexican authorities for information regarding the society called *los tecos* disappeared into the abyss of Mexican bureaucracy.

The Houston Police Department receded into the background, with great relief. Haydon, seeing how the investigation was being handled, tried to turn his back on it. In time, he knew, it would drop to the back pages of the newspaper, then disappear from public interest altogether. Still, he often found himself wondering how Negrete had escaped the intense police search that followed the killings at the Golden Way Motel, and how Blas Medrano had made his way out of the United States.

But he also had a more compelling interest in one of the key unanswered questions of the case. Celia Moreno's life had undergone dramatic changes. Haunted by the fact that she had been used by an unknown agency to gather intelligence for unknown reasons, she was preoccupied by the fear that eventually she would be killed for her role. She completely withdrew from her former fast-paced, high-profile life and moved home to live with her elderly mother in the little frame house under the pecan trees. She took a low-paying secretary's job in a complex of dentist offices and made every effort to become invisible.

Haydon tried to assure her that her fears were unfounded, but in truth, he wasn't altogether sure himself. He had his own ideas about the elusive Richard Elkin, and he initiated discreet but increasingly *urgent* inquiries through Mitchell

Garner to certain channels of the State Department. In the meantime, he stayed in touch with Celia. Every time she called the police to report strange cars in her neighborhood or dark figures lurking in the streets near her mother's home at nights, Haydon always showed up with the patrol cars and stayed afterward to listen to her rattled preoccupation with potential assassins. Celia became well known to the patrolmen whose beat included her neighborhood. None of the cars she saw, none of the license plates she recorded, none of the men she described ever proved to have any connection to each other, or to anything else that raised the least bit of suspicion. The conspiracy against her life became the special beast of her own imagination.

Then early one evening in late September, Haydon received a call at home from Mitchell Garner.

"Stuart, sorry to bother you, but I've got a man down here at my office who wants to talk to you."

Haydon's mind had been elsewhere. He gathered his thoughts, then felt a surge of adrenaline. "The inquiries?"

"Yeah, right." Garner's voice was dispassionately businesslike.

"We can talk there?"

"There won't be anyone here but the three of us."

"I'm on my way."

Haydon drove the Vanden Plas into the steamy, narrow streets of downtown, through slack traffic and walls of lights rising out of sight into the night above him. He parked in RepublicBank's underground garage, then took the elevator to the forty-eighth floor, where he approached a suite door with a nameplate that read simply "Law Offices." He pressed a black button beside the door and listened for the electronic click. Pushing open the door, he met Garner in the empty outer office.

"This could be what we've been waiting for," Garner said, standing close to Haydon, his voice low and portentous. His tie was undone, and the crisp white shirt under his braces was deeply wrinkled from a long day behind his desk. "Got his call about two hours ago. He said he wanted to talk to you about your inquiries, that he was with the State Department. I told him to come on over. When he got here he gave me a couple of names I recognized from the diplomatic mission in Mexico City. Told me to call them to check him out. I made the calls. He'd given me their *home* phone numbers.''

"And we can believe him?''

"We can believe the men who vouched for him,'' Garner said. "Although I don't think they had any idea why he was here. And they didn't ask. I got the impression they were used to these kinds of calls about this guy.'' Garner raised his eyebrows meaningfully, then turned and started walking.

Haydon followed his slightly rounded shoulders down a short corridor, past an empty alcove with armchairs for waiting clients, now eerily lighted by the indigo glow of black lights left on for the tropical plants. The city sparkled on the other side of the windows. Garner's office was at the end of the corridor. They walked through the receptionist's office and into Garner's suite.

As they came in, a man in his early fifties stood up from the chair where he had been sitting in front of Garner's desk. He was tall, maybe six-four, with neatly trimmed ginger hair shot through with gray. His ruddy complexion appeared to be suffering from overexposure to the sun. It wasn't the sort of skin that would ever tan. He seemed in robust physical condition, far better than most men his age; his eyes, pale gray and alert, were reading Haydon's curiosity with a curiosity of their own.

"Stuart Haydon,'' Garner said. "This is Karl Heidrich.''

Heidrich smiled unenthusiastically, locking his eyes on Haydon's as they shook hands. "Sit down, sit down,'' he said with a curt congeniality, urging Haydon to another chair as if the office were his own. Garner walked around behind his desk.

Though Haydon had initiated the inquiries, this man had asked to see *him*. He decided to remain quiet and let Heidrich take the initiative. It was something Heidrich seemed used to doing.

"I'm stopping over in Houston for only a few hours,'' Heidrich said pointedly. "I've got a flight out of Intercontinental at twelve-thirty, so we don't have a lot of time.''

He didn't say where he was from or where he was going. Haydon studied his face, which was settling into the heavier structures of that of an "older" man. It portrayed no uneasiness, and Haydon got the feeling that Heidrich's familiarity of manner was due more to the fact that he was a constant traveler accustomed to meeting people than to an extroverted personality. There was an air of self-sufficiency about him that had a larger dimension than that ordinarily exhibited by a confident executive. Haydon guessed he was a man used to walking into unstable situations, quickly assessing them, and taking control.

"I'll get right to the point, Mr. Haydon," Heidrich said. "Mr. Garner has already checked me out." The flicker of a smile again. "And I'm sure he's already told you I'm with the State Department. Some of the people there think you have a right to a degree of clarification regarding your inquiries. I'm here to try to answer whatever questions you have."

He stopped, looked at Garner, and then back at Haydon.

"That shouldn't be difficult," Haydon said. He wasn't going to say any more. He knew damn well Heidrich was thoroughly familiar with every communication Haydon had initiated. There was no use wasting time pretending otherwise. He looked at Heidrich in silence.

A subdued expression of bemusement grew slowly on Heidrich's face, then faded.

"All right," he said, crossing one leg over the other, giving it a boost with the help of a hand at the back of the knee. "You know you can believe what I have to say, but you're going to have to be satisfied with . . . abbreviated information. After I'm through here, we're going to assume your concerns have been satisfied. You understand that?"

"I think so," Haydon answered.

"Okay. I'm not going to give you a foreign-relations lecture," Heidrich said. "I know you're both aware of the administration's feelings about the importance of Central America and Mexico to our national security. It's not been an issue that's warranted a lot of media attention until the last few years, but that same attitude's been shared by every president in this century.

"As a result, U.S. intelligence gathering has a long history in Mexico. Our network of *orejas*—ears—down there is unsurpassed anywhere in the world. We pay them well for what they do. With their godawful economy the way it is, it's not hard to recruit them. We've got them in the trade unions, in the universities, in the dissident factions, in the police, in all levels of government . . . all levels. Very little happens there without our having seen it developing in advance. Sometimes, in small ways, we can influence events; sometimes we can't. Sometimes we want to, sometimes we don't.''

Heidrich reached into an inside coat pocket and took out a pack of cigarettes. He shook one out and returned the pack. From another pocket he retrieved a lighter. But he didn't light the cigarette. Instead he gestured with it, not in any hurry to smoke. Once again he cut his eyes at Garner, then brought them back to rest on Haydon.

"Benigo Gamboa," Heidrich said, "was one of these sources inside the Portillo administration. Inside the *tecos* . . . it was Daniel Ferretis.''

Haydon was jolted. Gamboa. Yes. He had speculated that. But Daniel Ferretis? Christ, that was unexpected. His mind raced back over the events. He couldn't make any sense out of Ferretis's role, considering what had happened. The truth, or the small part of it this man was about to reveal, was going to be complicated. He waited.

Heidrich pocketed his lighter. "When Portillo's presidential term ended in 1982, his administration left a wake of financial scandals. Some of the people we'd worked with, including Gamboa, were deeply involved. We helped them get out of the country. Many of them fled Mexico with enormous sums of money. We figured that was their business, Mexican business. We didn't get into the legal-possession question. This was four years before Marcos and Baby Doc. It was different then. They'd helped us, so we were returning favors. No moral judgments, just business. A number of them ended up here in the States, but they left a lot of enemies behind in Mexico.

"After the country had had some time to assess the damages, to see the real extent of its financial losses, the *tecos* appointed themselves avenging angels. The reasons are too complicated to go into, but we eventually got wind of the assassination plots . . . though not from Ferretis. In groups like the *tecos,* the more volatile, unpredictable organizations, we maintain more than one informant. But they work compartmentally, none of them know the others exist—that way we have the advantage of varying perspectives. In this instance it made all the difference. By holding out on us, Ferretis implicated himself. It took fast work to sort this out, to get a general picture of the setup, but we did it.''

Heidrich inhaled deeply from the cigarette and blew the smoke to one side. He seemed to be considering his words before he spoke again.

''That put us in an interesting situation,'' he said. ''The truth is, Mr. Haydon, Gamboa had become a problem for us. Since coming to the States he'd been acting as if our people owed him a lot of favors, even though we'd made it clear to him we considered the accounts between us squared away. He was strictly on his own. But Gamboa tried to milk an association he should have put behind him, using his former relationship with us as leverage in his business dealings. Very risky. Way out of line. He dropped a few names trying to put together some real estate deals. Too many names. He definitely had become a liability. This thing with the *tecos* . . . well, we decided if they got him, it wasn't something we were going to make a big stink about.''

Haydon was stunned a second time, amazed he was being told this. He looked at Garner, who stared at Heidrich with the unflappable composure of a trained psychiatrist. If he was shocked, he was determined he wasn't going to let it show.

Then Heidrich fell silent. He looked at Haydon and smoked, giving no indication he intended to continue. With what appeared to Haydon to be deliberate insolence, he was pretending to have delivered himself of all that he had to say. Perhaps he had sensed, and inwardly rankled at, Haydon's own haughty silence. Heidrich was not the kind of man to be bested in the subtleties of game-playing. He was not a subordinate, an errand boy coming to Haydon with his tall tucked apologetically between his legs to report on the State Department's indiscretions. If Haydon wanted something from him, he should by God ask for it. In all probability, Heidrich had bridled at having to come here in the first place.

''My concern,'' Haydon said obligingly, ''was for Celia Moreno. She *was* working for you, wasn't she?''

Heidrich lifted his head in a half-nod. ''Yeah,'' he said, ''she sure was. We had had our eyes on her for a while. We recruited her as soon as we could after we started suspecting Ferretis. Even though we already knew the assassination plots existed, we let her 'discover' them for herself. We, uh, thought that would give her a motivation she wouldn't have had otherwise. Besides, we couldn't tell her too much. It wasn't as though she were a professional. What we needed from her were the details. God knows we had too damn few before she got involved. But she got them for us. She was good, damn good.''

Haydon remembered Valverde's satyr's grin as he looked at Celia, bare-legged in the pink silk dress. He imagined the two of them naked on the nappy brown sofa, Valverde's pale buttocks, Celia's smooth knees. Every time Valverde took her clothes off, she'd said to Haydon, her body became Esteban's insurance policy.

Haydon forced his thoughts back to the present. ''Elkin was your man.''

Heidrich nodded.

''And the FBI really didn't know anything about it.''

Heidrich shook his head, but didn't elaborate. He went back to Celia. ''We know she's concerned about her safety,'' he said. ''She doesn't have to be. She was doing the right thing for the right people.''

The right thing for the right people, Haydon thought. Who the hell had put Heidrich in charge of morals?

''Why the charade, then?'' Haydon worked to keep his mind on track.

''Well, maybe that could have been handled better,'' Heidrich conceded. ''But we didn't have a lot of time. There was no way we could risk telling her more than we did.''

''And the tails I spotted at the Guadalajara airport?'' Garner interjected.

An uncomfortable half-grin crawled across one side of Heidrich's mouth. ''It looked like amateur night, didn't it? We weren't sure why you were going down there. That move was a bit of a surprise. And it put you way ahead in the game. Which was awkward for us. Up to then we didn't think you had a chance in hell to prevent the assassination.''

Haydon's mind was charging ahead, almost stumbling over itself as he tried to pull it all together.

"Then you knew about Blas Medrano, what he was planning, and when?"

Heidrich shrugged and narrowed one eye. "That's a touchy area. We did, and we didn't." He said nothing more, and he wasn't the least bit uneasy about leaving it at that.

"I guess it was your man who called in the tip about the motel, then," Haydon said. "I didn't have any luck tracing it."

"Right." Heidrich put out his cigarette in an ashtray on the corner of Garner's desk. "Negrete was going crazy. We were afraid he was going to get the information out of Arizpe in time to stop it. We knew you wouldn't be able to do that. You couldn't resort to those methods, and that was the only way anyone was going to get that Indian to talk. It was too bad Negrete got to him. We didn't think that would happen. Ironically, you two were trying to accomplish the same thing, but for different reasons."

"And you were betting on the *tecos.*"

For a moment Heidrich looked at Haydon in silence. Then he raised his arm and looked at his watch, then returned his eyes to Haydon. "That's about it," he said.

There were no more questions, only silence. Haydon looked at Garner, who had taken his ballpoint pen out of his pocket and was doodling on a piece of paper. His equanimity was gone. He seemed embarrassed, and didn't look up.

Haydon struggled with the welling anger, the several conflicting angers. Anger at himself for having this reaction, a piety he could not justify, an indignation that bordered on hypocrisy. The right thing for the right people. Heidrich played a complicated game on a large and complex scale, and Haydon reminded himself he was in no position to judge. He knew from experience that such contests sometimes required a fierceness of moral decision that, in retrospect, seemed to negate its original purpose altogether. And he knew that it was easier to criticize someone else for making those decisions than it was to make them yourself. He had no business feeling the way he did toward Heidrich. But he couldn't help it.

He gazed out the window to the city—lights like the sparks of scattered fires—and felt suddenly overwhelmed. There was too much to understand, and he understood too much. Too many secrets, too much fierceness. He stood, but couldn't bring himself to speak to Heidrich, even to look at him. He felt transparent, as if his alienation, his anger and emptiness, his distaste for Heidrich, were immediately apparent. Then he realized he didn't care, he didn't give a damn. No one said anything as he left the room, his movement silent on the carpet of the long dark hallway.

He hadn't returned intentionally, that is, he hadn't planned it. But his headlights caught the street sign, and he turned impulsively. In a few moments he was sitting across the street from the Belgrano walls, staring at them through the light rain.

It was the middle of November. The drought had broken in October with thunderstorms more reminiscent of spring than fall, their downpours washing the city like a ritual ablution. The steely heat, too, had been subdued by the storms, and wrathful summer, like a malevolent spirit, had loosed its grip. There was a period of clear days, cooler and cleaner days, renewal at the end of a long hot year. Then in the first week of November, gray, damp days descended in a mantle of fog and charcoal clouds. Rain was ever present. Haydon observed his forty-first birthday.

Looking across at the pitted wall darkened by the week of rain and shrouded in mottled shadows, he felt no heart-quickening recollections, no anxiety. He cut the Jaguar's headlamps, and the streetlights threw a leaden glow through the drifting mizzle. The windshield wipers were on intermittent. They swept in front of him, and he looked across at the gates through the polished glass. The rain would add more rust to the gates. He remembered Mooney commenting on the rust that morning. Mist collected on the windshield, and the iron gates grew indistinct, then distorted. A beginning rivulet hesitated at the top of the glass, then plunged crazily, followed quickly by a second one chasing it down. The wipers rose

and fell. The glass was clean, the gates were sharp and clear
again.

Haydon looked at the sleeves of his raincoat on his out-
stretched arms, his hands gripping the steering wheel. He
could smell the heavy, rain-dampened cloth. He could smell
his own cologne, which seemed to take on a second life after
he had been out in the rain.

The wipers rose and fell.

Haydon reached over to the passenger seat and picked up
his dark gray trilby. The lightweight felt was damp in his
fingers as he put it on, tugging at the front of the brim. He
opened the car door and got out, locking it behind him. It
was better outside. The closed car had begun to bother him.
As long as he was driving it was all right, but sitting in the
dark, in the rain, here, it was beginning to bother him.

No matter how much it rains in the barrios, the sidewalks
are always gritty. They never are washed clean. He walked a
little way, ignoring the stained walls on the other side of the
street, feeling the grit and moisture grinding under his leather
soles with each step. His breath floated around his face in the
November chill. He stopped, looked both ways along the deserted street, and stepped off the sidewalk toward the gates.
Twice he splashed through muddy puddles he could have
avoided had he been paying attention.

On the other side, he stopped. He looked through the
wrought-iron bars into the derelict grounds. With his hands in
the pockets of his raincoat, he held his breath and listened.
In the mottled gloom just inside the gates, water dripped
steadily on some hollow shell of a weed. Everything was just
the opposite. That morning there had been a bright sun and
a small crowd. The air had been parched dry and the dead
weeds were crackling with the sounds of insects popping
among the empty pods. There had been a dead man at his
feet. There had been Mooney. Now it was dark, and he was
alone. The night air was moist. There were no insects, and
the dried weeds were limp. There was no dead man, and only
the ghost of Mooney.

Haydon looked down at his waist where the two wings of
the gate came together. The chain was still looped through
the bars, but there was a different lock. He pulled a hand out
of a pocket and touched a water droplet hanging off the rusty

chain. He rubbed his fingers together and returned his hand to the pocket.

Looking up, he peered through the towering cypresses toward the upper story of the old house. It was difficult enough to catch a glimpse of the place during the day, and on this foggy night he had only a sense of its presence, but a sense that made it as real as if he had touched it, and walked in its rooms. Through the shadows and tangled brush and cypresses the streetlights picked up a glint from a glass pane in an upper-story window. Yes, the old place was still there, holding its breath, too, wanting him to go away, wanting to be left alone.

Haydon was aware of his wet feet. The thin leather of the Italian shoes was no good for walking in the rain. His feet were getting cold, and the unevenness of the sidewalk where it joined the brick drive under the gates led him to imagine that he was standing on the corpse of the Mexican. He had been right here. Exactly here. Haydon seemed to feel the flesh roll on the dead man's bones, could feel the shifting of the body fluids that made unsteady footing. He wanted to reach out to the rusty gate to steady his balance, to step down off the cadaver. In his mind he saw the Mexican moving underneath him, small twitches—for every motion there is a countermotion—animated by Haydon's efforts to maintain his balance.

He looked away quickly, far away down Chicon toward the solitary rosy orb of a tiny neon light in the window of a cantina. Jesus Christ. Why did he think such things? He turned, carefully, and walked away.

Haydon listened to his own footsteps as he walked toward the corner. He could hear the moisture, the grit, knew that though he did not walk carelessly, taupe flecks of mud were speckling the toes of his shoes. The graffiti going by his shoulder was illegible. The frail bare branches of tall shrubbery dangled over the top of the wall in several places, like shocks of coarse, wild hair, the mizzle dripping from the tips onto the sidewalk.

When he came to the corner he did not hesitate, but rounded the turn and saw the long stretch of wall broken at midpoint by the vertical recess of the doorway. At this angle he could not see the grilled iron gate, taller than he, that covered the doorway. He stood in the subdued pewter light cast from a distant lamp and took in the arena of Mooney's passing. The sidewalk was narrower than he had remembered, the street closer to the wall. He began walking. The wall was higher—he reached out a hand and let his fingers trail along the surface—and coarser. There were cracks in it he did not remember. He approached the gate and stopped in front of it. He did not remember the portal being so narrow.

He looked down at the sidewalk. A steady trickle of water ran off the brim of the trilby and dribbled at his feet on the spot where Mooney, alone, had experienced that final and incomparable sensation. From here he had stared up at the end of the world. Perhaps he had seen the night sky. Perhaps he had seen the stars before the rods and cones of his retina withered, trapping forever their sparkling images somewhere in the secret windings to his brain. Perhaps the sound of barking dogs had chased him into eternity. What had he smelled? What had he tasted? And what, in God's name, had he thought?

Making a quarter turn, he faced the gate. The smooth poles of bamboo glistened in the rain on the other side. Black bamboo. He stared into the dense stand, saw the thin individual stalks as though each were carved of brittle Mexican obsidian, a task of a lifetime, of two or three lifetimes. Dark and impenetrable.

His eyes focused on the gate. He never really had looked at it. He stepped forward. It was a beautiful piece of ironwork, intricate in design, the great swirl of its pattern following a centripetal course to its middle. Though he did not remember the gate itself, he did remember every detail of Mooney's death here. It had been the heart of the maelstrom, the four-day spiral of violence that had swept so many lives into the vanishing point of its center. He would remember. Memory never failed him; it cursed and blessed him, but never left him. Mooney's dying was as real as the rain, a timeless moment in the mind's eye.

He ran the fingers of one hand over the gate's ornate pattern, its iron turned scaly with rust, dripping with cold mist. Slowly, he put his fingers through the strange motif and gripped it tightly, watching the whorls of his breath float through its coils to the other side, toward the black bamboo.

Incredible.

Suddenly he rattled the gate once, sharply, and stood still, listening to the sound of chain and iron being swallowed by the moist, dark throat of the night. Then he turned and walked away.

"Western diplomats say almost offhandedly that they suspect that top officials made off with billions of dollars during the six-year administration [1976–1982] of former President José López Portillo, who is now said to be in Europe."

Newsweek,
August 12, 1985

"Wealthy Mexicans and their money are pouring into the U.S. . . . Mexico's central bank acknowledges that in 1977–1984, at least $33 billion flowed out of the country. Other economists say the total could be closer to $60 billion. . . . Some international economists estimate that as much as $5 billion has escaped this year [1985] alone. . . .

"In Houston, [one] law firm represents some 2,000 wealthy Mexicans who have invested more than $15 million each year since 1983 in U.S. assets ranging from restaurants to warehouses."

Wall Street Journal,
October 11, 1985

"[Mexico's] level of capital flight, estimated at more than $6 billion a year, may be the highest in the world. . . ."

New York Times,
May 25, 1986

"A controversial CIA study called Mexico the leading long-term foreign-policy concern of the United States because of the likelihood of widespread social turmoil."

Newsweek,
August 12, 1985

"Mexico's immediate stability is endangered less by a rebellion of the masses led by the Left than by a mutiny of the middle class inspired by the Right. . . .

"Most recently, a well-financed group known as *los tecos* in Guadalajara has emerged as the most extremist right-wing force in the country."

Alan Riding,
New York Times bureau chief in Brazil,
in *Distant Neighbors*
(Alfred A. Knopf, 1985)

"The private Guadalajara Autonomous University is home of Mexico's largest neofascist movement, known as *Los Tecos* (The Owls) for their unblinking vigilance of suspected leftists."

> Juan O. Tamayo,
> Knight-Ridder Newspapers,
> January 4, 1985

"I've dealt with these people [the Tecos]. They came to me when I was in the military and offered us their services. To show they meant business, they bragged that they had a death list of people in the States, people they wanted to get rid of. They were trying to work out the logistics then; I don't know if they ever got anyone."

> March 1986 interview with Col. Robert Eulalio Santivañez, former counterespionage chief in El Salvador.
> Scott Anderson and Jon Lee Anderson
> *Inside the League*
> (Dodd, Mead & Co., 1986)